Praises for *When The Serpent Bites*

"From debut author Clerge comes a n〔 ⟩ quest to survive prison and find ans〔 ⟩ The prison fear is vivid, the odds insur〔 ⟩ conclusion anyone's guess, though it cer〔 ⟩ ⟨ come easily. An arresting prison tale about penanc〔 ⟩

—*Kirkus Reviews*

"The characters have real depth—something I am big on—and the drama on the pages made me feel as though I was right there watching it. The book is fast paced and, in my opinion, downright amazing."

—*Bobbie Grob, Readers' Favorite*

"This character orientated drama benefits from a fully fleshed out protagonist, gritty writing, and psychological insight into a realistic psyche. The obvious sequel has a high bar to surpass........ *When the Serpent Bites* is a fantastic read for legal buffs, crime lovers, and readers who love a great story."

—*John Murray, Pacific book review*

"Nesly Clerge spins a convoluted web of human dynamics and sinister situations in his debut novel. Clerge's careful attention to character development and the cast's interactions with Starks is a main ingredient that keeps his story flowing. Clerge's cliffhanging chapters continually tickle the curiosity of thriller aficionados to keep turning pages to see what the final outcome will be. Clerge also maintains plot fluidity by alternating character scenes, backstories, and a plethora of twisted and suspenseful events."

—*San Francisco Book Review*

WHEN THE SERPENT BITES

NESLY CLERGE

WHEN THE SERPENT BITES

"When the Serpent Bites"

This is a work of fiction. Names, characters, places, and incidents are the product of the author's imagination or are used fictitiously. Any resemblance to actual persons, living or dead, events, or locales is entirely coincidental.

ISBN 10: 099650172X
ISBN 13: 9780996501729

Publisher: IngramSpark
Editor: Joyce Shafer (http://editmybookandmore.weebly.com)
Cover and Interior Book Design: Damonza.com

Acknowledgments

I WOULD LIKE to extend my sincere gratitude to my editor, Joyce Shafer. She was instrumental in the production of this book. I am grateful for her experience and expertise. I am also thankful for her patience and understanding. This book involved a huge amount of work; her guidance, her countless hours of coaching, and her attention to detail are unmatched. I've had the opportunity to consult with other editors, and by far you are the best, Joyce.

Special thanks goes to Dwayne Graham for guidance that provided relevant texture to specific topics, and to Makeda Crane for allotting time out of her busy law schedule to assist me. I am also grateful to attorneys David Shurtz and Hope Umana for taking the time to offer professional direction regarding the legal aspects included in the novel.

Evans Clerge, Danenia Smith and Dr. Rebekah Brown are among the few that provided their support. I am very thankful for their constant feedback. Without their contribution and support, this book would not have been written.

I also have to say a special thank-you to Tierra Guy for devoting her time and effort to helping me. I was able to complete this book because of the laborious and lengthy sessions held at our house. We complained about the late nights, but it was worth it. Your point of view as a reader, significant other, and critic made this book possible. Thank you for keeping me motivated.

CHAPTER 1

FREDERICK STARKS'S NEED gnawed at him like a painful, roving itch. He decided that this time he'd scratch it so it would go away.

He eased himself out of bed.

"Can't sleep, again?" Emma rolled onto her back and used her left leg to push the bedcovers down, revealing her nakedness. "Come back to bed. You know I sleep better when you spoon me."

"In a while. And then I'll do more than spoon you."

"Can't you just read until you nod off?"

"Fresh air clears my head."

Emma yawned. "All these late night drives. Should I be worried?" She stretched and purred in her own way then went still.

He crept to her side, checked to make sure she was indeed asleep then pulled the covers to her shoulders. He knew men who considered him one lucky bastard to have such a remarkable woman in his life. Luck had nothing to do with it; he didn't operate on luck, he operated on calculated risks and informed decisions. Nor did he feel guilty about any of his good fortune: He'd earned every bit of it. People tended to forget or never knew he'd had to do with less in his life and intended to never live like that again.

He dressed in the dark then went to his Bentley, waiting a few moments before turning the key in the ignition. Then, as he had so many nights for months, he drove off.

The moon was a pale sliver above him. Elm, cedar, willow, and holly trees, and anything else not under cover in the Boston suburb of Weston, were coated with frost that promised to be thicker by morning. The effect was one of an enchanted place, a serene place that sparkled in patches and swaths on the landscape. The stillness was broken only by the occasional nocturnal creature hunting prey. Scented smoke plumed from chimneys as fires below dwindled and died. Residents in this affluent town eagerly, or anxiously, contemplated plans for the upcoming Thanksgiving holiday just two weeks away, while children dreamed of the holiday to follow. In so many ways, it was a perfect night in a perfect neighborhood.

Until Starks went where he didn't belong.

Only a few houses still had lighted windows casting shimmering wide or narrow yellow strips on the ground. Starks drove by his home, the mini-mansion he'd taken such pride in, traveling slowly as he passed it; feeling his emotions ratchet up. Then he corrected himself—*this is no longer my home*. His wife, Kayla, and their three children still lived there, along with her latest boyfriend, Bret, and his two daughters.

Effects of escalated events over the past twelve months had taken a toll on him. Learning the full extent of his wife's deception had been the trigger, and was why he made the decision to go where he knew he shouldn't. His foot pressed down on the accelerator.

He and his wife, Kayla, had lived apart for most of that time, a reality still unfathomable to him. And even though he was now involved with Emma, his left arm went numb and his mouth turned dry when he saw Kayla and Bret nuzzling each other in a dark corner of one of the popular local bars earlier in the evening. They'd passed him on the road, unaware he'd seen them. He followed them, even though he knew it was the wrong thing to do; that it was best if he just got on with his life. Everyone made a point of saying this to him whenever he complained, which was often. But he couldn't let go of the long-held belief that Kayla belonged with him and to him, and only him.

If anyone knew what he was doing now, they would be puzzled. Especially Jeffrey. He'd say, "Bro, why go to Ozy Hessinger's house? If you need to vent some frustration, why not just punch Bret's lights out or puncture one, or better yet, all of his tires?"

It would be just like Jeffrey to try to diffuse tension building in the moment by suggesting something ridiculous, to make him laugh. Only he didn't feel like laughing. He hadn't felt like it for a long time.

It made sense that others would think his jealousy would or should, logically, be aimed at Bret, who'd seen what an easy mark Kayla was.

He doubted anyone would understand his reason for why he was going where he shouldn't be going, not at this time, not at any time: *Because Ozy should be made to pay for what he did to me, my wife, and my family.* They'd want to know why just Ozy. He'd be too ashamed to tell them.

He'd tried and failed to get over the humiliation of Kayla's preference for Ozy over him. The conversation they'd had still stung.

"I'm a bigger success and a hell of a lot wealthier than Ozy ever will be," he told her. "I own my businesses. He gets a paycheck."

Kayla opened a bottle of water, sipped, and stared out the French doors of their kitchen. "Aerospace engineering is a hell of a lot more prestigious than what you do."

"That's bullshit." He stuffed his trembling hands into his pockets. "Ozy can't give you what I do. He'll never love you—"

"The way you do?" Kayla glanced at him then away. Her grip on the water bottle tightened. "God, I hope that's true. For one thing, he knows there's more to life than money."

Starks' mouth dropped open. "That's rich, coming from you. You need to wake up and realize you're lying to yourself."

"You'd like to believe that." Kayla faced him with a jutted chin. "Ozy makes love to me in ways you'll never be able to. You'll never be that affectionate. Or intimate. You're too emotionally removed. Disconnected."

"One, if I became less affectionate, it's because I've used my energy to work my ass off for years to give you everything you need and want. Two, this is an affair you're having. For him, it's a way to get into your pants. You think he treats his wife the way he treats you now? You think after he's with you for a while he won't do to you what he's doing to her? If you think that, you're a bigger fool than I realized."

Kayla emptied the rest of the bottled water into the peace lily positioned on a stand near the French doors, left the empty bottle on the countertop then walked toward the family room.

Starks tossed the empty bottle into the trash compactor then slammed it shut. "Why do you do that? You know it annoys me." He leaned against the counter, folded his arms. "Why can't you just do the right thing?"

Kayla brought her lips into a pout. "Poor Starks. Doesn't like life to be messy. Tell yourself whatever you need to about what's going on. You always do." Her expression was one of regret. "I'm getting older."

Starks's face registered his confusion. "So am I. What's that got to do with anything?"

"I'm not wasting any more time on you and your delusions."

A vein centered on his forehead pulsed. "You're the one who's deluded. You end this nonsense—all of it—right now. I'm warning you."

Kayla laughed at him. "Go ahead and warn me all you want. What are you going to do, cut me off financially? Try it and see what happens. You're pathetic."

Her words echoed in his mind as he turned onto Tower Road. Perspiration beaded at his hairline. He pushed the sleeves of his cashmere sweater up to his elbows then wiped each sweaty palm in turn on his razor-creased pants. In the silent, pristine interior of the car, his grandfather's voice was so clear, the old man could have been sitting next to him—"You reap what you sow, Freddy. Remember that." Starks had been seven at the time, with no clue about what his grandfather meant. Sewing was for girls, was how his young mind had processed the statement. Now he understood: Ozy was about to reap what he'd sown, because he wasn't leaving the Hessinger house until Margaret knew what a cheating, lowlife bastard she was married to. He practiced a number of ways to say this to her as he got onto the MA-117.

He turned the heater off and rolled his window down all the way, letting the crisp autumn air attempt to dry his face and fail. Another thought prodded him: Turn this car around and head home. But the memory of pained expressions and pleas of his three young children for life to return as it had once been impelled him to keep driving.

Starks got off the MA-117 and made one more turn until he went directly to the correct address. He'd driven by the Hessinger house a number of times at different hours of the days and nights, each time trying to decide what to do or if he should do anything at all. Tonight, what he believed he should do was clear in his mind.

CHAPTER 2

OZY'S SUV WAS parked in the driveway at the top of the slope. The inside of the house was dark. A quick glance at the digital clock on the dashboard showed it was after midnight. He hadn't intended to go there this late; he hadn't intended to go by there ever again. But his thoughts ate at him, until he had to do something to make them stop. To make all of it stop. Seeing Kayla with Bret had pushed him to this edge. In the dark interior of the car he slammed his hands on the steering wheel.

"Fuck all of them. I'm taking back control of my life."

He parked at the foot of the driveway and got out. The temperature was dropping fast. Gusts of icy wind whipped at his face; treetops swayed and groaned. He leaned against the Bentley for several moments, shivering from cold and raw energy.

The grass crackled as he made his way toward the house, counting twenty-five steps as he dodged several children's toys that had been left out. He approached the front door where hay bales, pumpkins, and gourds had been arranged. He ignored the doorbell and pulled open the outer glass door to access the solid wooden one, noting there was no peephole, its absence an indication that Ozy wasn't afraid of what or who might come to his house. He raised a fist then held it back. There was still time to drive off, to just leave it all alone. Forcing an image of his children into his mind gave him courage. He swallowed hard then beat on the door without pause, until he heard someone turn the deadbolt on the other side.

Ozy wore his robe tied at his waist. His wife, also wrapped in a robe, and with hair flat on one side, stood behind him but to the right, eyes wide in fright at this disturbance.

Starks locked his gaze with Margaret's. "I'm here to let your wife know what you've been doing. That you slept with Kayla, *my* wife, for three years. Of course, *slept* isn't the right word."

Slurred voices of children disturbed from sleep came from behind the couple. Ozy yelled for them to get back to bed. He told his wife to wait inside then stepped over the threshold, closing the glass door behind him. Loud enough for his wife to hear, he said, "You have the wrong house, buddy. I don't know you or anyone named Kayla. Now get off my property, before I force you off."

Starks's expression darkened. His elbows pressed into his sides, his hands knotted into fists. The speech of well chosen words he'd practiced in his mind as he'd driven over vaporized.

"Liar! You've been screwing my wife in your car and anywhere else handy." He pointed at Margaret. "Who knows what you told your wife you were doing—going to the store, working late, and God knows what else. You think you can destroy my family, all I've worked for, and get away with it? I want your wife to know what a two-timing loser she's married to."

Ozy lowered his voice. "You're as stupid as you look standing here like a self-righteous ass. You've got a hot woman in your bed. You should be doing her instead of jacking off in front of my wife. Besides, there's no reason for you to be here. I'm done with Kayla, who, as you know, has another man polishing her chrome now. No reason for you to be here other than some misplaced pride."

"She was my wife!"

"What can I say? I'm a use 'em then lose 'em kinda guy."

Starks backed up a few steps, realizing how pointless it was to try to get Ozy to feel remorse of any kind. He'd done what he came here to do: Margaret had heard him. It was time to leave, time to return to Emma and her soothing warmth.

Ozy moved forward. "You don't know how to please a woman. Kayla was so fucking grateful that she couldn't do enough for me. If that new piece of ass of yours needs it done right, tell her to call me." He jabbed

Starks's chest with his finger. "In the bedroom Mechanical Man, you're a waste of space."

Starks had always seen himself as a rational man. But Ozy's arrogance overwhelmed him. The fact that he was no longer able to go home to his children, no longer able to kiss their foreheads each night as they slept, in effect, having been forced from sharing daily life with them because of this man, had festered inside him like a wound with no cure.

Howling, he charged at Ozy. Used his shoulder to ram the man into the glass door. Sharp shards rained down on both of them and scattered across the floor. Blood trickled from small cuts on both men. Margaret screamed.

Ozy yelled, "Upstairs. Call the police." He ran to the kitchen.

Starks ignored his instinct to leave and followed the man.

Ozy stood on the other side of the island cutting block centered in the room, with his back against the countertop. He edged his way left, his eyes fixed on Starks.

"I don't know why you're angry with me. You told Kayla you wanted her to be happy, whatever it took. It took me. She liked what I did to her." His grin was malicious. "Said she's been spoiled after having one my size. Said I knew what she wanted before she did. In fact, she liked what every man in my firm did to her. Liked me to watch." His face conveyed amusement. "Didn't know there was more than me? You're the loser."

Starks saw Ozy rest his left hand on the countertop. Saw him then move his hand behind him. He got distracted when Ozy said, "Are you upset that I did your wife or that sometimes a buddy and I did her at the same time? Get a fuckin' clue. Get your head out of your—"

Starks heard metal slide against wood. He saw the large knife Ozy held in a white-knuckled grip.

Adrenaline surged. Rage replaced reason. A heavy glass bowl rested on the counter near him. He took hold of it. Rushed at Ozy. Survival instinct and something he'd never felt before took over, blocking sound and sensation from his mind. He slammed the bowl into the side of Ozy's head. Fell onto the downed man. Used his fists to vent the tornado of emotions he'd held in for so long.

He didn't notice how much blood there was.

Or the absence of any defensive blows from his wife's former lover.

Starks, handcuffed, was dragged from the kitchen by two police officers. That's when he noticed two small children clinging to their mother's robe. Sight of them cleared his mind enough for him to see and hear their terror. Anguish and guilt and shame about how their innocence had been shattered—by him—caused him to cry out.

His eyes were wide and unseeing as the police hustled him out of the house. Starks stumbled and slid on the slick grass. The two policemen gripping his arms yanked him to his feet. Blue flashing lights drew his attention. He saw the ambulance. And wondered what he'd done. He remembered grabbing the bowl but nothing after that. He looked down; his hands, arms, and clothes were bathed in red. His stomach knotted, his skin went clammy.

The officer on his right cursed when Starks vomited.

County jail personnel bagged and labeled his personal items. His pants, sweater, and shoes were put into an evidence bag, his clothing replaced with an orange jumpsuit to wear, along with sneakers with no laces. A doctor cleaned him up and tended to his cuts and abrasions.

The only time he spoke was to ask to call his attorney. After a brief explanation of what had happened, he said, "Mike, my car." He felt guilty for worrying about it and relieved when his attorney said he'd take care of it.

He waited hours in a holding cell with—as he perceived them—unkempt, smelly lowlifes, before he was given a private cell. Once alone and he had time to think, he realized the tidy, organized life he prized and insisted on had taken a very wrong turn. The reality was that it had turned long before this night, he reminded himself. Denial was no longer an option.

The nightmares began that night. Violent, punishing images that yanked him awake, drenched him in sweat, causing one of the night guards to tell him if he didn't keep his mouth shut, he'd come in there and shut it for him.

He wanted to rewind time.

Too late for that. Time to get yourself out of this and move on with your life.

CHAPTER 3

ATTORNEY MICHAEL PARKER put his pen down and stood when Starks entered one of the interview rooms at the county jail. Starks glanced at the other man's appearance then down at the wrinkled orange jumpsuit that was two sizes too large for his average height and slender frame. "I was with you in London when you bought that suit," he said.

"I remember. You got a couple suits for yourself then. Lots of good times over the years, Starks. Good memories." Parker extended his hand.

Starks moved to shake hands—the motion was automatic—having forgotten about the handcuffs on his wrists. The color of humiliation climbed from his neck to his face. Parker cleared his throat; the two men took their seats across from each other at the heavy metal table.

Starks rested his elbows on the table's cool surface. "You got the Christmas gifts I asked you to? You got them to my kids?"

"Like Santa's helper on Christmas Eve. They were delighted." Parker pulled at his tie.

"But?"

"They miss you. Wanted to know when you're coming home."

Starks turned away. He wiped at his eyes then faced his attorney. "How was New Year's in Paris?"

Parker held his gaze for a few seconds then said, "I'm truly sorry you're in this position."

"What about my car?"

"Repaired. Like new. Jeffrey's keeping it in his garage. Starts it and runs it a few minutes every day."

"I'm lucky Margaret didn't torch it." Starks bounced his feet, realized he was doing this and stopped. "Okay. Let's get down to business."

"As I told you before, you're in a lot of trouble. The fact Hessinger pulled a knife with intent to use it works in your favor. That lets us claim self-defense to some of the charges. However, the problem is that no knife, much less intent to use it, is mentioned in the police report. I did report it after you told me, and they followed up, but it went nowhere."

"He pulled a big fucking knife on me."

"I believe you. Still—"

"It's up to you to make sure it's included."

"I will. But absence of any mention of it puts us at a disadvantage. It would have been better if you'd said something to the police while you were still at the scene."

"I told you, I was in shock. When I was able to think again, I thought it best not to say anything until I talked to you."

Parked sighed and nodded. "Your arraignment's tomorrow. You've got two things working in your favor: Your reputation in the community is solid, and this is your first offense. That may mean some leniency can or will be shown. Especially if I argue it as a crime of passion."

"Crime of passion is right."

"Still, the evidence is against you. You crossed unlawfully into the Hessinger house. That's considered breaking and entering—burglary is the official charge."

"I didn't enter the house; I fell through the goddamned glass door."

"I know, and I'll deal with that when it's time. However, even though you didn't go to or enter the house with a weapon, the Hessingers feared harm; now you've got burglary with assault tacked on. There was unwanted physical contact, which resulted in serious injury. That's battery, which has a stiffer penalty than if the situation had stopped at fear of harm. And because the attack continued after the police ordered it to stop, and Hessinger's in a coma, the D.A.'s going for attempted murder, premeditated."

Starks flung himself back in the chair. "Jesus. None of that was supposed to happen. I didn't go there to commit a crime."

"As soon as you touched Ozy outside his house, especially on his property, you committed one."

Starks pushed his chair back and began to pace. "I'm genuinely sorry about what happened. I never meant . . . All I wanted to do was shame him in front of his wife; to let her know what her husband was doing. He brought out something in me that wasn't me. Isn't me. I know how it looks but I want to plead not guilty. There was no intent to harm involved, and certainly not planned."

Parker pursed his lips. "That's not the way to go but it's your nickel."

"You mean my quarter mil. Paid upfront."

Parker cleared his throat.

Starks leaned forward. "I didn't mean to sound . . . Look, I know you can plead my case in a way that gets me off or doing community service . . . forever," he waved his hands in the air, "or something."

"I don't think that's how this is going to go, all things considered. You need to prepare yourself for that."

Starks raked his hands through his hair, his volume increasing with each word. "After all I went through . . ." He rubbed his forehead hard. "The things Ozy said to me, Mike. And he enjoyed every goddamn word. Took pleasure in driving the stake in deep."

"Calm down."

"Calm down? The one woman I believed was faithful turned out to be a slut. The mother of my children, for God's sake! Twenty years she's deceived me. And the personal things she told to . . . everyone, including that bastard Ozy. As if screwing him and others wasn't humiliating enough.

"And as for him . . . he used her. Kayla believed every lie he told her. Even after he said he'd never leave his wife for her, she still kept screwing him. And all the lies . . . all the lies she told me just to cover for that bastard."

He jabbed his right forefinger against the table. "For three years she came home to me and our children, knowing she'd been screwing him, knowing he was someone else's husband. Probably had a good laugh knowing I was inside her after he'd been there first. She betrayed me. My God, how she betrayed me. She sacrificed us . . . for him."

"This is why I'm going for crime of passion, even though, technically, it isn't a perfect fit."

"It's close enough, damn it. And, self-defense."

"All right. Much as I disagree . . . If you change your mind beforehand about the not-guilt plea—"

"I won't. I want a trial. I want the truth to be heard."

"Even if the truth is heard, you need to understand you'll probably have to serve some time in at least a minimum or medium security facility."

"Get this straight, Mike, I don't want to serve any time at all."

"I understand that. But the severity of the charges and the circumstances are what they are. You can probably get paroled early for good behavior." Parker linked his fingers. "That is, if . . ."

"If Ozy lives."

"That's the long and short of it."

"Pull out all the stops in my defense. There could be a big bonus in it for you."

Parker's expression was unreadable. He stayed silent as he put his notepad and file into his briefcase, which he snapped shut. He returned his pen to the pocket of his hand-tailored white shirt. "Any questions?"

"None that you can answer."

CHAPTER 4

STARKS TUGGED AT the neckline of the undershirt his mother had dropped off for him at the jail. She hadn't wanted to see him. He knew why: Members of the maternal side of his family were born with a pride chromosome. Lynn Starks loved her son but the extreme public humiliation resulting from his arrest was more than she could stand. He knew she'd forgive him one day, and that her ability to forgive tended to simmer until she was ready.

"All rise. The District Court of Suffolk County, State of Massachusetts, is now in session. Honorable Judge Harold Weaver, presiding."

The judge took his seat at the bench then shuffled through the case files in front of him, glancing up briefly at the line-up of people waiting to plead. "We'll begin with arraignments then move onto trials." In a monotone voice, he continued. "All persons are innocent until proven guilty. You have the option to plead not guilty, guilty, or no contest. No contest means you concede the charge or charges against you, without admitting guilt and without presenting a defense. I advise you against pleading no contest. You have the right to obtain counsel. If you cannot afford counsel, the court will appoint an attorney for you."

An hour later, it was Starks's turn in front of the judge. He flinched and his face reddened when the charges against him were read aloud. He also questioned whether his decision to plead not guilty would work in his favor or not. He'd always been able to methodically weigh pros and cons when it came to business matters. This, however, was unfamiliar, unpredictable territory.

He tried to give his full attention to what was going on but his mind wanted him in the past, a reverie that was broken when Parker nudged him to stand.

"My client pleads not guilty to all charges, your honor."

The judge looked directly at Starks then glanced at Parker with a quizzical expression on his face. He shook his head, checked the calendar and said, "Trial starts this coming Monday, 10:00 a.m."

"In the matter of bail, your honor—"

"No bail will be set."

"Your honor, in this instance, bail can be set quite high, which will ensure my client shows up for trial."

"Denied." The judge's gavel came down, putting an end to the matter.

Starks turned to Parker. "I don't want to stay in jail until the trial. Do something. Get me out, for Christ's sake."

Parker began to pack his briefcase. "This judge is a hard-ass. Plus, it's election time. You've seen the corporate scandals on the front pages of all the newspapers. Everyone, especially candidates running for office, are screaming for corporate criminals to be held accountable."

"I'm not involved in any of that."

"No." Parker shut his briefcase. "But you're considered one of them."

"Am I going to have to keep paying for the shit others do?"

CHAPTER 5

A HANDCUFFED STARKS WAS escorted by a bailiff into the courtroom from the holding cell. He shuffled directly to where Parker and the other top three of a long list of attorneys from Parker, Birnhaum, Bailey, and Todd sat at the defense counsel's table. He nodded at each man in turn. The chair next to Parker was empty, which the attorney pulled out for him.

"I see you brought your muscle," Starks said.

"Sometimes it makes a difference, especially for someone as high-profile as you are. But I'm lead counsel for your defense."

Starks turned to check out who was in attendance in the gallery. Behind the prosecutor's table, Margaret Hessinger glared at him. He looked away. Directly behind him and toward the middle sat his mother, his aunt Anita, and her son, Hank, who waved at him. Next to Hank sat Jeffrey Davis, who smiled and gave Starks the thumbs-up sign. Starks nodded, his own smile not reaching his eyes. He continued to scan faces, thankful that Emma had heeded Parker's advice and stayed away.

The one person he wanted to see wasn't there.

Where the hell is my wife? She should be here, supporting me.

After all he'd done for her; after all he'd sacrificed for her and their children. And after all, it was her fault he was here.

His jaw was tight as he turned to face the judge's bench.

"All rise. The Superior Court of Suffolk County, State of Massachusetts, is now in session. The Honorable Benjamin Solomon, presiding."

Once the formalities were taken care of, the prosecuting attorney walked to the jury box and began his opening statement.

Starks blanched at the words used to describe him. That person was unrecognizable to him: Extreme sense of entitlement, calculating, serial philanderer, a monster with a violent temper who'd planned his revenge on Ozy Hessinger—the victim of a deliberate, brutal, potentially fatal attack in front of his wife and two young children.

Starks rested his forearms on the table. Leaning to his right he said to Parker, "He's trying to make it sound like Ozy was the only victim."

Parker touched Starks's right forearm, making clear his message to stay silent.

Starks slouched in his chair and stretched his legs out in front of him. He crossed his arms and sighed.

Parker whispered, "Sit up straight. And get that expression off your face."

Starks did as instructed and glanced at the jurors, who listened with frowns on their faces as the prosecutor continued to speak. My God, he thought, I'm being branded as some rich CEO who believes the law doesn't apply to him.

Now he understood why Parker had advised him to keep his expression as blank as possible and not to look at the jury. He felt certain none of those people who were supposed to be his peers would think or imagine anything other than what they were being told to. None of them knew what he'd been through. How would any one of them feel if their spouse had cost them their self-respect, reputation, and family, and in the excruciating way his wife had?

Starks's head snapped up when he heard his name.

"Frederick Starks first attacked and injured Mr. Hessinger on his doorstep then entered the house unlawfully. Once inside the house, he hit the victim in the head with a heavy object then beat him repeatedly with his fists, in full view of Mrs. Hessinger and the Hessinger children, even though the victim was unconscious. Mr. Starks had to be forcibly removed and restrained by police." He paused for effect.

"I'm sure defense counsel will likely call this a crime of passion. Crime of passion is spontaneous, the result of something distressing happening in the moment regarding a spouse or partner and his or her illicit lover. It's designed to mean catching them in the act, which provokes the injured party to violence—in the moment. This attack happened almost a full year after the defendant and his wife stopped living together as husband and wife, and the defendant had another woman and her son living with him. So I ask you, what was the point of that brutal attack?

"Whatever image of the defendant defense counsel puts before you, ladies and gentlemen, evidence against Mr. Starks is clear and irrefutable, as well as the fact that he acted with premeditation, which prosecution counsel will prove."

The prosecutor returned to his chair, glancing quickly at the jurors. Pleased with what he saw, he didn't try to hide his smile.

Michael Parker made his way toward the jurors.

"Ladies and gentlemen of the jury, my client, Frederick Starks, went to the Hessinger house solely to confront Mr. Hessinger in front of Mrs. Hessinger so she'd know what was really going on in her life and marriage. Because my client felt she deserved to know that she, too, was being betrayed. That her family, as well, was on the brink of destruction. That's all my client intended. But Mr. Hessinger, rather than being truly sorry for his wrongdoings, chose to provoke my client, thereby inciting another form of passion: overwhelming frustration and a sense of helplessness to make right what had been made wrong, and this quickly became exacerbated by fear for his life.

"Today you'll hear testimony by prosecution's witnesses that make Mr. Starks appear one way. You'll also hear testimonies from witnesses for the defense counsel that claim Frederick Starks is known to be a mild-mannered, calm, non-violent individual.

"The fact is this: Mr. Starks had no harmful intention, no premeditation of an attack regarding Mr. Hessinger, but found himself in a situation where he had no choice but to defend himself."

Once Parker was seated, Starks said, "I'm not feeling confident about the jury's decision-making ability. The prosecutor hammered me."

"He's not the only one with a toolbox."

CHAPTER 6

THE PROSECUTOR CALLED his first witness.

A thin, angular woman clutching her handbag against her chest, moved with unsteady steps to the witness stand. She smoothed one side of her lank, dull hair before holding up her right hand to be sworn in.

Parker said in a low voice, "She's the prosecution's strongest witness. The longer she stays on the stand the more likely jurors will sympathize with her. That's problematic but not insurmountable. Don't let her testimony throw you."

Starks nodded and linked his fingers together, squeezing them hard to hide the trembling. He averted his eyes from the woman in the witness stand.

"Do you affirm to tell the truth, the whole truth, and nothing but the truth, under the pains and penalties of perjury?"

"I do."

"State your name and relationship to Ozy Hessinger."

"Margaret Hessinger. I'm his wife."

"Please be seated."

The prosecutor asked, "Mrs. Hessinger, do you recognize the defendant?"

Margaret Hessinger focused her gaze on Starks.

As much as he wanted to resist, he looked at her.

Her lips quivered then flattened into a thin line. "Yes. That's the man who tried to kill my husband."

Parker stood and said, "Objection. Witness's statement calls for a conclusion. Motion to strike the words after the witness identified the defendant."

"Sustained." The judge gave the order to the court reporter.

Starks's fingers felt something rough on the narrow front edge of the wooden table. He leaned back to see what it was. Someone had lightly etched a word into the wood: *Free*. He wondered if whoever had scratched it there had been found not guilty—innocent or not—and set free, or had it been a prayer by someone whose nerves had been as taut as his were now.

"Please tell the court, to the best of your recollection, what you witnessed and the words you heard exchanged between the defendant and your husband the night of the attack."

Margaret Hessinger repeated what she'd seen and heard, briefly halting her testimony while the glass bowl was entered as evidence.

"Please continue."

"There was a gap in what I could hear because I'd gone upstairs to the children. And to call the police, before I returned downstairs."

"Why did you return downstairs?"

"I was terrified for our safety, for all of us. Especially when I stopped hearing my husband's voice."

"Had you ever met Mr. Starks before that night?"

"No."

"Had you ever heard the names Frederick Starks or Kayla Starks mentioned by your husband at any time before that night?"

"No."

"How has this incident affected you and your family?"

The muscles of her face flickered as she twisted the strap on her handbag. "We're traumatized. My husband's in a coma, one he may never come out of. They just don't know. My children and I are in therapy five days a week."

"Your children were traumatized because they heard the violent commotion going on downstairs?"

"What traumatized them was that, even though I told them to stay hidden in one of the closets, they came downstairs. They saw what he, the defendant," she pointed at Starks, "was doing to their father. Saw their daddy covered in blood and not moving. My daughter, who's six, now wets her bed and suffers embarrassment about that. My son is five and now has panic attacks. Any loud noise, anyone knocks at the door, he curls up in the fetal position and stares at nothing."

Tears rolled down Margaret Hessinger's mottled cheeks. She took a tissue from her handbag. "They can't go to school. They can't leave my side. It was hell leaving them this morning with their grandmother. They cry day and night for their daddy. And when they can sleep, both of them have nightmares. They wake screaming in terror several times a night. Since the attack happened, we all sleep in my and my husband's bed. So none of us are getting the rest we need. Our family doctor suggested sleeping pills but I don't want to get them started on that habit and I don't want to be knocked out when they need me."

Starks rested his head in his hands and choked back a sob. He understood. There was no respite from his nightmares since that night, either.

Parker nudged him gently and said, "Remember what I told you."

Starks blanked his expression as much as possible and stared at his hands.

"Your witness." The prosecutor, wearing yet another slight smile, took his seat.

CHAPTER 7

PARKER REMAINED AT the counsel table. "Mrs. Hessinger, when you heard Mr. Starks state that your husband had been unfaithful to you with his wife, what were your thoughts?"

"I didn't believe him." She sat up straight. "I believed my husband."

"Do you still believe your husband?"

She glared at Parker but said nothing.

"We'll leave that for now. You were upstairs when the incident in the kitchen occurred?"

"For part of it. As I said, I was afraid for my husband so went back downstairs and heard them in the kitchen."

"You just said you couldn't hear your husband."

"I heard him," she pointed at Starks, "hitting my husband, and his foul language. Obviously, it meant my husband was there." She focused on Starks, her face contorted. "He—the defendant—was on top of my husband, beating him with his fists, over and over. He wouldn't stop. My favorite bowl that had been my grandmother's was on the floor." Her right hand went to her mouth. She swallowed several times then added, "With my husband's blood and hair on it."

"Did you at any time say anything to either Mr. Starks or your husband to get them to stop the altercation?"

"I don't remember. I was in shock. I may have screamed. And," rage found its voice, "there was no *altercation*. It was a vicious attack. The man's an animal. My husband was unconscious, unable to defend himself."

"So you have no knowledge of what happened before you went to the kitchen. When you went into the kitchen, did you see a knife where it didn't belong, say, on the floor or the counter?"

The prosecutor stood. "Objection. Beyond the scope. Defense counsel cannot ask questions about anything not entered in evidence or not covered in the previous line of questioning."

"Yes, counselor," the judge said. "Defense will refrain from—"

Parker faced the judge. "Your honor, my client has pleaded not guilty to attempted murder or any premeditation of such. We intend to prove his actions in the kitchen were in self-defense, after Mr. Hessinger grabbed a knife and—"

The prosecutor shouted, "Objection."

"Sustained. Defense counsel will follow the rules. Proceed."

"No further questions, your honor."

Parker took his seat.

Starks said, "We've got to get them to believe the truth about the knife."

"That would be easier if you'd spoken up at the time. However, we still have some good cards in our deck, and I intend to play them."

CHAPTER 8

THE PROSECUTOR CALLED to the stand the primary EMT who had attended to Ozy Hessinger in the back of the ambulance. "What was Mr. Hessinger's condition when you arrived at his home?"

"Mr. Hessinger's breathing was shallow and he was unresponsive."

"Did the defendant, Mr. Starks, require medical attention?"

"His hands were swollen, and he had some lacerations and contusions. Mrs. Hessinger told us some of his injuries were received when Mr. Starks attacked her husband and they crashed through the glass door at the front of the house."

The prosecutor asked, "Did you provide medical attention to Mr. Starks's injuries?"

"The police said they'd see to any medical needs of Mr. Starks. Mr. Hessinger's condition was critical, so we got him into the ambulance and to the E.R. as quickly as possible."

"Did Mr. Hessinger, at any time, regain consciousness from the time you arrived at his home until you released him to emergency room staff?"

"No."

"Your witness, Mr. Parker."

Parker kept his head down as he scribbled something on his notepad. "No questions."

The E.R. doctor was called to the stand. "The head trauma Mr. Hessinger received has the potential to cause long-term, severe neurological damage, possibly even paralysis. He's currently in a comatose state."

"Is this a medically-induced coma?"

"He was in a coma when we received him in the E.R."

"Can you offer any prognosis?"

"Not at this time. In situations like this, we have to wait and see. Fluctuations in brainwave activity indicate that consciousness may be possible at some point. But, not as yet."

"Your witness, Mr. Parker."

"No questions for this witness."

The judge raised his gavel. "The court calls a fifteen-minute recess."

The sharp crack of the gavel echoed in Starks's mind, as though the sound itself declared him guilty as charged, without waiting for the full story to be revealed. But he couldn't get the image of the Hessinger children and their suffering out of his mind. What's been done by all of us, he thought, has more repercussions than any of us ever bothered to consider.

He'd only wanted to humiliate Ozy. No, that wasn't true. He'd hoped to destroy Ozy's family, just as the man had destroyed his. Just, God, not in this way.

Now the proverbial Dominoes were tumbling, each one striking the next as they fell. And, it seemed this would continue, until none were left standing.

CHAPTER 9

THE TWO POLICE officers who had responded to the nine-one-one call were in the gallery, but only the one who had drawn his weapon at the Hessinger house was called to testify.

"Tell the court what you found when you arrived."

"The defendant and Ozy Hessinger were in the kitchen. Initially, I thought Mr. Hessinger was dead. He wasn't moving, and there was significant blood on the two men and on the floor, mostly on the floor. There was some blood splatter on the walls and cabinets. When checked, Mr. Hessinger still had a pulse, but it was faint."

"The report you filed said you drew your weapon. Why did you do that?"

"The defendant didn't respond to repeated orders to cease the attack. I also feared he might assault my fellow officer when he tried to restrain the defendant."

The prosecutor walked to the witness box. "Was it difficult to separate the defendant from Mr. Hessinger?"

"Yes, sir. He was obviously enraged and—"

Parker was on his feet. "Objection. Witness is stating an opinion."

The prosecutor said, "Your honor, I'd like to establish that this witness is qualified to state more than an opinion."

"Overruled. Proceed."

"How did you come to the conclusion that the defendant was enraged?"

"Twenty years on the job." The officer looked at the jurors. "I know enraged when I see it."

"How long did it take you to restrain the defendant?"

"At least a few minutes. It was a struggle to get him to the floor so I could cuff him."

"Did he try to escape?"

"Not escape, but . . ."

"But what?"

"He didn't take his eyes off Mr. Hessinger the entire time. Even while I restrained him, his hands stayed in fists, like he wanted to get back to the fight—not that it was a fair fight."

Parker stood. "Objection. Your honor—"

"Sustained. Strike the entire statement from the record."

"If you hadn't shown up when you did, do you think the defendant would have continued his attack until he killed Mr. Hessinger?"

Parker leaped up. "Objection. Calls for speculation."

"Sustained."

"I withdraw the question. Did you or the other officer find any weapons in the kitchen?"

"Not actual weapons, just the heavy glass bowl used to hit Mr. Hessinger."

The prosecutor picked up the bowl and brought it to the witness. "Is this the bowl?"

"Yes."

"How did you know for certain this bowl had been used to strike Mr. Hessinger?"

"The bowl was on the floor, near the victim and defendant. It had blood and hair on it. Later we determined fingerprints on the bowl were the Hessinger family members' and the defendant's."

"What color is Mr. Hessinger's hair?" The prosecutor turned and stared at Starks's nearly black mop that was months past his regular haircut. The jurors followed his lead.

"Blond."

"Was blond hair the only hair found on the bowl?"

"Yes."

"Was DNA on the bowl checked?"

"It was Mr. Hessinger's blood and hair."

Starks, head down, heard Ozy's voice in his mind—*Are you upset that I did your wife or that sometimes a buddy and I did her at the same time?*—then the sound of the knife being pulled from its slot. Felt again the fear followed by rage. What, he wondered, would any person in this room do if they found themselves in the same situation.

The prosecutor returned the bowl to the evidence table. "Did the defendant at any time mention to you, the other officer, or anyone else anything about a knife?"

"No. The only thing he said, when he finally decided to talk at the station, was that he wanted his lawyer. He told his attorney about the knife then his attorney told us."

"Was this information followed up?"

"My partner and I returned to the Hessinger house. There was a block of kitchen knives on the counter, but they were all in place. Mrs. Hessinger said that's exactly how they'd been before and after the incident."

The prosecutor faced Parker. "Your witness."

CHAPTER 10

PARKER GOT UP but stayed behind the defense counsel table. "You said that neither you nor the other officer found any weapon in the kitchen."

"No weapon other than the bowl, which was used as a weapon."

"Did you look for anything else that may have been used as a weapon?"

"Objection."

Parker said, "Your honor, we request leeway to continue this line of questioning."

"Objection overruled. Witness will answer the question."

The policeman sat forward. "We didn't look for other possible weapons. The bowl, obviously used in the attack, was in plain sight. Nothing else was out of place. There were no wounds on either man indicating any weapon other than the bowl, and the defendant's fists, had been used. Each man had small cuts, but we learned those were from when they fought outside the front door and the glass door shattered when the defendant shoved Mr. Hessinger through it. After it was reported a knife had been involved, we went back to the scene. We didn't run any tests on the knives, because we would have found logical fingerprints on them—the Hessingers's, I mean—since the defendant said he never touched the knife. And since the knife wasn't actually used, also according to the defendant, there wouldn't have been any blood."

Starks whispered to Todd, who was on his left, "The knife must have fallen under the island or behind it. I swear he dropped it when I hit him. When I saw he meant to use it on me, I freaked. You can be damn sure Margaret found it later, cleaned it and put it away."

The attorney gave one subtle nod of his head.

Parker was silent for a moment. "No further questions."

The prosecutor rose and said, "Your honor, permission for counsel to approach the bench."

"Granted."

Parker glanced at his law partners; they appeared as concerned as he was. He joined the prosecutor where he stood in front of the judge's bench. The words spoken couldn't be overheard but Parker's posture stiffened. He turned to look at the men at his table; his lips were pressed together.

The judge picked up the gavel. "The court will take a brief recess to meet with counsel in chambers."

Starks asked the other attorneys, "What's this about?"

Todd said, "We'll find out."

Everyone at the defense counsel table remained silent as they waited. Tension coiled up Starks's back and neck. He used his sleeve to wipe at the sweat that beaded on his forehead and wondered what reason there could be for a private discussion. He and the three attorneys watched the chambers door. And waited.

Fifteen minutes later, the door opened. The expression on Michael Parker's face made Starks's stomach flip. Once his attorney was back in his chair, he asked, "What the hell's going on?"

"I'm sorry. I tried everything possible." He looked at his partners. "The judge is allowing Kayla to testify for the prosecution."

Todd said, "A wife can't be made to testify against her husband."

"The judge is allowing it. Because Starks and his wife have been separated as long as they have, with obvious intent to divorce."

Color drained from Starks's face. "I don't believe it. I . . . I can't believe she'd do this. Not after all she's put me through already. Doesn't she realize she might take our children's father from them?" He shook his head. "It's not her." He pointed to the other table. "It's him, the prosecutor. He's forcing her to do this."

"I'm sorry. That's not how he made it sound."

Starks slumped back in his chair. Tears welled in his eyes. "My God. This is a nightmare that just doesn't stop."

CHAPTER 11

THE PROSECUTOR CALLED Kayla Starks as his next witness. Starks wrenched his head around and saw her rise from the last bench on the left, realizing she'd slipped into the courtroom at some point. Curious eyes, as did his, followed the petite, shapely brunette as she walked with measured steps to the witness stand.

Starks kept his voice low as he told Parker, "The bitch got a modesty make-over. No cleavage hanging out, no red lipstick. Mike, you know this isn't how she looks. If she's going to lie about that, no telling what she'll say up there."

"People get up there and swear to tell the truth. They usually tell the truth that works for them," he replied.

Kayla was sworn in. The prosecutor began. "Mrs. Starks, do you admit to having an affair with Ozy Hessinger?"

Kayla blushed, looking even more beautiful. She cast her aqua eyes downward and replied, "Yes."

Margaret Hessinger leapt to her feet and shouted, "You whore! You and your husband have ruined our lives."

The noise level in the gallery rose as heads turned to stare at the woman, whose eyes and snarl were more animal than human as she pointed a fin-ger at Kayla.

The judge slammed his gavel several times. "Order in the court." Once those in attendance settled, he said, "Mrs. Hessinger, you may stay if you remain quiet. Although the court understands your feelings in this situa-tion, another word and the bailiff will escort you out."

The prosecutor waited several moments then asked, "When did your involvement with Mr. Hessinger begin?"

"After my husband and I were separated."

Starks was on his feet. "That's a lie. You were screwing him long before we were separated. Three years. Three fucking years!"

The judge used his gavel. "The court will not tolerate that type of language. Mr. Parker, control the defendant. One more outburst and he'll be in contempt of court."

Parker stood. "Yes, your honor." He whispered to Starks, "Keep your mouth shut. You'll turn the jurors against you for certain."

Starks nodded and pressed his fingers against his eyelids.

The prosecutor faced Kayla. "During the time of your involvement with Mr. Hessinger, did you know he was married?"

"Not at first. We'd been involved several months before I learned this."

"How did you discover his marital status?"

"Ozy told me. Said he was sorry for not telling me sooner but he was afraid he'd lose me. He was as miserable in his marriage as I was in mine. He planned to leave his wife so we could be together. He knew how much I loved him, how much I needed him."

Soft sobs came from the gallery. The judge looked at Margaret Hessinger but said nothing.

"Mrs. Starks, was your relationship with Mr. Hessinger over by the time the defendant attacked him?"

"Yes. Way before. Ozy felt guilty about his children. Said he couldn't divorce their mother until they were old enough to understand. He thought it would be unfair to ask me to wait for him."

Starks told Parker, "This is exactly why I stayed in denial for so long. She's a convincing liar. People see the beauty, not the bitch."

Parker nodded. "I'll have my turn with her."

The prosecutor asked, "Did your husband—the defendant—give you any indication that he would seek revenge against Mr. Hessinger?"

Kayla hesitated. "Not exactly. But he had what I thought was an over-the-top hatred for Ozy. He was jealous of him, you see. Ozy told me he frequently saw my husband drive by his house, sometimes during the day and sometimes at night."

"So the defendant was engaged in a form of surveillance, or stalking, in Mr. Hessinger's regard."

Parker called out, "Objection."

"Overruled."

The prosecutor continued. "Did the defendant ever state any intention to directly engage with Mr. Hessinger, whether in conversation or in any other way?"

"No. But his temper—"

Parker was up. "Objection. Calls for a conclusion by the witness."

"Sustained."

The prosecutor smiled at Parker before turning back to Kayla. "Knowing the defendant as well as you do, why do you think he went to confront Mr. Hessinger?"

"Objection. Calls for opinion and speculation from the witness."

The prosecutor said, "Your honor, who knows a husband better than his wife who's lived with him as long as Mrs. Starks has lived with the defendant? She may not know his every thought, but she knows his personality."

"Objection overruled. You may answer the question, Mrs. Starks."

Kayla pursed her lips into a pout. "He has this over-blown sense of entitlement. He's so used to buying what and who he wants, he feels entitled to have whatever he wants, no matter what. And there's his double-standard about how men can behave and women can't. He considers me his property, just because I'm his wife. Thinks he can keep me in a glass cage and use and abuse me as he pleases."

Parker stood. "Objection."

"Overruled."

"You said 'use and abuse.' Did your husband physically abuse you?"

"There are other forms of abuse."

"Would you be more specific, please?"

"There's verbal abuse. Neglect is abuse." She glanced at the jury and said, "As is rampant infidelity." She faced the prosecutor. "Getting drunk and breaking things in the house is abusive, especially when the children are forced to witness it."

"Did the defendant display these behaviors throughout your marriage?"

"Not when we were first married. Back then, he was different. The more successful he became the more entitled he felt. And the more violent his temper became when he thought life—and especially I—shouldn't deviate from how he believed we should be. He's one for everything in its place, everything neat and orderly, including people. I tried to tell him life just isn't like that."

The prosecuting attorney dragged out Kayla's testimony about Starks's affairs—"the ones I know about," she said—and recollections of destructive outbursts of temper, both witnessed and not witnessed by their children.

"Prosecution rests."

Parker stood in front of the defense counsel table. "Mrs. Starks, do you wish to change your testimony about how long you were involved with Mr. Hessinger?"

"No."

"What about your involvement with other men?"

The prosecutor said, "Objection. The witness is not on trial."

Parker said, "Your honor, as the wife of Mr. Starks, at least still legally, the witness's behavior and the results of it are relevant to Mr. Starks's state of mind prior to that night and especially that night."

"Objection overruled. Witness may answer."

Kayla, head down, said, "I don't remember the question."

Parker stared at her, waiting until his silence forced her to look at him. "Were you ever involved with other men?"

"Only my husband."

"You mean until Ozy Hessinger."

"Yes."

Parker kept his eyes fixed on Kayla; she met his gaze. "No further questions."

Starks watched Kayla, who avoided looking at him, until the courtroom door closed behind her.

Starks's shoulders heaved. "Jesus. Did she ever love me?"

Parker had no reply.

The judge picked up his gavel. "Court will take a two-hour recess for lunch. Trial will resume at two o'clock."

"Mike, why didn't you ask her more questions? I thought you'd rip into her."

"That wouldn't have helped us. The Hayes's testimonies will."

CHAPTER 12

"DEFENSE CALLS JEFFREY Davis."

Jeffrey drew attention, as he always did, especially from the women in the courtroom, as he sauntered to the witness stand. His skin tone was almost the same as Starks's, but in his case it was a result of an African-American father and Caucasian mother. Like Starks, his hair was nearly black but his eyes were gold rather than dark brown like his friend's, and he was almost half a foot taller and twenty pounds more muscular. As he approached the witness stand, he smiled at one of the female jurors who automatically smiled back then blushed when she realized what she'd done.

"Mr. Davis, you and my client are business partners. Did you know each other prior to your professional association?"

Jeffrey smoothed his tie. "We've been friends since high school."

"When did you meet Kayla Starks?"

"Ninth grade. She was a student there as well. A new student."

"The defendant and his wife dated in high school?"

"Oh yeah. It was love at first sight—for Starks, at least." Jeffrey smiled. "He was bitten big-time."

"Did Mrs. Starks share his affections?"

"I don't know what she felt, exactly. I do know she said she liked him—girls talk, you know. Back then, Kayla came across as really shy, reserved even. But she knew Starks was interested; he made sure of it. She put him off for over a year, though. Not sure why she did that, but it worked. Made him crazy for her. He still is, despite what's happened. Maybe that was the point."

"Objection," the prosecutor said.

"Sustained."

"How would you describe Mr. Starks's usual behavior?"

"Loyal, supportive. He's a true friend and the best business partner you could ever have. The hardest working man ever. Great mind for business, a real leader. And he's an active, contributing member of his community."

"Would you describe him as a good husband and father?"

"He's devoted to his family. Busted his hump to provide only the best for them. And Kayla *always* insisted on the best."

"Objection."

"Sustained. Witness will refrain from offering opinions."

Jeffrey looked at the jurors. "That's not an opinion, it's a fact."

The judge said, "Mr. Davis—"

"Sorry, your honor." Jeffrey winked at Starks.

Parker continued. "Did Mr. Starks ever display signs of temper?"

"If you mean did he ever get upset like everyone else does, sure." Jeffrey glanced at the jurors. "Who doesn't when they have a good reason to?" He turned back to Parker. "But Starks has always been easy-going and good-natured. His ability to stay calm when the going gets tough is one of his most admired characteristics. So you can bet something big set him off that night."

"Objection."

"Sustained."

Parker continued. "You're saying that in all the years you've known my client, you never witnessed any displays of violent temper, especially toward his wife? Or abuse toward her?"

Jeffrey perched on the edge of the chair. "No way. He's not like that. Starks has never been confrontational or aggressive, especially not with his family. Assertive, sure, when it's called for, but he prefers to avoid conflict. Prefers to sort things out calmly and logically. He likes to keep the peace."

"Knowing Mr. Starks as well as you do why do you think he decided to go the Hessinger house that night?"

The prosecutor jumped up. "Objection. Question calls for speculation from the witness."

Parker said, "I withdraw the question, your honor." He hesitated a moment then asked, "From your personal knowledge of and or conversations with Mr. Starks, how did news of his wife's affair with Mr. Hessinger affect him?"

"Starks was devastated. I'd never seen him like that. Ever. Really felt for him." He tapped a finger against his right thigh. "But he wanted answers, not revenge. Especially when he learned the affair was going on a couple years before they separated, and that there were others before Ozy. Although, Ozy told him there were others at the same time." He raised his eyebrows. "You know . . . at the *same* time."

The prosecutor stood. "Your honor. Objection. The last part of the witness's testimony is hearsay."

"Sustained. Strike everything after—"

"Your honor," Parker said, "defense will be calling a witness who will verify much of this information is not hearsay, which means Mrs. Starks's testimony about her involvement with Mr. Hessinger, as well as other men, was false."

"You can present your witness but I will not allow the last part of that testimony. Objection sustained." The judge advised the court reporter about what to strike.

Parker turned to Jeffrey. "Mr. Starks told you the affair between Mrs. Starks and Mr. Hessinger was going on before he and his wife separated, not after, as Mrs. Starks testified?"

"Yeah."

The prosecutor was on his feet again. "Objection. Hearsay. Your honor, prosecution objects to defense counsel's line of questioning. Mrs. Starks is not on trial. Testimonies are in danger of becoming more like a divorce trial rather than a criminal one. Prosecution requests—"

Parker raised his voice. "Your honor, defense recognizes who's on trial. But as stated before, the behaviors of the defendant's wife have direct bearing on events, specifically regarding what my client's state of mind has been as a result. Crime of passion is the result of sudden anger or heartbreak regarding a spouse or partner who betrays the relationship. We believe it's imperative that it's made known that Mr. Starks was pushed to the limit that night by Mr. Hessinger's behavior and actions, and prior to that night by his wife's infidelities. Defense counsel is interested in the truth. We do not feel the jury can make an informed decision without knowing the background that put Mr. Starks into a fragile state of mind."

The judge hesitated. "Try to keep this line of questioning as contained as possible from now on. Objection overruled."

Parker faced Jeffrey. "How did Mr. Starks know this infidelity was a fact? Did he employ the services of a private investigator?"

"Later he did but not at first. He said he wanted more information but was too embarrassed about Kayla cheating on him. He also said he was holding out for the possibility Kayla would come to her senses and perhaps they'd reconcile. Paying a P.I. would make it more real. The proverbial nail in the coffin. Turned out he didn't learn anymore than he already knew. Just got confirmation."

"Then how did Mr. Starks first learn about his wife and Mr. Hessinger?"

"Richard Hayes. His wife told him. She's Kayla's best friend, or was."

The prosecutor said, "Your honor, if this witness's further testimony is to be based on gossip and hearsay, prosecution objects."

Parker faced the judge. "Your honor, I intend to call Mrs. Hayes as a witness for the defense. And, I have no more questions for this witness."

"Objection overruled."

The prosecutor moved to the witness stand. "Mr. Davis, after the defendant and his wife separated, did he become involved in another relationship?"

"He did. And he had a right to. He was miserable, broken-hearted."

The prosecutor smiled at the jurors. "Not so *very* broken-hearted, it seems."

"Objection."

"Sustained."

"Mr. Davis, would you say the defendant was faithful to his wife throughout their marriage?"

"Yes."

"Are you certain of this?"

"Women are drawn to Starks. Always have been. He treats them well.

You know, with consideration. He's courteous, even back in school. Maybe he flirts a little. Who doesn't? It's good for healthy self-esteem. But that's as far as it ever went."

"No further questions for this witness."

Parker called one of Starks's employees to the stand.

"Your honor, the prosecution would like to save the court time and money. We understand that defense counsel intends to call a number of Mr. Starks's employees as character witnesses who will swear to the integrity of the defendant and speak on his behalf. But as these people rely on the defendant for their livelihood, we feel their testimony may be slanted."

Parker asked, "Are you saying these witnesses would perjure themselves?"

"I'm saying prosecution allows that their testimony would likely, understandably, be favorable toward the defendant. And unless one or more of them were personally involved—were actual witnesses—to anything relative to previous testimony or this case—"

The judge nodded. "Your point is taken, counselor. The court acknowledges that defense can present numerable favorable character witnesses for the defendant. Mr. Parker, if you do have any witnesses on that list who have direct, personal testimony to offer, you may proceed."

Parker's shoulders sagged. "Yes, your honor. Then defense calls Jennifer Hayes."

CHAPTER 13

"HOW LONG HAVE you known Frederick Starks?"

Jenny Hayes ran a shaky hand through her auburn hair. In a paper-thin voice, she answered, "Since high school."

"How would you describe Mr. Starks?"

"Hard worker, all through high school and after. He's kind, generous. I'm not sure what else you'd—"

"Would you say, based on your observations and personal experience with the Starks all these years, that he was a good husband and father?"

She nodded. "Oh yes. He fulfilled his obligations as a husband and father. More than that. He gave them a secure, luxurious life. They'll never have to worry about anything they need. Or want."

"How long have you known Kayla Starks?"

"We were best friends in high school and after, until . . ."

"Until what?"

"Kayla made rude remarks about my husband and our family. Later, we made up. Then we ended the friendship for good. Because of her affairs and . . . other reasons."

Parker glanced at the jurors. "Affairs? Not just the one affair, as she testified?" He returned his focus to Jenny Hayes. "Do you know for a fact that Mrs. Starks had more than the one affair she stated she had with Mr. Hessinger?"

"After Kayla and I made up, she invited me to go out with her. Often. She flirted with men. A lot. Always wore low-cut tops and either tight pants or short skirts or dresses. She told me about what she was doing with other men. At first I didn't believe her. I thought she was just trying to show off; she always has to be the center of attention. Then I saw the truth for myself. I tried to get her to see reason and be faithful to Starks, but I couldn't. My husband began having trust issues about . . . my faithfulness. He asked me to tell him the truth about what Kayla and I did when we went out. I also told him about her affairs, including with Ozy. He insisted I end my friendship with her. I did, because I wasn't willing to lose my family."

"This going out—it occurred after Mr. and Mrs. Starks were separated?"

"Long before."

"What did you disclose to your husband about Mrs. Starks's interactions with other men during this period of socializing?"

"Everything, and that she'd lied to Starks about other men, going all the way back to college. They became a couple the last two years of high school, you see. Anyway, she told me she never wanted to marry Starks. It was just that he'd promised to spoil her and she intended to make him keep that promise. That once the money came in—and it was so much money, she wasn't about to part with it. She said Starks was having his fun so she was going to have hers. That he could just learn to live with it."

"When did Mrs. Starks tell you about her relationship with Mr. Hessinger?"

"Almost four years ago."

"That's a good deal of time prior to her separation from my client. However, it's important to know if you have any personal knowledge of their relationship, beyond what Mrs. Starks told you?"

"About two and a half years ago, I saw her and Ozy together. They were in his SUV, behind a restaurant. There's a side street I sometimes use. That's how I saw them. Her car was parked behind his."

"Were they having a conversation in his car?"

Jenny stayed silent but her face burned red.

"You may answer the question, Mrs. Hayes. It's okay."

"They were having sex."

"Please be more explicit."

"Kayla was moving up and down slowly, on top of Ozy. Her top was bare and Ozy was . . . he was nuzzling her breasts."

The judge banged his gavel to quiet chuckles from the gallery and several of the jurors.

"Did you tell any of this information to Mr. Starks?"

"My husband did."

"Why did he do that?"

The prosecutor said, "Objection. The answer lacks foundation."

"Sustained."

"No more questions for this witness."

The prosecuting attorney focused on his notes for a moment. "Mrs. Hayes, did Mrs. Starks ever disclose to you anything about the defendant's infidelities?"

Jenny squeezed her hands together. "Yes, but—"

"Did she specifically say the defendant had been unfaithful to her during the course of their marriage?"

"Yes. But—"

Parker jumped up. "Objection. Hearsay."

"Sustained."

"I have no further questions." The prosecutor took his seat.

CHAPTER 14

PARKER CALLED RICHARD Hayes to the stand.

"How did you and Mr. Starks meet?"

"Through my wife, who was friends with Kayla—Mrs. Starks."

"Your wife testified that her friendship with Mrs. Starks ended as a result of their social activities and how they upset you. What was it about their activities that concerned you?"

"My wife and I socialize together, whereas Starks and Kayla often socialized separately. At first I supported Jenny's going out with Kayla because I knew she missed the friendship they'd once had. But Jenny started coming home later and later at night. Then I found text messages on her phone, from men hitting on her, men she'd met while out with Kayla. That's when I insisted she tell me everything that had been going on. I wasn't about to let Kayla corrupt my wife."

"Were you surprised by the disclosure of these facts about Mrs. Starks?"

"Yes and no. Kayla's always been more independent than my wife. Almost to a fault. That's not accurate. It was to a great fault."

"What do you mean by independent?"

"She didn't treat Starks with the respect she should. I guess what I mean is that she isn't as traditional as my wife is. My wife believes in the sanctity of marriage. Kayla believes in doing whatever she wants."

"Objection. Witness is stating an opinion."

"Your honor," Parker said, "Mr. Hayes is speaking from personal knowledge of Mr. Starks and his wife."

"Overruled."

"Why did you tell Mr. Starks what you'd learned about his wife?"

"We'd become good friends. He had a right to know his wife was cheating on him, so he could deal with it."

"What did your wife tell you about Mrs. Starks and her affairs, including with Mr. Hessinger?"

"Kayla showed Jenny text messages from Ozy and other men from her workplace, which was Ozy's workplace as well, and also from men she met when she went out. A lot of the messages were explicit about what they'd done and what they wanted to do."

"You shared this information with Mr. Starks?"

"You're damn right." He glanced at the judge and said, "Sorry," then faced forward. "I felt he needed to know everything. I'd do that for any friend."

"What were your thoughts when you learned Mr. Starks confronted Mr. Hessinger about his affair with Mrs. Starks?"

Richard Hayes stayed silent.

"Mr. Hayes?"

"Starks has always been level-headed, even when I told him what Kayla was up to. He was understandably upset, but he wanted to save his marriage. I hesitated just now because I feel he has a right to be upset after all she put him through. I know how I felt when I thought . . ." His hands knotted into fists. "I'll say this: Starks says he went there to talk then that's what he did. He says the guy pulled a knife," Hayes slapped his right thigh, "then that's what happened."

The prosecutor glanced up from his notes. "Objection."

"Sustained. The witness's last two statements will be stricken from the record."

"Mr. Hayes, were you aware of any infidelities of the part of Mr. Starks?"

"My wife said Kayla told her about this."

"But you have no direct knowledge—no proof—that he was unfaithful during his marriage?"

"No. He's crazy about his wife. Or was."

"So Mrs. Starks's claims about her husband's infidelities may have been as false as her testimony about her relationship with Ozy Hessinger and other men."

"Objection."

"I have no further questions." Parker headed toward his table.

The prosecutor said, "No questions for this witness."

Parker, still standing, said, "Defense rests."

The judge raised himself from his chair. "Court will take a fifteen-minute recess."

Starks whispered to Parker. "Let me testify. Let me tell them what was really going on all that time, what really happened that night."

"I can't do that."

"Damn it, Mike, put me up there so I can tell the truth."

"The prosecutor will have you hanging yourself before his third question. You're too emotional, too volatile. Trust me on this."

"I feel like a fucking target." Starks pushed against the table edge. "All right. We'll do it your way. What's next?"

"Closing statements. Then the jury leaves to deliberate their verdict."

Starks's breathing grew rapid. Not since he'd been a young child had his fate been in anyone's hands but his. The complete lack of control was intolerable. It was a feeling he never wanted to experience again.

CHAPTER 15

THE PROSECUTOR FACED the jurors.

"Ladies and gentlemen of the jury, whether or not the affair between Mr. Hessinger and Mrs. Starks happened before or after the Starks separated, the defendant had no right to attack or attempt to murder anyone. Yes, Mr. Hessinger is still alive, thanks to his wife's quick action. But he's in a coma. It's unknown as yet whether he will ever recover. And if he does wake, it's possible that he'll never be the same again. Perhaps he didn't deserve his wife's affections after his indiscretions, but his children did not deserve to lose their father, because for all intents and purposes, he is removed from their life at this time, as a direct result of the defendant's actions.

He moved closer to the jury box.

"You heard defense call this a crime of passion, an act perpetrated in a moment of emotional distress. To successfully raise such a defense, despite what defense counsel wants you to believe, the defendant must have acted *immediately after* the provocation—meaning catching his wife and Mr. Hessinger in the act of sexual relations, and having—or taking—no time to calm down. If we eliminate premeditation, which is what the defense counsel wants us to do, charges against the defendant can be lessened. More than that, he can be acquitted. The defendant and his counsel would like that.

"But you cannot forget that the defendant deliberately went to Mr. Hessinger's house late at night, where his wife and children slept, and with the intent to confront Mr. Hessinger. Otherwise," he raised his hands in question, "why was he there? Defense wants you to believe it was to have a calm, rational conversation. Yet, the defendant's own wife spoke of his violent temper, how he destroyed some of their property in his fits of rage.

"Defense wants you to believe the defendant showed up at the Hessinger house on more of a whim rather than as a calculated plan, and that the situation went awry. How does anyone simply show up anywhere? It can't happen. A decision to go somewhere specific has to be made, unless, of course, the defendant wants you to believe he happened to be driving by the Hessinger house on his way to somewhere else late at night and spontaneously decided it was a good idea to—after nearly an entire year of separation with his wife—wake the Hessinger household and . . . have a chat."

He paused, taking a moment to meet the eyes of a number of jurors.

"That's not what happened. The defendant made a deliberate choice to go there. Whether that was five minutes before he went or five months or five years shouldn't matter. The result is the same: It was decided and planned in advance. You have to consider whether or not it's likely that a man with a violent temper, who selfishly puts his 'fragile' ego above rationality, planned nothing more than stopping by—after midnight—to make a statement such as, 'Even though my wife and I are no longer together, even though your affair with her has been over for months, even though she's made it obvious she no longer wants to be married to me, I want to get you in trouble with your wife.' And then leave."

Starks whispered to Parker, "Not true. She was begging me to come back to her. I'm the one who refused after finding out the truth."

Parker gestured for him to keep quiet then put his attention back on the prosecutor.

"Yes, Mrs. Starks admitted to being involved with Mr. Hessinger. Yes, the defendant and his wife did separate. And, the defendant," he turned and pointed at Starks, "was so broken-hearted about his wife that he immediately got into another relationship, which he's still involved in."

The prosecutor turned back to the jurors and smiled. "So why go see Mr. Hessinger? The word was used, ladies and gentlemen: Entitled. Rather than realize or admit his wife no longer loved him and had chosen to end an unsatisfactory and possibly inevitable violent relationship with her husband, the defendant felt entitled. But entitled to what? He was involved with another woman. Why not move on—or is the defendant not as rational and peaceful as we've been asked to believe?

"The defendant deliberately went to the Hessinger home late at night, catching his victim unaware. He deliberately attacked Ozy Hessinger on the doorstep of his home, an attack witnessed by Mrs. Hessinger. He then deliberately entered the Hessinger home and continued his attack, becoming more and more violent, not even stopping when two children watched the brutality he committed against their father. With the exception of his hands, which had minimal personal injury brought about by his own actions, the defendant had no defense wounds. No wounds at all.

"What Mr. Starks did was a grievous offense, one that has caused as yet untold, long-term damages to the victim and his family. The defendant is a highly successful businessman. A businessman used to analyzing his competition and doing what it takes to win. According to others, he's proven himself adept at calculating his wins. This time, he miscalculated: he was caught in the act by police.

"Defense counsel wants you to believe this was a crime of passion." He shook his head. "This was no crime of passion; it was a crime of violent temper.

"Ladies and gentlemen, I ask you to consider the evidence put before you today. There's only one verdict you can give, as I'm sure you realize: guilty of all charges."

Starks slumped forward. "God help me."

Parker said, "My turn."

CHAPTER 16

PARKER STOPPED WHEN he was even with the witness stand then faced the jury.

"Frederick Starks fell in love with his wife, Kayla, in high school. This was no schoolboy crush; it was deep, abiding love, evidenced by the fact that they have been a couple since those teenage years until a little less than a year ago. Mr. Starks believed he and his wife would spend their lives together with their children and someday their grandchildren. That dream was crushed. Not by Mr. Starks, but by his wife, the woman he cherished and provided so well for all these years. And this was abetted by the actions of her lover, Ozy Hessinger.

"The prosecution wants you to believe Mr. Starks is a calculating man. A good businessman has to be, in some measure. But you heard testimony that proves Mrs. Starks is even more so. It was said by her that she never wanted to marry her husband." He glanced at Starks. "She did, however, want to make certain he spoiled her, as he'd promised to do." He returned his gaze to the jurors. "Which he did. Whatever she wanted, she could have. She and their three young children have been well provided for, and will continue to be so, as a result of Mr. Starks's consistent efforts for more than two decades.

"Some people are harsh when it comes to people who have his level of success. But I ask you to consider what it's like to study hard and work your way through college so that you can support your family. And not just help your family, but be generous with friends and members of the community who are in need, as Mr. Starks has done. To build a business that provides employment and good livelihoods for others and their families. What type of character must this person have? Is Mr. Starks to be judged because of his success and his generosity ignored?

"How would it feel to struggle for years then have the person you trust and love most betray you in a way that devastates you and destroys the family you cherish and worked so hard for?" He waved his right hand. "This might lead to feeling crushed, angry even. Maybe you'd walk away from it; take your licks. Or maybe you'd feel justified in telling the person or people involved exactly what they've done. Let them know how their actions have harmed your family, especially your young children. And maybe during that conversation, you find yourself put in the position of needing to protect your life.

"I realize that crime of passion, as the prosecution stated it, and according to the law, refers to catching the person you love and trust in the act of infidelity. But the law also refers to heartbreak. A crime of passion due to sudden anger or heartbreak. Heartbreak doesn't always happen so conveniently in one particular moment. It can also and often does build over time. It happens when you learn of your spouse's betrayal, including that it wasn't just recent or minor—if betrayal can ever be deemed minor—but has been going on for years, as is the case in Mr. Starks's situation. Heartbreak happens when you are forced to live apart from your children, to watch their distress and be unable to do anything about it. To feel you've failed them or worry they'll think you have."

Parker moved forward until he was two feet from the jury box.

"Mr. Starks has been accused of being an unfaithful husband. No evidence was provided of this. In fact, testimony from witnesses who know him well stated it was not true. Where did this rumor come from? From his wife, who was unfaithful, egregiously so, and was so long before their separation. She admitted to being involved with Mr. Hessinger after the separation, but Mrs. Hayes, if you recall her testimony, who was at the time still her best friend since high school, stated this was not so. I realize Mrs. Starks is not on trial today, but her behaviors and how they affected Mr. Starks must be considered.

"And, yes, Mr. Starks did become involved in another relationship after he and his wife separated. For all intents and purposes, the Starks's marriage was over. Yet, he still held out hope for their reunion, especially for the sake of their children.

"People deal with emotional pain differently. Some turn to drugs or alcohol. Some shut down and isolate themselves. Some, especially in matters of the heart, may try to find intimacy with another person, as Mr. Starks did. Yet, his love for his wife and children, and the pain of what he'd lost, drove him to approach his wife's married lover, to let him know the results of his own infidelity.

"Could he have chosen a better time and place to speak with Mr. Hessinger, or abandoned the idea altogether? Yes, but who among us hasn't found our hearts deeply affected when we faced such loss then found ourselves making choices we wished we hadn't? It's human nature."

Parker rested his hands on the front of the jury box. "Mr. Starks was indeed pushed to his limit that night outside and inside the Hessinger house. And let's not delude ourselves into thinking we ourselves have no such limits." He smiled. "And this includes the prosecutor." He backed up a few feet. "Mr. Starks had, until that antagonistic encounter on the part of Mr. Hessinger, demonstrated remarkable restraint. And then it became a matter of self-defense. Please keep in mind that Mr. Starks did not enter the house intentionally: events unfolded that put him inside the house, where he never meant to go, and subsequently put his life in peril.

"The prosecution doesn't want you to consider the fact of a knife being present. And I realize the officer said neither he nor his partner saw a knife. He also admitted they didn't look for any weapons. Why? Because they believed the wounds, alone, didn't give them a reason to. Mr. Hessinger had a butcher knife in his hand, and when Mr. Starks saw the knife—when he realized Mr. Hessinger's intent to use it—he grabbed the bowl and struck in self-defense. The knife fell from Mr. Hessinger's hand. What became of the knife remains unknown. At this time, at least. And, yes, Mr. Starks did then strike Mr. Hessinger a number of times. But by then the chemical adrenaline was surging through his system. Fear for one's life will do that to a person. That's a scientific fact of human biochemistry, not a fault in Mr. Starks's character."

Parker retreated, until he was halfway between the defense table and the jurors.

"One thing you are obligated to consider is reasonable doubt. The prosecutor bears the burden of proof that his version of events is accurate, and he must have proven this to the extent that there can be no doubt in your mind that Mr. Starks is guilty as charged. And, this must be considered for each charge separately. I trust you will take this into consideration and make a fair and informed decision.

"Ladies and gentlemen, I ask you to think about what it's like to be betrayed by someone you cherish then taunted deliberately by the person your spouse betrayed you with—for the longest period of time. I ask you to consider what you would do, and how you might feel, if the person who had in fact already destroyed your family, pulled a weapon on you with intent to do bodily harm or even to end your life. Then I ask you to see reason, to grasp the fact this was a crime of passion and a matter of self-defense, and find Frederick Starks not guilty as charged, on all counts."

Parker returned to his chair.

"Thank you for that," Starks said. "I only hope the jurors really listened to you."

"You have to face facts. You're guilty of entering the premises, and of assault and battery, which the police witnessed. It's possible the jury will find you not guilty, but it's probable they'll find you guilty of something. Let's just hope their deliberation takes a long time."

"Why?"

"The longer they deliberate, the more in your favor they're leaning."

CHAPTER 17

"MR. FOREMAN, HAS the jury reached a verdict unanimously?"

"Yes, your honor."

"Please read that verdict before the court."

"On the charge of attempted murder in the first degree, we the jury find the defendant not guilty."

Starks grabbed Parker's arm.

"That's good," Parker said, "but that's just the first charge."

"On the charge of assault, we the jury find the defendant guilty."

Starks's grip tightened.

"On the charge of burglary, we the jury find the defendant guilty. On the charge of battery, we the jury find the defendant guilty."

The judge struck the gavel to quiet those in the gallery. "Will the defendant please stand."

Starks, shaking his head in disbelief, had to be helped to his feet by Parker. Birnhaum, Bailey, and Todd joined them as they faced the judge.

"Frederick Starks, in accordance with the laws of the State of Massachusetts, for the felony charge of burglary with assault, I hereby sentence you to the minimum penalty of ten years. For the charge of a battery resulting in serious injury, I hereby sentence you to the maximum penalty of five years. You are remanded to county prison while you await transfer to Sands Correctional Facility. Court adjourned."

Starks collapsed into his chair. "What does this mean?"

Parker sat next to his client. "I told you they weren't going to let you get away without some punishment."

"Oh my God." Starks covered his face with his hands.

Parker took hold of Starks's right arm and shook it. "Pay attention. From this moment on, you do everything right. You hear me? Especially at Sands. I'm pretty sure it's because of the extent of Ozy's injuries that the judge sentenced you to a maximum-security place rather than a minimum or medium one."

"Maximum? Jesus Christ."

"Listen. I repeat: You make damn sure you have a record of good behavior from now on. That'll improve your chances to get your fifteen-year sentence reduced and early parole. In the meantime, we'll get busy on an appeal."

"Fifteen years. Jesus. And if Ozy dies?"

"You're screwed."

CHAPTER 18

AFTER A BRIEF glance at their faces, Starks was deliberate about not looking at the other five prisoners being transported on the bus to Sands. Only two of the men wore ambivalent expressions. The others looked as terrified as he felt. He took a seat on the left side of the bus and stared out the window, ignoring the slate sky that hovered over the snow-covered landscape, and picked absent-mindedly at his cuticles. Despite the fact the bus heater was either broken or kept off deliberately, his clothes were soaked with sweat, and he stayed damp for the nearly two hours the worn-out shocks jostled the passengers over the paved and black-top roads that needed their own repairs.

After what seemed an age of road-racket white noise, one of the other prisoners said, "It's a damn fortress."

Starks swiveled his head right and saw Sands Correctional Facility for the first time. Acres of snowy ground unimpeded by trees or shrubs stretched between the road and the two-story concrete structure that squatted far back from the main road. Small patches of brown weeds poked through the bare expanse. Any prisoner trying to escape in that direction had no place to take cover.

A twenty-foot wall painted white interspersed with streaks of rust surrounded the grounds and was topped with strands of razor and electrical wire that coiled up at least one yard. Around the exterior perimeter of the wall was more razor wire, coils of it five feet high and four feet wide. Ten watchtowers loomed in various locations.

The bus turned onto the road that ran alongside the prison. A guard came out of a kiosk to speak with the driver before the heavy metal gate screeched open and the bus rambled through before lurching to a stop. The driver said nothing to them as he stepped out to meet the guard who joined him.

After a frozen fifteen-minute wait, two guards boarded the bus to get the prisoners. Starks followed the others through a mechanized door then through the next similar door once the first one clanged shut. He was brought to several holding rooms where he gave identifying details more times than he thought necessary.

It was in the last holding room he was brought to and where his shackles were finally removed that reality slipped yet another cog.

"Strip."

"What?" Starks read the name tag sewn onto the guard's shirt and added, "Mr. Jakes."

"That's *Officer* Jakes or CO Jakes, mister. Now strip. Or I can get a few inmates in here to get those clothes off."

Conscious of the pounding in his chest, Starks used fingers that threatened to go numb from fear to remove the slip-on sneakers. He stumbled as he stepped out of the jumpsuit. At a motion from the guard, he slid his underwear down, covering his genitals with one hand then the other.

Jakes pointed at the jumpsuit and shoes. "You wanna keep those?"

"Get rid of them." Starks grabbed his underwear, realizing he didn't have another pair. Something he'd have to take care of as soon as he knew how. He started to put the underwear back on but the guard told him not to.

The CO snapped on a pair of gloves. "Open your mouth." This was followed by "Bend over and spread 'em."

When Starks felt the probing intrusion, he said, "Jesus."

"No treat for me, either."

Jakes finished his exam then handed Starks a bar of soap and told him to follow him into an adjoining room, where he pointed to several shower heads mounted on the wall. "You got sixty seconds to suds and rinse."

Starks brought the soap close to his nose, sniffed, and recoiled. "What is this?"

"Disinfectant. Shower. Now."

Starks turned the water on and held his hand under it.

"Listen, Goldie Locks, no time for you to wait till the temperature's just right. Get your ass moving."

Starks's skin puckered under water that stayed frigid. Only since he'd been a boy had he showered so fast. And that was at a public pool where the rule required it before people could enter the water.

A prison doctor gave him a quick examination, asked him if he had any particular medical issues. He said he didn't.

Jakes handed him a set of yellow scrubs and a pair of lace-less shoes. Starks dressed in a hurry, grateful to end his exposure.

"Follow me." Jakes's walkie-talkie crackled. He listened a moment to the garbled chatter then turned the dial until the static stopped.

They entered yet another room. The CO said, "Hold out your arms."

Into Starks's outstretched arms were bundled a blanket, a coat, two more sets of yellow scrubs, a plastic plate and cup, toothpaste, toothbrush, and a bar of soap.

"What about deodorant?" Starks asked.

"Get your own in the commissary. Or stink. Personally, I don't care, but some of the inmates think stink is an aphrodisiac." He laughed at Starks's terrified expression. "Anything else you want you gotta buy."

Another guard approached them. Jakes said, "Officer Roberts here will escort you to your new home away from home." He turned to Roberts. "New fish is all yours."

Roberts held up a plastic-coated ID with Starks photo and prison number on it. "Always have this with you. If a CO or any authorized personnel asks to see your ID, even in the shower, and you don't have it, you'll be punished. It goes missing, you find the nearest correctional officer ASAP and get a new one."

He slid the ID into Starks's shirt pocket and said, "Follow me. A word of advice: Keep your eyes to yourself. Looking into anyone's cell can get you into shit you don't want to get into."

Starks kept his eyes aimed forward as Roberts led him through a series of sliding steel doors and corridors. He fought the urge to look around but was aware of certain things: Everything was gray—floors, walls, ceilings, and more doors with bars than he could count. Odors permeated the air: Sweat, human waste, soup, personal products, disinfectant, and some odors he had no inclination to identify. The stony silence of a number of inmates he passed was as loud as the shrieks of a few men Starks felt sure belonged in a mental facility.

Roberts finally said, "Cell Block C," then continued walking until he stopped at an open barred door two cells from the end of the corridor.

Starks stopped at the threshold to take in his surroundings. Bunk beds were mounted to the wall. The bottom bed was covered with a rumpled blanket, food wrappers, crumbs, but no person. A plastic chair was pulled out from a small desk next to the head of the lower bunk. The desktop was crammed with items that had spilled onto the floor. An overflowing plastic ashtray rested precariously at the edge of the desk. On the other side of the narrow enclosure was another desk and chair. He placed his items on top of the unused desk and studied what would be his bed with its thin, vinyl-coated excuse for a mattress.

"Where's my roommate?"

"*Cellmate*. This isn't college." Roberts checked his watch. "He'll be here in eight minutes. For the count."

"What's the count?"

"Unless you're someplace else you're authorized to be, you have your ass in this cell at eight, eleven, three, six, and ten every day. You're not here . . . maybe you don't want to find out."

Roberts turned and started out of the cell.

"What's my cellmate's name?"

"Ask him. I can't do every fucking thing."

CHAPTER 19

STARKS BELIEVED WITHOUT a doubt that he was not born to be an underling. Low man on the totem pole did not suit him at all. Yet, here he was, lower than he'd ever been. And this was only the first day of the next fifteen years. The only advantage he had in this god-forsaken place was money. Parker had greased a few palms to get Starks's prison number as soon as it was assigned. Jeffrey had then promptly deposited four hundred dollars into his prison account and set up automatic deposits of the same amount every two weeks, with the agreement that if more money was needed, it would be there.

He edged his way slowly around the fenced-in prison yard, pausing to grasp the mesh of the chain-link fence and look past it at the twenty-foot wall that was ten yards from where he stood. A crow landed on the wall. It stared at Starks, tilting its head in crisp movements, seemed to study him with one eye then the other. The black bird sharpened its beak on the concrete, cawed once then flew away.

Nearby, inmates played a rowdy game of football, while others used exercise equipment or otherwise occupied themselves. He'd learned from Parker that there were several hundred more inmates incarcerated with him than the place was actually designed to accommodate, which was already a large enough number. He wondered what the ramifications of that compression of bodies, mentalities, and egos would be, especially in the hot months. Fortunately, if one could consider anything about prison life fortunate, at least in Massachusetts, there were fewer hot months here than in the southern states. This did not ease apprehension about sharing his confinement.

Fifteen years was a long time. Especially in a maximum security prison. Unless he got out early for good behavior. This, he decided, was what he'd strive for, unless what he dreaded happened and his sentence became life.

"What happens to me if Ozy dies?" he'd asked Parker.

"You don't have to worry about the death penalty. Massachusetts no longer executes felons and hasn't since 1947. Some enthusiasts have tried overturning that decision. It's been up for a vote a number of times over the years, always defeated. Really, don't worry about it."

"Easy for you to say."

"I know it's a small comfort. I'm afraid you'll have to get used to small comforts. They'll keep you sane."

I'm in hell.

And I don't deserve to be here.

He desperately wanted to return to his former life. Wanted everyone to say that what he'd done that landed him in this godforsaken place had been justified, excused. That he'd done what any man in his situation would have done, and had a right to do—if he had any self-respect at all.

He thought about writing a letter to Jeffrey or calling him on the phone, realizing he had no idea how either process worked here—derided himself for not getting more of this kind of information from Parker before coming here.

Jeffrey would understand if he told him "I'm scared out of my mind, man. I'm always looking behind me, watching my back. Inmates stare at me. The fear of being raped or stabbed is more than a fear, it's a real possibility. If anyone other than a guard approaches me to talk, I don't know what I'll do. I don't trust anyone in here. And no one tells you anything, unless you ask. Even then, you almost wish you hadn't. You have to watch and learn what to do, not even knowing what the penalty might be for getting it wrong. Know what they call new arrivals, like me? New fish. That's how I feel. Like a fish out of water, flapping desperately on dry land, gasping for breath. It's a different world, Jeffrey. I'm seriously thinking of finding a way to kill myself." He knew his last sentence would seem dramatic, and he broke into a sweat when he realized some part of him meant it.

He let go of the fence and continued to walk, taking note as unobtrusively as possible of inmates in the yard. None of them looked friendly.

His cellmate had shown up for the count at eleven that morning. The man was short and wiry, as was his salt-and-pepper hair. He also spoke almost no English, though he seemed to understand it well enough, which Starks found out when he asked, "What happens if you're not in your cell for the count?"

"Big shit," though the man pronounced it *beeg sheet.*"

Then the cellmate had babbled in his native language, which Starks didn't recognize.

"Why the hell do they put people together who can't talk to each other?"

His cellmate bobbed his head several times and smiled, revealing the seven tobacco-stained teeth remaining in his mouth.

"Maybe that's a good thing," Starks added, as he climbed onto his bunk, where he lay staring out of the slit called a window.

His stomach grumbled in protest. How did anyone survive on the crap they served? As soon as he was brave enough to ask, he'd find out. The lunch meal, his first in prison, had not only been inedible but the entire process was confusing as hell. He'd had to watch others, and be careful how he did that so he didn't piss them off. It hadn't taken long to realize why trays were pushed anonymously through a slot: Who'd want to be blamed for the poor excuse for food. There had also been the matter of figuring out where to sit, which he quickly learned wasn't wherever you wanted to: Inmates had their usual tables and others were expected to treat this as a fact, if not practically a law. There was the discovery that he had to knock on the table before he sat and when he got up. He wasn't sure why, but every inmate did this, so he imitated them. And he'd learned he had ten minutes to eat in the chow hall, as one guard who poked him with his nightstick informed him. The dinner meal was no different.

That evening, after resisting using the exposed toilet all day, Starks went to the seat-less, coverless stainless steel fixture. It was bad enough he had no privacy, but his cellmate, whose name he still couldn't pronounce, had urinated on the rim and not cleaned it. The small attached sink was littered with spat-out toothpaste and beard hairs. Starks gagged. He wanted to shout at the man and tell him, "You're a pig," but he didn't want to be stuck like one while he slept. He also decided to keep his toothbrush far from this part of the cell.

Once he finally fell asleep, the nightmares haunted him: Ozy laughing as he plunged the knife in, Margaret's grandmother's bowl spilling blood over the rim like lava, and other disturbing images.

The third time he woke screaming, he heard from the bottom bunk, "Shut da fook up, you."

CHAPTER 20

"**G**IMME YA TRAY."

Starks recognized the man making the demand. He'd seen him strutting around the prison yard the day before, a man, he'd observed, inmates either avoided or deferred to. A need to know what the deal was led him to finally work up the courage to ask an inmate who seemed safe enough.

"That's Boen Jones," the inmate had told him. "Called Big Bo, which shouldn't be hard to figure out why. His gang's the largest and the worst. Controls big-time illegal shit on the inside, and on the outside. Only the brave or stupid ever mess with him. Or the insane. And, there *are* insane people in here. Rule is, always avoid them. As for Bo . . . he wants something from an inmate, he expects to get it. With a smile."

"I'm used to making demands, not receiving them."

The inmate had backed up, rocked his head back and forth on his neck. "Funny how stupid doesn't always look stupid."

Starks aimed his eyes at his tray. A large hand came at him from his right. The head of a tattooed white serpent began on the back of the hand and wound its way around the dark-skinned, muscular arm. He had to bend his neck nearly all the way back before his eyes locked with Bo's, and was immediately made aware there was a significant difference in seeing the inmate up close as opposed to at a distance. Everything about the man was enormous, except his voice, which was too high for the container it came from.

"I said gimme ya tray, motherfucker."

Bo reminded him of crazy Lenny, the grammar school bully who'd taken his lunch every day for a month, laughing at him in class when his empty stomach growled. He finally spoke with his grandfather about the bully. His grandfather patted him on the back and told him that any man without self-respect could never amount to anything; that he was better than that. The next day Starks came home with a black eye. His grandfather listened to the tale of how his grandson had kept his self-respect by bloodying the bully's nose.

"I meant the bully had no self-respect," he told his grandson. He cupped Starks's chin in his hand, examined the black eye and smiled. "But you did all right, boy. Never let anyone crap on you or your life. People will try to take what's yours, especially your ability to look yourself in the eye in the mirror. Take care of them and do it quick. Longer you wait the harder it is to do what you need to."

Starks stared into Bo's dark recessed eyes then at the fleshy round face wearing a self-amused expression.

"No."

Bo puffed out his chest. "Lookit, fellas, we got ourselves a spicy little fish. This new meat don't know my rules yet." His smile became a grimace. "You give me that tray or I teach you my first rule."

"I said no."

Bo's lips curled back over his teeth.

Starks stayed seated, kept his expression as one of being unimpressed, his debate about living or dying in conflict inside him. Confused as to which outcome he desired more, he stood and faced the inmate.

"I can't take a demand or threat seriously from someone with a voice that sounds like a squeaky-toy."

A number of inmates laughed. Some started to ease away from the table.

"You fucking sonofabitch. Nobody talks to me like that. Not if they want to live."

Two guards approached. One of them said, "Enough. Sit down and eat, both of you. Or we'll escort you back to your cells and keep you there."

Bo smiled and nodded at the guards then put his face close to Starks's.

"This ain't over, you little shit. You gonna learn what's what in here, and I'm gonna teach you."

CHAPTER 21

FOUR DAYS LATER, Starks worked up the courage to find the commissary. It wasn't anything like the upscale stores he was used to shopping in but it had the basics when it came to toiletries he needed. With a small amount of relief, he found some food options that were only slightly better than what was offered in the chow hall—everything was packaged, nothing fresh. He also bought letter-writing materials, envelopes, and stamps. He watched others for several minutes, discovering there were some items he could order that weren't kept in stock.

The inmate running the commissary told him, "Don't pin your happiness on your order always getting here on time. It'll get here. Eventually. But if your happiness depends on it . . ." He shrugged.

Starks dropped off his purchases in his cell, grabbed his coat then went to the yard, stopping at the exercise equipment. He pretended to check out what was available, keenly aware that Bo and several members of his gang were watching him from about five yards away. Bo said something to his cronies then, alone, started to move closer, until he stood a yard from Starks. The man's fists were clenched, his squint unblinking.

"When I tell you to gimme your tray, you give me the fucking tray, or anything else I want."

"Can't."

"Why the hell not?"

"I read the sign."

"What sign?"

"The one that says not to feed the animals."

"You going down, motherfucker."

Shorter and smaller as he was, there was no way he was a match to the bigger man. Nor did he believe that Bo was someone who believed in a fair fight. He could let the man take him out. It would end the pain and humiliation and nightmares once and for all. It might even make Kayla realize what she'd done to him. Let the bitch live with my death on her conscience, he thought.

Even as this inner struggle played out in his mind at high speed, one driving thought came to him: I have to live for my children.

So much had been taken from him. And they—Kayla, Ozy, Bret, and the others—had gotten away with it because he hadn't done what he needed to do. Just as it was with crazy Lenny and every other bully who'd ever crossed his path, this was a matter of self-respect but on a whole different level. His objective became clear: do anything and everything needed to survive—for the kids.

He waited until it wasn't safe to wait anymore then snatched up a twenty-pound dumbbell, slamming it into the man's solar plexus. Bo dropped to his knees and gasped for air. Starks threw the dumbbell to the side and with all his strength, kicked the man's face. Bo collapsed and curled into a ball. Starks leapt onto the man, using his fists to deliver devastating blow after blow to the man's face and torso. Blood splattered them and anything nearby. Like a man possessed, Starks pounded the downed man, until several prison guards pulled him away.

Starks stared down at the unconscious man.

Not again.

Guards on duty in the yard spoke with spectators, which included some of Bo's gang. Starks learned a valuable lesson as he listened: A code of silence was an unspoken rule. And he felt certain anyone who broke that rule would be punished swiftly and possibly fatally by other inmates.

Some of the spectators commented that he had a death wish. It became clear to him that rumors would spread around the prison, and that whatever inmates believed about his motivation for the attack, their consensus about him would likely be that he had to be insane.

He hadn't been here even a full week and he was already a feared man, or at least a man to stay away from.

A man repeating his recent past.

CHAPTER 22

THE GUARDS GOT nowhere with the informal interviews so dragged Starks inside. They shoved him into his cell then locked the door, which didn't put him in good with his cellmate.

An hour later a shackled Starks was escorted from his cell by two guards, to be questioned by the incidents council, one of them explained. They brought him to a room with a color scheme that hammered home the personality of the place: Gray—walls, linoleum, long metal table, metal chairs, filing cabinets, and five individuals covered in indifference.

Those five men stared at him from the other side of the table. In front of the man at the center was a desk name plate that read *Tony Spencer, Prison Incidents Investigator.*

Spencer pointed at the chair positioned three feet from the desk. "Sit."

Starks hesitated a moment then did as asked. All but Spencer, who stared at him over the rim of his eyeglasses, appeared bored.

"Frederick Starks. Hardly started doing your time and already you're in trouble. Not good. And not very smart to get into it with the inmate you did. So I have to ask, did Boen Jones threaten you? Is that why you attacked him?"

About two feet behind Spencer's head was a small window filmed with condensation. A bead of moisture swelled at the top of the glass then meandered its way down, revealing a sliver of reality on the other side. Starks followed its descent in silence.

"Starks?"

"No."

"*No?* That's your answer? Then why'd you attack him?"

"I didn't like the way he looked at me."

The investigator let silence hang between them for a moment. "You have a death wish, mister, or do you need your attitude corrected?"

Starks shrugged and leaned back in the chair. He could hear Parker reminding him to practice good behavior. Too late now.

"You're not going to tell me what's going on, are you?"

Starks remained silent.

"You're damn lucky Red Dot wasn't called."

"I don't know what that is."

"It means all hell's breaking loose. You hear that announcement, it means rubber bullets are about to fly. You cause a Red Dot call and you'll have everyone pissed off at you because everyone gets punished. You do that and they'll fight themselves to see who takes you out. If the trouble's bad enough, you get transferred to Red Onion, the toughest damn correctional facility in the U.S."

Spencer aimed his pen at Starks. "I've been prison investigator for eighteen years. I know the hierarchal structure of those incarcerated here. I know about every fight, or at least the ones reported to me. I know about some of the sexual assaults and about the drug trafficking—each impossible to stop. But you can help me to help you, if you just tell me what happened."

"Ask Bo."

"I tried. Went to see him in the infirmary, where he'll be for a while. He's not talking. But he's way more than angry. You humiliated him. He's not going to forget and forgive. Frankly, Mr. Starks, I fear for your life. One last chance to speak up."

Starks stared at his hands. He looked up when he heard Spencer confer in whispers with the other men at the table.

"You leave us no choice, since you admit to starting the assault. Thirty days in the SHU might make a difference. I hope for your sake it does." Spencer explained in response to Starks's puzzled expression, "Secure Housing Unit. Not a place you'll care to return to, I promise you."

The same two guards escorted Starks down more corridors than he could follow, to a windowless six by eight cell constructed out of concrete. The bed was a concrete slab with no mattress and no pillow, just a thin, scratchy blanket with holes and stains he didn't want to think about. At least, he thought, the toilet and washbasin will stay clean.

One guard stood watch with his charged taser in his hand. The other guard shoved Starks forward, chuckling when he tripped on the restraints around his ankles.

"Get on in there, asshole. It's not like we got all day." He laughed. "Oops. I forgot—you do got all day. Every day for a month!"

The guard was rough as he started to remove the restraints that had abraded skin on Starks's wrists and ankles.

Starks squinted up at the single blinking fluorescent light buzzing overhead. "Ballast needs to be changed."

The first guard yanked hard on the chain. "Showing off, prick?"

"You're going to fix it, right?" Starks asked.

"You may've been a big-time mucky-muck out there," the other guard said, "but you're nothing in here. Here's what you can count on, puke. Breakfast, lunch, and dinner shoved through that slot in that door. Maybe your food'll even stay on the tray." The other guard snickered. "One hour a day you'll be taken out to walk around. We might even let you shower so you don't stink up the place any more than you do now. The rest of the time, you can stare at the fucking walls, for all we care."

"What about the light?"

"Pretend you're in a fancy nightclub."

"What about my stuff?"

"Maybe some of it'll be waiting for you. Maybe not."

Just before the door slammed shut, Starks yelled, "There's no toilet paper."

His only response was a nightstick rapped against the opposite side of the door.

CHAPTER 23

THE NEXT MONTH went by in a disjointed combination of slow and fast for Starks: Thoughts flickered in his mind like a film of his life's worst moments. When he did sleep, he was roused by nightmares or the incessant screaming of other prisoners isolated as he was: Some of them yelled to get a CO's attention or to talk with other prisoners; others carried on because they were not in their right minds. Starks worried he might soon be one of the latter, especially because the anticipated hour outside each day had been prevented by blizzards, ice storms, below-freezing temperatures, and—he was convinced—a certain amount of lying on the part of the guards. He asked about going someplace inside whenever they said the weather was bad. They ignored him.

At the end of thirty days, he was released from the SHU but wasn't returned to Cell Block C. Instead, he was placed in yet another windowless cell almost exactly like the last one but in a different section. This time the bed frame was steel instead of concrete, bolted to the floor and wall, and with an even thinner vinyl-coated mattress. When he asked about this, he was met with silence and a shove.

Three times a day, he heard the steel flap on the door unlocked—the cuff, he heard one guard call it—and watched as gloved hands pushed a tray through, waiting until he was just about to grab the tray then letting it go. He usually caught the tray, sometimes he didn't.

And every day, he used the hard bar of soap to make a mark on the wall, to count the days.

After the first week, Starks pounded on the door and shouted, "I want to know why I'm in here. I demand an answer, damn it. I deserve an answer or to be put back in my regular cell. You're all a bunch of fucking sadists."

The cuff opened and the voice on the other side barked, "Stand in the middle of the cell." As soon as he'd done so, the guard said, "You don't get to demand shit. You're not behaving right, so you're gonna get a treat. Nutraloaf. You're gonna love it."

The flap was slammed shut, leaving Starks to wonder what this announcement meant.

He learned what it meant when the first heavy brick of the stuff was delivered instead of the usual slop for dinner. Starks picked it apart, able to identify cabbage, carrots, pinto beans, something that resembled shredded chicken, fake scrambled eggs, and way too much bread. The rest of it wasn't anything he could name. He spit out the first flavorless bite then pounded on the door.

"What the hell is this bullshit? I want something I can eat."

A guard tapped the door with his nightstick, opened the cuff, and spoke through it. "You figured out yet why you're getting it?"

"Has to be a form of torture."

"You're getting smarter by the minute. Now shut the fuck up."

No way could he eat it. He drank as much water from the faucet as he could stand but this didn't quell his hunger.

Breakfast was another brick. He was hungry enough to eat a fourth of the nauseous concoction, which was delivered to him twice a day for two more days. When a regular meal was finally delivered, he devoured it, barely chewing.

The food went down fast. It came up even faster.

After two months in the same cell, with infrequent one-hour respites outside the cell for exercise and showers, Starks used the plastic fork delivered with his dinner tray to rip at the veins in his wrists. It was a painful, pathetic attempt with a sad excuse for a tool but it landed him in the infirmary for treatment. And there, Starks saw an opportunity to surreptitiously acquire a small treasure.

He wasn't kept in the infirmary but was put on suicide watch and moved to yet another similar cell, one with a round-the-clock surveillance camera placed out of reach, and one of the usual thin mattresses on the bed. This time someone made sure he had his hour out of the cell each day, and he was told he'd have to meet with the prison counselor, as soon as it was set up.

Two afternoons later, on his way to the yard segregated for prisoners in isolation, Starks overheard a couple of inmates comment as he passed them: *He's on suicide watch; he's considered a wild card—stay clear of him; acts like he has nothing to lose; unpredictable—stay outta his way.*

Assumptions about him had run through the inmates like wildfire. They were right that at times he didn't care if he lived, but that feeling inevitably was replaced by a desire to survive. That his behavior was unpredictable was a fact, one he was having difficulty wrapping his mind around. That his value on life—his or anyone else's—being non-existent was erroneous, he was relieved to realize. If inmates believed, and advised others, that it was best to avoid him, that worked in his favor, as far as he was concerned.

The other twenty-three hours of silence every day were getting to him. Starks's grandfather had told him silence could be a refuge, a resting state for the mind, a friend of sorts. Silence was just another enemy he faced in his enclosure within an enclosure. With every moment of silence, he descended into an orgy of emotional hurts, sadistic analytical reasoning, and memories of a past best forgotten.

But he knew he wasn't going to be allowed to forget.

CHAPTER 24

"PICK A CHAIR. And try to relax. I'm one of the good guys here."
Prison counselor, Matthew Demory, had thought the name
Frederick Starks was familiar when he'd been instructed to start
sessions with the inmate. He'd reviewed the inmate's file, saw the photo-
graph included, and realized this was the CEO of Tendum Enterprises.
Starks, a mechanical engineer who'd graduated *summa cum laude* from
Massachusetts Institute of Technology, had accomplished a great deal in
his life.

Even without the file photo, he would have recognized Starks as soon
as he saw him. His face had plastered the front pages of newspapers for
months, and there had been numerous video clips of him holding his
hands in front of his face and his head down, as well as photographs that
captured the man's abject misery. The media had revealed damn near everything but the man's underwear brand and size. Starks was not the average
inmate. And to the best of his knowledge, Starks was the only "celebrity"
currently housed at Sands.

Demory told the guards escorting Starks to wait outside and to close
the door. Initially, they watched through the double-glassed pane on the
top half of the door, but he gave them a look that made them turn away.

He swiveled back and forth in the brown leather chair positioned
behind his desk. His paunch strained several buttons on his shirt that had a
fresh coffee stain on it, as well as a wet spot where he'd made a half-hearted
attempt to clean the spill. His hair, cut short, was the same color as the

leather, except for touches of silver at his temples. Robin's-egg-blue eyes watched with interest as Starks took in the decor.

It was an office quite different from any other at Sands, something Demory was proud of. He understood and insisted that this one space was to be something of a sanctuary. If an inmate was in need of his help, by damn they'd have a more pleasant place to get it in. What he kept to himself when he'd had this discussion with the warden was that he needed the environment as well; a depressed counselor was no good to anyone. The warden had told him if that's what he wanted, it had to come out of his pocket. Demory was happy to do it that way, and his accountant was happy to write off the improvements as a business expense.

So he'd personally painted over the gray walls with a soothing blue-white paint, adding a few wavy lines in aqua to resemble calming surf, and placed a large rug with a pleasing pattern under his maple desk. Two maple chairs with secured cushions were angled in front of the desk. Maple filing cabinets and book shelves filled one wall.

After Starks sat, Demory struggled to get him to speak. Some inmates were eager to talk, whether from loneliness, craving attention, or a socio-pathic need for control. Some were as reticent to open up as this one was. For the first several minutes, the most he could get from Starks was more often one-word responses than full sentences. The information was in Starks's file, but Demory had learned that with inmates hesitant to talk, it warmed them up if they believed they needed to confirm vital statistics and immediate family details—"For the record," Demory said. Starks wasn't as accommodating as most.

The counselor wasn't opposed to an unorthodox approach, if he thought it was needed. Too loud for the space between them, he said, "Frederick Starks. You go by Frederick, Fred, or Freddie?"

"Starks."

"You don't use your first name? Ever?"

"No. My father abandoned us when I was young. Understandably, my mother resented him. Most mothers use the kid's full name when they mean business. Not mine. Whenever I did anything that annoyed her or reminded her of him, she called me by his last name."

"Did you annoy her often?"

Starks shrugged. "I was a typical boy. Young boys get into mischief. Usually not harmful, just irksome to their mothers." A half-smile crossed his lips. "I got into mischief so often my mother started calling me that name all the time. More often than not, she'd smile when she did. I got used to it. So when people asked my name, that's what I told them to call me."

Demory paused to note in the file that talking about family, or at least certain memories, seemed to ease Starks's resistance.

"You founded and managed a huge firm. Tendum Enterprises. Very impressive. That kind of success requires certain things: Time, money, intelligence, stamina. I'm interested in hearing how you became so successful."

Starks blew out a long breath. "A desire for success earned through hard work was instilled by my mother, grandfather, and uncles. And they were strict about a good education. I learned to earn my merits and rewards. An opportunity presented itself. I borrowed twenty thousand dollars from family and friends to start my company. Worked three jobs while managing my start-up firm. After three years, I was able to start satellite offices."

"That's a lot of effort for one person."

"My wife and I both worked while my business was in the start-up phase."

"So she was supportive?"

Starks shrugged and picked at his cuticles.

Demory judged this response to mean the wife, whom he knew was on the way to being the ex-wife, was a trigger for Starks. It was too soon to get into anything deep just yet. When inmates held back as this one did, it was smarter to build into the heavier topics gradually, unless the inmate indicated otherwise. Those kinds of conversations required trust, something most inmates were in short supply of. Plus, he needed to get to know them better as well, observe them, so he could watch for inmates with behavior disorders who'd like nothing better than to dick around with him.

The session continued and ended on the same note it had started: general questions, nothing too personal, about Starks's family and life before prison, all of which Starks gave the briefest answers he could get away with.

Demory put his pen down and said, "Our introduction to one another is up. Twenty minutes. Not so bad, was it?"

Starks rolled his neck right then left then stood. "Felt a lot longer to me."

"The next session will be the full fifty minutes."

"Oh joy."

Demory watched Starks's stoop-shouldered stride to the door. These tough-to-reach inmates took time, but they were usually worth it. Even after years of being in practice, including at Sands, the depth of what people carried inside them and what motivated them to do some of the things they did could still surprise him.

Starks left the session confused, wondering if it was a joke. He'd expected questions about why he'd attacked Boen Jones, and why he'd tried to kill himself, among all the other probing questions he'd anticipated and dreaded.

The steel door of his cell clanged shut behind him. He stayed standing where he was and let his eyes scan the confined space. He chuckled, but not in amusement.

What a system.

His thoughts had led him to try to kill himself, and what did the system do? They put him in even more solitary confinement twenty-three hours a day, where his thoughts could eat at him from the inside one tearing bite at a time. He was relieved that, so far, they didn't know about his small *treasure*—the six-inch metal ruler lifted from the infirmary doctor's desk. The failed suicide attempt hadn't been a complete waste. He'd pretended his foot itched and hidden the ruler in one of his shoes. Every night when overhead lights were dimmed at eleven, he lay on his side, facing the wall. The metal strip would be removed from the slit he'd made in the underside of the mattress cover, right at the seam, where it wouldn't be obvious. Pretend snores covered the sound as he whittled metal against concrete, until he got drowsy. Then he'd slide the ruler back into its hiding place. A slow process, for sure, but soon he'd have a proper shank. If the guard on the other side of the camera noticed the subtle arm movements made in the dimmed light . . . well, let him think whatever he wanted to about that. When the shank was sharp enough, he'd use it.

Also sharp was the loneliness. It led him to ask himself questions like why had he fallen in love with and married Kayla. He'd loved and trusted her, and she repaid him by proving she was nothing more than a harlot. He'd been through everything with her. Had sacrificed so much for her. And this place—this *life*—was the end result of all he'd done. For her.

Thinking about her led to thoughts of Ozy and all that her involvement with him had resulted in, how many lives had been irrevocably altered.

He choked on the pain.

CHAPTER 25

WHY *HAD* HE gone to Ozy's home that night?

Why hadn't he handled the infidelity differently?

Ozy was still comatose, which left the man's wife without a husband. Their children were without a father, as were his own children. And as much as he knew it shouldn't matter in comparison, his actions had destroyed the reputation he'd put so much of himself into establishing. The good results of all his efforts had been more than diminished—they were now forgotten, having been replaced with his notoriety.

Mild-mannered was in the past as well. Now he was volatile, his behaviors irresponsible. His methodical thought process, so keen and beneficial when he'd built his business and the goodwill in the community he had enjoyed, was something he trusted less after experiencing how his emotions could take over.

The words of a TV pastor, heard while channel-surfing, came to him like a slap: "For every choice there is a consequence. Choices are life-changing; consequences are long-lasting. You can make a choice, you cannot choose the consequence. But you must be prepared to live with it."

Kayla's betrayal—on so many unimagined levels—had wrecked him and their family. Every day as he'd waited for and gone through his trial, and for far longer than he could believe possible that a story could or should hold interest, the print and visual media played with the headlines and stories about him. They amused themselves in order to squeeze words onto a page or give newscasters a reason to make witticisms at his expense:

Tendum Tycoon's Tirade. CEO's TKO. Philandering Philanthropist Penned. People were paid to think up these ridiculous sound bites. Other people paid to read them and the stories that followed.

With the exception of Jeffrey, his so-called friends had quickly distanced themselves from him. Sure, his mother, aunt, and cousin had gone to the trial, but neither they nor any other members of his family visited him in jail prior to and during the trial. They had, however, visited him before he left for this place. He'd pleaded for someone to make sure he saw his children before he began his long stint at Sands. Did he ever again want to hear from any of them was a question he had no definite answer for. For now, at least, he'd told the prison, in writing, to refuse all visitors he'd put on his list, unless otherwise notified.

Then there were his children. He ached for them. Not being able to see them, wondering how they were getting along without him, haunted him.

Blake, twelve, was old enough to understand what had happened, and to feel the shame of it. He'd always been affectionate with his parents, so found it especially difficult when they separated, and agonizing when his father was incarcerated. Tears welled in Starks's eyes as he recalled how Blake kept his arms pinned to his sides when his father hugged him good-bye before he was transferred from the county jail.

Nathan was ten. A quiet type. He rarely expressed his feelings, but the pain he felt when Starks hugged him at the end of that visit showed through his eyes, on his face, in how rigid he held his slight body. The boy had always internalized his feelings. Starks still felt stabbing guilt at not being able to console him.

His daughter, Kaitlin, was now seven—he'd missed her birthday since being here, and wondered if she'd asked for him. She hadn't understood more than that Daddy wouldn't be able to play with her for a long time. Soon she'd grasp the truth, and add shame as a feeling she walked around with.

What tore at him was the possibility that other children, and some adults, might be cruel to them all. Because of him.

He blamed Kayla but was still rational enough to own some of his share of that blame. It was his lack of self-control that led to this confinement and the, though still unofficial, end of his marriage. Should he have buried his pride and saved the marriage? Had there been anything left to save? None of this would have ever happened if he'd chosen that safer path. But he'd always prided himself on taking calculated risks and fighting for what was his, especially his self-respect.

One thing was certain: He now knew Kayla's true character. Knew she didn't have the ability—or chose not to exercise it—to use proper judgment about relationships. She could easily decide to continue to go from man to man—use them then lose them (to borrow Ozy's phrase), as she had done with him and the others. What if the silly bitch did man-hop, causing multiple men to interact with his children, possibly hurt them, with him unable to protect them. Or—the thought wrenched him—another man raised his children. Would they call that man Daddy as well? Or instead?

Coming from a broken home, Starks had promised himself that his children would never have that experience. A shattered promise, indeed.

He wasn't going to be able to teach his children about life, work ethics, or the importance of contributing to their community. And, God help him, what had his own actions taught them? He'd always been so careful to let them see only the best of his nature. A parent's right to deceive for a just purpose, or so he'd believed.

One momentary lapse in judgment had brought an end to being loved or at least admired by many, even those he'd helped financially. He'd created a mini-empire of engineering firms through hard work, dedication, and perseverance. Instead of a fine watch and shoes, he now wore shackles. Marriage, family, success, amenities that made life pleasurable—all of it gone.

He'd once read that the universe abhors a void. Create a space and the universe fills it, the author had stated.

Not this time, he told himself.

Nothing about his life now allowed him to believe the void in him would be filled with anything other than more emptiness.

A question came to him in his grandfather's voice: What are you going to do about your situation?

I'll think of something.

He was certain of this: What he was contemplating would have grieved his grandfather.

CHAPTER 26

THE SURVEILLANCE CAMERA in his isolation cell was positioned in the corner of the high ceiling and to the right of the door. Starks calculated where in the cell the camera, angled as it was, most likely could not see him. One narrow space in the corner opposite where the camera was mounted seemed the ideal spot. He stood there to see if his absence from view drew anyone's attention. With no clock or watch, he timed it by counting the seconds. Five minutes.

The door flap was flung open by a guard.

"You. Stand in the middle of the room."

Starks did as told.

"What the hell are you up to in there?"

"Meditation."

"Meditate on the bed, the bench, or with your head in the fucking toilet, for all I care, but stay out of the damn corner."

The time was now. He lay on the mattress, tossing and turning, pretending a poor attempt to nap, and removed the shank, keeping it hidden in his hand. For several more minutes, he continued to play the role of a troubled sleeper, all the while going deeper into the feelings that he was a disgrace to his family and friends, and that life was no longer worth living.

He went to the blind spot in the room.

Quick efficiency would do the trick. He positioned the shank against his jugular. One quick slice, and in a brief amount of time—he hoped—all his pain and humiliation would be over.

Sweat began to run in rivulets down his face. Moisture pooled in his armpits, his groin, behind his knees. *This hesitation is wasting valuable minutes.* His heart hammered, willed him to live. Then he sensed an inner voice asking him to trust. A sob wracked its way up from deep in his core.

He flung himself onto the mattress, careful about putting the shank into its hiding place without being seen.

After several minutes, the adrenaline rush was over. His head, arms, and legs felt leaden. His brain craved rest. He lay on the bed with his eyes open, unable to fight whatever thoughts demanded his attention, until a spider crawled across the ceiling and entered its small web in the corner. How had the spider gotten inside and when? And when had the industrious creature built its web?

It wasn't a typical web of geometric appeal. This web was coarsely constructed, its purpose of capture-and-keep and hide the truth within obvious by its opaque aspect.

The glimmer of an idea sparked: Create your own web. How to do that in here, though, eluded him.

He'd trust that something would come to him.

CHAPTER 27

TWO WRONGS DON'T make a right.

How often his grandfather had repeated that old adage while Starks was growing up. Perhaps that was the seed of the twisted tree his and Kayla's marriage had become, he thought. They'd each ignored the meaning of that phrase intended to make reasonable people pause before they acted. They'd both failed miserably.

Somewhere in the recesses of his mind he recalled hearing someone say, though he couldn't remember who, "Life is a series of natural and spontaneous changes. Don't resist them; that only creates sorrow. Let reality be reality. Let things flow naturally forward in whatever way they will."

Damn easy to say. Not so easy to practice.

His father's absence from his life was one he never meant to copy, and certainly never in this way. Starks's father stayed with his wife and son until Starks was three. Then he left; removed himself from their lives, as though he'd never existed.

Starks's mother had struggled to support them. When Starks was five, she moved them into her father's house, at his insistence, and where several other relatives lived within a small radius.

His grandfather had never gone beyond fourth grade—he'd quit school to help his family with their farm, which they lost—and was why he, along with his daughter, was strict with Starks about education. That time had formed habits and beliefs about a work ethic, which he demonstrated to a young Starks by rising each morning at five to get some chores done and to get to work a half hour earlier than his 7 a.m. shift at the clothing factory. He woke his grandson as well.

A sleepy six-year-old Starks asked, "Why do you get up so early. Why do *I* have to get up too?"

"Better to start early, Freddy. You get a lot done that way."

"But why do you go to work so early?"

"I go a half hour early because I don't own the factory. If I owned the factory, I'd go *two* hours early. It's a discipline you want to practice. You want to take good care of your family when you're a man, don't you? Want them to be proud of you, don't you?"

"I guess. Can I have some cereal?"

The old man poured cereal into a bowl. "You practice now so it becomes natural to you later." He added milk. "Practice now to build stamina and character. A man's character's his calling card in life."

Every weekend, holiday, and summer break, no matter the weather, Starks did yard work and chores at his home and for a few older relatives. His services were unpaid—"So you learn the true value of being paid for your labors"—his grandfather told him. The older and stronger he got, the more work the old man found for him to do, until Starks was legally old enough to get one or more part-time jobs that paid. He was allowed to keep a small amount of what he earned to use as walking around money. The rest went into savings.

The other relatives, for the most part, were old-school. This included how they felt about divorce: It just wasn't done. This, however, didn't prevent husbands from cheating on their wives and not being bothered about doing so. Even if the wives felt shamed by their husbands' infidelities, they shared the belief that it was even more shameful to divorce, and equally shameful to remarry. How many times had he listened to these matters discussed by the older relatives over coffee at their kitchen tables? They'd practically spoon-fed such beliefs to him.

Starks's mother, Lynn, remarried anyway. The relatives showed leniency in her situation, since her husband had abandoned her and her child. It was a short-lived union, lasting long enough to provide Starks with two stepsisters for a couple of years. The three children had been close, until the divorce and his stepsisters' move with their father to the opposite coast ended any interaction.

He still believed the philosophy of the men in his family, his role-models: satisfy your curiosity and appetites; no point in going hungry when life's a buffet.

They should have told him to be discreet.

And he should have listened to his family's initial opinion about Kayla.

* * *

He introduced Kayla to his family a few months after he took her to the prom. His uncles, aunts, and cousins had come to the house to meet her. They hadn't been invited; they'd been expected. Duty called.

All were polite to Kayla as they shared iced tea and a large sheet cake his mother had baked. Seemingly general questions were asked about her family and life. They listened attentively as Kayla, blushing, explained that her father had left them; that she couldn't remember him. They nodded in understanding, and some of the aunts patted her on the arm, since her story, in part, was similar to Starks's and his mother's own experience.

The family got animated when Kayla said she had five brothers, and contained their shock when she clarified her brothers had five different fathers.

Two hours later, when Kayla said her good-byes, the congenial ambiance shifted. Everyone was silent. All but Starks's mother looked everywhere but at him.

His mother's lips were set in a hard line. "This girl isn't for you. Just look at her family."

"Too similar for your tastes, Mom?"

"Don't you sass me, Starks. Her mother is like a revolving door for men. Consider what she's taught her daughter by example. Mark my words, 'The apple doesn't fall far from the tree.'"

The proverbial floodgates opened, spilling comments from the relatives that were much the same. Starks slouched in the chair, with his arms crossed at his chest, and kept his gaze focused on his sandaled feet stretched out in front of him. He listened in silence for the half hour they barraged him with arguments and pleas.

Red-faced, he leapt up, "Enough! All you care about is how who I go out with reflects on you. You're so close-minded. You're wrong about her. Wrong. This is the girl I want. This is the girl I love."

"You'll regret this one day." His mother stood with her hands on her hips and glared at him.

"What do you know about real love?" he said. "Look how that turned out for you."

"Frederick Starks!" His grandfather yanked him to his feet. "You're still wet behind the ears, boy. And here you are, acting like you know everything. Your mother's right. You continue to see this girl, to—God forbid—marry this girl, and the day'll come when you regret it."

"I'll *never* regret it. I'd only regret letting her go."

No, not a pleasant memory at all.

Not because of what they'd said, but because they had been right.

CHAPTER 28

FIFTEEN-YEAR-OLD STARKS CHOSE a desk near the window. English class. The first period of the first day of his freshman year at a new school.

The facility had taken three years to build, and merged students from two broken-down high schools that had been around for decades and would cost more to repair than to build one larger building.

He looked around the room to see who was familiar and who wasn't. Two rows over and one chair back, he saw her.

The dark-haired girl with pale skin and aqua eyes looked his way, saw him staring slack-jawed at her. Her smile was shy. Then she blushed in a way that made him feel a thirst that needed quenching.

In that brief moment, he was lost. He listened carefully when the teacher called roll: He had to know her name. Kayla Dixon.

He *had* to meet Kayla, *had* to go out with her or he wouldn't be able to eat or sleep ever again.

As Mr. Thorpe droned on about what they'd cover that school year, Starks planned how he'd catch up with Kayla in the hall after the bell rang; how he'd introduce himself in some intriguing way. By the time he gathered his books and thought of something sort of clever to say, she was gone.

That night he let his imagination run wild, creating one future scenario after another he wanted to share with Kayla, using a third of a new box of tissues in the process.

The next day, smitten even more after a night of fantasizing and convincing himself that she shared his feelings, he approached her.

"Hey, Kayla. I'm Frederick Starks. But everyone calls me Starks."

She stared at him with wide eyes and parted pink-glossed lips but said nothing.

"I was wondering . . . What I mean to say is . . . do you have a picture of yourself you could give me?" He realized how his request might sound, but it was too late.

Kayla covered her mouth with a hand and giggled. She didn't answer. No photograph was handed over. No promise to do so was made. Instead, she turned and walked away.

As much as he wanted to, he didn't trail after her. He refused to believe he'd blown his chances with her. He wouldn't allow himself to believe it. Whatever it took, however long it took, he'd make her his.

First period the following day, Starks sat in the same desk by the window. Tortured by his adolescent longings, he jabbed the arm of the classmate whose desk was between his and Kayla's.

"Cripes. Why you pokin' me?"

"I'll give you five bucks to swap desks with me." He pulled a folded five-dollar bill from his pocket, flashed it then held it in his palm.

"Sure. I don't care where I sit. Hand it over."

His plan was thwarted almost as soon as it started. Kayla reached the classroom door, saw where Starks now sat, and walked over to the teacher.

"Mr. Thorpe, I need to move to a first desk. My new contact lenses aren't in yet, so I need to sit closer to the board."

The teacher directed the student in the first desk of Kayla's row to move to another. Before taking her seat, Kayla acknowledged with a subtle smile the disappointment Starks expressed through his eyes.

Seating arrangements were finalized for the remainder of the school year. The student to Starks's left snapped the five-dollar bill and laughed.

Starks's further attempts to speak with Kayla or get a photograph or her phone number fell flat. Many times he caught Kayla and her best friend, Jenny Hamilton, with their heads together. They'd watch him watching them. They'd whisper to each other and laugh. And each time, Kayla would meet his gaze for a tantalizing moment, blush then look away.

Resigned that she was painfully shy and that he was ineffectual, he stopped trying to talk to her. He watched her from afar, suffering in silence and longing. He dated a number of girls but never seriously. And he never gave up on winning Kayla.

It wasn't in his nature to give up whenever he wanted something.

CHAPTER 29

ELEVENTH GRADE PROM was two weeks away. Starks was desperate to go with Kayla and terrified to ask her.

For two agonizing years, she'd given him lots of looks at school, but hadn't said more than a quick hello before rushing away. As far as he knew, she wasn't dating anyone in particular. If he waited too long, some other guy would hold her in his arms during the slow dances. Some other guy's lips would kiss her goodnight.

He'd never abandoned the idea of making her his. Especially after watching her grow more beautiful as the days, months, and years passed since the first moment he saw her. Summers and seasonal school breaks had been torture for him. All that time without a glimpse of her or hearing her laugh. He'd thought about finding out where she lived and knocking on her door to make her talk to him, but his grandfather and his part-time jobs kept him too busy.

He needed help. The answer came to him: Jeffrey.

Jeffrey was popular with everyone. He was charming, polite, genuine. Mothers adored him. Teachers loved him. Girls, especially, were crazy about him; he had a natural way with them, having grown up in a house full of females. He had a stable of girlfriends who knew they weren't the only ones Jeffrey dated and he still managed to keep all of them happy. Guys liked him, trusted him, were jealous of him and called him Jeffrey the Juggler. They'd learned quickly that the payoff for being with him and not against him was a better deal. That he was likeable took some of the sting out of his success with girls that most of the guys couldn't imitate.

It was Monday. Starks was cutting it close, but maybe he wasn't too late. He caught up to Jeffrey during a classroom change.

"I really need to talk to you. Can we sit away from everyone at lunch?"

"Bro, that's some serious face you're wearing. I'm intrigued. Meet me at the cafeteria door. We'll grab some eats and head out to the commons area."

Starks's shoulders relaxed when he finally saw Jeffrey ambling his way. "Can't you hurry up?"

"No problem, bro. But you should chill. Tension has zero sex-appeal. And the girls are always watching."

They found a bench in the corner of the outdoor area. Jeffrey chomped into his sandwich and asked, "What gives?"

For several minutes, Starks poured out his frustrations and desires. He took a breath and said, "I want to ask Kayla to the prom, but she never says more than hi to me, if that. I've tried. For a long time. What's with her? Does she have a boyfriend? I didn't think she did. Does she?"

"Well—"

"Is she going to the prom with anyone? Do you know?"

Jeffrey laughed. "You've got it bad, bro."

Starks stared at his unopened sandwich now squished in his clenched hand. "Tell me about it." He unfolded the wrapper on his sandwich then wrapped it back up. "How come *you* never went out with her?"

"She's not my type. I like 'em outgoing. Give me two days to ask around; I don't want to be too obvious."

Wednesday, they went back to the same corner bench outside.

Between bites, Jeffrey made his report. "From the girls, I learned Kayla's not dating anyone. But, she thought someone would've asked her to the prom by now. From the guys, some of them don't know if she's quiet because she's stuck up. No way they want to ask and be rejected. Some guys think she's too shy and won't be any fun, so they won't ask her."

"That's a relief. Thanks."

"Time to do your thing. By the way, I put in a good word for you."

"What'd you say?"

"Good stuff, I swear." He punched Starks on the arm. "Get a move on. Don't make this harder than it has to be, bro. *Pun intended.*"

Starks took a bite of his pizza slice, unaware of chewing or swallowing. And half-heartedly listened to Jeffrey talk about his plans for the prom.

CHAPTER 30

INSTEAD OF IMMEDIATELY asking Kayla to the prom, Starks watched her in every class they shared and followed her between classes like a predator studying his prey.

On Thursday Jeffrey told him, "Get a grip. It's like you're a stalker or something. Haven't you seen her walking slower or hanging around to give you a chance to ask her?"

"Yes, but—"

"But nothing. You're gonna blow it if you don't ask her soon."

Still, he made no move to speak with her.

Friday morning, Jeffrey cornered him between morning classes.

"Bro, time's running out. She's gonna need a dress. At least. You gotta figure out a suit or tux or something. What about a corsage? A limo? If you're gonna feed the girl, like you should, restaurant chairs at the good places are getting scarce. Unless you plan to take her to a burger joint, and wouldn't that make you the number one desirable date from now on."

Starks's jaw dropped. "I don't know what she likes to eat."

"I know how you can find out?"

"Yeah?"

"Ask her!"

"Everything has to be just right."

"Nothin's gonna be anything if you don't fricking ask her."

"She has to say yes. I can't make it through the weekend without knowing."

"Ask the girl. Give us all a fricking break."

The bell rang. Starks rushed from the classroom toward the cafeteria. Kayla, facing the other way, was by herself near the entrance. Jenny hadn't met up with her yet. It was now or never. He ran.

"Kayla!"

Startled, she swung around.

"I . . . um . . . that is . . ." He tucked in his tucked-in shirt. "Would you like to go to the prom with me?"

She held his gaze for a moment then lowered her eyes. "Yes."

"Great. That's . . . great. Let me get your phone number." He dropped his notebook, picked it up. Dropped his pen and retrieved it. "I'll call you after school. Four o'clock?"

"I'll be there."

The day could not end quickly enough. He sprinted home, grabbed a snack, and watched the clock. Usually he did his homework then played basketball for an hour. Not today.

He opened his notebook to the page where she'd written her number. Studied her handwriting, wished he knew more about that science. What secrets might he learn about her, if he knew what to look for?

He dialed, swallowed hard then panicked. He was about to talk to her and had no idea what to say.

"It's Starks. So, how's it going? What're you doing?"

"Homework."

"I can call back if you want."

"No! I mean . . . this is a good time."

Silence.

"Very awkward moment," he said.

She laughed.

Starks relaxed. "What are you wearing to the prom?"

"I'll get a dress this weekend."

"Great. Let's sit together at lunch on Monday, alone, if you can arrange it with Jenny. You can let me know what color your dress is so I can get the right corsage. I'll take care of everything. The limo . . . everything."

Someone said something to Kayla. "My mother wants me to get back to my homework."

"See you Monday. Lunch. Just us."

He had her phone number and could be expected to call her, was entitled to call her. And a week from today, he'd finally be able to hold her close. He prayed for more slow songs than fast ones to be played.

There was a lot to get done before the prom.

Then he cursed.

He'd promised her a special night but had spent his pocket money and wasn't allowed to touch his savings.

He had to wow her or risk losing her.

CHAPTER 31

AFTER SOME ENERGETIC teenager-style pleading, Starks's grandfather and several other family members agreed to help with prom expenses in exchange for extra chores.

That weekend, he got his suit, had his hair trimmed, shined his dress shoes. All other arrangements were made; though, it took a lot of frantic calls since he'd waited so late. The first three evenings that week, he put on his suit and shoes and practiced dancing in front of the full-length mirror in his bedroom. His grandfather told him, "If you don't stop doing that, that suit'll have to be cleaned and pressed and the shoes re-shined."

Thursday after school, he checked with the limo service, the florist, and the restaurant to make sure everything was in order. He called Kayla, hoping she shared his excitement, sighing in relief when she said she did.

After school on Friday, he picked up the corsage—one perfect white orchid. A wrist corsage, "So you don't damage her dress," his mother had advised.

Six o'clock Friday evening, a white limousine stopped in front of Starks's house. Corsage in hand, he made his way to the car, pausing to wave at his relatives who'd showed up to take pictures.

In the back of the limo, he took several deep breaths to loosen the knot in his stomach. Everything had to be perfect tonight.

Starks ran a hand over his hair, straightened his straight tie, and looked back at the chauffer. The limo driver gave him a thumbs-up. Starks returned the gesture, took a deep breath and knocked.

Kayla's mother opened the door.

"Mrs. Dixon? I'm Starks. Is Kayla ready?"

"It's *Ms.* Dixon. Better yet, just call me Jessica."

"Um . . . okay."

"I'll go up and check on her. Have a seat in the living room."

"I'll stand, if that's okay?"

"Suit yourself." Without looking back, she wriggled her fingers in a wave and said, "She'll be down soon."

He walked to the nearest window. The driver waited next to the back door of the limo, ready to treat the young couple like royalty, as promised. He'd told the driver all about Kayla during the ride over. The driver had given him some tips, when he could get a word in.

Starks glanced at his watch. Ten after six. At six fifteen he heard footsteps on the stairs. Kayla's mother came down first.

"She's ready."

Starks's gaze followed hers to the top of the stairway.

His breath caught as his eyes followed how the fabric caressed Kayla's thighs with each downward step, how the long dress hugged her body the way he longed to, how the dress matched her eyes—eyes that watched him watching her, and with an intensity that surprised him.

At the bottom of the stairs, she turned to show him the dress. Her waist-length hair moved aside, causing Starks to gasp again. There was nearly no back to the dress. His palms tingled as he imagined running his hands over her back as they danced or when he guided her to tables and through crowds.

"Wow. Kayla, you're . . ."

"You look nice, too." She focused on the clear container in his hands. "What a lovely orchid."

"It's a wrist corsage, so it doesn't put holes in the—" He gestured at the dress, searching for the right word.

"It's silk."

"I'll be right back," Kayla's mother said. She returned with a small cellophane package in her hand, which she gave to her daughter.

Kayla removed the white rose bud and pinned it to Starks's lapel. "One for you, as well."

"Um . . . thanks. Ready?"

"Remember, Kayla," her mother said, looking at Starks, "your curfew is one o'clock."

"I remember."

"Unless you feel you have a reason to stay out longer." She winked at Starks.

Kayla's face flamed red.

Starks, open-mouthed, looked from mother to daughter, wondering what was going on, and feeling somewhat embarrassed that his own curfew was midnight.

Outside, he offered his arm. "Shall I escort you to the limo, my queen?"

She giggled as she took his arm. "It's so elegant, Starks. Thank you."

The ride to the restaurant started out in silence. Starks noticed the driver frequently used the rearview mirror to check on them. After two minutes of dead air, the driver turned the stereo on. Starks mouthed "Thanks" into the rearview mirror, which got a nod from the driver.

"What should I order at the restaurant?" Kayla asked.

Starks took her hand in his. "Whatever will make you happy. I want you to always have whatever you want. I'll do whatever it takes to make sure you do."

He did everything Jeffrey had told him to do, to convey to Kayla that he was a gentleman who knew how to take care of a lady. Dinner went well, though a little awkward at first. By the time they ordered dessert, they were easier in each other's company. By the time they made their grand entrance at the prom, they were comfortable with each other, able to make each other laugh. By the time they danced to "If Only for One Night," he knew the lyrics that requested she let him hold her tight, even if only for one night, were wrong. One night would never be enough. He wanted every night with Kayla. Delicate, gentle, shy Kayla, who was opening up to him more and more.

Aside from the formal photograph each couple posed for, friends with cameras took pictures as well.

"One day," Starks teased, "we'll show these photos to our kids."

Kayla bit her bottom lip.

Starks stared at her mouth. No matter how much he wanted to kiss her, he'd follow Jeffrey's advice:

"Take it slow, bro. Practice delayed gratification. Don't rush the kiss. Wait until you take her to her front door. And nothing over the top. Just enough of a kiss to make her dream about you. Girls love that, especially on a first date."

Waiting to put his lips to hers was utter, delicious agony.

CHAPTER 32

STARKS'S ARMS WERE around Kayla. One hand held her close, the other gently stroked her back left bare by the dress. With restraint that ached, he kissed her. She responded. He kissed her again.

Someone on the other side of the door was opening it. Starks did not stop the kiss. The person slammed the door open.

The metallic sound forced Starks to open his eyes. His vision met gray all around him.

"Hey, prick!"

Silence.

Sorrow.

"I know you heard me. Answer when I talk to you. I'll be back in a half hour. Make sure you're awake and talking."

Isolation made it far too easy to get lost in memories. It was also easy to lose track of time, with no watch or clock or window. Not that he had a reason to track time. He knew whether it was day or night based on which meal was served and by lights being dimmed or brightened. Were it not for the one hour out of his cell every afternoon, he'd have no contact with natural light at all.

Moments were no longer moments; they were eternities, when he was awake, which was more often than not.

He heard the cuff open. Had it been a half hour, or were the guards messing with him again?

"Yo! You gonna answer me this time?"

Starks's grandfather had told him silence was sharper than words. He kept his mouth shut.

"You're gonna talk, whether you want to or not, butt-face. Shrink time in one hour. Be ready."

"If it's in an hour, why'd you disturb me earlier?"

"I was bored."

Accompanied by COs Jakes and Simmons, a shackled Starks shuffled along the corridor then through a number of barred and glass doors before they entered a corridor in the general population area.

Once even with one of the cells, Starks heard someone hiss at him. He recognized one of Bo's gang members. The inmate sneered at him and mouthed the words, "You. Die."

Starks halted, careful to keep any emotion from showing.

The gang member lost his smirk. "Hunh," was all he said.

Jakes said, "Keep it moving. And you," he said to the gang member, "back it up. Nothing to see here."

As soon as they were out of the corridor, Starks began to tremble. He was relieved that his game-face had showed up without any conscious thought on his part. It was the result of decades of practice with surly professors and later clients and their attorneys who wanted to see how far they could push negotiations.

But, he wondered, how long would he be able to fake it?

CHAPTER 33

D EMORY GLANCED AGAIN at Starks's file in the few minutes before his patient arrived. Police statements taken from people who knew Starks were consistent about the man never having previously demonstrated any violent tendencies. Family often lied, but not neighbors and business associates, who usually had no reason to hold back with the truth.

Kayla Starks's statement, of course, was derogatory. And, as expected, Margaret Hessinger's statement was scathing.

Having been through a bitter divorce himself, he knew that a person can be pushed beyond a rational point. Although he didn't condone the action, he could sympathize with Starks for snapping the night he went to his wife's former lover's house. The problem was he was still snapping. In here. The last place where he could or should do that. The last place he might ever live, if he didn't get a grip.

The inmate arrived one minute early.

Demory smiled and motioned for him to sit. Once the guards left and the door was closed, he asked, "How are you doing?"

Starks rubbed the back of his neck. "How do you think?" He rested his clasped hands on his lap and stared, unseeing, at them.

"Why'd you try to end your life?"

Starks looked him straight in the face and said, "You're kidding, right?"

Demory waited.

"You're familiar with my trial?"

"I followed the news, and I ordered and read a copy of the trial transcript after I knew I'd be meeting with you."

"Then you know what my wife did. Finding out what my wife really was—and that she willingly spoke against me—fucked me up bad. Everything I'd ever worked for, what it did to my kids . . . Then coming here, being locked in isolation for so long . . . I just wanted it to stop."

"What did you want to stop?"

"Pain, humiliation, memories that run on a loop. And feeling like I have to live in constant fear."

"I'd like to talk about the event that led to you being in here; what happened at the Hessinger house."

Starks's head jerked up. "I don't want to discuss it." He pointed at the file in front of Demory. "Anything you need to know about that night and what happened before that night is information you've already read. No need for me to repeat it."

"I'm afraid we have to discuss it. If I have to ask you each session, I will, until you tell me about it."

After a minute of silence, Starks answered. "I lost control, went over the edge."

"What sent you over?"

"He had no shame. Only wanted to shame me. Blame *me* for my wife cheating with him."

"How'd he do that?"

Chains rattled when Starks swiped at the trickle of sweat on his cheek. His gaze traveled quickly around the room, his breaths became shorter. Demory waited.

"It's a long story."

Demory's smile was sympathetic. "Time is on our side."

Starks nodded, looked away.

"Your file indicates you're still married but that you and your wife had been separated almost a year at that time. Why did you want to talk to Hessinger then? Why attack him then?"

The next forty minutes taunted Starks as he recounted what had been said and done that night. It was more words than he'd uttered since arriving at

Sands. More than anything, he wanted to lie on his poor excuse for a bed and sleep. And forget. Even for a while.

He relived events in his mind over and over each day and night, like a form of penance. Feeling forced to do the same in these sessions annoyed him. Although he still felt somewhat justified for what he'd believed was righteous anger and action at the time, he didn't want to reveal his shame and shameful behaviors any more than they'd already been revealed publically.

"There are no right answers, Starks, only true ones," Demory had said when he'd gone silent in the middle of their time together. "Answers like 'I felt betrayed' aren't enough."

"It's pretty damn simple, as far as I'm concerned. I was betrayed. End of story."

"You have to face your feelings if you're ever going to deal with them properly. You need to manage them, rather than let them manage you."

"If you want to help me, help me stop feeling so much."

"It's not feelings that are the issue; it's that you choose to feel them."

"Bullshit."

"We have to look at your feelings. We do that so we can look at forgiveness."

A spasm of contempt crossed Starks's face. "Fuck forgiveness. If you think I can forgive him or her after all this, you need to swap sides of the desk with me."

"Forgiveness isn't for their benefit, it's for yours. The moment you forgive yourself, and, yes, even them, that's the moment you can set yourself free of the feelings giving you such a problem now. You'll be able to stop carrying what happened in the way you have been."

Starks shook his head. He got up, noticed three balled-up sheets of paper on the floor. *Must have been from his last patients. Pigs.* He placed the papers in the small trash can then used his right foot to align the can with Demory's desk before returning his gaze to the counselor.

"You want me to forgive a woman who lied in court, knowing it could put me behind bars?" He sat back down. "Here's more that I can't forgive—that right this moment, she probably has 'em spread for that syco-phant she calls her boyfriend. That she and that freeloader are enjoying the expensive house that I built through my blood, sweat, and tears to provide for her and my children."

He dragged a hand back and forth across his chin and went back to pacing. "You want me to forgive her? Before I came here, she had the nerve to tell me Bret's going to take over my role as their father."

"Not the right choice of words for her to use. But do you doubt his ability or willingness to be a good stepfather?"

"Just like I don't believe a stepmother would ever care for my children like their biological mother would—or maybe I should say *should* care for them, I damn sure don't believe Bret will step up and be a good stepfather to my children. Kayla thinks Bret's going to do exactly that."

A vein in his right temple throbbed. "My children share a phone; my little girl uses it to play games. They showed me the photos their mother sent to them, of her and Bret acting inappropriately. Can you believe that? As if it wasn't painful enough for these children to go through this sordid mess. My kids had only known the security of a true family. I don't know what gets into her or why she can't see how foolish doing things like that is. More than foolish—hurtful and confusing for them.

"What message does it send to them when their mother is in bed with her boyfriend doing God knows what in the other room? How did I miss this about her? How did I miss who this woman really was? I call her foolish but I was the bigger fool. And this is the woman who'll be taking care of my children while I'm in here. If she hasn't used proper judgment so far, how the hell can I trust her to do what's proper for our children? God knows, I never wanted it to be this way.

"After all her nonsense with Ozy, she had the nerve to tell me she didn't do anything wrong. It's so much easier to forgive somebody who accepts fault. Somebody who doesn't point the finger at someone else."

"It is easy to point the finger, isn't it?" Demory leaned back and watched for what response might be given.

Starks whirled around. "What are you getting at? I know what I did to fuck things up in my marriage, but I never pointed the finger at anybody. I accepted my faults."

"Have you?"

"She's the one in denial. Look at the marriages she destroyed, that I know about, that is: Ours, Ozy's, and damn near did it to Jenny and Richard's. Jenny. Now she's a woman I'd find easy to forgive. She knew she made a mistake and did all she could to repair the damages, even though Kayla tried to convince her to lie to her husband because—Kayla told her—guys like us weren't capable of forgiveness." He shook his head. "I don't think I can forgive Kayla. I don't think I can do that."

"Do you realize how what you just said sounds?"

Starks wore a puzzled expression that lasted a few seconds then said, "That's not what I meant, and you know it. Jenny was contrite; Kayla wasn't. Still isn't."

"Forgiveness can't have stipulations and conditions. I can help you to find a way to forgive." Demory closed the file. "Same day and time next week?"

"I'll come. Because it's a diversion with a nicer decor. But if you're expecting a lot from me—"

"Just show up. We'll take it from there."

Starks left, debating in his mind which was worse: being isolated with his thoughts tormenting him or having some counselor doing it to him.

CHAPTER 34

THE GUARDS WALKED Starks past the gang member's cell on the return trip to the isolation block. The man stayed seated on his bed but the two inmates made eye contact and held it until they were out of each other's sights.

Simmons opened Starks's cell door; Jakes pushed him inside.

"Looks to me," Jakes said, as he unlocked the shackles, "like the only person wants to see you is the shrink. No visitors. No calls. No letters. No one here wants to see your butt-ugly face. Doesn't say much about you, does it?"

"Oh, I don't know," Simmons said. "I think it says a hell of a lot."

"Yeah, like nobody cares whether you live or die, *Mr. CEO*."

"That's not right," Jakes said. "The prison cares. They get paid for every body in here."

"Always more where he came from."

The steel door slammed shut behind the COs and their self-amusement.

Starks sat on his bed with his back against the wall and thought about his session with Demory.

What a load of crap.

He'd worked seven days a week to give Kayla everything she needed and said she wanted. All the while, she was screwing Ozy and who knew how many other men. All of them laughing at him, ridiculing him behind his back. She'd given little thought to him, their children, or their marriage.

Screw her. And Ozy and the others.

Screw this forgiveness nonsense.

Demory's demeanor indicated compassion but the counselor got to go home at the end of each work day. His exposure to this place, these people, was limited. In here, forgiveness and how the system expected you to act could get you killed. They wanted him to feel remorse. Well, goddamnit, he did. But he didn't want to wear it on a fucking T-shirt so others could feel appeased. They didn't need to know how often remorse nearly strangled him.

Jeffrey had said something once that had really pissed him off. But, maybe Jeffrey had been right. Maybe he *had* driven Kayla to do what she did.

He didn't want to think about that. Didn't want to examine it. It felt better to blame her for everything. She was certainly guilty. And, she was free. Probably whining about him with friends who trashed him over their martinis and hundred-dollar entrees, while the nanny comforted their children.

Starks dropped his feet heavily to the floor then began to pace.

Where were his children now? Were they okay? If only he could see them, hold them. He kicked the bench and fell to the floor, clutching his throbbing foot.

His grandfather and uncles had fed him the erroneous belief that if he always did what he should, he could control his life. They were wrong, possibly because none of them had ever imagined a larger life, much less lived it as he had. He'd believed and followed their guidance all these years, yet here he was, in this untenable predicament. He missed his grandfather, but thank God he was no longer alive to see his Freddy brought so low and the family shamed.

A scream escaped him as he punched the wall with both fists. Blood welled and oozed from broken skin. He was surprised to find this action had a calming effect. He limped to the washbasin, alternating his hands to hold the single spigot open to let cold water rinse away the red.

A knock came at the door. The cuff opened and green eyes in an unfamiliar, somewhat pudgy face looked back at him.

"Time to exercise and shower, Mr. Starks. You ready?'

"I stay ready."

Starks was curious to see who was on the other side of the door: no guard had ever called him mister, or knocked before opening the flap.

The steel door swung wide. "You know the drill, Mr. Starks. Stand in the middle, please."

The heavy-set guard entered the cell, shackles in hand. A CO named Camello stayed just inside the doorway. Starks had seen him around but hadn't ever dealt with him.

Starks noted the polite guard's nametag read *Landers.*

"Officer Landers, you just started working here?" he asked.

"Been here a long time, just in another area. I'm filling in for a guard on extended leave."

"It's nice to meet you."

Camello harrumphed.

Landers's heavy tread in the corridor echoed in Starks's mind. I'm like Pavlov's dogs, he thought, conditioned to anticipate my reward by the sound of footsteps leading me to sustenance.

Ten minutes later, Starks stepped inside the segregated yard large enough for several inmates to be active, even create a basketball game with two-person teams. But he was always the only one there. Only one prisoner allowed at a time, he'd been told. He didn't know how many others were in his isolation block. He could ask, not that he wanted to know. So far, he'd counted five distinct voices, finding the task as daunting as trying to identify different bird song.

Camello removed the shackles.

Starks squinted against the sun, lifted his face to the warmth, tasted the cold fresh air.

The guard carried the chains with him a few yards away, dropped them then lit a cigarette. He inhaled deeply and looked bored.

Officer Landers stood near a plastic canister that held a basketball, football, and soccer ball.

Starks dribbled the basketball. He held the ball still and said, "You're different from the other guards. They've been anything but polite."

"My mother raised me right. Do unto others . . . until they give you a reason to do otherwise."

Starks bounced the ball once. He lowered his voice and asked, "Can I know your first name?"

"That's not encouraged here." Landers glanced at the other guard then took a moment to decide. "Ted. Never use it where others can hear."

Starks dribbled the ball twice then stopped. He looked Landers in the eyes. "Thank you. Makes me feel somewhat human again."

For the next forty minutes, Starks dodged imaginary opponents and shot hoops with near-perfect accuracy from various distances until he heard, "Mr. Starks. Time's up."

Camello ground out his fifth cigarette then picked up the shackles and fastened them on Starks's wrists and ankles. "Now for the highlight of my day," he said. "I get to watch you shower."

Landers frowned at the guard. "That's enough from you. Let's go, Mr. Starks."

Starks heard a commotion. Over in the main yard, Bo postured like a bull contemplating a target. Even at this distance, he could see the gang leader's face was still healing.

Starks said, "If looks could kill."

Bo was playing it smart: He kept his mouth shut. But he elbowed the gang member next to him, who traced Bo's line of sight to Starks.

Adrenaline surged the message of fight or flight throughout Starks's system, as though he had a choice between the two. A new feeling came over him: He was goddamn tired of feeling afraid. People could sense fear, read it on a person's face, smell it on them. If he didn't get his act together, he risked becoming one or more inmate's bitch. Or be gang-raped. Or killed.

His thoughts raced and he resisted looking back as he made his way into the prison.

Landers impressed him yet again. The other guards always started the hour when they opened his cell door. If they could shortchange his time, even if by just a few minutes, they did. Landers had waited to start the hour once he got outside.

He'd always thought grand gestures were what made a difference. The significance of the guard's small kindnesses was like manna delivered in the desert.

He felt the first spark of—what? encouragement—something he hadn't felt in a very long time.

CHAPTER 35

THE TRUTH, STARKS realized back in his cell, was that he'd given little thought to Bo during his time in isolation, a true case of "out of sight, out of mind." Seeing Bo brought something home to him: if the gang leader didn't get him, one of his gang members would.

He'd caught Bo by surprise in that attack, and he knew that wouldn't be allowed to happen again. The inmate and his followers would be on alert from now on.

He could feel retaliation following him, waiting for him like something in the shadows. He was in prison for a long time. They all were. All Bo or anyone needed was an opportunity—or an arrangement with the right guards.

Sure, he'd demonstrated that he, too, was capable of violence but he'd never initiated it. He'd always been provoked.

Maybe he needed to make a concession in this case: Kill Bo before the man killed him. But that solution was fraught with dead-ends. Literally. One or more gang members would surely go after him, if he succeeded. The idea of taking Bo out was nothing but wishful thinking, with no basis in reality.

Maybe there were other gangs at Sands that would include him as a member, protect him? Of course not, he chided himself. No one opposed Bo. Not if they wanted to live. And especially not if they wanted the contraband he could provide that no one else could.

Maybe if he attacked a guard, they might extend his time in solitary.

But that didn't guarantee safety either, including or especially with the guards who'd probably avenge their own, one way or another.

And he was fairly certain the chance that another inmate would kill Bo, for whatever reason, was zero. Even if someone else did the job, that wouldn't mean Bo's gang would let him get away with what he'd done to their leader. Eventually, he'd have to be made an example of.

Every idea that came to Starks's mind was followed by a reason it wouldn't work. The only idea he couldn't argue with was that he should use some of his isolation time to build his strength. Letting himself get weak in any capacity wasn't a wise way to go. They couldn't keep him in isolation forever.

And, he decided, he should do something to strengthen his faltering nerve, as well. But that seemed harder to wrap his thoughts around.

He almost felt foolish for being so edgy. The rest of the week, after all, had been routine: meal trays of crappy food were slid into and retrieved through the slot; all the guards but Ted Landers insulted him; lights dimmed at night and brightened in the morning; one hour a day to exercise and shower.

It was during that one hour that he went on full alert. He felt somewhat safer when Ted was on duty, but knew not to trust that completely. Not that he believed Ted would betray him but that the out of shape CO could be overpowered, injured, or killed by another inmate.

That thought not only made fear return but intensified it.

He needed more people on his side.

CHAPTER 36

JAKES AND CAMELLO arrived to take him to his next session with Demory. Starks's was surprised at how much he was looking forward to it: it was time out of solitary, and in a more normal environment, even if the counselor usually annoyed him.

He'd have to pass by the gang member's cell again, so fixed his face into one absent of expression. Whether or not the man was waiting for him to walk by, or was even in his cell this time, it was smarter not to appear frightened or intimidated. And it wasn't just the gang member he needed to show this face to, it was for every inmate who stood by to watch the show. Enough eyes focused on him that he wondered if tickets were being sold.

Starks sat in his usual chair in Demory's office. As soon as the guards closed the door, he leaned over with his elbows rested on his knees. He took several shallow breaths then looked up. The doctor was watching him.

"How's it going?" Demory asked.

"I've had better days."

"Want to talk about it?"

"Not really, Doc." Starks leaned back, glanced around.

"I'm not a doctor."

"I know. If it's all the same to you, I'll use the moniker."

"Fine with me." Demory sat forward, pen poised over paper. "We'll get straight to it, then. Did you give any more thought to what we discussed last time? Feelings? Forgiveness?"

"Until you walk a mile in my shoes, Doc . . ."

"I can't help you if you won't talk to me."

"Help me to what? Forgive? Screw that. You have no idea what I went through in the past few years."

"I will, if you'll tell me. I have an idea that it was traumatic in order to cause a man of your intelligence and reputation to end up sitting across from me. Starks, c'mon. A violent attack on the outside. A violent attack in here. Attempted suicide. That's a drastic change for a man like you. If for no other reason, satisfy my professional curiosity."

Starks dropped his head into his hands and moaned.

Demory tossed his pen onto his notepad. "Start somewhere."

Starks stared at the restraints around his wrists. "I worked my ass off to give her and our children everything. Other than the long hours, she has no idea what it took for me to really build my first business then the satellite businesses, and to keep them profitable. She helped me at the start, sure. But at the first sign of success, she wanted more. I just never realized how much: Personal trainers for her and the kids, live-in nanny, Ferrari, mansion, expensive clothes and jewels—got them all. Stress-free life for her, burdens out the ass for me. Look how she repaid me."

"How did she repay you?"

Starks slammed his hands on the desk, ignoring the dents the wrist cuffs made in the wood, and the fact that Demory jumped back. "She lied and cheated with not only Ozy but with other employees at her job. Yeah, they worked in the same office. According to Ozy, every man in his firm had his turn with her. More than once. Who knows how many others she was with who didn't work there."

"Do you know for a fact that was true?"

"Even if it was just him—which it wasn't, it happened. And this went on for a long time. He told her he loved her and she believed him. And there I was, blinded by my faith in her and working my butt off while his only responsibility was to find a convenient place to fuck her then put his clothes back on and go home to the wife and kiddies. That's the man she chose over her marriage and family."

"Were her feelings for him the only reason for her choice?"

"She blamed *me*, as though I drove her into his arms and him between her legs."

He slammed his fists on the desk again. "Who did she call when a fire broke out in the basement of our house—her house now, damn her—after we were separated? Not the man who supposedly loved and cared more for and about her than I did." He slumped forward, and after a few moments said, "Ozy said she told him and every other man she was with that I never satisfied her in bed."

"And you chose to believe him?"

"She told someone else I know. Someone reliable."

"Doesn't mean it's true. Did she ever indicate this to you before all the—"

"Shit hit the fan?"

Demory smiled. "Did she ever tell you that she was displeased?"

"Quite the contrary."

"Sounds to me like it was all talk, to annoy you. And it worked."

Starks shrugged then stared unseeing at the ceiling.

"All that pain eventually went to rage when you felt betrayed, didn't it?"

Starks turned his head away and stayed silent a moment. He cleared his throat before turning back.

"Only the people we're closest to," Demory said, "can hurt us that much. Even if we never get close to anyone, if we live long enough, someone's going to hurt us. But if we never get close to anyone, that'll hurt us, as well.

"Starks, listen to me. Pain is a part of life. We'd like to escape it, but that's not the reality we live in. Emotional pain is worse than physical pain. We know what to do about physical pain. It can be healed or numbed. We rush to take care of it, get rid of it. Emotional pain is something we don't always know what to do about. We often feel ashamed when we feel it, which makes it even worse. But we can't escape it. Not in this life. And because we can't escape it, we have to learn what to do about it in a way that's constructive, rather than destructive.

"You'll stay in trouble here, as well as outside once you're released, if you don't come to terms with this and figure out a better way. Let me work with you to make it an easier road to walk down."

Starks stayed silent.

"Did you have any idea she was like this when you married her?"

Starks shook his head. "She wasn't like this. Correction. That's what she wanted me to believe. And I did. It was all an act."

"And now you're here."

"And now I'm here."

"I know it's easy for me to say, but you need to adapt to being here as best you can."

"I need to become or at least act impervious. To protect myself."

"That's not what I had in mind."

"Then why don't you tell me what the hell you're getting at."

"Do you think Kayla's life changed in such a way that, as a defense mechanism, she turned cold toward you, felt she had to protect herself, even if gradually, over time?"

"I still don't get your point." Starks's posture was rigid. "And you're pissing me off, if you want the truth. It's sounding like you're taking her side."

"Bear with me. I have a point, I promise. What was your and Kayla's intimate life like?"

Starks's jaw tightened. "None of your goddamn business."

"I don't want to piss you off. What I'm asking you to do is consider more than just your side of what happened. Wait," he held up his hand when Starks started to protest. "Let me finish. If the only side you see, if the only feelings you consider are yours, you'll never heal your emotional wounds or your relationships. And you can't deny you've been wounded; otherwise, you wouldn't be talking and acting the way you do. I promise you that I understand your pain and humiliation and every other emotion you feel but you'll never understand more than you do right now, about what led you to this moment, if you don't try to understand her feelings, too."

"Again, bullshit."

Demory frowned. "I'm not blowing smoke up your ass, Starks. I do get it. But we have to start somewhere. You can start by looking at the names you call her. I have no idea what you called her or said to her in front of your children but from now on, I want you to imagine the pain and shame your children would feel if they heard you speak about or to their mother that way. Even if you feel she deserves it."

"She deserves it."

Demory let a minute go by before he spoke. "Look, you can't erase the past. But you won't heal if you won't let it go. People make mistakes, just as you did. Most mistakes are made because people think it's their only choice, wrong or not. You want to look for that place in your heart that allows you to release judgment of them. For your sake, if not theirs."

"After what she did?"

"It's always easier to see what another person does. Easier than seeing what we do. None of us are perfect. If we expect perfection from anyone, we have to, in turn, allow them to expect perfection from us. It just isn't realistic. We can do the best we can, but we're going to mess up sometimes."

Starks swung his head up but remained quiet.

"Enough of that for the moment," Demory said. "We need to get to the root of what happened, before you got here and since. I think you need to talk about it with an impartial listener."

Starks fidgeted in his chair. "Fine. I guess we'll see how impartial you really are."

"I want you to keep in mind what I said earlier: There are always at least two sides to every story. It may be painful for you to travel that path, but I'm going to ask you to travel it, with me here to assist you. And I'll need you to be honest. We want to consider what you both did. We don't have time to get started with that today, but plan on it the next time we talk."

Demory closed the file then looked up to see Starks, head down, wringing his hands.

"What is it?"

"I'm scared, Doc. I don't think I'm going to make it here. Big Bo or one of his gang will kill me. I'm sure of it. One of them just recently let me know I should plan to die. By his hand or not, I know he meant it." Starks wiped away tears he'd fought hard to suppress.

"I'll report this so the COs can keep watch."

"You know how it is; it won't help. I'm a dead man. As much as if I were on death row."

"You riled up the wrong bunch of inmates, not that there's a right one.

They're used to dealing with life only one way. And I know from prior experience that talking with them—the way I'm talking with you—won't work. That's one reason I'm committed to helping you."

He locked his gaze with Starks's. "You use your mind. They use only muscle. The best thing for me to do is inform the authorities, or at least recommend they keep you in isolation until I say otherwise. I know that's not easy but it's safer."

"That'll keep me from being so exposed. But you and I both know that even in isolation, there're no guarantees. If—when—they get serious about getting me, they'll do it."

"We'll do whatever we can for now. Hang in there, Starks. I'll see you next week."

He watched Starks rise, thrust his shoulders back and hold his head up as he opened the door and left with the guards. Starks wanted to live; the suicidal tendency was fading, or so it seemed. But now this extra threat was hanging over his patient's head.

On one hand, he wanted to help Starks get over the violent behaviors that had emerged, but he knew that might be another form of suicide in here. Especially if Boen Jones and his gang intended to make good on their threat.

There was also a selfish aspect: This was the first time in a very long time that he was working with a redeemable inmate. Whether or not Starks remained here or was eventually returned to society—or God help him— faced life imprisonment, he wanted the man to live, and even die, feeling like a whole man again.

A system was supposed to be in place to protect inmates in danger. And although he couldn't name names for certain, he knew some of the guards were on Boen Jones's payroll, whatever form that took. The gang leader got away with too much; too many illegal activities had his name written all over them.

As counselor, he was obligated to report this latest threat to authorities. Doing so might lead to a sure death sentence for Starks, and soon.

His choice was obvious, as was his responsibility.

* * *

I have to survive.

The powerful feeling underneath this thought made Starks stop pacing in his cell. For the first time in untold months, he wanted to *live*—the word hammered in his head. But, what could he possibly do to guarantee it? He was an engineer, a problem-solver. This problem seemed like one without a solution. No ready answer came to him.

His attention was drawn to his mattress. The shank he'd taken so long to make as a weapon of self-destruction had, in an instant, transformed into one that might save him. For now, all he could do was continue his daily routine. And be vigilant.

Starks wondered if he was becoming paranoid. Each day, as the week crept by, he found he flinched more and more at every sound. When out of his cell for the one hour, he repeatedly looked over his shoulder. When he shot hoops, he missed and had to chase the ball every time. Then he had to listen to the derisive laughter and jibes coming at him from other inmates standing with Bo, who *managed* to be outside when he was.

Was it even possible to request transfer to another prison? If it was possible, would his request be denied, and word spread around that he wanted out? If transferred, he was sure he'd find a different version of Bo and his gang wherever he went. Who else filled the cells besides people just like them, or worse?

He imagined Demory's voice in his head saying, "Maybe you ought to look at that last question you just asked yourself. Maybe you want to ask yourself what kind of person you choose to be while you're here."

Maybe the counselor had a point.

CHAPTER 37

DEMORY TOOK NOTE of Starks's downward cast eyes and hunched shoulders. Everything about the man's demeanor was constricted, as though he was holding himself together, barely. He knew that Bo's eventual payback weighed on Starks's mind. There was nothing he personally could do about the actual threat, but he could help Starks emotionally, at least as much as the man would allow him to.

Demory picked up his pen and held it poised, ready to make notes. "You haven't received any visitors since you arrived here. I checked. You put it in writing that you didn't want to see anyone."

Starks shrugged.

"Why is that?"

"My family feels shamed. As for friends . . . I realized most of them aren't really friends. Except for Jeffrey. But I told him I didn't want any visitors, at least not for a while."

"Why would you shut out your support system?"

"The trial was humiliating enough. I don't want anyone to see me like this."

"Sometimes the way to become stronger is to talk with others you trust about how you feel. Give them a chance to assist you, let them show they care."

"Weakness is detested in my family. And damn dangerous in here."

"Getting what you need isn't a sign of weakness." Demory sighed. "All right. You don't want to see them. Yet. You're here now. Talk to me. Start wherever you want."

"Everything starts—and ends—with Kayla. I knew the first time I looked at her that I had to be with her for the rest of my life. At first my family rejected her, because of her mother. My mother said Kayla's mother was a loose woman. And it didn't matter how intelligent or polite Kayla was. Not to them. But I refused to give her up. Eventually, they grew fond of her, including my mother. My mother even told me how wrong she'd been about Kayla, something I never expected to hear."

"Were you physically intimate before you married or did you wait?"

"Long before."

"How did that go, for both of you?"

"We were teenagers driven by hormones. More obviously so for me but Kayla responded in her own quiet way. We were both curious about sex. We tried everything we could think of. Went at it any place we could find that was private."

"What else did you do as a couple?"

"Spent as much time together as we could. I'd pick her up in my Dodge and ride around, go to the park, or spend time at our houses. Then she got her first car. A Geo Metro. It didn't even have power steering." He smiled and shook his head. "I teased her about how she'd develop muscles driving that damn car.

"We didn't have a lot of money to spend, so we rented movies more than we went out to see them, which was a good thing because both our homes had finished basements used as entertainment rooms. We'd watch movies then get physical, if we could wait until the movie was over. Our parents believed we would never do anything until we were married, so it didn't concern them to leave us alone like that. We were in love. Or so I thought." He pulled at the collar of his shirt.

Demory leaned back in his chair. "What about after high school?"

"I wanted to be a mechanical engineer, so applied to MIT. Kayla applied to Boston University, with a major in information technology."

"How'd it go, being at two universities?"

Starks propped his elbows on the chair arms and stretched his legs out in front of him. "We had our disagreements from time to time, like all couples, but we stayed together. Until my second year."

"What happened?"

"I told her we were definitely getting married after college but that I felt we'd become a couple so young; that we should take a break from each other, apply ourselves to our studies. I thought I'd presented a logical suggestion; that she'd see reason. When I saw how upset she was, I tried to take it back, but she refused. We broke up."

"Was that your only reason for making that suggestion?"

"Kayla was the only one I'd ever had sex with. And there I was, surrounded by attractive, intelligent, fun women. I didn't want to eventually marry Kayla and feel I'd missed out or had regrets. But I didn't want to tell her the truth, either. She would never have come back to me if I had."

"How did you feel during the break-up?"

"It wasn't as easy as I thought it would be. Our families weren't happy, especially mine. Especially after all I'd put them through at the start of our relationship. But I felt if I didn't take a break from it and experiment a bit . . ."

Demory waited then asked, "Did you go out with other women?"

"I dated, but never got serious with anyone. In fact," he snickered, "the only woman I got physical with was a woman named Janisa. All those women I wanted to enjoy, and didn't. And even with Janisa it never went beyond heavy kissing and some groping. My heart wasn't in it. And no one was more surprised than me that my penis wasn't either. I wondered if something medical was wrong with me. I did get interested in one other woman, but not for long. Turned out I was a rebound for her. All she talked about was her ex-boyfriend. I couldn't stand to hear about him anymore."

"Did Kayla get involved with anyone?"

"Bernard Hazely. But it was brief. I saw to that. Jeffrey told me about Bernard. Told me I was going to miss out on a very nice girl, meaning Kayla, if I didn't get my act together. I did miss her, more than I expected to. And I didn't like how it felt to know she was with someone else." He rubbed where the gold band used to reside on his wedding ring finger.

"Were you and Kayla in touch during the break-up?"

"We spoke occasionally. Soon as I learned about Bernard, I told her I wanted her back."

"What did she say?"

"She wanted to know why she should take *me* back. I told her it was because I was the one for her, just as she was the one for me. That we both knew it. She said what I had done wasn't nice." He tapped a forefinger on the edge of the desk. "I told her that in this world nice guys finish last; that I never intended to hurt her. That I did it for us. I told her she'd always be first with me. That it might take a while to get going, get successful, but I'd be the one to give her everything she wanted or could ever want."

"Did she come back to the relationship then?"

"She went out with Bernard for another month and a half before she broke it off with him."

"How did you feel about that?"

"Pissed-off. Scared."

"Were she and Bernard intimate?"

"She said no. Told me I was the only one. It was a lie, of course."

"But at the time you believed her?"

"She wasn't the type of girl to sleep around." Starks placed his head in his hands. "God. I actually just said that."

"What was your reunion like?"

"We had some issues. Broke up a few more times, but always got back together."

"And then you stayed together."

"Yes. Soon after, the difficulty she was having with her mother escalated so Kayla moved into an apartment just off campus; I was still living at home. She was crap at managing money but I always found a way to help her out, even though I didn't have a lot. Had to tap my savings fairly often. I yelled at her about repeatedly overdrawing her checking account. I'd ask how she could mess up something so simple. Her answer was that I was the one who knew how these things worked; that I was the man. Even though I took over doing her bank statements, she still spent more than she had. I had to work overtime hours so I could deposit money into her account every month. All those damn overdraft fees."

"What was the problem between Kayla and her mother?"

"They argued. A lot."

"What about Kayla's father?"

"He deserted them when she was young. All she knew about him was what her mother told her, and it wasn't good. She didn't like to talk about him, so I didn't ask."

Demory took a few seconds to complete his note. "What about after college?"

"We graduated the same year. My family made a big deal out of celebrating our accomplishments. Her mother attended. It went well enough, considering.

"I got a paid internship with Gravitron Enterprises, which lasted a year. After that, I enrolled in the master's program at the University of Houston. Kayla also wanted to pursue a master's degree. Where she did that wasn't an issue for her, so we went to Houston together. Got our first, very small, apartment as a couple."

Demory looked up. "Were you married?"

Starks shook his head. "My family wasn't happy about that. All that mattered to us was that we were building our future together."

"Any chance you still love her?"

Starks shifted in the chair. He stared at the floor, took a few shallow breaths then said, "No."

Demory put his pen down. "We'll pick up next week where we're leaving off today. But I'd like you to consider pride before our next session."

Starks smirked. "As in 'Pride comes before the fall?'"

"Something like that. Pride can guide us but sometimes it's the enemy.

"I want you to think about this, Starks: The people who love us hurt us, whether they mean to or not. We hurt those we love, whether we mean to or not. And when we make one person the center of our world, perhaps put them on a pedestal, where they can't move without falling off, both get hurt. There's also the fact that people change over time. And they should; we're all meant to. Partners sometimes outgrow each other because of how they change as individuals. The strength of any relationship has everything to do with whether or not, and how well, the individuals ride the occasional storms these changes bring. One thing that makes a difference is being open-minded about the change life brings. We want to get you comfortable with exploring how to become more open-minded about what happened then and how you can move forward now."

Starks winced.

"What is it?" Demory asked.

"My own words—open-minded—coming back to haunt me."

CHAPTER 38

STARKS LAY ON his bed with one arm covering his closed eyes, contemplating the question that had come to him during the trial and again in his last session with Demory: had Kayla actually loved him during those early days, or had he been fooled into believing it— because he'd refused to believe otherwise?

Certain details of his and Kayla's start together in their first apartment in Houston were still clear in his memory. They'd been lucky to find the tiny, sparsely furnished place. Kayla wanted to decorate it, make it feel more like a home. When they had free time, they'd go to the local dollar stores, flea markets, and garage sales. They went to many such places because Kayla was very particular about her purchases: She did not want their furnishings to appear as cheap, even if they were. They had so little money then. Each of them had a small stipend from their financial aid loans, and his family sent a small amount each month. It was never enough.

Two months after they moved in, they lay entwined in the darkened room, spent after making love.

Kayla lightly traced his chest with a finger. "Tomorrow morning I'm looking for work. We could use the extra money."

"You don't have to do that. I'll find a way. Don't worry about it."

"You have to study."

"So do you."

"Your studies are more important. Your degree has more requirements than mine."

"That's true. But still—"

"Just a part-time job. It'll be fine. We'll have some extra for expenses and for some fun now and then." She nudged him playfully. "Tell me it's okay."

"I don't like it but if it's what you want . . ." His hand stroked her damp back.

She lowered herself on top of him. Her kiss lingered on his lips. "It is what I want. Now I'll give you something you want."

They both knew his groan of weariness was pretense.

Three days later Kayla had a job as a waitress in a diner. One month later, she took on extra shifts. Two months later, she took incompletes in all her courses and went to a better-paying job at an upscale restaurant. Starks was angry she'd dropped out of university without discussing it with him but knew that being without money made her unhappy, which she made clear when they argued about her decision.

They lived off her income, his stipend, and his family's small contributions for the next year. It became too much for his pride. He got a part-time job at a department store and worked full-time during breaks. They still squeaked by most months. Time together, aside from finally sharing a bed late at night, was infrequent, and more precious because of this. They made those times as special as they could afford to. Each left love notes for the other to find—in the book for his next class, pinned to her waitress uniform, next to key rings.

Together they'd done what was needed to create a better life then and for the future. There was true pleasure found in sharing a purpose and dreams, or so he'd believed.

Starks sat up, swung his feet to the concrete floor of his cell.

They'd been happier then, when they'd had nearly nothing. When they'd worked as a couple for everything they had. Had done whatever was needed to support each other, love each other.

During those early years, he never imagined how very wrong things could go.

Starks rose from the hard prison bed, went to the washbasin and splashed cold water on his face. He turned the spigot off. The scar on his right hand caught the light, bringing to mind the sharp teeth that had torn his flesh. It had happened up the block from the one-bedroom house he and Kayla had rented after that first apartment.

The house was wood-framed, on piers, and had been built in the late 1920s in a neighborhood filled with similar houses, along with apartment buildings. Three drooping wooden steps led to the tiny front porch. The exterior that had been painted white, back when someone cared, was covered in grime. Black paint flaked off the doors and shutters that sagged. Weeds neither of them wanted to deal with grew at the edge of the house but stopped where the packed dirt of their postage stamp-sized yard began. Rotting garbage littered the streets and sidewalks most days. Brackish water often pooled by drains no one bothered to clear. It was low-end living, for sure, but fit their restricted budget.

Gunshots, police sirens, and loud fights that went on nearly every night and especially on weekends kept him awake when he desperately needed sleep. Not Kayla, though; she could sleep through any noise, which he many times told her was annoying. She'd shrug and tell him she was sorry he couldn't sleep but wasn't sorry that she could.

The cocker spaniel Kayla had begged him for shared their space, oblivious to its surroundings and their struggles. She'd named the dog Fristo. Starks rubbed the scar, remembering how close they'd come to losing the frisky puppy when the pit bull owned by a guy, Devin, who lived up the street, had gotten loose and attacked the spaniel. In trying to pull the dogs apart, the pit bull sunk its teeth into his hand. The trip to the E.R. had taken all but the last thirty dollars in their account, too many days before more funds would come in. The dog's owner was apologetic and promised to pay all expenses if Starks would please leave the police out of it so his dog wouldn't be destroyed. Devin's promise was a lie.

So much of his life had been a lie.

If I had a scar for every lie Kayla's told me and the pain she's caused . . .

It was unimaginable.

But so was everything that had happened since and was happening now.

CHAPTER 39

ONE THING THAT wasn't a lie was an event that should have sealed their bond as a couple. Thought of that experience and the fear he'd felt for their safety sent shivers through him. No way could he have anticipated then that in the future, his escape from that element was temporary; that one day he'd be living among them; that he'd be considered one of them.

The gas gauge in Starks's Chevy had red-arrowed on empty while he was driving home.

If he used the bus as often as possible or car-pooled, he could afford to put five gallons in the tank, just in case, and fill it up when more money came in next week. He was okay about doing that, not that he had a choice.

The local convenience store with gas pumps was a half mile from their house and in an even worse neighborhood than where they lived. He was careful to grip and release the nozzle so that no more than those calculated gallons went into his fuel tank. He went inside, grabbed a couple packs of ramen noodles then stood second in line at the register, anxious to get out as quickly as possible.

A yard and a half away and to his left, a man keyed in numbers onto the ATM pad.

The glass door near the ATM opened. A young Caucasian teen wearing dark sunglasses and a hooded sweatshirt entered and glanced around, tapped at a few bags of chips but didn't pick one. The teen approached the ATM just as the machine dispensed the cash.

"Gimme the cash," he told the man.

"Fuck off." The ATM man slammed his right fist into the teen's jaw.

The teen pulled a .38 from under his sweatshirt and fired three times. Three twenties drifted to the floor. He scooped up the blood-splattered bills and ran out.

Behind the counter, the employee yelled into the phone, "Police! Shooting at—"

That was all Starks heard as he rushed out behind the thief. He jumped into his Chevy parked behind a truck at the other pump. Car in reverse gear he punched the gas pedal, burned rubber, and took out a post near the Do Not Enter sign.

He slammed on the brakes when he pulled into the dirt yard at his house, sending his satchel to the floorboard.

Starks grabbed his satchel and ran toward the door, where Kayla waited for him.

"What's the matter?" she asked.

"Lock the door."

"Tell me—"

"Lock the damn door. We've got to get the hell out of this neighborhood. I've got to find a way. Now."

"Tell me what happened."

"I just saw a man get shot. At close range. I'm pretty sure he was killed."

"Are you okay? Were you hurt?"

"Damn lucky I didn't get shot." His breaths were shallow. "Damn it!" He began to pace. "It was such a cold-blooded act. By a kid a few years from needing a shave. For sixty fucking dollars."

He hurried around in the small house making sure everything was closed and locked. Fristo, wanting to join the *game*, yapped and danced and followed Starks as he moved from room to room.

Kayla followed as well. "You're scaring me."

"I'm sorry. I just want you—us—to be safe. If anything had happened to me, you'd be here, in this wretched place, alone. Without my protection. Bad enough you're here at times by yourself."

"I know this is upsetting, but you need to calm down. Would you like some tea?"

"Damn it!"

"What now?"

"I dropped the noodles in the store. We don't have anything to eat."

"We have milk, cereal, bread, peanut butter. But I can go get a few groceries if you'd like."

"Hell no. I don't want you going out." He rubbed his forehead. "Besides, we don't have enough money. There's only eleven dollars and change in the account. Who knows what we may need it for before more money comes in next week."

"Strip."

"Huh?"

"Go to the bedroom and take off your clothes." She took his hand and pulled him after her. "You need to relax. We both do. Then we'll dine on cereal or peanut butter sandwiches, or both, by candlelight."

"Kayla, I'm the luckiest man alive."

It took several months of scrimping and working overtime, but they finally moved into an apartment in a town an hour away from his school in Houston. The neighborhood seemed to have nice-enough people in it and no crime to speak of.

Starks carpooled to the city to save even more money. Kayla got a sales job in a local upscale clothing store, earning more than she ever had, and she enjoyed the employee discounts. Sometimes too much.

But there was something she didn't like.

"I can't take your hours anymore," she told him. "You're out of the house by five thirty every morning. You don't get home until after midnight. You work weekends. All this and we still don't have enough money. And we never have any fun anymore."

"For now, it's necessary."

The blue glass vase she'd gotten from the dollar store—the vase she'd months ago stopped putting fresh flowers into once a week to brighten the apartment—shattered and sent shards flying when it hit the wall.

"This *sucks*, Starks. All of it."

He ran his hand through his hair and said, "It's the only thing that sucks around here these days."

Kayla twirled to face him. "You bastard. I handle everything around here. You think I have the energy for that? You think you deserve *that*?"

Starks glanced around at all the housework that wasn't being done. At her new outfit. At her fresh manicure and pedicure, which he knew she hadn't done herself.

"Damn it, Kayla. I'm doing the best I can. I know you're working, too, but I'm the one who pretty much gets home with time to shit, shower, and shave before I have to leave again."

She kicked at the broken glass. "This is not the life you promised me. How long will we have to live like this?" She collapsed, sobbing, to the floor.

He lifted her up, cradling her in his arms.

"I know it's not easy. I promise you that one day these tough times will pay off."

"You'd better be right because I can't go on like this much longer."

CHAPTER 40

THE PAPERWORK HAD taken months to fill out, submit, and be assessed, but Starks and Kayla received financial aid to attend Stanford University.

In response to Starks's query about a place to live, plus his hesitant comment about their finances, his guidance counselor said, "I know someone with an affordable place in Foster City. It's only fourteen miles from Stanford, give or take. It'll fit your budget. If you'd like, I can line it up for you."

They rented a do-it-yourself moving truck, hooked up the one car they kept to the back, and made the trip in three days. The sale of the other car provided enough money for moving expenses, the deposit and first month's rent for the one-bedroom efficiency apartment located not too far from one of the lagoons, and enough to tide them over for two weeks, if they were careful.

By the end of their first week there, each of them had found a job that worked with their school schedules. It would be tight no matter what, money-wise, but they'd be able to make it. Starks had created a strict budget they agreed to adhere to.

Near the end of the fourth month, Starks sat at the Formica-covered counter that separated their miniscule kitchen from the only slightly larger living room. The bank statement, checkbook register, and pocket calculator were in front of him. He checked the numbers twice then covered his face with his hands.

"We're overdrawn by thirty-eight dollars."

"That's not too bad," Kayla said. "I'm getting paid soon. We'll be fine."

"You don't get paid until next week. Rent's due three days from now." He threw the pencil down. "The late fee is a hundred bucks. A hundred bucks we don't have to spare. And there're the overdraft fees."

"Maybe we can get the landlord to excuse the late fee. It's our first time to be late."

Starks shook his head in frustration. It wasn't the first time rent was late but he hadn't wanted to scare her the other times. The late fees were killing them, as was her disregard for the budget.

He exhaled and said, "Sometimes I feel like I'm down a well with no way out. But I'll figure something out."

"You're so good at that, baby."

How could he stay angry with her when she believed in him so much?

The next day he saw a flyer on the community board in the student union: Car title loans. He grabbed the flyer and hurried to his car. It was worth it to skip a class or two.

Twelve hundred dollars and a thirty-day loan with hefty interest later, he paid the rent and other bills in person, and in cash. He treated a delighted Kayla to a candlelit dinner that night at a nice restaurant overlooking the water. The rest of the money was deposited into their checking account. They enjoyed a lobster a piece, and he relaxed, knowing this would be their easiest month since they'd been together.

The first of the month he went to the bank to cash a check for twenty dollars—the weekly allowance he split with Kayla. He requested a printed receipt with his account balance on it, headed for the door to leave then stopped. The balance amount couldn't be right. He got back in line and requested a printout of his account transactions.

"Oh God."

"Are you all right, Mr. Starks?" the teller asked.

He shook his head, his breaths coming fast, and left without answering.

Kayla had, yet again, forgotten to give him receipts so he could enter the amounts onto the check register, or to check with him before she spent, as she'd agreed to. The first loan payment was due, as was the rent. The funds to pay both weren't there. He could pay one or the other.

His grandfather's words echoed in his mind: "It's the man's job to handle expenses. A woman shouldn't be made to stress about such things."

He took out a new loan with the old principal added on, keeping this new loan hidden from Kayla, just as he had the original one. She didn't want to be bothered with such details, as she'd reminded him when he'd previously chided her about their budget.

Nor would he include her in such decisions that were his alone.

I'll think of something, he told himself.

* * *

Sitting in solitary at Sands, he brooded at how consistently Kayla had ignored his repeated requests to do what was needed to keep them out of the hole that kept getting deeper.

Could he really fault her for not doing better? After all, he'd failed to learn his lesson regarding her, and here he was, in a different kind of hole.

One he couldn't buy his way out of.

Then he recalled the glimmer of an idea he'd had recently and forgotten about. He glanced up at the spider's web. His foggy mental image was gradually taking shape, its edges beginning to sharpen.

CHAPTER 41

THE CUFF ON the steel door opened.

"Dinner. Get it now or it's going on the floor."

Starks sprinted to the door. He caught the tray just as it was about to topple forward. Slop again. A far cry from the lobsters he and Kayla had enjoyed that night long ago and all the times since. He'd been so proud about how he'd handled all those tricky money situations back then.

Maybe Demory had a point about pride; though, the counselor certainly didn't know the whole story.

The men of his family were all about pride. How could he or anyone expect him to be any different? It had been drilled into his mind that the man ruled the house. That responsibility came with ruling, no matter who, no matter what, was ruled. How could a man with no pride ever fulfill such obligations? Surely one required the other. Didn't it?

Yes, he was a proud man. Or had been.

Maybe there's more than one kind of pride, he thought.

This was a consideration he'd never made before. Had the wrong kind of pride been his undoing, cost him everything?

No. Kayla was at fault.

What had she been thinking, for Christ's sake? She'd listened to friends and family, even when their advice went against common sense, but balked at the idea of him telling her what she needed to do.

She should have known her place, as he had.

He picked up the bread roll on his tray, bit into it. Stale. Still, he chewed.

All he'd ever tried to do was make sure she had the life she wanted, and help her enjoy it, as well as do whatever it took to put them in good standing in their community.

His grandfather had told him that one of his responsibilities, especially once he'd become successful, was to help others, beyond just his family. He'd helped others. Lots of others. Lewis Mason, for one. Brilliant chemist, frail geek, annoying as hell. The man had gotten six years in Waltgate, in upstate New York, known to be one of the worst prisons anywhere. Mason had been sentenced for drug trafficking. It should have been for operating without any street sense. He'd begged Starks to help him avoid a heavy sentence.

He'd discussed with his grandfather whether he should or shouldn't help Mason.

"Freddy, you don't know when you'll need other people. When you help others, they owe you."

So he'd hired the best lawyers, practically funded Mason's entire defense. The little genius owed him, big-time. Mason had put his Purdue smarts to use at Waltgate and had become a force to reckon with. That made him the perfect person to offer advice about how to survive prison.

Jeffery was the only one he'd trust to contact Mason. But that meant he had to call Jeffrey

Two days before, he'd asked about using the phone and was told not as long as he was in isolated confinement, unless it was to call his attorney. That wouldn't work. He didn't want Parker asking questions.

Starks forced himself to eat the beans in congealed broth.

He feared going back into general population, but knew he had to. He was too restricted in here. After all, he was a target no matter where he was. Mason could tell him something that was useful, he was sure of it.

Next time he saw Demory, he'd ask him to call Jeffrey, or see if the counselor could arrange for him to make the call. He'd also ask Demory to recommend he be removed from solitary confinement. The sooner the better.

His brows drew together, his mouth turned downward. Putting his fate into the hands of others was not the way he'd been taught to live. Not the way he had lived.

One more discomforting feeling to add to the growing list.

CHAPTER 42

"UP AND AT 'em, Starks. Time for your hour in the cage."

Jakes and Simmons again.

He held his wrists out, grimacing when Jakes slapped the cuffs on. "I haven't seen Officer Landers around. Is he on vacation? Sick-leave?"

Jakes secured the restraints and said, "Not your business."

Starks shuffled to the door then stopped. He looked right then left.

Simmons shoved him into the corridor. "You don't have to look both ways here. This isn't a street corner."

During the walk through the corridors, Starks resisted checking behind him. The days of getting even minimum pleasure from being in fresh air and moving with more freedom seemed over. At least for now. The possibility he could be rushed at from the back, could be stabbed in the back, gnawed at him, as it had since the threat from the gang member. Bo staring him down during his outdoor time added to his fear.

This was not paranoia, he told himself; this was facing facts.

This time, however, neither Bo nor any recognizable member of his gang were outside at the same time.

Most of his shots made it through the hoop.

Maybe things were looking up.

* * *

Demory studied Starks for several moments.

"You look less upset today," he said.

Starks rested back in the chair, stretched his legs out in front of him.

"I'm not doing too bad, all things considered."

"Glad to hear it. Ready to start?"

"Ready when you are."

"At the end of our last session, I asked you to think about pride."

"I considered it. All in all, pride's a good thing."

"It can also be a five-letter word that leads to destruction."

Starks sat up straight, drew his feet under the chair. He frowned and said, "Granted. But pride also serves a purpose. Pride can keep people on the right track. It helps build character."

Demory relaxed in his chair. "Pride can be a good thing. But every coin has two sides. Misused, it can lead people to make unfavorable, even irrational decisions. If I said a wiser choice is made from reason rather than pride, what would you think about that?"

Starks looked at Demory straight on, stayed silent for several moments before he replied, "I can see that."

"Why do you think you're having these sessions with me?"

"I didn't control my emotions."

"Do you think pride had something to do with why you didn't or couldn't control them?"

Starks didn't answer.

"You waited a year to attack Ozy Hessinger. You were already separated from your wife. The male ego can be fragile, but do you see how pride played a part in that?"

"Damn straight." Starks leaned forward. "I had to honor my children and my family. And, there's her pride to consider. That woman's pride is why I'm in here."

"What do you mean?"

"She doesn't have any. How could a woman with any pride behave as she has?"

Pen scratched on paper. "Have you ever considered that perhaps she felt the same way about you?"

"What are you getting at?"

"People hold up mirrors for us. We don't always like what we see, and we blame them."

Starks willed himself to sit still.

"Do you think Kayla still loves you?"

"Seriously? Sometimes I think she'd be happier if I were dead. Besides, how the hell would I know what she feels? Sometimes your questions suck, Doc."

"What if your anger is just pride speaking?"

Starks lurched forward in the chair. "That woman hurt me in ways you can't imagine."

"I'm sure you hurt each other."

Starks stood up. He glared at Demory then began to pace with as much ease as the ankle shackles allowed.

"Listen, Starks, it's a hard fact to accept, but no relationship's problems stem from just one person. We're either part of the problem or part of the solution. There's no escaping that reality. But those problems are in the past. You need to find a way to become part of the solution, as it relates to now," Demory tapped his pen on the desk, "and the future. Not just about Kayla, but about being here."

Starks paced back and forth. "I'm doing the best I can."

"Learn from your past so you avoid repeating mistakes."

Starks dropped into the chair. "What the hell good is it for me to keep going back to my past? Thinking about my past only messes with me."

"The Danish philosopher Søren Kierkegaard said something that I'd like you to remember: 'Life can only be understood backwards; but it must be lived forwards.'"

"Fuck philosophers. They weren't married to Kayla. Neither were you. So, easier said than done, Doc."

"Life isn't always easy. But it doesn't have to be as hard as we sometimes make it. Listen, Starks, if you want to regain control of your emotions rather than let them control you, you're going to have to heal some wounds. Otherwise, your attention stays on them, and that's where you'll base decisions from. No one likes to hear this, but it's true. Although, you'll have to do what's needed; no one else can do it for you. This pride you let guide your choices and decisions all this time . . . how's that worked for you so far?"

Starks's shoulders raised then sagged.

Demory sat forward. "It's a lot to take in. Give it time. One of our goals is to get you to a point where you make better, wiser decisions, ones not based solely in pride.

"Maybe that's enough about that for now, unless you want to discuss it more. No? Okay. Talk about whatever you want to then."

"Kayla. She surrounded herself with the wrong people. Poisonous people. She lacked the discernment to understand that some people don't have your best interest at heart; they only add fuel to the fire."

"Are you referring to friends or family?"

"Both. But I can't blame them completely. Kayla manipulated them. She's very good at playing the victim. I told her repeatedly that she needed to keep them out of our personal business. She never told them about all the crap she did or was doing. With only one side of the story, they found fault with me."

"Why didn't you tell them the truth?"

Starks's hands went to his face; he rubbed the skin hard as he shook his head.

"Pride. My family would have seen me as the failure, not her. Of course, that's how they saw me, anyway. It was a no-win situation for me."

"Didn't you have a close friend or friends you could confide in?"

"Friends . . . ha! They're right there with you when things are going well, when they can benefit from your success or they need something. Want to know who your friends are? Go broke. Get ill. See how long those friends stick around. Sure, they'll give advice, but when you need them the most, they desert you."

"Did you have one or more bad experiences with people you believed were your friends?"

"Haven't we all? The older I got, the fewer friends I kept. But, Kayla? She thinks her so-called friends really care about her. The same people she's been pouring her heart out to, and lying to, are the same ones judging her and laughing at her behind her back now.

"One of her friends told Kayla second marriages are so much better. You know, the old grass is greener on the other side bullshit. Why didn't she advise Kayla to put her pride aside and work on her marriage, the marriage Kayla vowed to stay in, as I did, for better or worse? Senseless damn fool. These are the people she's listening to."

"So you don't think Kayla has a mind of her own? You believe she's that easily influenced?"

"Everyone can be influenced by other people. Some more than others. Even me. Look how I let her do it to me all these years."

Demory steepled his fingers. "You're right that we're all open to being influenced by others but it's less likely to happen if we have a strong personal foundation. It's possible that you both had faulty foundations."

"I don't give a damn about foundations, Doc. She went looking for a Prince Charming rather than working things out with me. Instead, she got Ozy, who used her, and then she got a man and his daughters who are living with her on her nickel. Correction, on my nickel. Initially, I wanted us to start over. Forgive and forget, you know? But after Ozy . . . no way. I no longer respected her. Soon as I pulled away, she wanted me back. I couldn't do it. And frankly, Doc, I wish to hell you'd stop nagging me about what that damn woman thinks or feels. I don't give a fuck."

Demory put his pen down. "I can see this is making you angry so let's move on. Continue with where you wanted to go with what you were saying."

Starks picked at his ragged cuticles. "We struggled in college. More than we needed to. I've always said my family could send only so much to help us out. That's not true. They sent what I asked them for. I didn't want to ask for even that much, much less more."

"But they would have sent more, if you'd asked?"

Starks nodded.

Demory twirled his pen. "All that stress on both of you could have been avoided then. If they could send more and would have, why'd you choose to struggle?"

"I lied to Kayla about that. Otherwise, she would have insisted I ask for more. If she hadn't always spent more than what came in, we could have made it. It would have been tight at times, but nothing like what it was."

"Despite tight money, were you happy as a couple back then?"

"We had some very happy times together, or at least I thought we did. Because we were in it together."

Demory nodded. "It's hard to face the fact that you shared a history, and now that relationship is broken. Our belief about how life should go tells us such an outcome isn't right. People don't tend to like change, don't find it easy to adapt. Some do a better job of it than others because of what they tell themselves."

"Some changes are unnecessary, so why the hell should I adapt to them?"

"What if I said everything happens for a reason?"

"That's some philosophy, Doc. I can't see any reason for what she did. Not after all I did for her."

"Sometimes it takes time, even years, before we understand. We come together for growth. Sometimes it's for life, sometimes it's not. We often get signs that something needs to change. When we don't pay attention to the signs, life changes in spite of us. Transitions are more painful when we ignore the signs, when we resist the inevitable."

Starks waited for Demory to look at him. "Speaking of change . . . I'm ready to go back into general population."

"Last week you wanted me to keep you in solitary as long as possible."

"I know. Because of Bo."

"What's different?"

"I realized I have to deal with it."

"How are you going to do that?"

"I'll think of something. Our sessions are helping." In response to Demory's raised eyebrows, Starks said, "I mean it. I'm getting a lot out of what we're doing."

"I'll think about it. I'd like to feel confident about making the recommendation."

"I understand. One more thing. Can I have visitors, or make a phone call?"

"That is an improvement. Visitations are limited for people in isolation, but I can see about arranging it. I'll check on the phone call, as well. Anyone particular in mind?"

"Jeffrey."

"The friend you mentioned. What about what you said about friends?"

"I should have excluded Jeffrey from my comments."

"I'll see about getting approval for you to call him."

"What about his visit?"

"I'll see to that, as well. If they agree to let you call him—and I'm going to push them to agree, have him contact me."

"I appreciate it, Doc. One thing: I put it in writing that I didn't want visitors until further notice. How do I change that?"

Demory handed him a tablet and pen. "Write it and sign it. I'll sign off on it and get it to the right person."

Starks wrote out his request, signed it, and watched Demory add his signature.

"I'll take care of this today. And, our session's up."

"You're making a difference, Doc. See you next time."

Demory leaned back in his chair, tapped his pen on the open file in front of him. He didn't want to discourage Starks by telling him he didn't think the man was ready to leave isolation. But facts were facts. Nor did he want to put the man's life in jeopardy. Or was this Starks's way of putting his own life at risk with yet another form of suicide? His comment that he'd handle Bo was suspect; Starks didn't stand a chance. Or was he underestimating his patient, especially considering what he'd done to get himself thrown into isolation in the first place. That, however, was a one-time deal. Bo's gang would never allow it to happen again.

Something felt wrong. He'd do what he could to arrange for the phone call and visit, but not the release from solitary confinement. It was too soon.

He couldn't shake the feeling that something was up.

CHAPTER 43

STARKS'S CELL DOOR flung open so fast and hard it hit the wall. He leapt from his bed, landing in a crouch.

Jakes laughed then sneered. "Let's go," the CO said.

"Go where?"

"Phone call."

"I've got a call?"

"We don't take calls, asshole. You asked to make one."

Demory had come through for him.

Simmons came in with the shackles. Starks held his wrists out and fought the urge to grin. No point in letting them think he was excited about this opportunity. He felt in his gut that any sign of enthusiasm on his part might lead them to muck everything up.

Eager to speak with Jeffrey, he had to focus on not tripping on his ankle restraints during the long walk to the few phones mounted on the wall. His shoulders slumped; each phone was in use and several inmates waited their turn.

"I just dial out?"

Jakes's sneer returned. "Why don't you learn what's what here? You gotta call collect. The person's name has to be on the list you turned in. Name's not on the list, you can forget it."

Jakes told him to mind his manners, before they left him and went to talk to the guard in the enclosed booth.

He hadn't been around this many people in so long it felt as though he'd entered an alternate reality. Realization of the role human interaction played in a person's life struck him. Fear or no fear of retaliation, he needed to get out of his solitary hole.

Inmates in the area stared at him as he waited his turn.

He heard one of them say, "That's the fool that fought Big Bo."

"He may be a fool, but that little dude is quick," the inmate near him said. "You saw how he kept punching Big Bo's ass. Like in the movies."

"Movies, my ass. This Big Bo we talking about. That little dude is crazy."

Starks put a scowl on his face before he turned around. "Mind your fucking business."

The inmates moved away. Two other inmates took their place in line behind him. Starks's glare made them back up a few feet. He stood with his back straight, tried to look relaxed and on alert at the same time. The inmate in front of him ended his call.

Starks lifted the receiver and punched zero for the operator. The buzz of conversation in the area distracted him; a quick look back showed inmates were keeping their distance but kept their eyes on him the way people watch a lit firecracker.

He heard a voice on the line he recognized.

"Bro, how the hell are you? Everyone keeps asking about you. Everything okay?"

"I need you to visit me as soon as possible."

"Are you in trouble?"

"You could say that. No time to explain. You need to call and arrange a visit. But call Matthew Demory first so he can tell you what's involved. That's D-e-m-o-r-y. We talked about you coming here."

"Who's he?"

"Prison counselor."

"The what?"

"I need to go. Please. Just do it. As soon as we hang up."

"I'm on it."

Starks stepped away from the phone. The two guards joined him to take him back to the confinement unit. Murmurs from inmates were heard as he passed their cells. He slowed to see if he could catch what was being said.

Jakes yanked hard on his wrist restraints. "Get moving."

"Pull on me one more time and see what happens."

"I'd like to see what happens." The guard shoved him.

Starks narrowed his eyes and stood with controlled stillness.

Jakes pulled out his nightstick and whacked the palm of his hand with it several times. "You wanna play, asshole? Let me tell you how it'll go: you'll lose."

Starks snickered and resumed walking. It was all for show, for all the inmates watching his every move.

He couldn't afford to drop his façade. Not until he was alone in his cell again. Not until he was safe in isolation.

It had been a long time since he'd heard Jeffrey's voice. He hadn't believed he'd miss anyone from his former life, other than his children, but the brief call with his friend proved him wrong.

Now he had to wait.

* * *

Jeffrey stared at the phone. Why was a counselor involved? What the hell was going on with Starks? Whatever was happening, he'd do whatever he could to help.

The first call was brief because Demory had another patient showing up in minutes, said after that session he'd get the ball rolling about a visit.

It was an anxious hour and a half before Demory called him back.

"What's going on with Starks?" he asked.

"I can't tell you. That would be a breach of confidence. Let him answer any questions you have when you see him. If you're ready, I'll give you the details about how to make that happen. The paperwork should be faxed to you today. I set it up so that if you fax the forms back ASAP, they'll rush it so you can see him next week."

"Fire away."

Jeffrey ended the call. He cracked his knuckles and swallowed hard.

CHAPTER 44

N O WORD HAD come from anyone as to whether or not the visit would happen; though, he was sure Jeffrey had made the call to Demory, as he'd said he would.

Frustrated, Starks sat on the concrete floor opposite his bed and shut his eyes to close out the bleakness of the cell. He rubbed his chin; heard the scratch of skin across bristle. Ran his fingers through his shoulder-length hair. If Jeffery could visit, he hoped it was at a time after he'd showered and shaved. His friend had always teased him about seldom having so much as a hair out of place. There was no way he could look as presentable as he had in the outside world, but neither did he want to be scruffier than necessary when he saw his friend.

Thank God for Jeffrey.

His friend always came through for him, like the time he wired three thousand dollars to him and Kayla when they lived in California. Jeffrey had added in his note that no payback was required or would be accepted.

Kayla was thrilled to get the money.

"That's a good friend you have," she said.

"He's always been generous and concerned about others, especially his friends."

"You looked so relieved when you opened his envelope."

"You bet. The bills are piling up. His timing was perfect."

The extra money was gone by the end of two months, and they'd been back to where they usually were when it came to money.

On top of the tension they'd been feeling was the diagnosis Kayla's doctor had given her the week before.

The doctor looked over the rim of his glasses at Kayla. "You have fibroid tumors in your uterus."

Eyes widened in shock, Kayla said, "Is it dangerous?"

Starks squeezed her hand.

"It's a common condition. Almost never develops into cancer." The doctor fixed his gaze on Starks. "As a disclaimer, I want to add that no one can know what will happen until it happens." He returned his focus to Kayla, "But your fibroids are benign."

"Can I get pregnant?"

The doctor took off his glasses. "It does pose some difficulties, given the location. However, each individual is unique. I've had patients with this condition who had no problem getting pregnant. There are, however, some risks with the pregnancy. But that can be monitored and dealt with."

Starks chewed at a cuticle. "Can't you give her some type of medication?"

"There's no drug treatment that will cure it. We often recommend oral contraceptives to help with the menstrual bleeding associated with it. But that won't shrink the fibroids. Surgical treatment is probably the best option, especially in her case."

"Is that risky?" Kayla asked.

"Every procedure has some type of risk. It's best if you discuss this with a surgeon." The doctor scribbled something on a tablet, tore the sheet off and handed it to her. "This is the surgeon I'll refer you to. I'll have my nurse call and make an appointment while you wait."

On the quiet ride home, Starks stopped to buy the cheapest palatable wine they could afford. Once home, he poured two glasses of merlot and sat with Kayla at the small table in the kitchen.

Kayla turned her glass slowly in circles. Tears welled in her eyes fixed and unseeing on the dark liquid. "This explains a lot. All these years without using contraception and I never . . . How long have we talked about a house blessed with lots of children?" Her eyes met Starks's. "Is that dream over?"

"The doctor didn't say it was over, just more complicated than we imagined. Listen, we'll get a second and even third opinion. We don't want to risk your health, so we'll get enough information to make an informed decision. We'll get answers. I promise you."

Kayla's smile quivered.

He took her hand in his. "You know that whatever you need or want, I'll find a way."

Other doctors they'd seen had confirmed the diagnosis, but also said pregnancy wouldn't be as high a risk as they had feared, given the size of the fibroids. One doctor had winked and told them to keep trying, and to enjoy it. Somewhat relieved, Starks and Kayla began to relax.

But their love-making was not as it had once been. Before, their intimate moments had been about them and their pleasure. Now the possibility of no children weighed on them.

"Look, my doctorate is almost completed," he told her. "Instead of worrying about this, focus on your degree and let me be the only one working. The doctor said you need less stress."

"I'm afraid I'll lose everything."

Something stopped him from asking what she meant. But he needed to talk to someone so sought guidance and commiseration from his mother.

"Get married," she said.

It was as though she hadn't heard anything he'd told her.

Then the first child came. Then the other two. Then the behaviors, and now this.

Starks eased away from the concrete wall. The back of his shirt was moist with sweat. He crossed the brief distance to his bed and sat, groaned in frustration and got up again. Escaping his thoughts about Kayla was impossible.

He chided himself that his focus should be on what he'd say to Jeffrey, what the message he wanted delivered to Mason should be. The visit had to happen and soon. He couldn't ask Demory to give the message to Jeffrey: Demory would want to discuss it. Worse, Demory would decide to keep him in isolation.

He had to get out of this gray pocket of misery.

A man could go crazy.

CHAPTER 45

STARKS LOWERED HIMSELF into his usual chair in front of Demory's desk.

"Before you ask, I'll tell you—I'm doing well today. At least, better than I was."

Demory's pen wasn't working properly. He opened the center desk drawer for a replacement. He smiled at Starks. "Any particular reason?"

"You know why; I got to make my phone call. Thanks for helping with that. It was good to talk with Jeffrey again."

"I was happy to do it. The visit's being set up."

"That's great."

"I knew you'd be pleased. But what I want to know is what it felt like to be around other inmates when you made the call."

"It felt good."

Demory linked his fingers and rested his chin on top of them. "Are you saying you had no anxiety about being around other inmates? No fear about—"

"At first there was some of that then I relaxed. Isolation isn't easy." Starks stared out the small window. "It's getting to me. What I'm telling you is that it felt good to be around others. Even chatted a bit with a few of them."

Demory picked up his pen and started writing. "That went well?"

"Better than I'd hoped. And when I got back to my cell, I didn't have to worry about my thoughts."

"Which thoughts?"

"Angry thoughts, especially about Kayla. I'm not saying I don't have moments of anger, but I'm not feeling it like I was before."

"What are you thinking or feeling instead?"

"Old times with Jeffrey. And what it would be like to be back in general population. What it would be like to have a cellmate I could talk to now and then."

Demory leaned back in his chair and fixed his gaze on Starks. "What about thoughts of killing yourself?"

Starks shook his head. "I'm not going down that path ever again."

"You sound sure."

"I have to live, for my children. My recent example of behaviors . . . let's just say that's not what I want to teach them. I have the opportunity to rectify that. Or I will, once I'm back in general population and can have visitors. I know it'll be difficult for my kids to see me in here, but I'd hate to miss seeing them grow up."

"It hurts to be away from them."

Starks lowered his head, focused on his hands. "More than anyone knows."

"You said you're looking forward to having a cellmate to talk with. You had a cellmate when you first got here. How'd that go?"

Starks leaned back, tried to cross his legs and remembered the restraints prevented it. "It was hard initially to adjust to the setting. Having no privacy when I used the toilet took getting used to. Plus, he spoke almost no English."

"And you think it'll be easier now?"

"Anything is better than isolation, Doc." He shrugged. "What other choice do I have but to make the best of it? I can't serve my entire sentence in the Hole. I'd lose my mind."

Starks leaned forward. "Listen, the time before I went into business was tough, and my first two years in business were hell, but I didn't give up. I had to adjust. Had to find a way, and I did. It's the same here. I have to find a way to make it work. I'm here for a long time."

Demory scribbled on his notepad.

"What do you think, Doc, about my return to general population?"

Starks chewed on a cuticle. He stopped when he saw Demory watching him.

"I promise I'm giving it serious thought. Let's get to work. What do you want to talk about today?"

Starks scooted back in his chair. "Okay. California was the end of the race for me. Well, that particular race. End one, start another."

"What do you mean?"

"Once I was close to completing my degree, I started getting offers, ones I could seriously consider. I knew it was just a matter of time before all the financial suffering would end."

"You were both working and going to school, weren't you?"

"At first, but that shifted. Kayla went to school full-time and I had a job while I worked on my degree." Starks shook his head, grew quiet.

"What are you thinking about?"

"About when we decided to get married. We didn't want anyone to ever tell our first child that we had to get married because of him or her. Not that that's treated the way it used to be. But we both felt the same about it."

Demory smiled and asked, "After all that time together, how did you propose to her?"

Starks's expression went blank for a moment then his cheeks flushed. "I see what you're asking. I didn't do any kind of formal proposal or celebration. We just decided to get married. And it didn't make sense to have family come to the West Coast for the wedding, so we got married in Massachusetts. My mother, grandfather, aunts, and uncles all chipped in and paid for everything. Between what Kayla and her mother wanted, it became an elaborate affair. Thirty thousand dollars."

"Did her mother or relatives pay anything toward the wedding?"

"Her mother didn't have the money. And none of her other relatives contributed."

"What about the honeymoon?"

"We had to get back to school and work. But time in bed was more passionate. I do remember that. Kayla was so pleased that I was her husband. That we were legal, as she put it." Starks paused. He smiled but the amusement didn't reach his eyes.

"What?"

"Kayla used to say that what we had was special and sacred. If I had a dollar for every time she said that I was the only man she'd ever been with . . . She got pregnant sooner than either of us expected. We were overjoyed.

"I continued with my studies and work. I also wanted to save some money before our first child, Blake, was born. I got an extra job delivering pamphlets. I had a specific area and a certain amount of time to get them delivered to all the residences. Got up at five every morning and drove to a particular block, parked, and loaded my arms with as many as I could carry. One morning, when Kayla was three months pregnant, she drove the car, while I put the pamphlets at the houses. After that temporary gig was up, I got another job."

Starks's smile was slight. "She was so worried that she wasn't ready to be a mother. When Blake arrived, her maternal instinct kicked in. She did just fine."

"How did you feel about becoming a father?"

"I couldn't wait. Kayla stopped going to school because of the pregnancy; she didn't want to risk it. And she wanted the first few months with Blake. School and work took up most of my days. But once he was born, I'd come home at night and stare at him in his crib, get up with him during the night so I could have time with him and so Kayla could rest. Any spare time I had, I spent with him."

"How was your life after several months with a baby in the house?"

"More involved, of course. I had my doctorate by that time, so looked for more promising work. Got several serious offers for jobs on the West Coast, but they wanted two- and three-year contracts. Kayla and I spoke about this and realized we wanted to return to Massachusetts. We wanted Blake to grow up around his larger family. So there I was, a Ph.D. cleaning carpets." Starks shook his head and laughed. "Didn't need a doctorate for that. But it paid the bills and more. That work was physical. But my days were usually no more than nine hours, which was a nice change." He stared at his hands. "The heavy machinery was difficult to maneuver. I complained about how stiff my hands, wrists, and arms felt after a day at work. I was only twenty-six, but sometimes swore that I had arthritis."

"Did Kayla go back for her degree?"

"Eventually. There were only a few credits needed to complete her master's. At first she was concerned about leaving Blake, but I told her the classes she needed were offered in the evenings. That I could watch Blake after work. She tried to use the excuse that she was too old to go back. I reminded her she was only twenty-five.

"Around the same time she got her degree, I got an offer from Focus Designs. It was located back home and was the perfect opportunity. A six-figure job. We went back East, but decided that instead of paying rent, we'd live with my grandfather and mother. We used the basement, so we could have some privacy. We did what was needed to fit the three of us in that one room. Fortunately, it was an adequate-sized room. At least, temporarily."

Demory nodded. "How was your romantic life after Blake was born?"

"I've never really been what you might call a romantic person, but I took care of my family. I was a good provider."

"A woman's emotional needs sometimes alter after she becomes a mother. She may need some romancing so she knows her mate still finds her desirable."

Starks spoke through tight lips. "Look, Doc, Kayla knew how I was." He slumped forward in the chair. "I know where you're heading with this. Okay. Maybe I became somewhat complacent, in some people's opinion. I'd call it focused. I had a lot to take care of. Kayla knew how I felt about her, or should have. I was there, wasn't I? I was supporting her and our son, wasn't I? A person can have only so much expected of him."

Demory put his pen down. "Women—all of us, really—need to feel loved. Those in a relationship need to figure out how their mate needs to be told or shown they're loved, not just how they themselves express love."

"I'm not following you, Doc."

"Even if we think we're communicating our love, our mate doesn't always hear it, because it may not be their way to feel it. For instance, you worked hard to support and supply your wife and child with what they needed. And to you that was your expression of love."

"Damn straight. I don't know how she could perceive it any other way."

"Some people need to hear words to feel loved. Some need their mate to spend quality time with them, even if it's not a lot of time. Others feel loved when they receive gifts. Not necessarily elaborate gifts, but small, thoughtful ones that let them know their partner pays attention. Others feel loved when things are done for them, like a man taking care of certain things around the house without being asked, or a woman doing certain things that make the man feel special, respected. Some people need to be touched to feel loved, and I don't mean just sexually. They need hugs, kisses, their hair stroked, massages—that kind of thing. Is any of this making sense to you?"

"Sure, but it's so damn complicated." Starks sank his face into his hands. "I guess I can see why she fell for Ozy, or any guy that did things I didn't do; made her feel the way she needed to feel, especially if they caught her in a vulnerable moment."

"It's important for you to see this. That kind of attention is the basis of any strong relationship."

Demory jotted a quick note then put the pen down. "We're done for today. Before you ask, I'd like to wait just a bit longer before requesting a transfer into general population."

"Doc, please. I can't stay in isolation any longer."

"Let's wait at least one more week." Demory raised his hand to forestall a protest. "I have some news you'll be happy about. Jeffrey will be here tomorrow."

Starks leapt from the chair. "What time?"

"Visiting hours are from eight in the morning until two in the afternoon. Jeffrey said he'd be here by ten. Once he's waiting in the visitation room, a guard will get you and take you there."

"Doc, I appreciate all you're doing for me."

After the door closed behind his patient. Demory added a few notes to the notepad, one of them being *General Population*, with several questions marks behind the words.

CHAPTER 46

EVEN THOUGH EXCITEMENT disrupted his sleep, Starks hopped out of bed early with vigor that felt more like his former self.

He went to the small metal sink, wet his hands and smoothed his hair into place, promising his reflection that he'd get a haircut as soon as he was back in a regular cell. Shaving resulted in several nicks brought about by trembling hands. He stripped off his scrubs and did the best he could to freshen up using the hard stub of soap and cold water then put on his only other clean set of scrubs once his skin dried.

Breakfast was, as always, uninspiring, but he ate every bite, mostly by rote. His mind was too full of what to say to Jeffrey and how his friend might react to seeing him.

The wait seemed interminable. Several times he got up to pace then changed his mind. He didn't want to work up a sweat.

Finally, he heard a knock on the steel door. Starks smiled. Only Ted Landers would knock.

The door opened and Ted said, "Mr. Starks, your visitor's here."

"Officer Landers, good to see you. It's been a while. Everything okay with you?"

"Had a nasty case of flu. I'm better now. I noticed this is your first visitor since you've been here."

"I'm looking forward to seeing a familiar face."

Jakes entered the cell and scowled as he listened to the exchange between guard and prisoner while putting the restraints on Starks.

It was a long, shuffling walk down one corridor to another and another. Starks glanced at Ted. "What's the visitors' room like?"

Jakes answered, "It's not for you; that's for damn sure."

Ted told him, "That's enough from you."

Starks halted and turned a puzzled face toward Ted. "What does he mean?"

"You have a different set-up. Because you're in solitary." At Starks's confused expression, he continued. "You have what's called a non-contact visit. You're going to a booth that has a glass partition separating you and your visitor. You'll be able to see and hear each other; you use a phone to talk.

"We need to keep walking, Mr. Starks. Don't want to keep your visitor waiting."

Starks raised his hands to wave at Jeffrey and watched his friend's smile fade when he saw the restraints.

"When you're ready," Ted told him, "we'll come back to get you."

Another guard was seated several yards away. "He'll monitor the visit," Ted explained.

Starks sat in the hard plastic chair and lifted the modified telephone receiver, waiting for his friend to do the same. "Man, is it ever good to see you."

Jeffrey rested his elbows on the counter. His left hand held the receiver in a tight grip. "What's with the long hair?"

"Not my choice. I'll get it cut as soon as I can."

"How're you holding up in here, bro?"

A moment of silence followed before Starks asked, "Any chance you know how my family's doing?"

"I check in with your mother once a week to see if she needs anything. They're all fine but they want to visit you."

"No way. My mother would be too emotional."

"I get why you wouldn't want Emma to come here. But your family? Even if your mom acts like herself . . ." Jeffrey shrugged.

"I've humiliated them. And I damn sure don't want them to see me like this. Bad enough you have to. They wouldn't be able to keep their disapproval from their faces. I couldn't take it."

Jeffrey nodded. "Yeah, I know how they are. But they care about you. I think they'd put pride aside so they could see you; see that you're safe."

Starks leaned toward the glass and lowered his voice. "I'm not safe. I got into a fight with a gang leader, and now he wants to kill me. He'll either do it himself or get one of his soldiers to do it. Already got a death threat. I'm in isolation, but the guy or someone he pays off could still get to me, one way or another. That's why I asked you to come here. There's something only you can do for me."

Jeffrey's face paled. He imitated Starks's posture and moved his face closer to the partition. "Shit, bro, this is serious. What's being done about the guy?"

"It doesn't work that way here. Once you cross the threshold of a place like this, the rules change."

"What can I do?"

"Remember Lewis Mason?"

"What about him?"

"If you recall what he said about his time at Waltgate, he became a threat so no one bothered him again."

"I'm not following you."

"I want to know how he did it. Talk to him. Ask him to visit me, tell him why I want to see him. Help him arrange the visit. That reminds me, I need to add his name to the list. I'm trying to get moved back into the general population, but I don't know when that'll happen; it could happen as early as next week. I need to talk to him before that happens."

"I'll see what I can do." Both men were quiet then Jeffrey said, "I have some good news."

"I could use some."

"Hessinger's out of his coma. And get this. While he was unconscious, his wife got the scoop on his extracurricular activities. She's filing for divorce. Waited because she didn't want anyone judging her for filing against a comatose husband."

Starks sat motionless for a moment then his chest heaved. "Thank God. A life sentence is no longer a threat. The icing on this is that his wife learned what a loser she's been married to. I'm sorry for her and the kids, but they're better off without him."

"I was relieved when I heard. I want you to get out of this place."

"Anything else?"

"Spoke with Kayla."

"What'd she want?"

"Primarily to tell me about Hessinger."

"I wonder if she'll cheat on her new lover and go back to Ozy."

"Kayla's not the type to deal with damaged goods."

"I'm in here because of that cheating bitch."

Jeffrey rubbed the bridge of his nose. "I love you like a brother, but you know I'm all about fairness. I kept my comments to myself when you slept with all the women you did, spent all the money on them that you did. I'm not saying what Kayla did was right. But your score is way higher than hers. Maybe you need to ease up on the anger, for everyone's sake."

Starks strained to compose himself. "You're taking her side?"

"No way. But facts are facts."

"Facts are facts, huh? I may not make it out of here alive. Because of her. Having an affair is one thing; nobody's perfect, including me. Maybe my affairs didn't help the situation but she's been lying and cheating for years."

"Again, sorry, but . . . glass houses, bro."

"I can't believe you, Jeffrey. You *think* you know Kayla? You don't know shit about her. She fucked Bernard Hazely in college. Did you know that? After being with him for just a few months. But according to her I was the only one. How about the guy on Twitter that she fucked? How about the fact I caught her more than once looking for a hotel room? Not to mention all the inappropriate encounters with all those men at her job. What about all of that?" He let out a breath. "The red flags were there. I was just an idiot for not paying attention." His gaze fixed on Jeffrey. "She's a liar and a manipulator. You're making me think maybe she has you fooled."

"Bro, your anger's going to eat you alive if you don't do something about it. And, I'm not fooled. I'm trying to be fair. You may get pissed off with me for what I'm about to say, but it needs saying. You didn't make it easy for Kayla. She knew about the strippers and the flings. You're damn lucky she never found out about Cathy and Kyle."

"That's enough!"

"Maybe it is, and maybe you need to look at the bigger picture. How do you think she'd feel and react if she found out you had a child with Cathy; that you paid toward his care and hers? What about Michelle? You fell in love with her while married. Got me involved with covering for you with Kayla more times than I care to remember, until she found out about her." Jeffrey pointed at Starks. "You don't think any of that was painful for her or would be if she learned the whole truth?"

"Yes, everything you said, and more, happened. Cathy was a mistake. A big one. And I did what I had to do to end it with Michelle, which was to call her in front of Kayla and say I was going back to my wife. Because that's what Kayla wanted me to do. I did love Michelle, but I was wrong and accepted it; did what was needed to save my marriage and my family. What happened when I told Kayla to do the same about Ozy? You remember her response?

Jeffrey nodded and murmured, "Yeah."

"That's right. She told me no. First she contemplated it but then she started talking to her friends and family. All of a sudden it's, Why does she have to show her love for me?"

"I'm probably going to piss you off again, but why was her calling Ozy in front of you so necessary? If you loved her, it wouldn't matter where she did it."

"Are you fucking serious? After all the crap she'd been involved in, she couldn't—wouldn't—compromise and make that call to save us, like I did? When I think of all the compromises I made for this godforsaken marriage . . ."

"If she'd done what you asked, would you have gone back to her? I mean, let's be honest, she wasn't the woman you thought she was."

"You're missing the point. I did it for her when I screwed up. She was supposed to do the same for me. That's what people do in a marriage. Compromise. Do what you have to do to make it work. And one more thing, I never spoke negatively about Kayla to any of the women I was involved in. Not like she did with Ozy and others about me. And I always made it clear from the start with any woman I got involved with that I was married and not leaving my wife for them. I told them we could have some fun and they'd be spoiled for as long as it lasted. That they should count on it not lasting. I gave them a choice."

"And that made it okay?"

"Maybe not. And maybe you think I'm overreacting about everything—then and now. But I'd like to see how you or any man would feel if he found out his wife told her friends that being physically intimate with him made her want to vomit. That shit's not easy to hear.

"She had the nerve to tell me she wasn't wrong to do what she did. Said it was just my bruised ego I was concerned with, not with her. Said I was furious because she liked having sex with another man, and that she could sleep well at night because she didn't feel guilty about meeting her needs, because I couldn't. She didn't say wouldn't. She said couldn't. Kayla actually asked me what made me think she ever wanted Ozy to leave his wife. Can you believe that shit? At least common street whores respect themselves enough to get paid."

"She was probably angry and hurt when she said—"

"She said it deliberately, to crucify me."

"Maybe so."

"And another thing. I read her and Ozy's text messages to each other. He talked to her like she was a prostitute, and she accepted it. I never could have gotten away with that. She thought he treated her so well, with respect. Hunh. I read one of her texts to him about how wet his kisses made her, how much she loved his body and how it felt to touch him, have him inside her. What a load of crap. And after she poured that and more out to him, do you know how he responded? 'It was fun.' And those *sweet* words made her hot for him?"

"Bro, you're torturing yourself. You need to stop."

Starks lurched upward. His chair fell over; its clatter to the floor echoed in the room. "She was my goddamned wife!"

The guard shouted, "Keep it calm or end it."

Starks righted his chair and said to the guard, "It's fine. Just got some bad news." Seated again, he pressed the received hard against his ear. "The only thing I did wrong was care too much about her. I wish I could be as cold-hearted as she is, but I can't."

Jeffrey chewed on his bottom lip. "I remember how you felt when you found out she was in that accident and got knocked unconscious."

"I called everybody until I found where she was, so I could make sure she was okay. She ignored me, refused my calls; told my children to tell me not to call her. Then the very next week, she needed money. Suddenly, she found the phone to get me to sign papers to release more money for her."

"You know Kayla's stubborn."

"Stubborn my ass; it's a lot more than that. She only asked for more money because she had that parasite at the house." He clamped his jaw tight and gritted his teeth. "The thing is I was genuinely worried about her. If something more serious had happened to Kayla, who was going to step up to take care of her, besides me? Bret? He would have left at the first sign that his cash cow was down."

"You did the right thing in that situation; she didn't behave appropriately. But this is Kayla we're talking about. I know you still care about her—maybe not for her, but . . . If you didn't, you wouldn't get so worked up when the topic of her comes up."

"Fuck it. I've gotten to the point that I can't even look at her, don't want to hear from her. Even when that woman's name is mentioned, it only brings up hurt and pain. I don't want to talk about her. Kayla's dead to me. Don't mention her to me again."

"Listen, the fact is this: Nobody involved in this mess is innocent. But you're right. Let's not talk about her. There's something else I need to bring up. Cathy contacted me. She needs money."

"Give it to her."

"I will." Jeffrey looked down. "She still talks about Kyle."

"I think about him too. Five years old when he drowned. All because of Cathy's negligence. What a waste of a life. Still, she's not a bad woman. Give her whatever she wants. She knows I'm in jail. Who doesn't? Just don't mention or discuss anything about me with her."

"Emma's been calling me nonstop since . . . since the incident. She loves you, bro."

"The word love used to mean something to me. Kayla crushed all meaning out of it."

"I get why you feel that way but life without love is—"

"Don't be a fool, Jeffrey. I was."

"Being a fool for love isn't the worst thing that can happen to a guy."

Starks motioned with his hands. "Look around. Maybe you want to rethink that."

"So, what about Emma?"

"Besides you, and Mason, I don't want anyone else to see me like this. Don't get me wrong: Emma's got a good heart and admirable qualities." He chuckled. "I use to say the same thing about Kayla. Look, Jeffrey, life is just fucked up. You have the right formula—stay single as long as you can or forever."

Jeffrey checked the wall clock behind Starks. "Had to store my watch with my other stuff in a locker. Took everything but my clothes so I could pass inspection. Sorry, bro, I got to get moving. I thought I could stay longer but my schedule changed at the last minute."

"You reach Mason yet?"

"Yeah. But he told me to wait to talk when we meet, which'll be soon."

"You'll take care of everything?"

"Absolutely. And so you know, the business is doing well." His smiled faded. "We had to remove you from the board of directors. But your portion of the profit is going into your mother's account, the one you're the beneficiary of."

"I'm not worried about any of that now, but thanks for looking out for me."

Jeffrey stood. "I'll get back with you as soon as I can."

"Thanks for coming. You're a good friend."

Jeffrey nodded. He kept his gaze fixed on his friend. "Take care of yourself."

"I'll do my best."

With a final wave, Jeffrey, his lips pressed together, walked to the door on his side of the partition. He didn't look back before walking through the door the guard opened for him but Starks knew his friend well. The stiff set of Jeffrey's shoulders said enough about how his friend was feeling.

CHAPTER 47

TOO MANY PAINFUL things had come up during his conversation with Jeffrey, including rage he now wished he'd suppressed. But what the hell was Jeffrey doing? He said he wasn't taking Kayla's side but he'd never commented about Starks's actions before. He had no idea Jeffrey even had those thoughts.

Kayla. The woman was like a hot rash: He felt compelled to scratch it, or rub it raw. Would his anger finally have dampened fifteen years from now, he wondered? A larger question loomed: did he want it to?

Then there was Kyle. What a bad start and finish that poor, beautiful boy had been given: illegitimacy then early death by drowning.

And Cathy. Tears had streamed down her cheeks when he'd yelled at her, "How could you leave a five-year-old unattended? Just how fucking careless are you? You were careless enough to get pregnant then careless enough to let him die. Like that." Her guilt and his money had kept her from revealing that he was Kyle's father.

Had been. Past tense.

Jeffrey was the only other person in his life who had known about Kyle. Except for a few drunken, tearful episodes with his friend, he'd had to go through his grief in silence. He certainly hadn't wanted to share that grief with Cathy. Nor had he gone to the funeral—he couldn't afford to be seen there. He'd gone to the grave a week later, alone.

The relief he'd felt when Cathy moved to Rhode Island six months after the funeral had been beyond description. The last thing he wanted was to ever see her again. Her face had become perpetually etched with guilt and loss and was more than he could stand. It dragged him down. Anything or anyone in his life that did that was removed or modified to his liking. It had to be that way. Otherwise, life became too cluttered, something he couldn't and wouldn't tolerate.

Maybe his notion about true friendship was flawed. Jeffrey had always been and still was a true friend, right from the start. Especially when it came to keeping secrets.

God, I'm such a hypocrite, he thought.

He'd judged Kayla for her secrets, for her indiscretions, while his own life was rife with both. Nor had he been as careful as he could have when it came to keeping his affairs secret from her, just as she'd been careless. Demory would probably ask if their carelessness was deliberate. He shook his head; such a question made no sense.

Cathy, of course, had been the exception, because of Kyle. Poor Cathy. She'd loved him. She still loved him because he was the father of her child. But he'd never loved her. He had loved Kyle. Or was he lying to himself about that? Did his feelings for the boy have more to do with pride at fathering another son, instead of love?

Maybe Demory was right about how judgmental he was, about how he thought more about his feelings than what was going on for others. All this time he'd condemned Kayla when he'd been doing her dirty. Maybe faulting Kayla had become a habit. Something, he was beginning to realize, he relied on too much, like an addiction. Or maybe trashing her was keeping him sane. He didn't want to think about what Demory would say about that.

He didn't want to think about any of these things anymore. At least not today. He wanted to entertain different thoughts, like getting tips from Lewis Mason; like getting transferred out of the Hole and back into a regular cell.

Life had become an endless loop of problems needing solutions.

In the recesses of his mind he heard Demory ask:

How many of your problems are of your own making?

CHAPTER 48

STARKS WAS HALFWAY across Demory's office when he asked, "Have you given the general population matter more thought?"

Demory glanced up. "I know you're eager to get out of isolation, but I need to believe it's the right move."

Starks flopped into the chair. "I don't know how much longer I can stay in isolation without losing it."

"I get that. Let's see how today goes." Demory held his pen poised over his notepad. "How'd the visit with Jeffrey go?"

"Good. A little tense at times, but I guess that was to be expected."

When nothing more was added, Demory asked, "Want to talk about it?"

"Not really. I mean, we were happy to see each other. He caught me up on business and such."

"I heard you got upset at one point."

Starks puffed air through his lips. "It wasn't anything. Just something about a difficult client. I felt bad about not being there to help out. That's all." He jiggled his feet up and down then stopped and leaned forward. "Look, Doc, the thing that's on my mind is getting back into general population. I know what you just said, but being alone as I am gives me too much time to think about the past. Talking with Jeffrey . . . I was always so social. Having no one to talk to most of the time is affecting me, and there's nothing to do. I've never had nothing to do. At least in general population I can get a work assignment or get into some programs. Anything to get my mind onto other things."

"Aside from the potential threat from Bo and his gang, I'm hesitant because I think you're not ready to—"

Starks sat up stiffly. "What do I have to do to prove to you that I'm ready?"

"What I was going to say is that I don't think you're ready for a cellmate."

"I'm as ready as I'll ever be. I'd already started to adjust before I got put into the SHU. I need something to do. I need to be more active and engaged. And I want visitation and phone rights again. I'm ready to see family and friends."

"There's also the other issue: you tried to kill yourself."

"We talked about that. I'm not ever going to do that again, for the reason I gave you." Starks paused. "You want to know why I tried?"

"I do."

"The isolation and silence torment me worse than facing anything or anyone out there." He gestured toward the door behind him. "Doc, I realize there's risk out there. It's prison, for Christ's sake. No one is exempt. But out there I have a chance to avoid it, deter it, or defend myself against it. Isolation is the guaranteed winner every time, and I can't even put up a fight."

Demory chewed on the end of his pen as he kept his gaze on Starks. "Your argument's logical. I'll get back to you. Let's talk. You know what to do."

Starks got as comfortable as he could in the chair. "I lied to Kayla about the real amount of my salary."

Demory looked at him with raised his eyebrows. "Sounds like you made a habit of lying to her. Especially about money."

"It was a necessity. I lied about my salary so I could save for a house. Kayla wanted a home of our own; so did I. I took away her checkbook and gave her an allowance she could use for herself and the baby. I paid everything else. Her allowance was more than she'd ever had before, and she knew that if she wanted her own home, she had to go along with the arrangement. It took about a year before I had what I considered enough money. The first house we bought was practically a mansion. Life was good."

"Did your romantic life improve as well?"

"I told you I'm not the romantic type. But if you mean sex, it did get better, once we had our own place. It's a little off-putting to have your baby next to you and relatives just upstairs, if you know what I mean."

Demory nodded and smiled. "That can spoil a mood."

"Yeah. But something else spoiled it even more. The second year we were in the house, the two owners of Focus Designs had a falling-out. I and the other staff members couldn't make out the words, but we could hear them shouting at each other in the conference room. That was on a Monday. By the end of the day, we were advised the company was filing for bankruptcy, and not the restructuring kind. Everyone was out of a job. The doors were locked the following week."

"What did you do?"

Starks laughed. "You mean after I panicked?" Demory nodded. "I started looking for other jobs, but none of them paid as well. And to add to that, we learned Kayla was pregnant again, with Nathan. It was a complicated pregnancy. She had to be careful. Couldn't exert herself."

"What happened about a job?"

"Jobs. Plural. Day and night shifts, but none of them paid enough to cover everything . . . mortgage, household bills, all the medical bills for Kayla. I wasn't about to get on that fucking merry-go-round again. And this is where what I told you in our first session comes in, about the twenty thousand I borrowed from family and friends." Starks grinned. "I took over the goddamned company that closed.

"The money wasn't enough to cover everything; I'd thought the extra needed funds would come in from the old accounts receivable. That didn't happen. But I was familiar enough with the accounts and contracts to feel confident I could succeed, and I changed the name to Tendum Enterprises, to try to improve goodwill."

"Was Kayla pleased or proud that you went into business for yourself?"

"She was against it, at first. Afraid I didn't know enough to take it on, but I knew I had it in me, so went for it. The first few years were hell. I wasn't able to pay my bills on time. Got eviction notices several times.

Sometimes I had to ask employees to wait to deposit their paychecks. It was a small staff, thank God, but still."

"Was Kayla supportive?"

Starks rested his elbows on his knees and flexed his fingers. "I didn't tell her. She knew something was going on, though, when I got to a point that I couldn't pay our mortgage or our bills. I lied and told her I'd had to use the money to cover business expenses. But I wasn't able to pay them on time either. Told her it was temporary." He looked up. "Doc, I'd go downstairs in the middle of the night and pace. Did that nearly every night. I felt like such a failure. But I wasn't going to give up. I just kept borrowing money from whomever I could, to maintain the business. Thank God people believed in me."

"What about your personal bills?"

"Mortgage modification carried us for a while. It was slow, but money did start coming in. I worked twenty hours a day, seven days a week, to get out of that sinkhole. Then one remarkable day, the business was in the black. There wasn't much extra after the bills were paid, but I made payroll from then on, and was able to pay my personal bills. Nathan was three and Kaitlin had just been born when the business became profitable and grew from there."

"So your time and energy was focused on the business while Kayla took care of the house and children. Did this affect your marriage?"

Starks pressed his lips into a tight line. "That was when I began to suspect Kayla was cheating on me."

"What made you suspicious?"

"It was eleven at night when I heard a text message come in on her phone. She was sound asleep. I got up, went to where her phone was on her side of the bed. Someone with a number I didn't recognize had wished her good night. I went downstairs to look at our account call log online. That's when I saw that she'd been texting this person on a regular basis. I wrote down the number and called it the next day. A man answered. When I asked him what was going on, he said nothing; that he and Kayla just talked. When I asked what about, he said about our marriage problems. Said I wasn't paying enough attention to my wife the way I should. I was too shocked to say more to him than to leave my wife alone."

"Did you speak with Kayla about this?"

Starks nodded. "She said nothing was going on; that he was a co-worker and a good listener. Said she felt more comfortable talking to a stranger than with someone who knew us. I told her I was sorry about all the time spent on the business but that I was doing it for us—for her and our children—so we could have a better life. She said she understood."

"Did you believe her?"

"Yes. She reassured me that . . . God, I was such a fool."

"That was the end of her interaction, and yours, with the man?"

"I didn't communicate with him again, but I told her that married people shouldn't have friends of the opposite sex, especially not ones they tell such personal things to. She got angry and said I wasn't around to talk to about what was going on with her. I got angry and told her that guy was pretending he cared, was waiting for the perfect moment to get into her pants."

"What'd she say?"

"Said she'd stop talking with him. I asked her to be patient with me; that one day my time would free up and we'd both be happy with the result of my efforts. I did check the call log a week later. His number wasn't there. And things did get better between us."

"How does it feel to talk about that time?"

Starks focused his eyes on the ceiling. "I don't feel as angry as when we've talked about the past before. So, I guess it feels okay."

"It's never good to dwell on the past, but it can be cathartic to talk about it. The more you tell it like a story the more new perspectives can come from it. A new perspective can help you let go of the past, because you see what happened, and the person or people involved, and even yourself, differently." Demory put his pen down. "That's all for this week."

"What about the transfer, Doc?"

Demory smiled. "I'm going to approve it. You should be back in general population within the week."

Starks whooped. "Thanks, Doc. There's more I want to say, but, thank you. You won't regret it."

"I hope like hell you're right."

CHAPTER 49

THE CELL DOOR slammed behind the guards.

Starks took several moments to figure out how to hide the shank he'd made under the lining of his left shoe without being observed by whoever was monitoring the surveillance cameras.

He needed to stay armed from now on. Any moment now, he'd be moved to a cell in one of the general population blocks. Demory had always done what he said he would. No reason to doubt him this time.

The moment arrived the afternoon of the third day, about an hour after his dinner tray was pushed through the slot.

One guard, not two, came to get him. The pat-down was quick and free of rude comments from CO Simmons. As anticipated, Starks's shoes weren't checked. No ankle restraints this time, just handcuffs. Along the way, he decided he needed to at least seem like a tough guy then questioned whether that was necessary: inmates had decided he was one of the crazy ones.

Starks struggled to calm his breathing when he entered the cell block; he had to appear in control, self-assured. The guard in the security booth was watching him. He nodded at the guard, who turned away.

Simmons stopped at a cell at the center of the block. The metal barred door was open.

At the far end of the new cell were two metal bunk beds bolted to the wall at the sides and heads. The mattresses were only slightly thicker than the one he'd had in solitary. But at least there was the standard long, couple-inches wide window centered on the far wall.

A metal shelf was bolted to the wall next to the head of each bed. Two metal desks, each with a hard plastic chair were positioned against the opposite wall. The same model of steel toilet and sink combo were near the entrance, with a small mirror bolted to the wall above the sink.

Limited as it was, Starks felt relief about finally being freer to walk around in the block or to go outside to the prison yard, when it was allowed, and for longer than an hour. He'd have to remember to be in his cell for the count. He'd forgotten about that routine.

The top bunk was already taken. The bottom bunk was unmade, but a folded blanket and a pillow had been placed at the end of the bed.

His new cellmate was reading in bed, and looked up when the two men entered the cell.

Simmons removed the handcuffs and said, "Someone will get your clothes and stuff to you before dinnertime." His walkie-talkie crackled. He listened then left.

The cellmate sat up, dangled his legs over the edge of the bed. He rubbed a hand over his shaved head, nodded, and said in a gravely voice, "Mike Lawson."

"Starks." He wanted to act confident, cocky even, knowing it might be a risk but one worth taking. Better than acting as scared as he felt. He had nothing to put away yet that would occupy his attention and nothing to look at other than Lawson. He walked to the unused chair and sat in it, stretching his legs out in front of him. Wanting to appear calm and relaxed, he linked his hands behind his head and stared at the opposite wall.

"They call me Weasel." Muscles rippled everywhere when the man leaped and landed like a cat on the concrete floor. The overhead fluorescent light highlighted a long, pale scar on his left cheek. Lawson was stocky and a few inches shorter than Starks.

Starks looked away for a moment then focused his eyes on the man, who was being more pleasant than anticipated. He steeled himself to follow his plan. "Why do they call you that?"

Lawson chuckled. "Because I can weasel out of damn near anything, especially when it comes to the guards."

"Maybe. Or maybe you're a snitch. Maybe you're a lying, cheating bastard."

"What the fuck's up with you?"

"I'll tell you what's not up with you. I want the top bunk."

"Forget it. I was here before you."

"You must not know who I am." Starks stomped to the bed. He grabbed the pillow and blanket from the top bunk and threw them on the floor.

Lawson reached for Starks, who grabbed his cellmate's collar with both hands then shoved him against the wall.

With a grim smile, he said, "Come on, Weasel. Challenge me. The only thing I've had to toss around for a long time was a basketball." He pushed Lawson again; made his eyes wild and said in a low voice, "Challenge me. Please."

Lawson raised his hands and said, "I know who you are. You want the top bunk, it's yours." He moved his possessions from the upper bed tray to the lower one.

Starks tossed his bedding onto the upper bunk.

"Listen," Lawson said, "We're gonna be cellmates. We can't be fighting like this."

Starks leaned against the wall with his arms crossed. "I can see that."

"In case you're interested, I'm in here for manslaughter."

Starks didn't respond. He climbed onto his bed, removed his shoes and placed them where he could easily reach them.

Lawson talked fast and nearly non-stop about his family, his past, and his trial, with no input from Starks. On the one hand, Starks enjoyed listening to someone other than the voices in his head doing the talking—it was a welcome change. On the other hand, he needed to keep his charade up.

After another hour, according to Lawson's desk clock, Starks said, "Not that your life story isn't riveting, but it's time for you to shut the fuck up."

"Sure thing. But there's one last thing I want to say: Bo deserved what you gave him. So did that guy who was doing your wife."

Starks stayed silent, kept it to himself that hearing someone finally say he was in the right was like finding water in the desert.

He would drop the tough-guy act with Lawson: Lawson understood.

His eyes stayed open most of the night. As soon as possible, he had to deal with the fears that kept him awake: Sleep was vital if he was to keep his mind and body strong.

The last thing he wanted to dwell on was negative thoughts about his cellmate. However, one thought had nagged him as his cellmate had prattled on: He seemed too smooth a talker.

Starks turned his eyes to the narrow strip of window. A northerly wind blew a cloud across the sky, revealing the nearly full moon.

He thought about how easy it is to feel exposed.

CHAPTER 50

SIX O'CLOCK. THE lights went on and the barred doors opened. Lawson yawned then said, "You want first dibs on the john?"

"It's all yours." Starks had used the toilet and washed his face while Lawson was still asleep.

They went to the chow hall together. Starks sat at the very end of a bench at one of the tables not claimed by a gang; his cellmate sat across from him. Bo and some of his entourage came in and sat three tables away, sometimes glaring at Starks and sometimes snickering at him.

The standard count of four guards walked the perimeter.

Behind Starks, an inmate said, "They put the CEO with the Weasel. That fucking guy'd betray his own mother."

"Know what you get when you put a Weasel and a CEO together?"

"I dunno. What?"

"How should I know? But you can bet it's slippery." All at the table laughed.

Lawson said, "Ignore them. There's not a whole half a brain between them."

Starks kept his head down as he pushed at the muck on the tray. "Need a spoon for these so-called eggs."

"One day you need a spoon, the next day you need a drill."

A shadow fell over Starks. He turned his head and peered into light eyes bulging at him from pale skin.

"That's my place. Move your ass, punk."

"Doesn't have your name on it." Starks turned back to his tray.

"You in the mood to have your ass whupped or something?"

"No, but you seem to be."

The inmate slammed his tray down on top of Starks's. Starks grabbed the man's wrist and twisted. The inmate attempted a headlock.

Lawson swung his tray, hit the intruder in the face; food ran down the inmate's scrubs.

The inmate lunged for Lawson, who jumped on him. They fell to the floor, fists connecting to faces and torsos.

Two guards pulled them apart. The other two guards meandered their way to the table.

"What's going on here?" a guard asked.

Another said, "Lawson jumped this one," he jerked his thumb toward the inmate whose face dripped oatmeal and eggs.

Starks looked at Lawson, who indicated with a subtle head shake to keep quiet. No one spoke up; the code of silence held firm.

"Well, Lawson, maybe more time in SHU will straighten you out."

Lawson grinned at Starks before two of the guards took him away.

Starks dumped his and Lawson's trays then returned to his cell.

His new cellmate had acted on his behalf when it wasn't even his fight. The man could have cleared himself by saying who'd started it.

It would be—what, a comfort?—to develop a real friendship in here.

The rest of that day and the next, Starks ate alone. If anyone shared his table, they sat a yard or more away from him. A few minor scuffles happened when new inmates tried to sit at tables spoken for by others.

Starks heard comments as some passed near him, all pretty much the same: "Crazy motherfucker."

And each time in the chow hall, Bo and his cronies sat in the same place, but no confrontations were started.

How long would this odd peace last?

He could almost hear the ticking.

CHAPTER 51

TWO DAYS LATER, Starks lay looking out the slender window when he heard footsteps of more than one person coming toward his cell. He hung his legs over the side of the bed, reached for his left shoe then stopped when he saw Lawson and a guard at the threshold.

"All right, Lawson," the guard said, "See if you can keep yourself out of trouble."

"You bet," Lawson answered. "Had enough of the SHU."

"Right." The guard looked at Starks, shook his head then left.

Starks slid to the floor and held his hand out.

"Thanks for what you did. You took my punishment."

Lawson looked surprised but shook hands. "I did hit the guy. But, hey, we should look out for each other. If you'd spoken up, a lot more shit would've gone down. There're penalties for that in here. You did the right thing."

"Thanks. I mean it."

"Was I missed at chow time?" Lawson laughed.

"No one fought to take your place."

"No problems?"

"Bo and his band of thugs kept their eyes on me. The guards kept their eyes on them."

"What are you gonna do about Bo?"

"I'll think of something."

"Better think quick. Bo's itching to pay you back."

"I have a friend who dealt with this kind of thing in Waltgate. I'm hoping to get some tips from him."

Lawson whistled. "Even rougher there than here."

"He's out now but he survived; earned respect or, at least, no one messed with him after the first few attempts."

"I bet you and me can figure something out. Two heads . . . you know?"

They spoke on and off for hours, sometimes going quiet to think their own thoughts. For Starks, it felt like the metaphorical floodgates had opened.

During the conversations, Lawson admitted to cheating on his wife more than once, which had led to divorce. Starks admitted his own infidelities.

"Man, I didn't like my wife," Lawson said, "but you were married to a serpent. Women like that . . . you don't see the attack coming and then *wham*!" Lawson slammed his fist into his palm. "That serpent's pumping its poison into your system. Pain's followed by confusion. Confusion's followed by—"

"Prison?"

Lawson barked a laugh.

"You know," Starks massaged his temples, "I never thought of it like that. You're right. I was snake-bit the first time I saw her. It just took a couple decades for the poison to fill my bloodstream."

"Know what the real bitch of it is?" Lawson leaned in. "No matter all that cheating shit you did, you loved the woman. Know how I know? Because you're still hurting, man. You don't care anymore, you don't hurt anymore. Her fangs are still latched onto your balls."

Starks pounded his forehead with his fists. "You're right. She's pretty much all I think about."

Lawson sprawled onto his bunk, punched his pillow a few times to shape it. "I gotta get some shuteye."

"Thanks, again, Lawson."

Starks hoisted himself onto his bed. He propped his arm behind his head and lay looking at the moon. His cellmate had called Kayla a serpent: She was. But she'd loved him initially.

Was he absolutely sure of that, or did he need to believe it so that his entire life didn't feel false, or so he didn't have to face the fact he could be deceived so easily by others, and himself?

Kayla had deceived him from early on in their relationship. But there was no denying he'd put her through a lot as well. And his indiscretions had been more public, at least at first. The realization that his actions may have caused her to stop loving him stung.

Starks drifted off to sleep with one final thought: he and his wife were both serpents in their own way, and each had been poisoned by the other.

CHAPTER 52

THE NEXT MORNING after breakfast, Starks waited in line for five minutes to make a call. Jeffrey answered his cell phone after one ring.

"Hey, bro. Listen, I'm sorry about saying what I said."

"Forget it. About Mason—"

"Talk about your perfect timing. I'm with Mason right now."

"Let me talk to him." He heard the phone being handed over.

"Long time, Starks," Mason said.

"It has been. I don't have a lot of time. You know my problem?"

"Jeffrey filled me in. There's a situation about my getting approved for a visit, though, since I was inside once."

"I didn't think about that. Maybe Jeffrey can get it worked out. But that could take longer than I may have. Tell me something I can use now."

"Not a good idea to communicate that here and now. You understand me?"

Starks closed his eyes and rested his head on the phone. He'd forgotten that Mason, after he'd finished his time in prison, had told him that phone calls were often listened to. "Thanks, Lewis. Put Jeffrey back on."

"Great to talk to you. Here's your buddy."

"I'm back, bro."

"Do what you can to get Lewis approved for a visit, as fast as you can. Call Demory, see if he can help. Maybe since he sped up your approval, he can do something about Lewis's."

"What should I tell Demory?"

"The truth. That Lewis has been there and can offer a type of support no one else can. No offense, Jeffrey."

"None taken."

"I have to go. The line behind me is getting longer."

"Wait. I . . . I have some unpleasant news."

Starks gripped the receiver. "One of my children?"

"No. They're fine. It's Kayla."

"What about her?"

"She's filing for divorce."

"Damn her. Not what I needed to hear."

"There's more. It's worse."

Starks ran a hand through his hair. "What could be worse than that?"

"She's pregnant."

Starks hit the wall with a fist.

"Bro, you okay?"

"No. But I will be."

"You're taking it better than I thought."

"It is what it is. I've got bigger, more immediate problems. See what you can do about getting Lewis here."

"I'll do what I can. And, bro, stay safe."

"Do my best."

Starks hung up but held onto the receiver for support. He struggled to breathe, felt his knees go weak. The truth he'd denied to everyone, including himself, gripped him, staggered him: Despite all that had happened, despite all his anger and bitterness, he'd believed he and Kayla would stay married. For better or for worse. She was filing for divorce and carrying another man's child, at her age. What the hell was she thinking?

He'd told himself that she and Bret were nothing more than infatuated with each other. That Bret was a rebound relationship—from him, though, not from Ozy, who'd never intended to marry her.

He sucked in a ragged breath. His family was truly broken.

The inmate behind him said, "Yo! Let go of the fucking phone."

Starks nodded and walked away.

When he looked up, he realized he was standing in front of his cell, unaware how he'd gotten there. The last thing he could afford to do was walk around in a daydream. He needed to get a grip.

Too many people and issues were throwing him off these days.

If he continued to let that happen, he might as well paint a bull's-eye on his forehead.

CHAPTER 53

STARKS PAUSED IN front of his usual chair in Demory's office then lowered himself into it like a man in pain.

Demory watched and waited a few moments before speaking. "Is everything okay?"

"Never better."

"Is there a problem with being back in general population? With your cellmate?"

"No and no. This guy's okay. Take my word for it."

Demory tapped the end of his pen on his chin. "You want to tell me why you're so low?"

"Lack of sleep. Adjustment, you know. But it's fine. I'm fine. Let's get on with it."

"It's your call. What do you want to discuss today?"

Starks slouched in the chair and stared at a spot on the ceiling. "When I first noticed a shift in our relationship. For me it was work and more work. The business went through a patch where it needed even more of my attention, which didn't sit well with her. Months went by with no sex, even though I begged her."

"What went on in your mind about that?"

"At first I thought she was just pissed off at me. Then I started thinking about that guy with the text messages. Wondered if she was cheating. Wondered if I wasn't getting it, maybe it was because she was giving it to someone else. I told her as much."

"What'd she say?"

"That I was paranoid because I was guilty. Guilty of never being available except for quickie sex. When I told her she should be good to me because of all I was doing for her, she said my lack of attention had turned her off from wanting sex with me."

"That had to be difficult to hear. Did you feel her complaints were valid?"

Starks looked directly at Demory. "Of course there was some validity, but I loved her. I was doing everything I could to provide for my family. That's how I show love, you know, like what you said before. I made sure she had a nice car and house and money to shop whenever she wanted or needed something for herself or the children. I worked my ass off to make sure she was comfortable."

"But providing for her and your children wasn't enough for her."

"Everything I did should have shown her how I felt. Exhausted as I was, I still wanted to have sex with her. She owed me that much." Starks got up, paced behind the chair. "It's easy for a man to tell a woman he loves her and that he desires her. It's another thing for him to be there for her and provide for her. And not just provide the necessities, but the luxuries, as well. Working seven days a week was how I showed my love." He thumped the toe of his shoe against a chair leg. "I've worked seven days a week for as long as I can remember. It's how I was raised."

"But it wasn't her way to feel loved. She needed more. Did you ever call her during the day to ask how her day was going?"

Starks stared at his handcuffs. "I didn't have time for that."

"Is it possible that even something as simple as that one call a day might have made a difference?"

"I suppose."

"How was Kayla behaving at that time?"

"Abrasive. Confrontational. She went through nannies; couldn't get along with any of them, which I know wasn't their fault, because she was getting into it with her friends as well. Even with some of my friends. She even damaged her relationship with her best friend, Jenny."

"How did you handle the changes in her behavior, as well as the lack of sexual contact?"

"Michelle Cooper. Complete opposite of Kayla. Listened when I spoke; great personality. We had chemistry. Sex with Kayla was non-existent at that point. I couldn't take it anymore. Michelle was happy to fill my needs."

"Did Kayla know about her?"

"Eventually." Starks snickered. "Used my own tactics on me: Checked the call log. Saw how much time I was on the phone with the same number. She called it from a pay phone. When Michelle answered, she hung up.

"Kayla was furious with me. She called Michelle again, from our home phone, to make Michelle think it was me, and told her she was going to make her life a living hell if she didn't leave me alone."

"Do you understand why Kayla felt hurt?"

"Sure. But it's only now that I understand how she might have felt."

"What about the fact that you made the time and gave the attention to Michelle that Kayla had been asking you to give to her? What message do you think that communicated to her?"

Starks glared at Demory then relaxed his face. "I never thought about it like that. Maybe she did feel an emotional connection with Ozy, especially if he made her feel the way she needed to. But their relationship was a farce. I loved Michelle."

"You were okay with loving two women at the same time?"

"I had no problem with it."

"Couldn't Kayla have felt the same way?"

"She only thought she loved Ozy, and that he loved her. He was just using her for sex. They'd meet in parking lots. Who the hell respects a woman who'll put out in a parking lot? Over time, it became *wham-bam* sex. Kayla accused him of no longer caring about her. She badgered him, and when he didn't change, she got furious with him. He called her unstable. Told her if she didn't start behaving better, he'd have to end it."

"How do you know all this?"

"Jenny's husband, Richard, told me some of it. Plus, Kayla confirmed most of it, as well." He cupped his head in his hands.

"What is it?"

"She got involved with Bret after we separated and now she's pregnant."

"How do you feel about that?"

"I can't explain what I'm feeling. It's not that she got involved with him or anyone. Our legal separation agreement stipulated we could see other people. It's just . . . although I've said it was over between us, it wasn't until I heard this news that I realized it was mostly my anger talking. And your favorite word: Pride. But, I guess this means it really is over."

"Not easy to realize, if you believed something else."

"Especially not while in here, where I can't do anything about anything, not that there's anything I could do." He lowered his head and looked away. "In a way, I feel like I'm dying."

Demory nodded. "That's understandable. It's like getting an unfavorable diagnosis. First comes denial. Then maybe there's praying or hoping everything will work out. Eventually there's acceptance.

"Despite all you've said about Kayla, I believe you still love her, at the very least, because she's the mother of your children. And as difficult as is may be to accept, your life is traveling in a very different direction from hers now, and will for quite a while, if not permanently. It may hurt but as soon as you can, you need to think about your children. If Kayla can truly find happiness, your children will benefit.

"Starks, look at me. It may not seem like it but you will come to terms with this, over time. If you allow yourself to."

"Right now it feels like a cluster-fuck."

"I'm sure it does." Demory put his pen down. "I'm sorry to end our session here, but time's up."

Starks nodded and made his way to the door.

"Starks, I know it seems like unpleasant stuff keeps coming at you. There's always a way to figure out what to do, how to manage yourself during such times. You need to believe that."

"Don't worry, Doc. I'll think of something."

CHAPTER 54

S TARKS FELT BREATHLESS as he returned to his cell in silence. Larson put his magazine down and said, "Man, what's that face about? Bad session?"

"I don't want to talk about it. But I do want to thank you again for what you did for me."

"Taking one for the team, you mean?"

"Yeah. I'm wrung out. I'm going to catch a nap."

Starks climbed into his bunk, resting his head on both arms placed behind him on the pillow. Images of Blake, Nathan, and Kaitlin flashed through his mind. He saw them as newborns, toddlers, and as they had grown. It struck him that the slideshow-like quality of the images was because his memories were mostly from photographs taken during special events in their lives and candid moments captured on film by Kayla and others, moments he hadn't been around for most of the time.

He'd missed so much because he'd stayed on the periphery of their lives, never realizing that he was doing it, convinced that what he did for them was more important than being with them. These next years, photographs would be all he'd have, if he could even get them. The children would grow up and into their futures, while he'd stay stuck here. Would they even want to have anything to do with him once he got out? Or while he was in prison?

His situation was certainly not the same as a parent who'd lost a child, but was similar in one significant way: That moment when the parent saw a friend of his child years after the loss. When the realization stunned him that the friend had continued to grow, while his own child was forever framed in the mind as the age when his or her young life had stopped. He was sure it would feel nearly the same for him when he saw his children again, all those years later.

Starks clutched at his chest, remembering that he did know what this was like. Tears welled in his eyes.

Kyle.

How often he forgot to remember the boy tore at him.

He swiped away tears. Breaking down was not the thing to do. Not here. Not now. He took in several deep breaths to calm himself.

A new future for his three living children was beginning, after they'd gone through hell for so long. Not that the tough times were truly over, with their father labeled as a convict. He wanted them to be happy but he no longer had any control over how that happened. As difficult as it might be to have them visit him, it was a matter he needed to reassess. Of the two choices, not seeing them would be worse. He needed to find the courage to face them.

He woke when it was time for dinner; nodded as though listening, as Lawson chatted through the meal. Starks ate but didn't taste.

Once back in the cell, he made his excuses before climbing into his bunk and falling into a heavy sleep punctuated by disjointed dreams.

Among the many dreams that caused him to toss about and tangle his limbs in the blanket was Kayla panting on top of Ozy in the back of his SUV, both of them laughing at him as he beat on the window and shouted for them to stop.

He dreamed he saw Emma standing in the prison corridor, and that he went out to meet her. She smiled at him and held out her arms. He rushed to her, embraced her. When he stepped back to look at Emma, her expression transformed into one of malice. She grew taller, darker, larger, until it was Bo's hands bruising his forearms. One hand let go and became a knife, which Bo took his time dragging across Starks's neck, laughing as the lifeblood gushed out of him.

Starks bolted up in bed, became aware his skin, hair, clothes, and blanket were saturated.

Rain pelted the window. He tried to calm himself, tried to remind himself he'd been dreaming. He watched the rain stream down the glass and attempted to sleep again but couldn't. The dreams had rattled him, and he was afraid they'd return. That was the only reason he could fathom for what he felt impelled to do.

In the bed below, his cellmate snored. He called for Lawson, but couldn't wake him. Starks slid out of his bunk, grabbed a pen and two sheets of paper, and in the dimmed illumination of the overhead lights, and in his small, concise script, he wrote two notes.

Kayla,

I'm truly sorry for the hurt I've caused. I've hurt you, our children, myself, and so many others. I'm sorry for how I reacted to the Ozy situation. I'm sorry I didn't provide what you needed—and deserved. I equated providing material things with love. I now understand you needed more from me. I was disappointed that you'd deceived me in so many ways, and for so long, but who am I to judge you? I had my own secrets and my own indiscretions. I will always care for and about you, and I understand now that being together is no longer possible, because of the pain we've caused each other. Please know how very sorry I am about everything. Please watch over our children and tell them I love them.

Emma,

You were there for me throughout this emotional roller coaster, and especially when my grandfather passed away. I'm sorry for being so guarded about seeing you. I'm dealing with a great deal of pain from my past and, unfortunately, I feel I need to be careful, for now at least, about whom I let get close. I couldn't take being hurt again, not while I'm trying to heal from all that's happened. You have all the qualities I need and want in a woman but who knows what the future will bring. It isn't fair to ask or expect you to wait for me. Just know that I truly care about you. If I make it in here, it would be wonderful to one day call you my wife.

He'd apologized to Kayla and given Emma an out, if she wanted one. Maybe now he could sleep.

Starks folded the papers, placing them under his pillow. He settled as best he could and kept his eyes focused on the window until, at some point, he fell asleep to the hammering drops against the glass.

He didn't dream.

CHAPTER 55

THE NEXT MORNING, after going through the motions at breakfast, he slipped the two envelopes into the mail drop.

Lawson wasn't in the cell, so Starks did what had become his habit: He removed the shank from his shoe and slipped it inside the slit he'd made in his pillow. It hadn't taken long for him to realize that when he was in his cell, it made more sense for the shank to be in easy reach. There was no perfect system for this, especially when out of the cell, but he couldn't think of another way.

He was lying on his bunk when a guard he'd never seen came to the cell and said, "Phone call."

"Who's calling me?"

"Do I look like your secretary?"

"Not on her worst day." He sat up. "Where do I go?"

"Go to the central station. The guard will hand the receiver to you through the slot."

Starks had never been called to the phone before. In fact, he recalled another guard telling him they didn't take calls for inmates. His puzzlement turned to fear about one of his children. The thought of an emergency, with him trapped in prison, made him leap from the bunk.

"No running," the guard reminded him.

Starks went in one direction. The guard went in the other.

He reached the center station in what felt like hours rather than minutes. "I'm Starks," he told the guard inside the enclosure.

"What's it to me?"

"I have a phone call."

The guard stared at him. "No you don't."

"I don't understand."

"If you're stupid, that's not my problem."

Starks was relieved there was no emergency after all, but if this was a practical joke, it sucked.

The time on the clock inside the enclosure showed that lunch started in five minutes. He'd told Lawson he'd meet him in the chow hall and was eager to see what his cellmate thought about this fake call business. Speed-walking got him there with a minute to spare. Lawson was waiting. They got in line together for their trays.

The bench where Starks usually sat was full across from him, so Lawson sat to his right. Bo and his gang sat at their usual table three rows away. And as usual, they watched him, glared at him, laughed at him.

He glanced around. There were only two guards on duty instead of the usual four. Certain more guards would show up in a few minutes, he began to eat, staring, unseeing, at the food on his tray.

The room grew quiet.

Starks looked up and to the left, and watched as the two guards exited through the door.

Nearby inmates stood and started to move slowly in his direction.

"Lawson, stay sharp. Something's going on."

Lawson laughed. "Can't put anything over on you."

Starks felt pressure then searing pain in his right side. He directed his eyes downward and saw lines and numbers on a metal strip and recognized his shank, which had been driven more than halfway in. His cellmate's hand was still holding it.

A dark stain began to spread on the fabric of his shirt.

"Lawson? What the fuck?"

The crowd around them was larger now, and more inmates hurried to join them, forming a human tent over the action, limiting the view security cameras would have.

Lawson drew the shank out and thrust it into Starks's abdomen.

Starks grabbed Lawson's hand and shoved at him, punched at him, but

Lawson kept pulling the shank out and finding another place to drive it in, sometimes shallow, sometimes deep.

Blood mixed with food, dripped from the stainless tabletop, ran in streaks down his cellmate's face and arms and hands.

Inmates shouted. Some rushed in the opposite direction. Most held the circle tight, broken only when Bo came forward and started choking Starks.

Starks, growing weaker, clawed at the large hands that then smashed his head into the table several times before letting him go. He twisted and fell, landed on the concrete floor, on his side, unmoving in his blood.

The alarm began to wail. "Red Dot" was shouted over the intercom. Armed guards ran into the room, shouting orders for inmates to stand with their faces to the wall, hands clasped behind their heads.

Starks saw Lawson move into the crowd with Bo not far behind him.

Ted Landers reached him first.

"God *damn* it! Someone get the doctor and a gurney. Now!"

Starks eyes met Ted's. He found the strength to grasp the CO's arm and say with difficulty, "Kayla. Emma. Children," before everything faded to black.

CHAPTER 56

DEMORY HAD A half hour before his next session began. He skimmed through his notes on the inmate he was to see and jotted down topics he wanted to cover. It was only their second session, and as often happened, getting anywhere took time.

There was a knock on his door.

"Come in."

The guard who opened the door didn't enter.

"Got some news for you, Demory. One of your patients just got offed."

He put his pen down. "Oh God. Who was it?"

"Frederick Starks."

Demory's arms fell flaccid at his sides. "Are you certain?"

"Saw him myself. He wasn't moving. Had a pulse too faint for him to last much longer. And all that blood."

"What happened? Where?"

"Chow hall. Stabbed a bunch of times. The fucking place is gonna have to be hosed down with bleach."

Demory glared at the man. Decided it was a wasted effort to comment on his callousness. "Who did it?"

"Nobody saw nothing. You know how it goes."

"Didn't any of the guards see anything when it started? For Christ's sake, if he was stabbed multiple times, you'd think they'd notice. What about video?"

The guard shrugged. "You know what they say: don't kill the messenger."

"Jesus." Demory slammed his pen onto his desk. "I can tell you who you should look at for this."

"Gotta run. Lots to do." The guard pulled the door shut.

Demory, devastated, leaned back in his chair and squeezed his eyes closed. He felt as guilty as whichever inmate had attacked Starks. An attack by Bo or one of his gang had always been a matter of opportunity. But if he'd just kept Starks in isolation longer . . . No, it could have happened any time, which Starks had known.

The proper prison authority would contact Starks's family. Whether the person would choose to contact the wife the man was separated from or his mother was an unknown.

Jeffrey Davis came to mind.

He pulled Starks's file from the cabinet, remembering that Jeffrey was listed as the contact person in case of emergency, which meant he probably wouldn't get in trouble for placing this call ahead of the formal one. He dialed the cell phone number provided.

"Hey, Big D! Sorry if I sound winded. I'm rushing to my car. Running a little late for an appointment. I was just getting some goodies to bring to Starks. Approved stuff only, I swear." He laughed. "What can I do for you? What does my friend need? Anything at all, it's his."

Demory ran his hand back and forth across his forehead. "There's been an incident." He heard a car door close and outside noises disappear.

"What kind of an incident? Is he okay?"

This was more difficult than Demory had anticipated. "I'm afraid he's . . . Starks was attacked. He's dead."

Silence, then, "No. I don't believe it. I . . . Jesus! I can't wrap my mind around this. Are you certain?"

"A guard just reported it to me. You're listed as the emergency contact person in my file, but I think in this case the proper official for this will notify the family instead. I thought you should know as soon as possible. Once his family's been told, I know you can be of assistance to them. I'm sure they'll need it."

Jeffrey was silent for a few moments then cleared his throat. "What did they do to him?"

"I'm not comfortable telling—"

"What the *fuck* did they do to him? Tell me, goddammit."

"He was stabbed."

"Aw, Jesus." He was quiet for a moment then said, "It had to be to the heart. Too fast for him to protect himself. One stab wound just anywhere wouldn't have killed him, right?"

Demory paused then decided to tell the truth. Too many incidents happened behind prison walls that got covered up. "It was multiple wounds. That's all I know."

Demory heard wracking sobs coming from the other end of the line.

Then the line went dead.

CHAPTER 57

JEFFREY WIPED AT his eyes. He ignored the heat building in the closed car. He ignored the sweat that dripped from his face onto his shirt. It wasn't that he wanted to think about practical matters, but that he had to. Starks and he were business partners.

Had been.

One hand scrubbed at the back of his neck when he thought about Kayla, who was going to be furious when she learned how Starks had changed his will after she'd stuck it to him during the trial. He'd witnessed the revision and had a copy of it in the small vault in Starks's office. Kayla could no longer get her hands on the business or the children's trust funds; Jeffrey had been made trustee. He wasn't looking forward to telling her about the changes. First things first: he had to tell her about Starks.

He'd either call her tonight or in the morning. It was best to give the prison official or Starks's mother time to notify her, depending on which one of them the official called. He also needed to make sure his head was on straight before he had the inevitable discussion with her. He'd seen Kayla's temper unleashed, and the new will and trust were likely to set her off.

Jeffrey dropped his head to the steering wheel and wondered how drama-free the funeral would actually be, considering what the media might do, and considering what he knew about Kayla and Starks's mother. Those two together at such an emotional time practically guaranteed a nasty scene.

He cracked his knuckles.

Still sitting in his car, he cancelled his appointments for the remainder of the day. He wasn't expected back at the office until just before noon the next day. It was better to break the news to the staff in person.

Jeffrey drove home, grabbed a bottle of Scotch and a glass then went out to his terrace that abutted the large koi pond. He dropped onto one of the padded lounge chairs, oblivious to the soft breeze that ruffled leaves on trees on the other side of the water.

After a strong shot of alcohol to help him do what he knew he must, he called Emma, Cathy, and Mason, advising them to keep the information of Starks's death to themselves, explained that the family possibly hadn't been notified as yet; that it should be sometime today, but he didn't know exactly when. Each of them asked for more details, which he didn't have. He gave them Demory's office number and thought about calling the counselor back, but didn't. Kayla could give him more information when he called her at six o'clock, or he'd get them from Starks's family when he contacted them, if they didn't contact him first.

Jeffrey moved back and forth from the terrace to the house to the garage, unable to land in one spot. When he staggered, he realized the Scotch was having more effect than desired or useful. He managed three bites of a sandwich before tossing it.

At four o'clock he fixed a pot of coffee and drank all eight cups over the next two hours.

One minute to six, he poured half a glass of Scotch and downed it.

Then he pressed the house number on speed-dial.

CHAPTER 58

THE LANDLINE AT Kayla's house rang four times before someone picked up.

Bret answered.

"This is Jeffrey. Let me speak with Kayla, please."

"What do you want with her?"

What the hell's the matter with him?

"She'll know. Please put her on."

"Listen, bub, you called *my* house and I want to know what your business is with Kayla."

His patience was already thin, but this was inexcusable behavior from this asshole, especially under the circumstances.

"Let me set you straight, Bret. It's Kayla's house, not yours. It's the house Starks built for her. The marble floors you're walking on, the bed you climb into with her—all made possible by Starks's money. Now, put her on the phone."

Jeffrey jerked his phone from his ear when he heard the receiver slammed down.

"Son of a bitch!"

He hit the number on speed-dial again. This time Kayla answered.

"Kayla . . . Honey, how are you and the kids holding up?"

"We're fine. You sound like you have a cold. Hey, was that you who just called?"

"Yeah."

"You nearly got me in trouble with Bret. He started ranting about someone named Jeffrey insisting on talking to me. Said you cursed him out. I reminded him who you are; that it's okay if—"

"Pardon me if Bret's feelings at such a time are insignificant to me."

"What do you mean?"

Kayla's light banter was now making sense—she hadn't heard yet, which didn't make sense, unless they'd contacted Starks's mother, who'd decided not to tell Kayla.

Crap.

"I really thought you would have . . . I have bad news."

"Oh God. Did something happen to the business? Is the money okay?"

"Forget about the money for one damn minute, will you?"

"What is wrong with you, Jeffrey?"

"It's Starks."

"What about him?"

Jeffrey gulped a shot of Scotch. "I'm so sorry. Starks was attacked. He was killed."

"If this is a joke, it's a cruel one."

"Kayla—" His voice broke.

"No. Jeffrey. No! He can't be."

"I know that underneath all that happened, you cared about him."

Kayla broke down.

Jeffrey brushed at own tears.

"I'm so sorry, honey. I can't believe it either. I can't believe he's no longer with us."

Jeffrey heard Bret ask her what was wrong.

"My husband's dead! He's dead. Everyone will hate me even more now. They'll blame me. Because of Ozy. None of this would have happened if I'd—"

"Kayla," Jeffrey said, "the person to blame is whoever did this."

"It doesn't matter. Everyone will blame me. But they weren't there. They weren't on the receiving end of his verbal abuse, how often he told me I was undesirable, that I was never good enough for him. And all the times he left me alone because he was too busy or was with one of his whores.

I begged him to treat me like he once had, to love me like he had in the beginning. He practically shoved me into the arms of another man."

Through clenched teeth he said, "Kayla, this isn't the time. As far as I'm concerned, anything he did to you, or you think he did to you, he's now paid for. With his life."

Kayla's weeping eased after a few moments. "You know I loved him, don't you?"

"Yeah, you loved each other but you both got lost along the way, and neither of you could find your way back."

"You don't understand how I tried, Jeffrey. No one does. He stopped caring about me. I told him over and over that he was my king and I was his queen, and that he should treat me like one, but he ignored me. Oh God, I want to die. My husband is dead."

"This is not helpful. You need to pull yourself together, for the children."

"I don't know how I'll tell them. I need to go see his family, tell them how sorry I am."

Jeffrey gripped the phone. "I don't think that's a good idea just yet. I plan to speak with them tomorrow. Let me see how they're doing, first. I'll come see you after I see them."

"This can't be real, Jeffrey. It can't be."

"I know. You two were together most of your lives. Even when it got bad, you always knew the other was still around."

Jeffrey's sigh was deep. "Listen, it's going to be hectic for a few days. And, Kayla, if you or the kids need anything, call."

"I will."

The phone was still pressed to his ear. He heard her sobs begin again before the call was disconnected. Some of her behavior was understandable, some of it wasn't. Kayla was filing for divorce, giving up her right to call Starks her husband, yet that's how she had referred to him. And what was Bret going to say about her word choice, considering she was carrying his child? That was a conversation or argument he was glad to miss.

What an unholy mess.

CHAPTER 59

J EFFREY DRAGGED HIMSELF out of bed at first light, rubbing at eyes red and swollen from intervals of weeping at the thought of how his best friend had been killed, an image he wanted to shake from his mind but couldn't. More tears mixed with water from the showerhead.

An old electric razor was pulled from the back of the drawer; his hands were too unsteady to use a regular razor. The piece of toast and several cups of strong coffee consumed in the kitchen weren't tasted but were tolerated out of necessity. He nearly regretted not being married, of being between girlfriends. Anytime something bad or tragic had happened before, he'd turned to Starks. Emptiness filled him.

It was a long wait until eight thirty, a time he felt was appropriate to call Starks's mother, Lynn. Especially after the night she must have had. The loss of any child was devastating, but Starks had been her only child. Someone she relied on, especially after her father had passed away.

Lynn answered after the first ring. "It's my other son. How are you? When are you coming to see me?"

Jeffrey cleared his throat and thought, My God, what is going on with that prison?

"I'm okay, Mom. I have some important news for the family. Would you please get them to your house so I can speak to everyone at once?"

"I'll get as many as I can. Work and school, you know. How's four o'clock?"

"That's fine. See you then."

"Jeffrey, I think I know what your news is. A happy announcement I've been waiting to hear, maybe?"

"It's not that, Mom. I'll tell you when I get there at four." Jeffrey shook his head, now dreading meeting with the family even more.

He'd hoped to get this part of it over early but the delay until four o'clock gave him some needed time, as long as the media didn't reveal what had happened before he could speak to Lynn.

There was so much to think about, a lot to address and many details to be taken care of. A quick call was made to his now confused secretary to tell her he'd be unavailable the rest of the day. No way would he tell the staff about Starks until Lynn and the rest of the family knew.

He turned off his phone and mourned.

CHAPTER 60

JEFFREY DROVE PAST Lynn Starks's house. Cars he recognized filled the driveway and were parked up and down the street in front. He found a place to park a few houses down, but remained in his car, trying to prepare for what was about to happen. He turned his cell phone off and prayed that the prison had already broken the news to them.

His knock on the door was anemic. No one responded. Straightening his posture, he knocked harder then stuffed his shaking hands into his pants pockets.

Lynn opened the door, wagged a finger at him. "Phone calls are appreciated but it's been too long. I know you stay busy, but you need to make time to visit." She kissed his cheek. "You look tired. Let me get you something to drink."

He heard conversations and laughter coming from the kitchen.

They still don't know.

Jeffrey crossed the threshold and moved through the foyer into the living room. He hugged her hard and said, "I promise to do better." Especially now, he thought, when you're really going to need me; not that I'll ever be able to take your son's place.

She patted his cheek.

Family filtered into the living room, inundating him with hugs and arm taps and punches and hellos.

Starks's aunt Anita pushed her way through the group. She frowned then broke into a wide grin as she dragged him to her and bear-hugged him. "Jeffrey, how are you?"

No longer able to meet their eyes and smiles, he looked down. The exquisite bamboo floors came into focus. "I'm so sorry. I forgot to take my shoes off."

Lynn pretended to chide him. "After all these years. Give them to me. I'll put them up."

So befuddled by sorrow and at their enthusiastic reception based in ignorance of the reality, Jeffrey had missed the racks littered with shoes and sandals in the foyer. Shoe removal in this house was a routine he knew all too well.

One of the uncles shouted for Lynn to get Jeffrey some Scotch.

"Water's fine, actually," he replied.

Lynn touched his arm. "Sit, Jeffrey."

Starks's cousin Hank sat next to him on the sofa.

"Yo, Jeff. What's up, man? Haven't seen you since the . . ." The word "trial" hung unspoken.

Jeffrey shook Hank's hand. "I always expect to see the little boy who stole French fries from my plate. How's college?"

"I'm enjoying my engineering courses. Only two years left."

"You know you have a job with us waiting for you, if you want it." He flinched when he remembered there was no longer an *us*. "The company will be happy to have you."

Hank laughed. "Yeah. Nothing like family being in the business. Some call it nepotism. In this family, we call it prudent."

Lynn returned with a glass and a pitcher of water. "Enough, you. Jeffrey's not here to discuss that."

She poured water into the glass and handed it to Jeffrey. Smiling, she asked, "What's this important news?"

Jeffrey took a sip of water. Tension caused him to choke when he swallowed. He recovered and said, "If everyone would take a seat."

Lynn didn't move. Her smile dropped away. "What is it?"

"It's bad news about Starks."

Silence filled the room. Jeffrey put the glass down and stood. Placing his hands on Lynn's shoulders he said, "I can't believe no one contacted you. Something has happened and . . . I'm so sorry. Starks is dead."

The glass pitcher crashed to the floor, fragmenting into shards; water pooled then seeped into the bamboo.

"They killed my boy. They killed my baby!"

Jeffrey drew her into his arms, held her while she beat his chest with her fists, her mouth open in a silent scream.

The room erupted in chaos of weeping, questions, curses, and denials.

Lynn collapsed against Jeffrey.

He stroked her back. "I can't believe it, either."

Lynn slowly pushed herself from him. "This isn't right. Someone made a mistake. Until I see his body, I refuse to believe it."

"I'm sorry, Mom. Someone from the prison called me."

"I don't give a goddamn who called."

Jeffrey flinched.

Lynn focused on his face and the pain etched into it. "Oh God . . . This can't be happening."

Jeffrey held her as her waves of weeping and growing quiet went on for several minutes.

Once she was still, he said, "I spoke with Kayla—"

Lynn stiffened and stepped back. "Don't mention that whore's name to me. This is all her fault. I told him. I warned him. But he *had* to have her. Even I believed her innocent act. I hope she rots in hell!"

"They did love each other. Once. Even after all this, I think they still did."

Lynn's lips curled a snarl. "She loved his money. She loved leading him around by his balls so she could get anything she wanted from him. And then after all he did for her, she . . . she became the whore she really is. Even with someone right here in our basement."

Jeffrey's posture went rigid. "What do you mean?"

"And now my son is dead. She killed him." She grew quiet. "If she thinks she'll get away with this, she's wrong. I'll make her pay. It's time she pays for all she did to my boy."

"Think about the children, Mom. They just lost their father. If anything happens to their mother . . ."

He'd had non-stop emotional turmoil for over twenty-four hours and was feeling it. The urge to leave now was palpable. He pulled one of his business cards from his pocket, with a name and phone number he'd written on the back.

"An official from the prison will be calling you, soon, I'm sure. In the meantime, this counselor was helping Starks cope in prison. This is his office number, if you want to call him now. I'll help with any of the . . . any of the arrangements."

He held Lynn's hands in his. "If you'd like, I can be the go-between with the prison about what's to happen next."

Jeffrey glanced at the faces focused on him. "I have some things to take care of but I'll be back. Probably not today, unless you need me."

Lynn nodded and took the card. "How did my son die?"

Jeffrey decided to lie. "I don't have details. I'm sorry."

He urged her to sit. Leaned over and kissed her cheek. "I'll be in touch soon, but call me if you need anything, yes?"

Staying silent, she nodded.

Jeffrey went to the foyer as family gathered around Lynn. He slipped on his loafers, went out, and stood on the porch, gulping in air.

Hank joined him.

"Thanks, Jeffrey. I know that was tough on you."

Jeffrey cracked his knuckles and tried to calm the thumping in his chest.

After a few moments, Hank said, "You know, I used to go to Starks for advice and he'd tell me to talk to you."

"You never came to me for advice."

Hank shrugged. "That's going to change now, if that's okay with you."

Jeffrey put an arm around Hank's shoulders. "Any time. Listen, that card I gave Mom . . ."

"The counselor."

"If any of you want to talk to him about Starks, about his time there, I'm sure he'll answer any questions he can."

They shook hands.

Jeffrey walked to his car, wondering what else could go wrong.

He reminded himself that no one should ask a question they don't want the answer to.

CHAPTER 61

JEFFREY OPENED THE windows of his car and turned the air-conditioner on high, even though the early May temperature still bore a chill. The air blew on his face but it didn't cool the heat that flushed his skin.

He turned his cell phone back on. More messages insisted on his attention than he was ready to give them.

There was one person and task he couldn't avoid.

He started his car and drove to Kayla's house.

The doors to the triple-wide garage were closed. No cars were parked in the semi-circular drive. He pulled the car level with the ornate front door then shut off his engine.

Every square inch of this house was as familiar to him as his own home. A muscle in his cheek twitched at the recollection of Starks's fixation on getting the man cave in the basement just right. Together, they'd drawn up the plans for where the bar would go and how to arrange the theater room. The times they'd had down there—either with party guests or just the two of them reminiscing almost as often as they made plans for the future.

It was time to stop avoiding the inevitable.

Bret answered the doorbell.

Jeffrey had never met Kayla's new love interest, but had seen them out together. How could she tolerate a man who didn't or wouldn't work? What did she see in him?

"Kayla's expecting me. I'm sure she told you I was coming by sometime today."

Bret replied with a grunt.

Kayla, puffy-eyed, came to the door.

"Come in, Jeffrey." She glanced warily at Bret.

Jeffrey crossed the threshold. "Where are the kids?"

"At my mother's. I haven't told them yet." Kayla fell, sobbing, into Jeffrey's arms.

Bret glowered at him; Jeffrey glared back. "Have a little compassion, man," he said.

Bret swiveled and stormed into the living room.

"Let's sit down and talk," Jeffrey said.

Kayla glanced toward the living room. "Best if we go into the family room."

Jeffrey followed her down the wide hallway punctuated with framed family photos, to the room adjoining the kitchen.

She gestured toward the sofa. "Have a seat. I'll be right back."

Kayla returned with two bottles of designer water, gave him one then took a seat in an adjacent chair.

"I still can't believe it," she said. "What will you do without your partner in crime?"

Jeffrey shook his head. "I'm still in denial. I don't want it to be real. Everything should stop, but it doesn't."

Tears streamed down her face. "I go back and forth between disbelief and anger and . . . blame." Tears turned to sobs. "I did this. I killed him. How can I live with myself?" She wept into her hands.

"There's nothing simple about any of this." Jeffrey stood and paced. "But for God's sake, it's not going to help anyone if you keep saying you killed him. Least of all your children. Never let them hear you say that. It'll destroy them. You're the only parent they have now. Besides, you didn't kill him. Someone inside that goddamned prison did."

"I spent most of my life with him." With a tremulous smile, she added, "You remember how we got together, don't you?"

"He involved me right from the start."

"I worshiped him. Even when we had almost nothing. And then he put me after everyone and everything: The business, his family, his women, his friends." Her eyes met his cold stare. "Twenty horrible years."

"You know damn well it wasn't always bad."

"You're right. But I put up with a lot from him. Don't deny knowing about Michelle, his *soul mate*. Bullshit. He told me if it wasn't for our kids, he would have left me for her. All the attention I begged him for—that he said he didn't have time for—he had it for her. It was a knife in my heart, Jeffrey. Can you understand that? Do you have any idea how lonely that was?"

"You had the children. And he always came home to you."

"It's not the same and you know it."

"You wanted the good life. He gave it to you."

She waved her hand. "Who doesn't enjoy nice things? He certainly did, just as you do. He knew what I was like before he married me. But I wanted him, as well as all this."

Kayla's eyes met Jeffrey's. "I still love him. I think I always will, but he made me fall out of love with him. The only thing that got him interested again was when he found out about Ozy. And it wasn't love that stirred him up, it was ownership. He believed he owned me. Then he tried to pay attention to me but I was done. After years of mistreatment and verbal abuse, I couldn't take it anymore."

"That's the second time you've mentioned verbal abuse. That's news to me."

"I'm not surprised. Why would he paint himself in a bad light? But he did it . . . about my weight, how he was no longer attracted to me, and more. Is it any wonder that when someone treated me like I was special and precious, I responded?"

Frowning, she pointed a finger at him. "I'm not proud of what I did, but I'm so damn tired of people trying to crucify me for what was done in the past." She punched her thigh with her fist. "It's in the past, damn it."

Kayla leaned back in the chair and looked away. After a moment she turned to Jeffrey.

"Ozy made me feel real again. Not like a shadow the way Starks did."

"That wasn't love. You only think it was."

Kayla raised one hand and studied her nails. "Whatever. All I know is it felt good."

Jeffrey perched on the edge of the sofa. "Listen, I know no one's perfect. Not me, not you, not Starks. You probably don't know this, but he used to brag about how you were a virgin when you two got together. Some men don't care about that but it was important to him. He also bragged that he knew he could trust you to be faithful and loyal. I don't want to take sides, but try to imagine the pain he felt when he learned that for twenty years, everything but your virginity was a lie."

Kayla lurched forward in the chair. "Who the hell are you to judge me?"

"I'm not judging you. But improper is improper, whoever does it."

"I'll tell you what's improper. Come to think of it, I don't have to, do I? I'm certain you know even more than I do about what Starks did to fit that label. And how dare you bring up being loyal to me. People in glass houses, Jeffrey."

Jeffrey's shoulders slumped. "I said those very words to Starks."

"Related to what?"

"Doesn't matter now. You know, we all made mistakes. And now Starks is dead. I can't even imagine . . ."

He pulled a handkerchief from his pocket and wiped his eyes and nose. "I spoke with Starks several days before he died."

"I'm sure he mentioned me."

"He felt what you did was the ultimate betrayal."

"See what I mean? I had an affair with a man. He fucked *how* many women? Did you or he ever count them? Did the two of you compete for numbers?"

"*A* man, Kayla . . . or men?"

"Fuck you, Jeffrey."

"My point is—"

"You men stick together. It's okay for men to cheat, but not the women they promised to be faithful to." She pointed a finger at him. "It's all bullshit. Men and their double standards."

"Starks was crushed to learn your cheating went all the way back to Bernard Hazely."

Kayla swept loose hair behind her ear. "Bernard was another lifetime ago. Starks and I weren't even together then. He was off doing his thing with other women, if you'll bother to recall. Gave me a lame excuse about why we needed to not see each other for a while. So I had sex with Bernard. Big deal. I'm sure Starks banged any woman who'd let him."

"The big deal was that you lied to him about it. You let him believe all these years that he was the only one."

"He called me a used mattress. What a damn hypocrite."

Jeffrey rested his elbows on his knees and focused on his linked hands.

"Try to understand his perspective. He was living a lie that you told him. You knew him well enough to know how learning the truth would affect him."

"That's one of the reasons I didn't tell him about Bernard. He would have ended our relationship for good if I had, despite anything he was doing or had." Kayla tapped a finger on the chair arm. "He'd made promises to me and I was going to make sure he kept them."

"He believed you were virtuous."

Kayla threw her hands up. "I'm so sick of hearing that word! He convinced himself when we met that I was this demure, perfect creature. I played along; let him believe it until he forced me to burst that bubble."

"You should have been straight with him from the start."

"Why are you putting all of this on me? He's just as guilty. You're not innocent, either. Now leave me the hell alone."

"Even after he knew everything, he still wanted you back."

"He wanted me *on* my back. All those times he came here for sex after we separated then later called to curse me out. He wanted to use and abuse me. That's not love. You don't know what the hell you're talking about, Jeffrey. You're coming at this from only one side: his."

"He shouldn't have done that, given you mixed messages. I'm sure it was his way of coping, even if it was misguided. It's much harder for a man to accept that his wife cheated."

"Ugh. I'm also sick of hearing about the male ego. Cheating hurts women, as well."

"But you did more than cheat; you trashed him to your friends. And to Ozy. You humiliated him."

Kayla shrugged. "If a man doesn't want his woman to trash him, he shouldn't give her a reason to do it."

"You hurt him in a lot of ways. He told me about your text messages with Ozy."

Kayla leaned back and crossed her arms. "I never should have unlocked my phone. He kept bugging me to. I knew he couldn't handle what he found. He should have left it alone."

"You're still not getting what it did to him. Or you just don't care. It was like he kept getting bombarded with one hit after another. It sent him over the edge. He lost some of his common sense."

"Then he should have backed off. I'm sure his own text messages and conversations with Michelle and all his other women were pure as fucking snow."

She stood and began to pace. "That goddamned Jenny couldn't keep her mouth shut. And her dominating husband. It's their fault for what Starks did. Up until he attacked Ozy, I believed that after an appropriate amount of time, I could fix it. I always did before."

"It's no one's fault but yours and Starks's."

"Betrayal's a bitch."

Kayla stopped in front of the French doors opened to the expansive back yard. She crossed her arms and stared at the swimming pool. "I wish I could jump in the water and wash everything away. Cleanse . . . everything."

She faced Jeffrey. "I'm not proud of what happened. But he made me fall out of love with him because of things he said and did."

"It was like you two couldn't or wouldn't stop punishing the other one. Like watching a battle where both sides are determined to win or die trying."

"He punished himself. He punished me. He punished Ozy. Everyone's trying to put it all on me. It isn't right."

"Jesus. The father of your children is dead, and you're still concerned about yourself. I just said it was both of you." Anger from loss filled him. "I'm not going to keep quiet any longer. What is it with you, Kayla? Do you ever sit back and look at yourself? Are you ever wrong? Starks was there for you when it counted. Maybe you've forgotten that. He's always been there for you. Even after he found out about Ozy, he continued to care and take care of you. Who do you think is ever going to care for you the way he did?" He pointed toward the living room. "Bret? Wake up and smell the coffee. Starks tried his best to fix things between you when he was wrong. Instead of pointing your finger at everybody else, you need to aim it at yourself, for once."

"Why are you here, Jeffrey? If you're only here to condemn me, get the hell out of my house."

Jeffrey drew in a deep breath, hoping to calm himself. "Actually, I'm here to talk about something else, something specific." He gestured at the chair. "Please sit."

Kayla crossed the room and returned to the chair. "Fine. I'm sitting. What is it?"

He looked at her then at the floor. "The will and trust."

"I know all about it. There's a copy in a file upstairs."

"Those documents are obsolete. Starks changed them before going to prison. I'm afraid what I say may shock you."

He covered the changes, aware of how often Kayla's expression, body language, and skin color changed as he spoke. He ended with, "And he doesn't want you to attend the funeral. The kids, of course, but not you."

"When did he say that?"

"Before he went to Sands. Said if anything happened to him—"

"Always had to have the last damn word. I knew he'd grow to hate me; would feel he had to punish me. Didn't know he'd do it from the grave. About the will and trust, it may surprise you to know Starks brought me up to speed. He meant to rub it in so called me right after he changed it."

"He's a—was—a good person. Not a saint, but look at how generous he was with everyone, all the philanthropic things he did in the community. He deserves credit for that."

"Yes, we've all seen the civic awards cluttering the walls of his office here and at headquarters. Starks never did anything generous without an agenda. True generosity doesn't come with strings. He's all about the strings. If he ever did anything generous just to do it, no one would be more surprised than me."

"You're being unfair."

"You're being loyal. And naïve."

"You're wrong about what he did and why."

Jeffrey stood with his usual fluid movement. "I need to go, need to try to get some sleep. Have to go to the office tomorrow and break the news, plus, see about helping with final arrangements. If or when you or the children ever need anything, please call me."

Kayla went to him and placed a hand on his arm, flashing the same innocent expression she'd used since their high school days. "I will. And, Jeffrey . . . don't be a stranger."

CHAPTER 62

DEMORY FACED OUT in the doorway of the hospital room. He stretched and looked both directions then slogged to the end of the hall where, beneath the large window, a folding table was set up with coffee and cups. Torn-open packets of sweeteners with grains of spilled powder, used plastic stirrers, and dried coffee splatters littered the surface. His throat grew tight when he imagined Starks scowling and commenting about the mess, if not cleaning it up himself.

Window glass reflected a disheveled man with mussed hair and clothes that looked like he'd slept in them. He had. For two nights. It was a rough vigil but he was still glad he'd told his ex-wife to stay in Switzerland with their daughter, assuring her everything was fine and that he wouldn't leave their son's side. He'd just hung up with her again. He'd stop counting her calls after the twelfth one.

He pushed the thermos nozzle and watched coffee dregs dribble into the last clean Styrofoam cup. He sipped; the brew was cold and bitter. He'd ask someone to keep up with making a fresh pot throughout the day and night, because he'd need it; a request he'd remind himself to make before he went down to the cafeteria to get better coffee and breakfast to go. It was okay now to be away for the short time this errand would take. His son was sleeping soundly.

Demory placed the cup on the window ledge and pulled his cell phone from the pocket of his rumpled suit jacket.

A number on speed-dial was hit, and the calls on his prison office voicemail startled him. All the messages were from people who'd called about Starks. This was a man who'd said he had only one real friend.

Three messages in particular stood out: Two from an Emma Guyson and one from a Cathy Lorton, who'd obviously been distraught—both women's messages were interrupted by bouts of loud weeping and unintelligible words. The third message was from Jeffrey Davis, asking—shouting—what the hell was going on, and what kind of a fucked-up system went on at that prison, and why the hell wasn't Demory returning his calls.

Every person who'd called wanted answers about some aspect of the incident. Why from him? Why hadn't the person from the prison who contacted whomever, provided this, and then *that* person pass on the information?

One more thing to be concerned about.

Demory saved each message. Despite his own current situation, guilt flowed through him. Circumstances had caused him to be remiss about finding out details about the attack on Starks. He may not be able to do anything about what had happened, but he could make a call to the prison.

Even though the attack had occurred two days ago, his callers might still expect to hear back from him. And, even if in his absence they'd learned the facts they needed, he had to return their calls. It was the right thing to do.

He wanted more information before he called anyone back. Jack Wilson, senior doctor in the prison infirmary, would have examined Starks and signed off on the death certificate. He was the person to call first.

"Infirmary. Dr. Wilson speaking."

"It's Demory."

"You poor bastard. Sorry about your troubles."

"I appreciate it. I called to get cause of death for Frederick Starks."

Silence was followed by, "You want what?"

"Frederick Starks. I know he was stabbed multiple times. I just want your official word on cause of death."

"Who said he's dead?"

Demory hesitated then said, "A guard told me that . . . What's going on, Wilson?"

"He's not dead, he's in a coma."

Demory placed a hand on the wall for support. "Holy mother of God."

"I can't tell if you're relieved or upset."

Demory blew out a ragged breath then asked quietly, "What's the prognosis?"

"Poor. Significant blood loss, of course. I heard surgery was a bitch. And there's some brain swelling from direct trauma."

"I wasn't told about a head injury. What are his chances?"

"Slim. But the trauma unit at Grace is exceptional. They'll do their best."

Shaking his head back and forth in disbelief, Demory muttered, "Thanks, Wilson."

"Sure thing. When are you coming back?"

"Unknown."

"Maybe it's none of my business . . . maybe I shouldn't ask . . ."

"Ask what? It's not like you to hesitate."

"You know how the rumor mill spins around here. Anyway, someone told me a guard heard you screaming in your office before you left. And—"

"Yes, I was yelling. For good reason."

"As I was saying—"

"For God's sake, spit it out."

"I'm sure it isn't true, but . . . word is you're losing your license because you slept with one of your patients here."

"That's a damn lie. There is an issue with my license. A typical system screw-up. I'll get it taken care of."

"That's a relief. Hope to see you soon. Gotta run. A patient just walked in."

The line disengaged.

Demory rested his hands on the window ledge and leaned forward to study the pewter sky. Gusts blew tree tops back and forth below him. The wind picked up speed.

What term had Starks used? Cluster-fuck. It certainly fit this situation.

As soon as the guard had told him Starks was dead, and as soon as he'd ended the call with Jeffrey Davis, the desk on his phone had rung with more bad news: His son's appendix had burst. The boy had been rushed to emergency and was being prepped for surgery.

After he'd quickly locked away his next patient's file, and as he was picking up the phone to let administrative staff know he had an emergency, he learned the bad news wasn't over: An inmate who worked in the mailroom dropped an envelope onto his desk; urgent was stamped in red on the front. Inside was a letter about the license issue. After a few moments of yelling in frustration, he'd stuffed the envelope in his jacket, made his call announcing he'd be out and would have to let them know when he'd return then sprinted to his car.

His son had developed peritonitis and was getting a strong antibiotic, along with several other meds, pumped into a vein in his arm.

Demory had been awake now for a little over forty-two hours.

He shook his head in exhaustion and frustration, pulled out the small notebook and pen in his pocket then hit the same number on speed-dial for his office voicemail.

Names and phone numbers on the notebook pages taunted him. Demory dragged a hand through his hair. God help him. He should have checked with the infirmary before making that disastrous call to Jeffrey.

After stepping into his son's room to check that he was still asleep and all was okay, he dialed the first number.

No hello from Jeffrey, just "Why the *hell* has it taken you so long to call me back? What the fuck is wrong with everyone? No one's heard from anyone. At least the media hasn't made a circus out of this. That's something to be grateful about."

"There's something else you can feel grateful for."

"Yeah, you finally called back."

Demory stayed silent.

"Listen, Demory, I'm sorry I yelled. I'm a wreck."

"I'm the one who's sorry, sorrier than you know. The most succinct way to say it is I screwed up. I should have checked the facts before I called you. There's really no excuse. Right after I spoke with you, I had a family emergency—my son. I've been at the hospital since then. It wasn't until a few minutes ago that I found out what really happened."

Jeffrey hesitated for a moment. "You've lost me, Demory. What facts? What did you just find out?"

Demory raked a hand through his hair. "I don't know who knows what anymore."

"Get to the point."

"I'm talking about the fact that Starks isn't dead."

"What the hell?"

"I just learned he was gravely injured and is in a coma. I was told by a guard that Starks was dead. I was trying to take the news in when I got the call about my son. I called you then zoomed out of there."

Demory rubbed his right hand over his forehead. "They moved Starks to the trauma unit at Grace. No visitors, though. That's their policy for a prisoner in his condition." He heard Jeffrey hit his fist against something hard.

"I don't fucking believe this." After a moment of silence, Jeffrey said, "Look, I'm sorry about your son, but you're goddamned right you should have checked. Jesus! You have any idea what all of us have been through? Family, friends, staff, for Christ's sake?"

"I haven't stopped imagining it since I heard."

"What exactly is his condition?"

Demory repeated what Wilson had told him. "I'm truly sorry for the confusion. I should have checked—would have checked—at the infirmary before I called you."

Jeffrey exhaled a ragged breath. "At least I know he's still alive. That's something. I hope to God he pulls through."

"So do I."

"I gotta go. I've got a shitload of calls and visits to make, and fast."

The last thing Jeffrey said before hanging up was, "And I'm giving them your cell phone number!"

Demory checked once again on his son then hurried to the elevator. He needed several moments to think, so shut off his phone. He would enter what was sure to be a viper's pit after he got some food into him.

Demory turned his phone on and found message after message from a number of people who'd been on his original call-back list. A new but familiar name was added to the list: Kayla.

He called her first and let her rant for a while, believing she had a right to: Her children had been traumatized "yet again," which she repeated often, at full volume. He apologized to her several times for his error in judgment, as he later did with all the others, before asking her what it was, specifically, that she wanted.

Kayla, Cathy, Emma, and Starks's mother all wanted the same thing: Visitation with Starks in the trauma unit. By rote, he explained to each person why the hospital wouldn't allow it, at least, not until Starks's condition stabilized or he regained consciousness—if they'd allow visitors at all, since he was an inmate. He explained the prison policy that required strict vetting for visitor approval, even for this situation, and assured each of them that family could call the hospital for updates.

He shut off his phone and plugged it in to recharge. A hand placed on his son's forehead indicated the fever was dropping.

Demory slumped in the chair next to the bed and drifted to sleep, unable to stop the voices in his head from chastising him.

CHAPTER 63

THE TRAUMA NURSE replaced Starks's empty saline bag and checked his I.V. The monitor next to his bed indicated his oxygen level, heart rate, and temperature were improving each day. As she had every day over the last two weeks when she was on shift, she spoke to him in a cheerful voice, telling him about the weather, her family, the latest romance novel she was reading—anything to possibly trigger a response from him. She even sang to him.

The I.V. was in good condition so she moved to check his catheter. When she touched the skin around the tube to check for irritation, his left leg moved slightly. At first she thought she may have imagined it. She touched the area around the tube again. Two fingers on his right hand twitched.

"Looks like you may be trying to wake up, Mr. Starks. Let's see what the doctor says. Lucky for you, he's making rounds now."

She pressed the call button.

"Yes, Ana?"

"Please tell Dr. Baker that Mr. Starks just moved his leg and a few fingers. They weren't large movements, but it's something."

"He's just walking up. I'll tell him."

Less than a minute later, Baker joined her.

"Was anything specific happening when he moved?"

"I was checking his catheter."

Baker's eyebrows raised then he smiled. "Maybe you have the magic touch."

He laughed when Ana blushed, and pulled a penlight from his pocket. Gently, he lifted each of Starks's eyelids and flashed the light back and forth. "No change."

He used a sharp-tipped probe, sticking each leg, arm, and foot with it. "Must have been a reflex. But it's the first movement since he's been here."

"That we know of."

"I want him checked every half hour. If there's any more movement, we'll try a few other tests to see if it's just reflexes or if he's trying to wake up."

"I'll see to it."

"Any new movement, whether I'm on duty or not, I want to be notified."

CHAPTER 64

ANA RAMIREZ WAS on the trauma unit's work roster for the next three days. The first two of those days, Starks had a few more reflex movements, but no response to the pen light or probe. Every day, orderlies bathed and shaved him, and changed his diapers, as well as did what was needed to keep his muscles and skin healthy.

The third day was her last before she had two days off. She assisted the orderly during the bath and saw no extraordinary response from her patient. As she walked away, the monitor began its loud beeps for attention. She pressed the reset button, checked the readings, and turned to leave. The monitor went off again. Thinking that maybe the monitor was going bad, she unplugged it at the wall then plugged it back in, resetting the monitor.

"Sorry about the racket, Mr. Starks. These things beep when they need to be replaced or when a patient moves the arm with the I.V."

She realized that his left arm, which she'd placed several inches from his thigh, was now next to it and that his fingers lightly scrabbled at the sheet. Ana rushed to the nurse's station, looked up Baker's number, and sent him a text message.

He called her back in less than thirty seconds. "I just walked in. Getting on the elevator now. Grab a Glasgow chart and wait for me."

Doctor and nurse hurried to Starks's bedside. Starks eyes were open but not for long.

"Were you doing anything special this time that caused him to move?"

"No. The monitor kept beeping. I was checking it when I realized he'd moved his arm several inches. I'd positioned it after his bath. And he was moving his fingers.

"Good thing you were paying attention. Let's see how our patient scores on responses."

Baker pressed hard on the base of one of Starks's fingernails. "His eyes opened but he didn't jerk his hand away. He didn't look at me, either. Give him a score of three for now."

Baker leaned in closer, speaking loudly. "Mr. Starks, can you look at me? Can you speak?"

Stark's mouth barely opened. He moaned, but none of his sounds formed words.

"Score a two for verbal response.

"One more test, Mr. Starks. Sorry if it doesn't feel good, but it has to be done."

Baker poked the probe at specific body points. There was some pulling away and extension of each limb, but it was slight. "That's another two. I want these tests done four times a day. Track his scores."

The nurse's excitement flagged.

"What's the matter?" Baker asked.

"I was just thinking about when he wakes up. What he'll wake up to. He looks like he's a nice man."

"Just remember he's at Sands because he did something that put him there." Baker patted her on the arm. "I want his scores texted to me."

Ana placed her hand on the arm her patient had moved. "I feel for you, Mr. Starks. You're in a tricky place: damned when you wake, damned if you don't."

***

Sixteen out of every twenty-four hours were spent in a medicated fog from painkillers, but each day, Starks responded a little better, became a little more alert. By the seventh day, he was doing better at moving his limbs on his own, and was beginning to speak, though mostly with single-syllable words or he broke syllables up as though they were words. When it became clear that he understood most of what was said to him, Baker ordered all conversations with the patient to be kept light.

On the eighth day, Starks smiled and winked at the young female orderly giving him a bath.

And then he remembered his reality.

CHAPTER 65

"GOOD MORNING, MR. Starks."

He studied the nurse's staff ID clipped to her uniform.

"Ana. You're one of the nurses who've been looking after me." He extended his right hand. "Thank you."

Her cheeks colored as she shook his hand. "You're welcome. And that was a complete sentence. Very good!"

She held up a folded gown.

"I know your bath was ten minutes ago. Sorry you had to wait for a fresh change. Let's do that now."

As she was tying the strings at the back, she said, "You need to get ready to work hard."

"What's that mean?"

"Physical therapy. Time to get your muscles stronger and your coordination back."

"Sounds good to me."

"It'll hurt but it's what's needed. You start tomorrow. And I'll be here to assist for the first round. Dr. Baker wants me to monitor and report on how it goes. When you're strong enough, someone will take you to the P.T. room."

"You're very pretty, Ana. Are you married? Any kids?"

"Are you flirting with me?" She smiled.

"No. Hope that doesn't disappoint you."

Ana turned to the monitor, pretending to check readings she'd already checked.

Starks raised the head of the bed a few inches. "Sorry. I didn't mean to make you uncomfortable. I don't mean anything by it. I'm not the typical inmate. Not a violent criminal. I mean, according to the system, I'm a criminal, though I still can't see myself that way. But I'm not violent. What I mean is . . . Forget it."

Her expression softened. "I know who you are. Anyone who watches the news or reads the papers knows."

She could see he was distressed. Compassion won. "I'm divorced, and I have four children."

"Are you and your ex still friends? Do you get child support? I'm making you uncomfortable again. I don't mean to. I have a reason for asking."

"I'd rather not discuss it."

"Sorry."

"There are more important things to focus on. Like getting you well."

Starks faced away. "Well enough to return to hell."

CHAPTER 66

DEMORY CARRIED A tray with scrambled eggs, toast, and orange juice to the bedroom his son used when he stayed with his father.

"Eat every bite and you can have your choice of ice cream as a snack this afternoon. I'm going to get a quick shower."

"Can't I have cereal, instead?"

"You need to build your strength. And," he ruffled his son's hair, "we don't need to have this conversation every morning."

In his own bedroom, Demory grabbed a pair of underwear from the chest of drawers and went into the adjoining bathroom. He placed his cell phone on the countertop and reached to turn the water on. The standard ringtone sounded. Someone not close to him was calling. He started to ignore it, but reminded himself that things ignored have a way of kicking a person in the ass. Lately, his ass. He recognized the number.

"Wilson?"

"Thought you'd like an update on Starks."

When the brief conversation ended, Demory grinned at himself in the mirror, punching the air with his fist. He got into the shower. His son would be improved enough in a few days for it to be safe to get a sitter for an hour or so. He wanted to visit Starks at Grace, certain the inmate would need his kind of support now more than ever. His exuberance flagged when he imagined how that conversation might go.

The following week Demory was free to visit Starks, who'd been moved to a room in the locked-down mental ward, which was standard practice for hospitalized maximum-security prisoners, he'd been informed. It had been fairly easy to arrange the visit since Starks was his patient, a fact the hospital had taken twenty-four hours to verify before telling him he was approved.

He stepped out of the elevator on the top floor at Grace and headed directly to the nurses' station.

"Mathew Demory. I'm here to see my patient, Frederick Starks."

After checking a list, she said, "ID, please."

Satisfied he was who he said he was, the nurse escorted him to a set of wide double doors, punched in a code then took him the rest of the way to the room Starks was in. She needn't have bothered to go the small distance beyond the doors, he thought; only one room had a guard posted outside of it.

"The guard will unlock the door for you," she said before she left.

The guard turned the key in the lock. "Knock when you're ready to leave, or if you have a problem."

Demory hesitated. Even though the report was that Starks looked good, all things considered, he steeled himself for what he might see: People's opinions about how someone looked were often relative. He wasn't disappointed; Starks's looked *almost* like himself again.

He had several seconds to study his patient before Starks realized he was there. As soon as he was spotted, Starks quickly shifted his dark expression to one that revealed nothing about whatever thoughts had been shelved.

Starks propped himself up on one elbow. "Doc! I can't tell you how good it is to see a familiar face."

"I can imagine. I've been really worried about you. How are you?"

"Watch this."

Starks sat up. He tried to hide the grimace on his face but couldn't as he slid from the bed.

"You're in pain?"

"They said it would hurt for a while. Scar tissue, you know."

"Are you taking anything for pain?"

"They want me to take meds on a regular schedule but I told them no.

I'm not getting trapped into that loop. If I really need it, I take one. The last thing I intend to do, as appealing as being in la-la land can be, is to be out of it at Sands. I learned my lesson. I need to be able to see and hear what's going on at all times."

Starks walked back and forth. "It took a lot of hard work and some agony to get to this point, but I did it."

"That's excellent progress. Looks like they're treating you all right here."

"It's as much a prison as the other one, but slightly more pleasant. For obvious reasons. I've even learned to appreciate hospital food." His grin widened. "And, there are women here. A nice change, I can tell you."

Starks's brow wrinkled. "Sorry to say it, Doc, but you look like hell."

"Got some personal issues I'm dealing with. And my son had an emergency the same day you were . . . attacked. He was hospitalized for awhile then had some recovery time at home. That's the main reason I haven't been to see you before now."

Starks returned to his bed. "I'm sorry to hear it. Is he okay?" He gestured toward the single chair in the room.

Demory lowered himself into the armless chair. "There were complications right after the surgery, but he's nearly a hundred percent now."

"As a parent, I know what a relief that is to you."

Starks's gaze locked with Demory's. "Doc, have you heard from my family or Jeffrey?"

Demory shook his head and said, "You don't know the half of it. They were disappointed to learn about the stringent visitation policy here. I was able to get in because of who I am."

Silence filled the space for a few moments. "How do you really feel, Starks?"

"I told you."

"I mean about what happened."

Starks avoided Demory's eyes. "I don't want to talk about it."

"Understandable. But at some point we'll need to."

Starks flexed the fingers of both hands. His face and voice showed no expression when he replied, "Believe me, Doc, I've given the matter a lot of thought."

Demory studied his patient, who kept his face averted. The skin on the back of his neck tightened.

Starks gave one firm nod of his head then looked at Demory. "Thanks for your concern, though."

"I care."

"I know."

"You've improved so much I don't think they'll be able to keep you here much longer. How do you feel about going back?"

Starks's lips twitched. "It is what it is."

Demory didn't miss the odd smile, and knew if he asked about it, he wouldn't get a straight answer. "As soon as you're back, we'll continue our sessions."

"Can't wait."

"Whatever your opinion is about the sessions, you need that time more now than ever." Eyes fixed on Starks, he leaned forward, as though that simple action would add import to his words.

Starks faced Demory. "Believe me, I know what's needed."

Demory stood and walked to the bed, extended his hand. "I'm sorry this is all the time I have. Don't want to leave the boy too long just yet, more for my sake than his."

Starks's hand clasped Demory's. "Thanks for coming to check on me."

"Take it easy."

"That's the only way in here, Doc."

Demory knocked on the door. He nodded at the guard as he pulled the door shut behind him and waited for the *click*. All the way to the double doors, where he buzzed to have the locked doors opened for him, all the way down the elevator, and all the way to his car, he wondered how worried should he be about Starks's enigmatic expression and comment: *I know what's needed.* As a counselor he knew how he preferred to take it.

There was also the way he preferred not to take it—the way he didn't want to think about.

CHAPTER 67

STARKS LAY BACK in bed, shifting his position several times, unable to get comfortable. He raised the head of the bed until he was almost sitting up, keenly aware of the closed wounds that pulled and jabbed whenever he moved. He would have preferred no pain but had decided to let the sensations act as motivation.

To get stronger mentally and physically.

To get even.

From this position, his reflection was captured in the small rectangular mirror secured in a recessed part of the white wall. He saw more than his unkempt image; he saw a night when he was pushed nearly to his limit.

That night, when more than a mirror was broken, uneasiness had settled in his bones as his fingernails bit into his palms.

"Where the hell are you going?" he'd said.

Unfazed, Kayla had smoothed the crimson silk of the dress that enhanced her curves. She watched his reflection in the mirror, watched as his eyes followed the slow trail of her hands.

"I've never seen that dress before," he told her.

Kayla turned slowly, taking in her appearance in the full-length mirror. "It's new."

"It's indecent. If it were any shorter, it'd be a shirt. And since when do you show that much cleavage?"

Her cell phone rang; she answered and said, "I'm on my way," then disconnected the call.

"Who was that? You tell me where you're going dressed like that."

"It's just Jenny."

"The two of you are going out way too much lately; I don't like it."

"You go out. No reason I shouldn't."

"You leave this house now, especially dressed like that, and I swear to God I'll change the locks."

With a hint of a shrug, she said, "Do what you want. That's all you ever do, anyway." She patted her short, dark hair. "Don't you have a woman panting to see you tonight?"

She picked up the small beaded handbag she'd tossed onto her side of their king-size bed then left the room and a furious Starks.

He listened to the fast-paced snaps of her stiletto heels move along the hall floor then down the stairs. Heard the expertly carved front door of their small mansion shut behind her. Starks rushed to the window facing the front of the house and watched the taillights of her car disappear into the night.

Body rigid, he stomped down the stairs then went to the built-in bar in the family room. He took a bottle of Scotch and a glass with him to the room he used as his office. He typed in information onto his computer, read, drank, swore, drank more. The printer hummed as whiskey burned his throat and added to the fire in his gut.

Although this latest round of winner-loser had started when he found her in their bedroom, dressed and perfumed as she was, he kept the results of his latest checking up on her to himself. Especially that he'd yet again figured out her e-mail and Twitter passwords. She'd changed the ones he'd been allowed to have before. Over the last week, he'd checked her messages daily on each.

There was more than one man she was in contact with. Some had responded recently and some hadn't. And the messages were ridiculous, in his opinion—*I had an x-rated dream about you last night. I need to smell your special scent again.* And on and on such messages went, some of them as inane as these were; some of them lewd. None of these men were the co-worker she'd previously pulled her shenanigans with.

He didn't change the locks as he'd threatened; they both knew it was an idle threat. That she knew this annoyed him even more. He wanted her to come home now so he could confront her, so he could call her a cheating bitch.

The latest nanny answered the in-house phone in her upstairs bedroom when he buzzed her.

"Keep the kids up there until morning," he said.

He waited and planned what he was going to say to his wife. He drank more than he should have, especially when the grandfather clock in the foyer struck twelve then one then two.

At two-thirty, he made a pot of coffee but forgot to drink it.

At three fifteen, the garage door opened and Kayla's Ferrari growled its way into the enclosure.

He was ready.

CHAPTER 68

KAYLA ENTERED THE house through the kitchen door. Starks was seated at the marble-topped dinette table.

"You shouldn't have waited up," she said. "I'm surprised you were able to stay awake, considering how empty that bottle is."

"Who the fuck is McSean Dwest?"

"How should I know?"

She paused, waving her hand in front of her face. "I can smell the whiskey from here. You need to watch how much you drink. It's making you delusional, and less than your usual charming self."

"You're a fucking tramp."

"You're drunk. I'm not going to waste time talking to you when you're like this."

Starks pulled a folder from where he'd hidden it on the chair seat next to him and slammed it on the tabletop. He turned the file to face her, opened the cover and pointed to the printed sheets. A vein in middle of his forehead throbbed blue against red.

"Lying bitch. These are your Twitter messages with him, along with a number of other men." He rose and stood inches from her. "What do you have to say for yourself?"

She pushed him away. "Get out of my face."

His arm swung back, his fist ready to make contact.

Kayla stood firm. "Go head," she told him. "Let our children see what

Daddy did to Mommy. Show our sons that it's okay to beat women. Teach Kaitlin it's okay for men to hit her."

There was a mirror behind Starks. Kayla glanced at her reflection, checked her hair and lipstick.

Starks needed an outlet for his rage. He yanked the mirror in the gilded frame from the wall and threw it as far as he could. The mirror connected with the French doors. Wood splintered; glass flew in all directions.

One brief moment of silence was followed by doors slamming open from above and feet pounding across the landing, down the stairs, and finally to where Starks and Kayla stood.

Starks whirled around; saw the nanny shielding Kaitlin with her arms, saw Nathan fighting to control his tears, and Blake with his mouth pinched tight.

All eyes were on Starks. A keening grief rose in his chest.

Kayla slid the folder into a drawer of the china cabinet. She pulled her cell phone from her handbag, dialed then stepped outside to talk.

When she came back into the kitchen, Starks said, "I'm leaving. And I'm not paying for anything anymore. You're on your own, slut."

Kaitlin began to wail. The boys looked from their father to their mother, waiting for one of them to say or do something that would restore their sense of security.

It was Kayla who spoke first. "Your father isn't feeling well. He has a fever."

"Yeah," Starks said, "and you fucking gave it to me."

The officer glanced at Kayla, noting how the long robe she wore was wrapped extra tight around her and belted to stay in place. He saw how she clutched the thick fabric closed near her neck. She had on stockings, but no shoes, and kept shifting from one foot to the other.

"Mrs. Starks, maybe, especially since your husband's been drinking . . . maybe there's someplace you and the children can go tonight. Let things calm down. He's still pretty upset. And drunk."

"We don't need to leave. Just . . . if you would, put him in bed upstairs. I don't want to . . . I can't manage him up the stairs. I think it's better if he's up there and we're down here."

"We can do that."

"Turn left at the top of the stairs. It's the room at the end of the hall."

She glanced at the children and their nanny unmoving on the sofa in the family room. "If there's anymore trouble, I'll get the children away from here and call you."

He flipped his notebook closed. "Okay, ma'am."

The officer, with Kayla following him, went to the formal living room, where his partner had taken Starks who was passed out on the floor.

"Let's get him tucked in for the night. His wife says it'll be okay."

"Yeah. He's done for the night.

CHAPTER 69

STARKS FLUNG A hand up to cover his eyes from sunlight. Kayla, damn her, must have opened the drapes all the way. On purpose.

He needed liquid to thin the muddy feeling in his mouth, and something to make his head stop drumming.

Body revolting as he moved, he lurched to the east window and closed the drapes. Flashbacks from the previous night started up. Some were hazy, some were clear, especially the way his children had looked at him. A moan escaped his dry throat.

The digital clock next to his side of the bed read 10:21. That's when he realized he'd slept on Kayla's side of the bed; his side was untouched. Someone other than his wife must have put him in bed fully dressed, he noted, except for his shoes.

No sounds came from inside the house. Heart pounding, he raced to the first of his children's bedrooms. Closets and drawers were still full. Cherished items were still in their places. It was the same for the other bedrooms. Then he remembered: the children would be in school at this time.

He leaned against the embossed wallpaper in the hallway, waiting for his breathing to slow. One sleeve of his shirt that still smelled of Scotch was used to wipe perspiration from his face. Steps imbued with frustration carried him to the master bathroom.

Starks downed two pills for his headache then stripped. In the shower he alternated steaming and frigid water. Shaved and dressed, there was another task he wanted to take care of before heading downstairs for desperately needed coffee. Instead of finding what he thought he would, he got a surprise. Anger surged; he made his way to the kitchen.

Kayla was at the table, coffee mug in hand as she read the newspaper. She didn't look at him. "Coffee's made. I'm sure you need some."

The hot beverage was too strong, the way she liked it. He drank half a cup while leaning against the cabinet, watching her deliberately not look at him.

The spot on the wall where the mirror had been was a blank space framed by paint exposed to more life than the covered surface. He glanced left and saw that new French doors had been installed.

He downed his coffee and turned to go back to the counter to refill his cup, stepping on a small mirror shard missed by whoever had cleaned up the mess. The uncomfortable quiet was broken when his weight crushed the ragged piece into dust.

Eyes aimed downward he said, "Your cell phone's no longer in service."

"I cancelled it."

He poured the coffee, took a sip. "I know you're not going to go without a phone. I want the new number and your password."

"I don't think so."

Kayla turned a page of the newspaper.

Starks slammed his cup down on the counter. "You give me the goddamned number and password or our marriage is over."

Finally, she looked at him. "Whatever."

"You'd rather end our marriage?"

"I'm not afraid of illusions." She looked away. "You're welcome to go." And he had.

Seven months he'd lived at his mother's house, until his relatives persuaded him to return home, hammering the belief that family and pride were fruits of the same tree.

The reunion between him and Kayla had not been an easy one. Only the children seemed comforted at having everyone under the same roof.

And for a while, he too had thought shared space was enough.

CHAPTER 70

S TARKS HAD CANCELLED his plans for that first Saturday night after he'd moved back home. The children were put to bed after ten, bathed, happy, and exhausted from a full family day. Their nanny retired to her room after tucking them in.

In his favorite chair by the fireplace in the master bedroom, Starks slipped off his alligator loafers, leaned over to remove his socks, all the while planning the right thing to say to Kayla that would persuade her to let him enter her and enjoy what he was entitled to as her husband and provider—an experience she'd withheld from him since he'd returned. He missed the feel of her, the taste of her.

Earlier in the day, she'd been more relaxed than he'd seen her in a long time, with many moments where she laughed at the children's pool play out back. At one point he brought his mouth close to her ear and whispered things he wanted to do to her. Her eyes stayed on the children, her smile was non-committal. But she didn't said no.

The shower had stopped a quarter hour ago; she was taking extra time getting ready tonight. He imagined Kayla's exit from the bathroom, her dressed in his favorite satin nightgown, her skin wafting the delicate citrus scent of the lotions she applied to every inch of her body each night. Her mouth taking him in. He thought about kissing the small, red heart-shaped mole, with its point directed to where he wanted his tongue to travel to. The thought made him hard.

He started to unbutton his shirt just as the bathroom door opened.

Kayla came out dressed in second-skin jeans, a low V-cut cashmere sweater—no bra, and high-heeled boots. Slinking to her vanity table, she spritzed her neck with some of the expensive perfume he'd given her a few weeks ago. She glanced over her shoulder at him. One of her eyebrows went up at the rise in front of his slacks. She smiled then walked out of the room.

She's teasing me, he thought, pleased with what the outcome was sure to be. It was how she liked to play it with him: Tease him then drive him wild. What she was going to get downstairs was a mystery, but knowing Kayla, it would add *flavor* to their experience.

Naked, he waited on the bed. Ten minutes later, he wondered what she was doing, what was taking so long. He wrapped his robe around him and realized that had to be the game: She was down there wondering what was taking him so long to figure it out. He was grateful the children and nanny were settled in for the night. He didn't want any of them to see how the front of his robe protruded.

His anticipation surged as he checked the living room, family room, kitchen. He stood at the French doors, straining his eyes in the dark, certain she was near the pool waiting to be ravaged. She wasn't there. Nor was she in the pool house. He checked the garage. Her Ferrari was there. His Bentley, with its quiet engine, was gone.

He wanted to believe she'd needed something special from the store but knew better.

Bitch.

How long did she think he'd tolerate such disrespect?

Starks linked two fingers around the neck of a bottle of Scotch, grabbed a glass with his other hand then went up to the master bedroom. A shot of whiskey was swallowed in one gulp before he stepped under the showerhead, where he relieved his pressing need as hot water pulsed down on him. Minutes later, his back propped against the headboard, he ordered a two-hour movie, poured glass after glass of whiskey until he fell asleep.

The garage door woke him when it hummed open at three thirty.

The uneven clomp of her boots grew louder as she made her way up to their room. Without looking at him, Kayla staggered to the bathroom and shut the door.

He waited for the lavatory water to turn on. Waited for a toilet to flush, or worse, another shower to be taken. None of these sounds came from the bathroom. Fifteen minutes of silence passed before he got up to find out what she was doing.

The door wasn't locked. She'd lowered the toilet lid, sat, and fallen asleep. Her mouth hung open, spoiling the air with her breath.

Furious, disgusted, he left her there and slept in one of the guest bedrooms.

Seven o'clock Sunday morning, Starks went to the master bedroom. Kayla wasn't there. He slid on jeans and a T-shirt and padded barefoot downstairs. The aroma of coffee reached him when he entered the family room. No one else was awake yet.

He poured a cup of coffee and sipped.

Kayla stood two feet away. Without looking at him, she said, "I'm making toast. Would you like some?"

"You have a fucking nerve."

"Fine. Fix whatever you want yourself."

"It's not about toast. It's about you leaving me when you knew what I wanted. It's about you coming back in the middle of the night so drunk you fell asleep on the toilet. It's about you disrespecting me in my own house. It's about the example you are to our children."

He grabbed the china plate Kayla had set aside for her toast and hurled it against the wall.

She crossed her arms in front of her and glared at him. "Like you're such an example of right behavior." Her voice softened. "What is it with you and destroying beautiful things?"

Doors above them opened. Footfalls on the stairway grew louder.

Her shoulders sagged as she looked down at the sharp-edged fragments on the floor. "One of these days, maybe you'll start cleaning up the messes you make. Maybe you'll stop making them."

"Maybe you'll stop giving me reasons."

They heard their oldest, Blake, as he entered the family room ask of no one, "What is it *this* time?"

Starks kicked a piece of the plate, sending it across the room. "I'm done with this shit." He avoided Blake's eyes and the eyes of his other children as he passed them. "Just an accident. Wet hands and china don't mix." He forced a chuckle, rubbed his son's head in passing, and cringed when the boy ducked from his touch.

His home office was downstairs. It was quiet in there. It was a place where he usually could get his thoughts straight. Slouched in his armed leather desk chair, he felt relieved he hadn't hit Kayla. It had come close. The impulse was stronger every time she gave him reason to get angry with her. He'd raised his sons to never hit a female, just as he'd been told by his grandfather, unless it was done in indisputable self-defense.

God, but that woman made it difficult for him to abide by that rule.

It was time to face facts: The marriage was over.

He'd have to be the one to leave. No way would he uproot his children. And whatever their mother was, it was best they stay with her. The nanny would look after them when their mother wasn't around, especially when she went out at night to degrade herself.

Kaitlin's lower lip trembled. Tears welled in her brown eyes. In her small voice she asked, "Daddy, where are you going?"

Nathan held his sister's hand, his eyes wide, disbelieving.

Blake scowled and followed his father's movements as the packing continued. "He's leaving Mommy. For good this time."

Kaitlin pulled her hand away and ran to her father, wrapping her arms around his legs. "No, Daddy. Stay."

Nathan ran to his room to suffer in silence, as he always did.

Blake gently pried his sister from their father, who stood rigid, eyes aimed upward.

"Come with me, Kaitie. I'm sure Daddy will tell us goodbye before he leaves. C'mon. I'll let you play on my computer."

Eyes and nose leaking, Kaitlin took her brother's hand and let him lead her away. In the doorway, she turned.

Starks, straining to keep his expression impassive, watched her. Her small mouth formed a silent "Daddy."

Until that moment, Starks had believed he knew what a broken heart felt like.

He'd been wrong.

CHAPTER 71

THE DOOR TO Starks's hospital room opened and the usual physical therapist entered smiling.

"Good morning, Mr. Starks. Time for you to show me your stuff."

Starks stepped onto the floor. "I've been practicing the exercises on my own."

"You've done a good job. Came a long way since we started."

During the next forty-five minutes, the therapist focused on every flex and extension of each of his patient's limbs.

"Perfect score, Mr. Starks. You've reached maximal medical improvement."

"Great. What does it mean?"

"You're done with therapy."

"What's next?"

No longer smiling, the therapist said, "You'll be released soon."

"I see." Starks held out his hand. "Thanks for everything, and for your encouragement."

"I wish circumstances were different for you."

"Circumstances can always be changed, one way or another."

That afternoon, the nurse on duty came in to check his vital signs.

"How am I doing?" he asked her.

"You're back in good working order. In fact," she glanced at him, "you're being released tomorrow."

Starks slumped back. "It had to happen sometime. I appreciate all you and everyone here did for me. One thing: Would you do me a favor? It's important."

"If I can."

"There's a nurse in the trauma unit—Ana Ramirez. She was especially kind to me during those rough first weeks. Would you let her know I'm leaving? Ask her to take a few minutes to drop in to say goodbye? I want to thank her."

"I can do that."

"How do I get back . . . to Sands, I mean?"

"The prison van will pick you up. They said to have you ready around one o'clock."

"Any chance I can have lunch before I leave?"

"Food's that bad?"

"You have no idea." He laughed. "Please ask Ana to come by before then, okay?"

"I'll get a message to her. But I can't guarantee anything."

"My beliefs about what's guaranteed in life have changed."

Sunshine filtered through the security glass of the high small window in Starks's hospital room. The sky was cloudless.

He pushed the tray table away, having eaten every bite of breakfast. *Like a last meal.*

At nine o'clock, Ana Ramirez knocked, called his name from the doorway then came all the way into the room.

"Mr. Starks, you look healthy, and strong."

"I feel pretty good. Especially now that I see your lovely face."

Ana blushed and studied her shoes.

A quick glance in the mirror across the room from him reflected mussed hair and stubble. "I didn't know if you'd come or not. Sorry I'm not more presentable."

"Don't worry about that. I'm sure I don't look so good myself. I'm just off my shift. Dropped by before I go home and get some sleep."

"Even after working all night you look better than I do."

"Flattery and charm."

"If we'd met years ago, you'd have been the only woman in my life."

"I would've considered myself fortunate."

"When's your birthday?"

"Why?"

"Humor me. Please."

"July 24."

"What year?"

"I'm thirty-three. Why do you want to know?"

"I promise my intentions are honorable. You're a respectable woman, Ana. And I want to do something to thank you for all you did, and for your kindness."

"There's no need to do anything. Just did what I was supposed to." She checked her watch.

"You need to leave."

"Sorry I can't stay longer. I'm back on shift tonight. I have errands to run and I need to sleep."

"Is it okay if I give you a hug?"

"It's not allowed, because . . ."

"I won't tell if you won't. It'll be the only hug I've had for a while. The only one I'll have for a very long time."

Ana leaned over, giving him a solid hug, though not a lingering one.

"I wish you the best." She knocked for the door to be unlocked then waved before pulling the door closed behind her.

Starks had showered the night before and didn't feel like shaving. He put on the blue scrubs the hospital had provided for him. The yellow scrubs he'd arrived in, he'd learned, had been bagged and returned to the prison as evidence, along with his shoes. He slipped the skid-proof socks on that all patients received and waited.

And he put his mind to work.

CHAPTER 72

"STRIP."

"Seriously? You guys just hauled me here from the hospital. I was searched before I could leave my room."

"Gotta follow procedure."

Starks huffed, and with compressed lips, removed all garments, revealing multiple ruby scars puckering his skin.

Officer Roberts whistled low at the sight. Other guards in the area stared and murmured comments.

Starks held his arms straight out to the side and turned in a slow circle. "Go ahead," he said. "Get an eyeful."

Roberts said to the gawkers, "Show's over." To Starks, he said with less of a bite to his tone, "Bend over."

"Do you understand that's going to hurt like hell? Do you care?"

"Gotta do it."

Starks bent over slowly, sucking in his breath from the pain. He rested his hands on his knees and cursed when a gloved finger was slipped inside.

"Open your mouth."

He did as instructed, fixing his gaze on the assisting CO who used a small flashlight to look inside his mouth.

"He's clean."

The guard pointed to a nearby metal table. "New scrubs. New shoes. Get dressed."

"No disinfecting shower?"

"Not this time."

Roberts went along the built-in shelves that lined one wall and pulled out bedding, a pillow, extra scrubs, and toiletries from various shelves, stacking these in Starks's arms to carry. He motioned for Jakes to join them, told him which cell to escort their prisoner to.

The last thing handed to Starks was a small box. It contained his few personal items that someone had packed after he'd been sent to the hospital.

"Officer Jakes will take you to your new cell."

Starks wasn't as yet out of earshot when he heard one of the other guards say, "Don't think he'll be going shirtless at the beach when he gets out. That's a lot of scars, man."

Roberts replied, "Tip of the iceberg. You can bet the real damage goes deeper."

CHAPTER 73

I T WAS A different cell in a different block, and it came with a different cellmate.

Jakes motioned for Starks to go in but stayed outside. "I'll let you introduce yourselves," he said then left.

The inmate was African-American, and looked to be around forty, but Starks had never been good at guessing people's ages. The man was reading a real book, not a comic book, which Starks hoped was a good sign.

He studied Starks for a moment then grinned. "Name's Ronald Jackson. I know who you are. Nearly everyone here does."

"I don't give a fuck."

"Just saying."

Starks stared at the empty upper bunk, debating whether or not to ask for or insist on the lower one. Every movement still brought pain. The idea of having to climb up and down to get into and out of bed didn't appeal to him. The idea of letting anyone know how weakened his condition still was appealed even less. Plus, the P.T. guy had explained that normal range of motion, along with the exercises he'd learned, might hurt but would help get rid of the stiffness in the mended tissues and skin, as long as he didn't overdo it. As he'd told Demory, he wasn't going to use the prescription for painkillers, unless there was no other choice and only at night when he was locked in his cell.

Starks used the chair to stand on to pile everything in his arms on the upper bunk then climbed up. He stacked his extra clothing on the shelf mounted to the wall, made his bed then eased onto his back, hoping his cellmate would go back to reading so he could catch a nap. Exhaustion was setting in, and he wanted to escape the pain for a while.

"I'm a mentalist," Jackson said. This got no response. "What's that, you didn't ask? I'm like a magician. I read minds."

"I'm not in the mood."

"Check it out." Jackson hopped up and grabbed the deck of cards on the table next to his bed. Fanning the cards face-down in his hand, he said, "Pick a card."

"Leave me alone."

"Let me just show you . . ." He shuffled the cards several times then pulled a card from the deck, looked at it then showed it to Starks.

"Queen of Hearts, right? That's what you picked, isn't it?"

Starks fixed his gaze on the card, the card he'd thought of, even though he hadn't meant to. "Don't make me tell you again to leave me alone."

"I was right, though. Wasn't I?"

Starks turned on his side and looked out his part of the window.

Jackson stayed where he was. "That's why I'm in here. Used my talent to trick people out of their money."

"Good for you."

"Started playing for bigger stakes with . . . certain people. Just tricked the wrong person."

"I'm not interested. And you're not listening."

"I get it. You have trust issues. Who wouldn't, right? I mean, your wife cheated on you. People close to you betrayed you. Your last cellmate was a piece of work. And . . . ha! You really like that nurse that took care of you."

Starks rolled over and said, "Who the hell's feeding you information?"

Jackson held his hands up and backed up a few feet. "I told you. I'm a mentalist. We don't reveal our secrets."

Starks moved to get down from his bunk, but stayed where he was when Jackson said, "Hey, for you, I'll make an exception."

He used his right forefinger to tick off fingers on his left hand as he spoke.

"First, your story was all over the news, including how your wife's cheating made you go after that guy. Yeah, some of us in here read. Not smart how you did it, though—you got caught. But, attaboy. Second, there are very few secrets in this place. Third, you attacked Big Bo. That was big fucking news. Fourth, despite the code of silence and the crowd ploy they used, security videos showed Weasel was the one who attacked you. After that," he shrugged, "too many bodies to see who was doing what. He was the only one they could pin anything on. He's a blabbermouth, which is how I learned a few other things about you before the shit hit the chow hall fan. Nobody in here keeps their trap shut when they're under Big Bo's thumb or if they think knowing stuff will put them in good with others. And in case you're interested, Weasel's been in isolation since that day." He laughed. "On a diet of nutraloaf."

"They went too easy on him."

"And, fifth," he pressed his finger to his thumb, "you think I'm gonna betray you, too. Wanna know why?"

"Enlighten me."

"You'd be a fool not to think that. Not after all that went down."

"Glad we got that settled. Now, leave me alone."

"No problemo." Jackson crawled into his bunk, picked up his book and waited.

"How'd you know about the nurse?"

Jackson chuckled and got back up. "I have a sensitive nose. Her scent is still on you. Not strong, but there. Only one place that happened and it wasn't here. You see," Jackson continued, "that's why men are seldom good at cheating. They forget how a woman's scent clings to skin."

He aimed a forefinger at his temple. "They don't think with this head." He pointed to his crotch. "They think with this one."

Starks shrugged. "Parlor tricks."

"Okay. What about this? Close your eyes and think back."

"You can forget closing my eyes."

"Then just stare at a point on the ceiling."

"If it'll get you to shut up. Fine. I'm staring."

"That test you took in school . . . remember how disappointed you were when you got that low score?"

"There was only one low score ever. How'd you know about that?"

"I didn't. I made a general statement. Who doesn't get at least one low or bad grade in his life, right? That's called misdirection. Phony psychics use it all the time. There's all kinds of general statements you can make to get people talking. Listen," Jackson continued, "it's about being observant. It's about watching facial expressions, mannerisms, body language, reactions. Do that and you learn how to read people without them realizing you're doing it."

"That's a handy skill. Now tell me about the card trick."

"If I told you, I'd have to kill you." Jackson laughed.

Starks didn't.

"Sorry, man. Wrong choice of words." Jackson kicked at his bunk. "All that card trick is, is another form of misdirection. Misdirection is what life's based on."

"I don't follow."

"You went to school to become an engineer, right?" Starks nodded. "People wanted you to focus on good grades and everything that goes with that, and you did. But the real focus was always on what comes later: money, prestige, rewards. You follow?"

"Not really."

"What do you call an engineering major who graduated last in his class?"

"A failure."

Jackson laughed. "Nah, man. You call him an engineer. He gets his degree and people think they're hiring one kind of engineer, when they're hiring another kind. Misdirection. It wears all kinds of masks."

"You make it sound like there's a thread of logic in there, but I'm not up to pulling that thread to see where it leads. I need to rest. I'd appreciate it if you'd stop talking."

"One last thing. I think you're a man who knows how to settle a score. I know you don't trust me—probably won't trust anyone in here ever again—but it's just possible, when you're ready, that I can help you settle that score." Jackson scratched at his scalp. "I was one happy dude when I heard we'd be sharing a cell."

Starks hesitated a moment then said, "Whatever."

Starks clasped his hands behind his head on the pillow.

Jackson had mentioned trust several times to him. It seemed like every time he trusted someone, they betrayed him. Eventually. Jeffrey was the only person who'd never done that or given him a reason to doubt him. And in here, Demory was the only person he could trust, though he preferred to remain a bit cautious about that, as well. The counselor was nice and all, but he was on their payroll, not his.

He rolled over, punched his pillow into shape.

Jackson was right about his intention to settle the score. If he didn't, he'd either be killed a lot sooner than later or become a repeat victim in this place. A bit over fourteen more years in that role wasn't going to happen.

Frederick Starks might get knocked down but he doesn't stay down.

Not as long as he can still get up.

It was time for a new Starks to emerge. One more focused on winning, as he'd been before coming here. How to accomplish this still needed to be figured out, but he was good at that.

Bo or Lawson, or some other gang member, would go after him again. He was as certain of that as he was that his scars would never disappear. It probably didn't look good on their *resumes* that after all they'd done to him, he'd survived.

Jackson had demonstrated some skills it would benefit him to learn.

The big question was this: was Jackson just another one of Bo's hired help?

He made a point of not changing his shirt where Jackson could see his scars. He wasn't ready for that yet. Soon, he'd have to hit the shower. He wasn't ready for that yet, either. Sponge-baths would have to do. It wasn't just the idea of being gawked at, it was how vulnerable he'd feel— still felt—without protection in the shower. Something had to be done about that, as soon as he figured out what to do. His shank was long gone. Getting a new weapon would be nearly impossible.

He could hear his grandfather telling him, "Choose your weapons carefully, Freddy. Use your imagination."

CHAPTER 74

STARKS IGNORED WHISPERS and stares as he waited his turn for a phone.

He tried not to fidget like the anxious man he was, even though his muscles tightened and his scars throbbed and itched. After ten minutes he was finally able to hear the voice of the person he most wanted to talk to.

Jeffrey let out a *whoop*. "Welcome back to the land of the living. How the hell are you, bro?"

"Better than I was. Guess I'm not that easy to kill."

"Man, when I heard you were dead—"

"Wait. You what?"

"Yeah. Demory called me with the news. Everyone freaked and—"

"Christ. He didn't tell me that. Wait until I see him again."

"He fucked up, for sure, but don't be too hard on him. That's what he was told, like a few seconds before finding out his kid needed emergency surgery. Soon as he heard you were actually in a coma, he called everyone and made it right. Well, as right as he could."

"My family. My kids! Crap. They had to be scared. Are they okay?"

"All good. Worried about you. Everyone wants to visit, including Kayla."

"As far as for Kayla, tell her I said no. Regarding my family: Not yet. You can tell them I called and that I'm well. For now, at least."

"What's that 'for now' business?"

"I know who attacked me and who was behind the set-up. I don't think they're going to crawl into a dark corner and leave me alone."

"They're not still walking around, are they? You reported them, right?"

"Not how it's done here."

"What're you gonna do?"

"You were working on getting Lewis Mason approved to see me."

"Roadblock, because he's an ex-con. Not that they don't allow ex-cons to visit. But then the attack on you happened and a big red stop-sign went up."

"That's unfortunate but not insurmountable. See if you can meet with him. Tonight, if you can. Get him to tell you what he did to protect himself while he was in prison. Anything he can suggest will help, even if he thinks it won't. Then visit me as soon as possible."

"I'm on it."

"One more thing. Ana Ramirez was one of my trauma nurses at Grace. She went out of her way to be more than nice to me." He gave Jeffrey the details he'd gathered from her. "Get Jim to investigate what went on when they were married and what's going on with her now. Tell him there's a bonus of a grand if he can get it done before you come here."

"What's this about?"

"I take care of people who take care of me."

"You always did."

Starks ended the call then turned to head back to his cell. It was unsettling to have to wait longer than he liked for information and action. He'd always delegated whatever tasks he could or should, and staff learned quickly that it paid to deliver what he'd requested sooner than later.

Caution would have to be his watchword until Jeffrey came to see him.

* * *

"Breakfast sucked," Jackson said when he entered the cell, "but you gotta eat something."

"Chow hall left a bad taste in my mouth," Starks replied.

"Then get your ass to the commissary. I get why you don't want to go near the chow hall, but you're gonna have to do it sooner or later or people here gonna think you're easy pickings."

Jackson opened one of his books then closed it. "Heard something you may be interested in."

"I doubt that."

"Really interested in."

Starks sighed and turned his face away so Jackson wouldn't see him grimace as he plopped into his chair. It cost him to move that way, but the cost would be higher if word got out that he wasn't as healed as he looked.

"Word is Big Bo's scared."

"Of?"

"You, man. He knows you're back and he's afraid."

"You're full of it."

"That's the scoop."

"Why are you so interested in my Bo problem?"

"I hate that bastard."

"Get in line."

"I know how it sounds, but Bo's scared. He's sure you're going to go after him."

Starks stayed silent.

"Well, are you?"

The call for the count came over the loud-speaker. Sounds of shoe soles slapping against concrete, books and papers being put away, and toilets flushing filled the wide corridor as inmates started lining up.

Starks saw and felt inmates on his block glancing his way, though no one said a word. Maybe that was a good thing, maybe it wasn't.

Time would tell.

* * *

Silence erupted as soon as Starks entered the chow hall for lunch.

He appeared calm as he took his tray but he was on full alert, not that he believed anything would be tried so soon, and not with four guards paying better attention than they had previously. Still, he made sure his facial expression let those in front of and behind him know they were to keep their distance. He noticed that Jackson had lost his place directly behind him, which did happen when inmates moved to get in line, but it caused him to fight suspicions that wanted to surface.

He didn't doubt that some new plan was in the works by Bo and his followers, especially once word had gotten out after the attack—and it was sure to have gotten out—that he was not dead but recovering in the hospital and would be back.

And now he was.

Tray in hand, he went to the farthest table, the one closest to the door. No one was sitting at it yet. He took a seat at the end of the bench, also near the door, and faced in, where he could watch everything and everyone.

Lawson, according to Jackson, was still in isolation, so that's where he'd get his meals. And he hoped it was true that the Weasel was fed nothing but nutraloaf. He deserved it.

Bo and his bunch were absent from the chow hall. Maybe Jackson would have information about why they weren't at their usual table at the usual time. For now, it was a temporary reprieve.

No one sat near Starks. Jackson had hesitated before sitting down midway in the rectangular room, his indecision about whether to join his new cellmate or not evident on his face for only a moment.

Inmates facing Starks's direction couldn't help but stare briefly before looking away. Others initially turned to have a quick look at him then turned back to their trays.

Starks ate with moderate speed. Grateful the experience was uneventful he turned his tray in and returned to his cell, where he pondered one payback scenario after another, ditching each one in turn as their flaws became evident.

He was sure there had to be a way.

CHAPTER 75

C O TED LANDERS entered the cell smiling.

"Mr. Starks, you okay?"

Starks sat up in his bunk and grinned. "Good enough. What about you, Ted?"

The guard patted his stomach. "Except for my not-so-little middle, I'm still in pretty good shape."

Ted stretched his arm up and handed over a note that read *Jeffrey— call ASAP*.

"Thanks. I'll call him now. I'm just glad you didn't tell me they were holding a caller on the phone for me at the guard's desk."

A puzzled expression crossed Ted's face. "We never do that. We take a message and get it to the inmate."

"That sick ruse was played on me shortly before the attack." Starks stopped himself just short of revealing why he'd been tricked out of his cell.

"I didn't know. Sorry about what happened." Ted stared at his feet. "I was the first one to reach you that day."

"You must have done something right because here I am."

"All I did was a lot of hollering and cursing. I used my shirt to try to stop the bleeding. There was so much . . ." Ted looked up. "Sorry. You don't need to hear that. Sure you're okay?"

"Stronger than I was before."

"I'll walk with you to the phones. Make sure no one tries anything. Whenever I'm on duty, I'll check on you. Offer whatever protection I can."

Starks jumped off the bunk with his back to the guard to hide the fact the act rendered the pain nearly intolerable. He adjusted his expression and turned around.

"Ready when you are."

They walked in silence for a moment then Starks said, "I appreciate you offering protection, but I don't want you to compromise yourself."

"Let me worry about that. I've been at this prison a while. There's lots of shit going down. Always is. In the short time I have left here, I'll do what I can."

"You're leaving? When? Why?"

"Two weeks. I can't afford to work here anymore. My wife and I have twins. My mother took care of them while we worked. Couldn't afford childcare, even with my wife working full-time and part-time. My wife . . ." He cleared his throat. "My wife was diagnosed with cancer last year. She kept working while getting treatment. Then my mother died. My wife's gotten worse. Can't work anymore. I've arranged to work two jobs so I can pay for childcare, get some help taking care of my wife, and pay on medical bills insurance isn't covering." Ted stopped walking, looked up and rocked on his feet. "I can't lose her, Mr. Starks."

"I'm truly sorry to hear this. It's obvious you and your wife are close."

"Love at first sight for both of us. My wife's got a smile I can't wait to see first thing in the morning. Smiles even with all she's going through. And," he chuckled, "she can't tell a joke right for anything. Never could. But she loves to laugh." His expression softened. "She's my best friend."

Starks started walking again but at a slow pace. "If things were different—financially, I mean, would you stay here?"

"And not work two jobs? Believe it. I hate the idea of having even less time with my wife than I do now."

"You've always treated me with respect. And, you did what you could to help me that day, so I'm going to help you." He held up the message. "I'm going make sure you and your wife are taken care of."

"I don't know what you mean."

"I've done this before, help people in real need. My friend Jeffrey will set it up so you can continue to work here. Childcare will be taken care of. So will getting someone in to take care of the house and whatever your wife needs while you're at work here, and even when you're home, if you'd like. I can't guarantee your wife's recovery, but she'll get the best medical care and other services available."

Ted's face registered surprise then his brow furrowed. "As much as I'd like to accept, I can't. I can't accept anything from inmates that might be taken as a bribe."

"That's not what's happening here. This is an opportunity you can't pass up, Ted." He fixed his gaze on the guard until the man's eyes met his. "Do this for your wife, for your children. There's no reason we can't keep this between us. We're almost to the phones. What's your decision?"

Ted paused and surveyed the area. Without looking at Starks, he said, "I have to. For her. I don't know how to thank you."

"No need to thank me. I always return favors and kindnesses."

All the phones were in use as they approached, but an inmate ended his call soon after. No other inmates waited a turn.

Starks positioned himself at the phone then said, "I'll tell Jeffrey what to do for you. I'll set it up, but call him anyway, so he knows how to contact you." He looked around. "Call him at Tandem Enterprises, but not from here. Never from here."

"I understand."

"You don't have to stay with me."

"I'll wait over there and walk you back to your cell. At least this time, since I'm here."

"I won't be long."

Ted went to the observation desk and struck up a conversation with the guard encompassed behind bullet-proof glass, while Starks waited for the operator to complete his call.

"Jeffrey, any news?"

"Lewis Mason understands the urgency. Says he'll have something for me to give to you, but his team has to get it ready."

"That's not exactly what I asked for but—"

"He went on and on about how he's not a brilliant chemist for nothing, and that you're going to owe him big-time."

"I'll set him straight about what I owe him later. Any idea what he's cooking up?"

"Said he'd explain when he sees me. I'm approved for a visit tomorrow. Lewis said he'll have his creation ready tonight. Not sure how I can give it to you if we're separated by glass."

"We won't be. That was the arrangement then because I was in isolation. Now that I'm in general population, I get to meet with you in the visitation room. We just have to be careful about how you pass anything to me."

"They'll search me before they let me in. I'll figure something out, as soon as I know what to figure out."

"Really appreciate it, buddy. If I owe anyone, it's you."

"You don't owe me, bro. The day you made me a partner changed my life. I was heading down a bleak financial vortex. You saved my ass. Did it in a way that saved my self-respect."

"You're my best friend. That's what friends do."

He heard Ted laugh and turned to glance his way. "There's something else I need you to do."

"Name it."

"Ted Landers. He's a guard here who's treated me right, especially when I was attacked."

Starks explained what was going on and what he wanted Jeffrey to take care of.

"What about Ana Ramirez?" he asked. "Did Jim get anything on her?"

"I'll give you the scoop when I see you tomorrow."

"Looking forward to it. Jeffrey . . . thanks."

"I'm grateful you put me in a position to be able to do it all."

"Can't wait to see what Lewis has up his sleeve."

"With him, there's no telling."

* * *

"For crying out loud, Jackson, turn off that damn light and go to bed," Starks said. Instead of a click, he heard another page being turned.

"It's a tiny light clipped to my book. It can't possibly bother you up there."

"I can hear the pages turning."

"I'll try to turn more quietly. Reading is fundamental."

"All you do is read."

"You should read this one when I'm done. *How to Influence the Mind*."

"Not interested."

"It pays to fill your mind with useful material."

"My mind's full enough."

Tonight it was full of images: How he and Jeffrey and sometimes a few others got together for drinks after calling it a day at the office. The well-endowed—by nature or silicone—topless cocktail waitresses who'd serve their drinks at the high-end strip clubs, and who were ready to serve Starks in other ways to get the generous tips he gave them. The ease of how his Bentley responded on the road. How parking valets at his regular hangouts rushed to assist him, eager for the hundred-dollar tips he gave them for taking care of his car.

Other images wanted to occupy space in his mind but he brushed them away, allowing himself to slip into oblivion. As he fell asleep, the sounds of pages turned below him became more like gentle, slow-motion waves touching the shore.

And in that dream place, he smiled as Kayla, dressed in the tiniest bikini she could find, splashed in the waves.

CHAPTER 76

STARKS BLOCKED THE sunlight shining directly in his eyes. "It's already morning? Damn."

Jackson yawned loud and long from his bunk. "You're in a mood. Not that that's unusual."

Starks rubbed his face hard with his hands. "I can't get that damn woman out of my head. Are the images ever going to stop?"

"The ex still disturbing your sleep with her *nightcapades?*"

"Legally, she's still my wife."

"Nothing more than a paper fallacy at this point."

Jackson shuffled to the toilet, did what was needed then prepped his toothbrush. "Same dream about her each time or different ones?" He brushed his teeth, using the mirror to watch Starks slip his scrub shirt on over his undershirt.

"They're usually different, except this brief dream does happen often, like a film clip played over and over." He paused then went on. "We were back in high school. Waiting at the bus stop. Kayla tripped and fell, but wasn't hurt. I reached for her hand to help her up, which didn't go smoothly, because we were both laughing so hard. I slipped and ended up on the grass next to her."

"Did that happen for real?"

"Yes. I don't know why that moment is significant enough to repeat as often as it does."

Jackson added water to his mouth, swished it around then spit. "I think you still have a thing for her."

Starks climbed down. "You're wrong."

"I mean it, man. Not to be nosy, but who actually cheated first? I know from the media that it wasn't lack of funds that upset the marital bliss. You're loaded."

Starks looked straight at his cellmate. "The bitch never blames herself for anything she ever did. If she'd stayed faithful—"

Jackson snickered. "You know what's funny?"

"Can I stop you from telling me?"

"Men dish it out but they can't take it. Most men will have sex with any number of women. But as soon as their girlfriend or wife does anything," he shook his hands in the air, "the balance of their universe is upset."

"Let's kill this conversation."

"Truth bites, doesn't it?"

"That's enough, Jackson."

"Chomp, chomp."

"I mean it."

Grinning, Jackson said as he slipped his shoes on, "You want it your way, fair or not."

"Stay out of my head."

* * *

"Look at this sad excuse for eggs," Starks said. "No way they came from a chicken. Stale toast hard enough to be a hockey puck and mystery meat that came from God only knows what kind of animal."

"Yeah," Jackson said. "Food like this makes you glad to wake up in the morning."

"I wouldn't feed this to a dog."

"That's what we are in here. Dogs." Fork in hand, Jackson pointed around the room. "You got your pit bulls, your Chihuahuas, your weenie dogs—"

"I get the picture."

"Hey, there's five guards here today instead of four."

Starks scanned the room, stopping when he reached a particular table. "And I think I know why." He gestured with his head. "Bo's here today."

Jackson followed the direction Starks's eyes were aimed at until he spotted Bo at his usual table.

"Yeah. And he definitely knows you're here." He leaned forward. "No worries. The guards are watching. Even Bo's too smart to do anything in here again. And I'll tell you something else. We gotta get Bo before he can get you."

"I don't know what this 'we' business is about."

"I'm in it with you, man. I told you I hate that sonofabitch."

"What are you going to do, magic man? Pull a rabbit out of your ass?"

Jackson chuckled. "Either I will or you will."

CHAPTER 77

STARKS WAS LYING on his bunk when Ted Landers came to the cell and told him he had a visitor.

"Thanks, Ted." Starks slipped on his shoes and climbed down.

"If you don't mind, I'll walk with you."

"I don't mind. How's your wife doing?"

The two men walked side-by-side and a foot apart.

Ted lowered his voice. "No change. I called your friend, though. The one waiting for you. We're meeting tonight. He said he'll handle everything from now on. All I have to do is let him know what we need and he'll see we get it. I still can't believe this is happening; that you're doing this. My wife and I are still stunned, and grateful."

"Glad I can help. I hope it makes a difference."

"It already has. Peace of mind. For both of us."

They stopped at the entrance to the visitation room.

Starks said, "I wish I could introduce you to Jeffrey, but obviously that's not a good idea. I don't know if you saw him yet but that's him in the corner, in the brown suede jacket."

Ted gave the briefest glance in that direction. "Got it. Now I gotta go."

Starks wound his way through the round vinyl tables surrounded by plastic chairs.

Jeffrey bounced up and gave his friend a brief hug.

"Bro! Glad to see you walking and talking."

"Takes more than stabbing me eleven times to keep me down."

"Eleven? Damn."

"Maybe it was an even dozen but who's counting?"

"You may not be huge, but you've always been tough. Tougher than I realized."

Jeffrey added in a low voice. "Let me sit first then you take the chair to my left." He positioned himself so his back was toward the wall. His expression became earnest. "How do you feel? You all healed up?"

"I feel good, except for the scars. They sometimes hurt like a sonofabitch."

Starks lifted his shirt and undershirt with both hands. "Look fast."

Jeffrey's mouth dropped open. "Jesus."

"Yep. Scarred for life. Literally and figuratively." He straightened his clothing. "My own fucking cellmate did it. Someone else did the head damage."

"Can anything be done to make sure nothing like this ever happens again?"

"That's the plan."

"You have to survive, bro."

Starks locked his gaze with his friend's. "I have to take out the bastards who did this. That's the only way to guarantee—as much as that's possible in here—that I continue to live, and in one piece, at least as far as my safety directly involves them."

"Mason agrees. He said he didn't think what he did would work for you, because he never had what happened to you . . . you know. That's why he wanted to whip up something special." Jeffrey glanced around the room as nonchalantly as possible. "I have it with me."

"Can't wait to find out what that means."

Jeffrey placed both of his hands on the table, palms down. Smiling, he said, "Do you see them?" He cast his eyes toward his hands then back at his friend.

Starks looked at Jeffrey then at Jeffrey's hands. "See what?"

Jeffrey spread his fingers apart. "Look again, but more closely. Just try not to be so obvious about it."

Starks placed his forearms on the table and leaned forward. "I'm looking but I don't see anything."

"You're not supposed to see anything, unless you know what to look for." He checked the guards, who were paying attention elsewhere.

Starks's eyes widened as Jeffrey used the forefingers on each hand to rub at the base of each thumb then slowly push upward: his thumbs seemed to lengthen a quarter inch.

Whispering, Jeffrey said, "Fake thumbs, bro. Made from the highest-grade latex rubber. Looks just like skin, especially with the thinner bottom edges."

"I'll be damned."

"Stop staring at them. And stop looking shocked." Jeffrey leaned forward. "They passed the search I went through before I was allowed in. Good thing our skin tone's nearly the same. No one will see them on you, either."

"They look real, all right, but what am I supposed to do with them?"

"Magicians use these for disappearing and appearing tricks. You can hide things in them, say, a small handkerchief or scarf. How Mason explained it is this: People watch what the magician misdirects them to watch. With a lot of practice, he learns how to make it a now-you-see-it-now-you-don't moment. He puts the scarf or handkerchief into his palm then gets people focused on something while he pushes the cloth into the fake thumb—or pulls it out, and, *voila!*"

"I wondered how they did that." Starks sat back, crossing his arms. "How the hell does Mason think *this* is going to help me? I don't get it."

"You're gonna love it."

Jeffrey rested his hands on the table and folded his fingers together, hiding his thumbs in his palms. It took only moments to remove the fakes and hide them in his lightly closed right hand.

"Do exactly what I tell you to do." Jeffrey leaned back. "Mason had me practice this over and over, until it was smooth. I'm going to get my handkerchief out of my left front pants pocket, unfold the handkerchief once, pretend to use it then slip the thumbs inside. When I go to return the handkerchief to my pocket, it'll drop to the floor between us. Pick it up. Carefully. Like you're grabbing a clump of something. Do your best to get the thumbs without anyone seeing. Place the handkerchief on the table so our hands don't touch then put your hands in your lap and under the table so you can slip the thumbs on. Got it?"

Starks nodded.

Jeffrey's movements went as planned. "Oops. Missed my pocket."

"I'll get it."

"Good thing I used my handkerchief before it hit the floor."

Both men laughed.

The handkerchief in Starks's right hand was placed on the table. His hands went onto his lap. A few seconds later, he rested his arms on the table, linking his hands together. "I can see the edges."

"Press down on them . . . gently and without looking like that's what you're doing. Body heat makes the latex adhere to and blend with the skin."

Starks did as instructed. His left eyebrow went up. "Tell Mason he's a genius. They're invisible." He studied the thumbs. "There's something inside these things."

"That's the other bit of magic he whipped up."

Jeffrey placed his right elbow on the table and turned his head toward his friend. "Inside each thumb is a small balloon with powder in it."

"What am I supposed to do? Blow it into someone's face? Drop it into their food or drink?"

"Just listen. The powders are not the same; by themselves, they're nothing special. You mix a small pinch of each powder together then add just enough water to moisten it into a paste. Put the paste on anything sharp. Doesn't even have to be large. You could use something as small as a sewing needle and it'd still work. Here's what you need to know. The mixture isn't toxic on its own. Blood's the catalyst for that to happen. So make damn sure you don't have any open wounds, especially on your hands, when you mix and apply this stuff. Once it mixes with the bloodstream, it's lethal shit, bro. And, it dries clear, so don't forget what you put it on. You have enough powder there to last you awhile, if you don't waste it."

"This is Mason's solution?"

"He said you have to get the guys who got you. It'll put off anyone who even considers going after you, especially once they see what would happen to them."

Jeffrey shifted in his chair. "C'mon, bro. This oughta give you some peace of mind."

"That's the second time I heard that phrase today."

Both men were silent for a moment.

Starks studied the thumbs. "You said it's lethal."

"What's even better is it takes forty-eight hours to kill once it enters the bloodstream. How fast the person loses consciousness, and doesn't ever come out, depends on body weight." Jeffrey drummed his fingers on the tabletop. "You're nowhere near when they bid adios to this life, if you can call it that."

"I just have to come up with a way to introduce it into the blood." Starks rubbed his thumbs together. "What's in the powders?"

"You really care?"

Starks shook his head.

"I didn't think so. Leave the chemicals to Mason. He knows his business."

"Okay, let's say this works. I still have to put myself in danger in order to get it into someone's system. I could be beaten to a pulp or taken out long before the mix kills the person."

Jeffrey twisted his lips in a wry smile. "Nah. That's the beauty of it. The moment this stuff gets into the blood, it causes unbearable pain. The person's too incapacitated to fight or care about fighting. You just have to act before the other person can do any damage to you. Mason said the ideal scenario is to cause some minor wound, even a pinprick, and do it with enough witnesses for word to get out that you're not taking any shit from anybody. Unless, of course, you want to keep your attack secret. But Mason said that's not the way to build a reputation."

"If it causes that much pain right away, won't I get busted? The infirmary doctor would probably run a tox screen, and then I'm S.O.L."

"Mason said it's untraceable once it enters the system. I didn't understand everything he told me, with all his techno-jargon, but the basic principle is this: Once it's in the body, it comes across like if the body's fighting a bacteria or something. Only this stuff acts super fast, and with more punch, instead of over time." Jeffrey, grinning, leaned back. "It's fucking brilliant, bro."

"Any inmate finds out I have this, they'll kill me for it."

"Nobody will know unless you tell them. What you have to do is give some thought to what you can do and how you can do it. The fake thumbs let you hide or transport the powders, in case you have to mix them in a certain place. Mason said you can use your spit if there's no water available. Long as you don't have any open skin on your thumbs, not even a ragged cuticle, you can carry the mix inside one of the thumbs. He said to carry a thumb in each pocket when you don't need or want to wear them. If there's a chance they'll be found, put your hands in your pockets and slip the thumbs on in a flash. Just remember to give the bottom edges a rub so they blend with the real thing."

"What if I'm caught with them?"

"First, don't get caught. You're a smart guy. Figure it out. Second, if you're caught, they won't see the powders because the balloons are small and the same color as the thumbs. Third, if they find the powders, they look identical. Unless they know the formula, both powders register as inactive if tested. If you're caught, come up with a damn good lie. Or, swallow the shit and pray you don't have a bleeding ulcer."

"Swallow it. Great advice, Jeffrey. Really appreciate it."

"Don't get caught."

"Can I wear them when I shower or put my hands in water?"

"It's best not to do that. Although, Mason said as long as the edges have adhered to the skin, the whole thing is waterproof. But not forever. And you have to watch not to get them caught on anything that could pull them off. Like I said, you've got some thinking to do about this."

"It's risky, but worth it. Thanks, Jeffrey. And thank Mason for me."

Jeffrey grinned and said, "I'll tell him you gave his idea two thumbs-up."

"That was sad."

Jeffrey's smile faded. "I miss being able to hang out with you, bro."

"There's a lot I miss, and some things I don't."

"Speaking of what—or who—you may or may not miss, Kayla wants to bring the kids to visit you."

"I don't want her anywhere near me. If my mother wants to bring the kids, that's different. I miss them, and her." Starks grew quiet. "I'm scared to let the kids see me in here, but at least visiting in this room should be less frightening for them than the first set-up you and I saw each other in."

"Glad you said that because your mother said she's coming, whether you want her to or not. She's eager to see you, especially after what happened. As for Kayla . . . I'll relay the message but it's out of my control."

"I decide who sees me and who doesn't."

"It's almost worth it to let her find that out on her own."

"What about Ana Rodriguez."

Jeffrey nodded. "Oh yeah. Jim verified the stuff you told me, plus a few other facts. She filed a restraining order against her husband for domestic disputes. Recently filed for bankruptcy. Car repossessed six months ago. Evicted from her apartment five months ago. She's living with her mother, which is putting a strain on all of them." He shook his head. "Her life's sucked for a while."

"She needs help. Figure out a way to give her fifty thousand."

"That's a lot of money, and tricky. But I'll figure it out. Wonder what she'll write in a thank-you note? Hey, maybe she'll ask to visit you to thank you in person." Jeffrey grinned. "Or is that your plan?"

"I'd rather she doesn't know it's from me."

Jeffrey's eyebrows went up. "All right. If that's what you want."

"It is. One more thing. It's important, so the sooner done the better."

"Name it."

"Have Jim check on my new cellmate. Ronald Jackson."

"Just being cautious, or has he done something to make you suspicious?"

"Yeah. He's nice to me. Last time someone in here was that nice to me—aside from Ted—I ended up in a coma and leaking like a sieve."

"I'll call Jim from my car and tell him he's in for another big bonus."

Starks fixed his eyes on the far wall. He rubbed his fake thumbs together and said, "I'm into giving special treats these days."

CHAPTER 78

THE WALK FROM the visitation room back to his cell was awkward as Starks fought the urge to keep his hands in his pockets but felt subconscious walking with his hands out, as though the rubbery items might at any moment glow like a neon sign with an arrow pointing where to look. Terrified the fakes would fall off he kept his thumbs pressed against his forefingers.

Jackson lay on his bed with an open book covering his face. He lowered the book and asked, "How'd your visit go?"

"Fine."

Starks started toward his bunk.

"Before you climb up, would you mind handing me the yellow highlighter on the far side of my desk? I'm too lazy to get up."

"Seriously?"

"I promise to return the favor."

Starks handed the marker to Jackson.

Jackson's eyes focused on Starks's right hand then on the left. He sat up fast; his expression became animated. "Whoa! Where'd you get the fake thumbs? What're they for?"

Starks froze in place. "I don't know what you're talking about."

"I told you I studied the magician's craft. Not as much as someone who performs professionally for a living, but enough to recognize fake thumbs when I see them."

"How—"

Jackson grabbed Starks's hands. "Someone did a beautiful job. Professional. The hand-painting is exceptional. What gave them away are the cuticles. They don't match your other ones. Whoever made these obviously didn't have a current reference, so did the best they could."

Starks yanked his hands away and backed up several inches. His breaths were rapid, his eyes wide.

Jackson held up his hands. "Don't panic. I doubt anyone here but me has this knowledge. I had a set myself that I played around with. But they weren't anything like this quality."

"I'm fucked before I even leave the gate."

Jackson pointed at the chair pushed under his desk. "Sit. You look like you're gonna keel over."

Starks pulled out the chair and sat facing his cellmate.

"Okay, Jackson, what are you going to do with this?"

"What are you gonna do with those?"

Starks didn't answer.

"Relax," Jackson said. "I'm not going to do or say anything about them." He held up his right hand then crossed his heart. "Magician's code of honor. But if this is part of your plan to get Bo, I want in."

"I'm going to have to trust you. I don't like it but I don't think I have a choice." Starks exhaled a shaky breath. "You said you could deliver Bo to me. Were you serious?"

"More than serious—committed."

"How do you plan to do that?"

Jackson moved to the edge of his bed. "I've been working on it a long time."

"You didn't answer the question."

"I'm getting there. It's about paying attention to routine, being aware of your surroundings. I pay attention to how many guards are on duty and their shift changes, as well as what creates distractions for them." He picked up his book and reclined on his bed. "There's more I could explain but it would cause you too much anxiety. You don't need that right now. Hard as it may be, trust that I have the details under control."

"That scares the shit out of me. But it's not like I have a choice."

"You're really going for Bo?"

"His is the first name on my list."

"I like it." Jackson clapped his hands together.

"What did he do to you?"

"Let's just say the bastard rubs a lot of people in here the wrong way. There are more people here who'd like to see him taken down than you might think."

"Let's talk, then."

"First, why don't you tell me *exactly* what it is you have up your thumbs?"

CHAPTER 79

TWO DAYS LATER Starks, with the thumbs in his pockets as instructed, took a seat across from Jackson in the chow hall at lunchtime. He observed how his cellmate glanced around but not in an obvious way, could practically see the man making mental notes about the environment and the people. Starks's amusement was interrupted by a conversation behind him.

"Demory? You sure?"

"That's what I heard."

"You know which inmate he did the nasty with?"

"Nah. Just one he was supposed to be treating."

"What are they gonna do to him?"

"It's done, man. He lost his license. He's out."

"I had some sessions with him when I first got here. Dude was cool."

"Got what he deserved, far as I'm concerned. Self-righteous prick."

"I didn't know you did time with him."

"Only once. I walked out on him. Told him to shove his questions up his ass."

Starks put his fork down. "I don't believe it."

Jackson's fork stopped midway to his mouth. "Don't believe what? Why are you looking like that? What's wrong?"

"Nothing. I was thinking about something. Didn't realize I said anything."

"You need to learn to control your thoughts, and your mouth. Keep your focus."

Jackson lowered his head but kept his eyes firmly on Starks's. "It's tomorrow, man."

"What is?"

"Showtime." Jackson wiggled his eyebrows up and down a few times then put the forkful of food into his mouth.

"Shit."

"Yeah. It's gonna fly."

CHAPTER 80

STARKS'S MIND REELED. The two bits of news he'd just heard had him walking back to his cell in a stupor. He didn't want to believe what he'd heard about Demory. And, Jackson wanted the attack on Bo to happen in less than twenty-four hours. It had been his intention to wait for Jim's information on his cellmate before planning or doing anything. That idea was blown, especially if Jackson insisted that tomorrow was the day.

No. He was calling the shots. Jackson would have to accept that.

Starks climbed onto his bunk, wrapped his arms around himself, clenching his hands to hide how much they shook.

Jackson, hands on his hips, stared at him. "What's the matter with you?"

"Why tomorrow?"

"I thought you wanted to get the bastard."

"I do."

"Then tell me why you're looking and acting like a man who's ten minutes away from the needle."

"Maybe this doesn't have to happen. You did say Bo's too scared to attack me."

"Doesn't mean he won't get someone else to do it. I've been here five years. Believe me when I tell you that if you don't attack sooner than later, you'll live—and I use that word sarcastically—to regret it. I can see it on your face: Don't even think of backing out. Especially not after all I've done to set this up."

"What kind of set-up?"

"A damn good one. You back out now, you better use that poison on yourself. Too many people—people you don't want to piss off—are counting on this going down."

"Won't fingers point to me if I attack him now?"

"Possibly. But you're not the only person in here who'd like to deal with Bo. Listen, suspicion is not conviction. They need evidence to convict someone, and inmates ain't gonna talk. You know that."

"I know that's how it's supposed to go but this is Bo we're talking about. Some of his people may talk."

"Your opinion of Bo is too high. He's a conniving, double-crossing sonofabitch who's pissed off a lot of people. Even some of his own people. People who'd pay the price of admission to see him get what's coming to him."

"Including you."

Jackson hesitated then said, "Especially me. And before you ask again, my why isn't important. My commitment is."

"It would help a lot if you'd tell me what he did to you so I understand why you want to get him back."

"Maybe one day. For now," he reached up and used a forefinger to tap Starks's forehead, "stay focused. Let me give you all the details. I'm sure that'll help you see why this is gonna work."

"You have to promise something."

Jackson narrowed his eyes. "What?"

"If this is successful, you have to tell me what he did to you."

Jackson scrubbed at his face with his hands. "Jesus. Sure. Back to business. The four guards who'll be on duty in the chow hall tomorrow are not in Bo's pocket. There's a problem, though. That guard you talk so friendly to is one of them."

Starks's shoulders and face relaxed. "I should be able to handle that."

"How?"

"Don't worry about him."

"Wish I could be as confident about that as you. Anything you wanna share?"

"No. Go on."

"I'm gonna get it lined up so you can strike and not get caught."

"If you can do that, you are a magician."

Jackson grinned. "I'm gonna use part of his own plan against him. One of his gang will start a fight. The guys I've lined up are gonna place themselves in such a way that Bo's cut off just enough from his gang so you can do your stuff."

Starks stared at Jackson several moments before speaking. "You're telling me one of his soldiers is going to betray him? Are you out of your fucking mind? If the man said he'd do this, it's a trap. You must know that."

"You have a steep learning curve ahead of you. There really is no honor among thieves. If you think those misfits are more loyal to Bo than afraid of crossing him, you're wrong."

Starks combed his fingers through his hair. "How'd you manage that?"

"You concern yourself with the wrong things at the wrong time. What you need to concern yourself with now is that this is likely going to be the only try you get. If this nosedives, who the hell knows when you'll have another chance."

"If it fails I'll be killed."

"No maybe about it."

"There's one flaw I see in this plan: cameras and guards will see me move in."

"Ye of little faith. I have that covered."

"There's a lot I don't know about this, and it's scaring me."

Jackson's sigh sounded his frustration.

"I'll need a shank," Starks said. "Lawson used mine on me."

"Too bulky." Jackson winked. "I've got something better." He slid his hand under his mattress, feeling around until his hand found what he was searching for. "*Ta-da!*"

"What is that?"

"Child-size knitting needle—same color as the scrubs so it won't be seen. Don't ask how I got it. It's sharp enough to make your point, if you'll pardon the pun."

"Where am I supposed to hide that thing?"

"In your shirt hem. It'll go here." Jackson pointed to the left side of his shirt. "Let your arms hang at your sides so it's blocked from view. It'll work. I promise." He smiled. "It's been tested."

"I hope you're right." Starks wiped his sweating palms on his pants. "What if they search us after the attack? What am I supposed to do with the needle after?"

"I've planned a disappearing act."

CHAPTER 81

STARKS AND JACKSON positioned the chairs in their cell so they faced each other as they went over the plan several times for the next two hours.

When Jackson said they'd covered everything often enough, Starks climbed into his bunk. "I can't believe I have to do this," he said.

"You know what'll eventually happen if you don't."

"Because of that fucking woman I've destroyed my reputation, faced death, almost killed a man, and now I'm going to deliberately take a life."

"She may have been the trigger for what put you in here but what you do inside is all about you. The sooner you get that the better off you'll be. It's about power, man. In here or out there, you either let others have power over you or you have power over them. That means you gotta have power over yourself. Time to play the cards you've been dealt and make the best of it. You play blackjack?"

"You and your cards. All right, where are you going with this?"

"If you ever got dealt a sixteen, it was a shitty combination because you have to take a hit and see how it goes. What you get is all about chance, or a cheating dealer. This is your time to turn the hand you were dealt in your favor."

"Until a few years ago, I always believed I knew which direction I was heading in—to the top—and that I was in control. Then up became down and down became up. It's even more so in here."

"And look where you are."

"What do you mean?"

"You're at the top." Jackson laughed. "Top bunk. Get it?"

Starks punched his pillow and faced the wall. "Sometimes your sense of humor is goddamned annoying."

"But my assessment of people is always right. You like everything neat and tidy. And, you like to win. You have to win or you become a miserable bastard." Jackson tapped Starks's bunk. "What are you thinking?"

"I'm thinking . . . what are the odds?"

"Which odds?"

"All of them."

Jackson stretched and said he'd be back in a half hour or so.

Starks lay on his bed, staring out the window. He'd never considered himself a cold-blooded killer. Yes, he'd gone after Ozy, but that was in a fit of rage, which Ozy had incited with his comments. It was an attack he'd never intended. This was something altogether different. He'd always judged, and harshly so, people who committed acts of pre-meditated murder. It was an ugliness he'd viewed as far-removed from his nature.

This was a steep decline from the days when his primary concerns and goals were to have success, a family, a home he could be proud of, and the freedom to live his life as he chose.

But Jackson was right: This was a matter of kill or be killed. If Bo was as scared as Jackson said he was, especially since his and Lawson's attack had failed, he wasn't going to let this status quo go on much longer. Otherwise, Bo risked losing his position as leader, maybe even his life, if his gang and others saw him as weak. Already, at least one of them was willing to betray him.

Starks prayed it wasn't all a trick. Again.

CHAPTER 82

STARKS CONTINUED GOING over the plan in his mind and trying to assess possible pitfalls. His mental exercises were interrupted when Ted Landers stopped at the door.

"How're you holding up, Mr. Starks? Everything okay?"

"Things are as good as they can be in here, I suppose."

"You look like you have something on your mind."

"I need to ask you something, but I don't feel easy about it."

"Ask, and we'll see what's what."

"I need a favor. It's life or death, or I wouldn't ask."

Ted's smile faltered. "If I can help, I will."

"You know my situation here. You know my life is on the line."

"Boen Jones."

"Yes."

Ted stepped two feet into the cell and leaned against the wall, crossing his arms in front of his chest. "Go on."

"If I don't take care of it, I'll be killed for certain. You know it as well as I do."

Ted massaged the back of his neck. "We shouldn't be having this conversation. If you want me to hurt someone, I can't do that." He stood straight. "Time to get back to my rounds."

"Wait. Please. That's not what I'm asking. How about if I talk hypothetically?"

"Okay." Ted stepped out of the cell for a moment. He looked in every direction before resuming his position against the wall. "What is it?"

"Hypothetically speaking, do you have access to the cameras in the chow hall?"

Ted stared at Starks, pausing before he answered. "Every camera in here is controlled internally from one room. In order to do anything to the cameras—hypothetically speaking—the guard who'd control them on a given day would have to be involved. That would put me, and him, in a bad situation."

"Understood. Staying in the realm of theory, if I needed the ones in the chow hall to malfunction tomorrow, could it be done? Could it be done for five thousand—cash, untraceable—for each of you?"

Ted cast his eyes downward. "Payback time, is it?"

"I wouldn't do that to you." Starks leaned forward. "I'm afraid for my life. You know I have every reason to be."

Ted stayed quiet for a moment then nodded. "When and what time?"

"Breakfast tomorrow."

"I'll see what's possible. Hypothetically speaking."

"Ted . . . I know what I'm asking. I know this isn't easy for you. If you can, you can; if you can't, you can't. And if you can't, or don't want to, nothing about our arrangement will change. I need you to know that."

Ted nodded and left, nearly running into Jackson as he entered the cell.

Jackson stopped at the entrance to make sure the CO kept walking then went up to the bunks. Frowning, he said, "I heard some of that. That wasn't smart."

"Insurance is always smart."

"Insurance? You're gonna get us fucked; that's what you can be sure of. He's probably on his way to the warden right now."

"He isn't."

"You know that, how?"

"I'm more sure about that than I am about a lot of things."

"You don't get it, do you? You don't trust people in here, especially not guards. Especially not the ones who treat you nice. Even if, like Bo, you think you own a guard, you still don't trust him."

"You want me to trust you."

"I'm on your side. Listen, I adapted to this shithole long ago. You're still in training pants, man. I'm trying to help you. Your success is our success. A lot of people are counting on you. They're risking their necks for you."

Starks's knuckles turned white as he gripped the edge of the bunk. He lowered his voice and said, "In case you think you're smarter than me, let me assure you that I'm ten steps ahead of you. You don't know why I can trust that man, nor do you need to."

Jackson raised both hands in submission.

"Okay. Okay. You're a genius and I'm a schmuck. You'd be the last person who wants this to go south. I'm gonna have to trust you." He pointed toward the corridor. "And him."

CHAPTER 83

RAIN STRUCK THE window hard. Seven in the morning and it was so dark the outdoor lights were on. Jagged lines of lightning were quickly followed by cracks and rumbles. The hair on Starks's arms lifted. This storm's going to last a while, he thought.

From the bottom bunk, Jackson said, "Hey, you up?"

"I've been up."

Jackson clapped his hands once, saying, "Today's the day. How're you feeling?"

"Not as chipper as you sound."

"You focused?"

"You can shove your focus."

"You're about to perform your first magic trick—a very elaborate trick. You damn sure better be focused."

Jackson got up, went to the lavatory and filled a plastic cup with water. He returned to the bunk and handed the cup up.

"Here. Might as well play chemist now. Give the stuff time to dry."

He got the knitting needle from the slit in his mattress and handed it to Starks.

"During the night, I sharpened the point. Good, huh?"

Starks sat up. "You're full of surprises."

"I used the point to make a hole in your shirt hem. Now, do your thing. I'll watch at the door."

"You had a busy night. I didn't even hear you moving around." Starks held up the fake thumbs. "Did you tell anyone about this stuff?"

Jackson turned back and stood at the edge of the bunk. "You must be crazy if you think I'm going to let anyone know you have those" he pointed at the thumbs, "in your possession. You said you're smarter than me. Act like it."

"Jesus. You'd think it was you who had to do this."

"I'm the one orchestrating it. My ass is on the line just as much as yours. Now get a move on."

Jackson took watch at the door.

Starks used the smooth surface of the narrow window ledge to mix the powders, stirring the concoction with the needle. It took a few attempts to get the paste just right. He ran the knitting needle through the paste, turning the needle so that the mix covered the entire surface starting at the point and going up three inches. He blew on the needle until he felt certain the mixture was dry. A couple of tissues moistened with water removed any remnants of the powders from the sill.

"It's ready."

Jackson picked up Starks's scrub top and slid the needle into the hole he'd made in the hem on the left side.

Starks jumped down, going straight to the toilet to flush the tissues away.

Jackson held out Starks's shirt. "Put this on and let's make sure the needle's unnoticeable."

Starks slipped the shirt over his arms and torso then stood back. "Can you tell?"

"Not with your arms down."

"I have to hand it to you for saying the needle needed to go on that side."

"You're right-handed. It's the only place it could go."

"Like a soldier drawing his sword."

Jackson sat on his bunk to slide his feet into his shoes. "Finish getting ready. It's almost time to go."

Starks drew in a deep breath, held it then exhaled.

Jackson frowned at him. "You gotta relax, man. You look tense. Don't look tense. You'll draw attention to yourself."

Starks stood in place, shaking his arms and his legs. He rolled his head in slow circles, rotated his shoulders.

"You ready for this?" Jackson asked.

"I just hope nothing and no one screws up. Especially me."

CHAPTER 84

STARKS HAD HIS arms as loose as possible at his sides. He forced himself take slow, deep breaths and kept his eyes, wide with anxiety, cast downward all the way from the cell to the chow hall.

In line for their trays, Jackson elbowed him. "Put your fucking gameface on, man."

"You're right."

As planned, a few seats were available at the table next to Big Bo's, but at the opposite end from where Bo and his gang sat. Jackson sat on Starks's right rather than across from him.

Memory of the last time a cellmate sat to his right flashed through Starks's mind. Sweat beaded on his upper lip. He wiped the moisture off with his hand and tried to assure himself this wasn't a repeat performance. This time the weapon of choice was in his possession. Unless Jackson had something hidden on him.

Several of Bo's gang looked his way. One of them nudged Bo, who turned his head. He locked eyes with Starks. Grinning, Bo raised his right hand, fashioned like a gun, which he pretended to fire. He turned back and said something to his soldiers, which sent their small crowd into laughter.

"Okay," Jackson, looking left, said. "I just got the nod. Stay alert."

Starks felt the skin at the back of his neck tighten and his bowels try to loosen.

This is it.

He heard someone shout, "Keep your spic eyes off my tray, shitbag."

The Hispanic man at the next table replied, "What the fuck you on about, *maricon?*"

Bo's gang member stood and said, "What the fuck you call me?"

"What you are. Someone who prefers pricks. Didn't your mamacita tell you that's a one-way street?" The others at his table laughed.

"You going down, motherfucker."

Bo's gang member launched his tray at the man, causing food to fly and hit a number of inmates at the table. Everyone at both tables, except Bo, stood up.

The table where the Hispanic man sat emptied of inmates as they rushed forward. Inmates positioned around the room started toward the area, leaving those who stayed behind shaking their heads. Guards shouted and tried to move in but were blocked by more and more inmates encircling where the action was. No one was doing anything more than posturing and throwing out insults.

Jackson said into Starks's ear, "Go now. Stay low. Make it count."

Inmates created just enough space for Starks to move along their human tunnel, just as Jackson had promised. He wondered if the hands that propelled him forward, as Jackson had also promised, were in fact assisting him or speeding him toward a trap.

Hidden by the bodies, Starks reached where Bo still sat eating and laughing and believing himself immune.

Starks's hands shook so much that it took three attempts to remove the knitting needle from the shirt hem. His right elbow drew back then thrust forward; he felt the weight of extra hands helping him. The needle pierced skin in the area of Bo's right kidney. Starks saw a hand pull the needle out, but not the inmate who did it. And he saw Bo's right hand reach around to touch the spot on his back where he'd felt the jab.

Bo turned his head and saw Starks. Lips in a snarl, he stood and reached out. Some of the inmates jumped Bo. Others propelled Starks back toward his starting point. The gang member sitting to the left of Bo turned; saw his leader fall to the floor. Saw feet kicking Big Bo, who was on his side, curled into a tight ball.

"Big Bo's down," he shouted. He shouted it several times before others in his gang realized what was happening.

Four masked guards rushed into the chow hall and up to the tangle of inmates.

Starks slid onto a bench a few tables away. He watched a few inmates dump their trays then head toward the exit, which they were prevented by a CO from reaching.

Inmates closest to the action shouted, cursed, and gasped as mace was sprayed into their faces, causing their eyes to stream and noses to drip. Some inmates and guards slipped in the mess. Nightsticks were used to pummel those still standing and even some inmates writhing on the floor. Several inmates screamed, twisted, and fell to the floor as rubber bullets fired by masked guards hit them. Tasers caused others to collapse. Over the intercom the call "Red Dot" came, causing the clot of men to disperse and run.

Inmates not involved tried to leave but couldn't. The chow hall was in lockdown.

Three minutes later, every inmate stood with his hands pressed to the wall and high above his head. All except Bo, whose shouts, moans, and profanity prevented the silence demanded by the guards.

One of the additional guards removed his mask. "What the hell happened?"

No one said anything for a moment then Ted spoke. "It started as a food fight, but I couldn't swear which inmate triggered it."

The guard pointed to Bo. "What's the matter with him?"

"I don't know. He was in the middle of the fight. Couldn't see him."

"None of them is going to tell us what happened, goddamnit." The guard stood on a table. "All right, you cocksuckers. First you're gonna be searched. Anyone holding anything is in deep shit. You other bastards will go back to your cells. And you'll stay there until dinner time. All privileges revoked until then."

He turned to the guards waiting for instructions.

"Somebody get a stretcher and get that man to the infirmary. *Move. Move. Move.* I fucking *hate* days like these."

* * *

The electronic door to the cell closed and locked.

"We did it," Jackson said. "Why are you pacing?"

"We're fucked."

"What do you mean?"

"Bo saw me standing behind him."

"Crap."

"Yeah. He'll talk, if he hasn't already."

Jackson shook his head. "I don't think they'd believe him. By the time the crowd started to move to the walls, it was obvious you were sitting far enough away—like you hadn't joined in. They'll think Bo's making it up, to get you in trouble."

"Maybe."

Both men looked at each other then away. Silence filled the space.

Starks dragged himself onto his bunk. If there was any energy left in his body, he couldn't feel it.

Had he done the right thing? What if Bo did name him, and was believed? As soon as Bo died, it would be a murder charge. And life in prison.

Jackson walked to the bars and gazed out, tapping his teeth with a fingernail. He turned, went to his desk and sat in the chair. "There's a chance he'll pin it on you but I don't think that's going to happen."

"No way you can be sure about that."

"I'm pretty sure he's not gonna say shit; that's if he's even still able to talk. For all we know, he may be paying tribute to a morphine drip. You think he'd want his rep damaged by breaking the code? No way. They'd take him out. Even if he has some lucid moments, he's going to be planning how to get you once and for all. The thing is this: we know something he doesn't."

Starks turned on his side to face Jackson, who was grinning. After a brief hesitation, Starks said, "He's only got about forty-five hours to live, most of them unconscious."

"*Abra-fucking-cadabra*, man."

CHAPTER 85

IN THE CELL the next day, Jackson watched Starks as he tidied his desk for the second time in an hour.

"Know what I think?" Jackson said.

"You're the mentalist, not me."

"I think if an election was held right now, you'd be voted top man."

"What the hell are you talking about?"

"Don't you realize the coup you just pulled off?"

"I didn't do it by myself."

"True. But you did the most important part."

"Don't blow smoke up my ass, Jackson."

"I'm not blowing smoke. I'm telling you—"

From the door came, "Hey, Mr. Magician."

Starks and Jackson looked at the Hispanic inmate standing at the threshold. He motioned at Jackson with his head. Jackson got up from his chair and walked over. The inmate whispered something then left.

Jackson stayed where he was, staring into the corridor. His fists balled up. "Well, fuck."

Starks shifted forward in his chair. "What?"

"Rumor is that Bo's conscious. Someone said they saw him walking around in the yard."

Starks sat back in his hard plastic chair, linking his hands behind his head to hide how much they were shaking. "Calm down. You look like you're about to freak."

Jackson turned around. "I'd think this news would make your balls shrivel."

"You said it's a rumor, not a fact. I'm confident the stuff worked." Starks jutted his legs out in front of him. "Get a grip."

"You get a fucking grip. If it's true . . . You said he saw you. He'll include me by default, because I'm your cellmate."

"It wouldn't be just by default, though, would it?"

Jackson stomped to his desk, picked up a book and threw it against the opposite wall. "Don't be a fucking fool."

Starks launched himself from the chair then grabbed Jackson by the front of his shirt. "Don't call me a fool again. You hear me? Now calm the fuck down."

Terror that the news might be true coursed through him, but he needed to appear unafraid and in control. Otherwise, he feared, Jackson might snitch in order to save himself.

He returned to his chair. "You made me a promise. Fill it now."

Surprise caused by the statement showed on Jackson's face. "What are you talking about?"

"If I succeeded—which I did—you'd tell me what Bo did to you."

"You want to talk about *that* now?"

Starks leaned back in the chair and crossed his arms in front of his chest. "Sit down and start talking."

Jackson stared at him in disbelief then pulled up his chair, where he sat twisting his hands and wearing a pained expression.

"My first month here, Bo and four of his soldiers cornered me when I was alone in the shower. The CO making rounds in there was in Bo's pocket and left when Bo came in. Bo wanted all the money from my account. I refused. His guys moved in."

Jackson's face sank into his hands. "They shoved me against the wall and kept me there. One of them grabbed my balls and twisted. I kicked and punched and tried to get away. They beat me, the four of them, while Bo watched and laughed. Then he said, 'Give him the special.'"

"They forced me onto my stomach and held my legs apart. One of the guys dropped his pants and said, 'Four treats for you today, you little prick. Only our pricks ain't little.'" Jackson shuddered. "The only reason they didn't succeed was five members of the Hermanos came in. They hate Bo and Bo knows it. But they liked my card tricks. I amused them, like a pet.

"Bo and his four left me lying there in my blood. The Hermanos looked for the CO, but he'd made himself scarce. They wrapped a towel around me and carried me to the infirmary. It took me a month to recover. Physically, that is. After that I did favors for the Hermanos, which they expected. Still do favors for them. Over time a mutual respect formed, at least, as much as that can happen in here."

"I wondered how you got them to cooperate. But I think you're holding something back. What they did for you in the chow hall wasn't simple."

Jackson looked up. "I needed protection. And about what I had to do to get it—you can forget about me telling you that."

"I think you should tell me."

Jackson stood up, kicked his bed frame. "You're missing the goddamn point."

"What's your point?"

Their conversation was interrupted when a CO approached their cell, sliding his baton against the steel bars and walls as he neared them. Both men sat quietly and waited for him to pass. But he didn't.

The CO was Jakes and he eyed both men in turn, before saying, "Frederick Starks."

Starks said, "It's just Starks."

"Like I give a crap, asshole."

Starks glanced at Jackson and said, "No respect."

"You want respect in here," the CO said, "you can find it in the dictionary."

Starks's smile didn't travel to his eyes. "Did you want something or just dropping by for a chat?"

"You got a meeting with the counselor in three days."

Starks sat up. "With Demory?"

"You got a problem with that?"

"No. No problem."

Jakes banged his nightstick against the door then left.

What the hell was going on? If Demory was actually still employed, and seeing him in three days, that was good news. But where did the rumor come from that he'd lost his license to practice? As far as Demory having sex with an inmate . . . that was so far out of character for the man, Starks hadn't believed it for a second.

". . . are not taking this seriously, man. You have to get real about this, and fast."

Starks looked up. "What?"

"Where's your head?"

"I'm thinking about a phone call I need to make. While I'm gone, get your shit together."

"I'm together."

"Then act like it."

Starks's pace was quicker than usual as he made his way to the phones. His face contorted as he passed Crazy Rodney's cell—the man was writing on the wall with his feces again. Why the hell did they have to transfer that guy to their block?

Jeffrey answered his cell phone on the first ring, accepting the collect call.

"Bro! How are you?"

"Muddled."

"What's up?"

"I'll say more when I see you again."

"Got it. What can I do for you?"

Starks glanced around to make sure no one was in earshot. Lowering his voice, he asked, "Did Jim get anything yet on what I asked for?"

"Still digging, but here's what he has so far. Let me get my notes. Here we go. Several arrests. Tax evasion, mail and wire fraud, impersonating a federal agent, second-degree murder, and aggravated assault."

"He stayed busy."

"A real piece of work. Jim says some of the charges didn't stick. But he learned Ja—"

"*The guy.*"

"Got it. The guy tried to trick some mafia wannabes out of a big chunk of change. They went after the guy. He did what he thought was necessary."

"Did the guy snitch?"

"Kept his mouth shut. Would've gotten a lighter term if he'd spoken up. He didn't want to risk it."

"He could have snitched and made a runner. I wonder why he didn't."

"No information about that, bro."

"He said he used to perform. Jim get anything about that?"

"Yeah. He had some gigs. Is that important?"

"I was just curious to know if he was being straight about that."

"Jim said the guy was good and that most of his acts were funny. Mostly local places, but he did have a couple of shows in Vegas."

"A touch of the big-time."

"Anything else you need? Are you sure everything's okay?"

"Yes. Just watching my back. You can never be too cautious."

"What about—"

"That's something else I'll tell you when I see you. What else is going on?"

"Your mom scheduled a visit for next week, on Thursday. It'll be her, Anita, and Hank."

Starks ran a hand through his hair and sighed. "You know how I feel about that. But I won't block the visit. Gotta get a move on. Thanks again, Jeffrey."

"I got your back, bro."

CHAPTER 86

"HEADS UP." STARKS tossed a packaged sweet roll to Jackson. "Maybe we should eat breakfast in here this morning."

Jackson yawned and sat up. "Wrong move to make. We gotta show our faces. You, in particular. Besides, I want to get the latest on Bo."

"You can do that without me."

"Get your ass up and go with me so people don't think you're hiding out. You gotta show your face, as well as not make the guards suspicious."

Starks slipped on a set of scrubs, followed by his shoes, slid the needle into the hem and a fake thumb into each pocket. "Nothing's ever simple here."

"Nothing's simple anywhere. And hold your head up. None of that staring at the floor thing you do when you're antsy."

Ten minutes later they took a seat at a table with several other inmates. Starks glanced around, his expression impassive, before focusing on the food.

"Breakfast is crap," he said.

"See. Some things are simple in here," Jackson replied.

"No amount of salt and pepper can make this shit easier to eat." Starks dropped his fork into the food. "I can't eat this. I'm going back to the cell."

Starks lifted his fist to knock on the table as he started to stand but was stopped when an inmate sat next to him and said, "Sit down."

The inmate kept his head lowered. "You-know-who puked his guts out all that first night, ran a fever so high they iced him down. They thought he had some kind of nasty virus. Then he went to sleep."

Jackson asked, "What are you saying?"

"Bo's dead."

Starks's gaze met Jackson's.

Jackson winked and sang soft so only those closest could hear, "Ding-dong, the dick is dead."

"Meet me in the cell in two hours," Starks told him.

He knocked on the table as he got up then dumped his full tray. On the way out, he passed the table where three Hermanos from his block were sitting. Each of them gave a subtle nod of their heads.

He returned the nods and wondered if their attention was a good thing or the opposite.

Starks kept checking over his shoulder, as well as scanning the face of every inmate and guard. This was as much about keeping an eye out for any of Bo's soldiers who might try to approach him as it was to make certain his small contingent of Hermanos were sticking with him. The guys who'd nodded at him in the chow hall kept their distance but made it evident they were watching his back.

He needed something to do, something that would take his mind off matters for a while. The first thing that came to mind was the commissary, where he filled three bags with foods and other essential items. He made sure his followers were still with him then headed for the library, indicating to the Hermanos that they should follow him inside. He placed the bags on a table, nodded at the bags then walked off. Once he was at the back of the room, he turned to see them going through the bags. All three men were smiling.

The library was a decent size and seemed to have a fair collection of books, magazines, and newspapers. He watched one inmate close the book he'd been reading then leave the library. Starks waited a few moments for the inmate to return but he didn't. He picked up the book, checking the label for the filing number, found the shelf where it belonged, and put the book in its correct place. Several other books were shelved out of order, which he corrected.

An inmate approached him. "You don't work here."

Starks faced the man. "So what?"

"Looks like you know what you're doing. There's a work assignment just opened up, if you want it."

Starks glanced around. "I wouldn't mind working here. This place looks like it could use some organization."

"Set it up. Start as soon as you can; I need the help. Name's Sam Carson. I'm like the head librarian or something."

Starks nodded. "Starks."

"Know who you are."

"Then I'll see you soon. Hopefully tomorrow."

CHAPTER 87

"WE DID IT," Jackson said, when he bounded into the cell.

Starks leaned back in his chair, blew out a deep breath and crossed his arms. His expression went blank and stayed like that for several moments.

Jackson slapped him on the arm. "Time to celebrate, man. Why are you looking like that?"

"I'm thinking about life."

"As in life in prison?"

"As in I can't believe this is my life."

Jackson pulled his chair around. "It is what it is. Shake it off. C'mon, you saved your life and probably the lives of who knows how many others Bo had in his sights."

"Still . . ."

"Face it, Starks, some people need killing."

"Still doesn't sit well with me."

"Sit well or not, some people don't give you a choice. That's the crack Bo put you in. You had to get out of there or get buried."

"On the count" was shouted over the intercom.

Starks groaned but got up and went to the door of the cell, followed closely by Jackson.

CO Simmons made his way through the block, pausing to hand out mail to inmates. "Starks, mail."

"Wonder who it's from," Starks said as the envelope was handed over.

"Maybe Santa Claus is writing to *you* this year."

"Nothing like a CO who's funny," he replied.

Starks read the front of the envelope as he went back to his chair. He stayed standing. "It's open."

Jackson nodded. "You're surprised?"

"Never got mail before."

"All this time and this is your first?"

"They read it?"

"There's no privacy in this shithole. You know that."

"I thought it was a federal offense to open and read someone's mail. Especially from someone's wife."

"Not in here. Use your head."

Starks unfolded the letter and started to read. He collapsed against the wall and slid down.

"Bad news, Starks?"

He folded the letter and slipped it back into the envelope. "That bitch." Face flushed, his brows knitted together, he ripped the letter in half and threw it onto his desk. "Fuck it. It's over."

This time, Jackson didn't need to be told to stay quiet.

CHAPTER 88

OFFICER JAKES STRUCK the cell bars with his nightstick. "Starks, get your ass up and follow me."

He wasn't supposed to see Demory until tomorrow. But he was eager to find out if there was any substance to the rumors about the counselor. He also wanted to talk about Kayla's letter announcing he'd soon be served with divorce papers.

Jakes said, "You're looking pretty happy for a guy who's gotta face the council."

Starks stopped smiling. "The council? Why?"

"Did you go stupid during the night? Let's go."

Starks glanced at Jackson then back at the CO.

Jackson said, "I'll be here when you get back."

"Don't hold your breath while you wait," the CO told him.

"And you," he said to Starks, "get the pleasure of my company as I escort you to Spencer's office."

Tony Spencer was scribbling something on a tablet when Starks arrived. He gave a brief glance up then back at what he was writing. "Sit down, Mr. Starks."

The same additional four men present his first time in front of the council were seated at the table in their exact places as before.

Spencer put his pen down. He leaned back, his gaze fixed on Starks. "You're aware of recent events, of course."

"Which events?" Starks kept his expression blank.

"That's how you want to play it?"

"I'm not playing at anything."

"C'mon, Starks. You know I'm talking about the attack on Boen Jones."

"I'm aware of the attack."

Spencer aimed his pen at Starks. "You were there."

"So were a lot of guys. I was nowhere near him."

"I think you did it."

Starks fought the sudden nausea that threatened to sabotage him and said, "You can think whatever you want. Doesn't make you right."

He rested against the chair back, splaying his legs out in front of him. "I'm not sure what your game is, Mr. Spencer. All you have to do is check the video. That's the purpose of the cameras, right?"

Spencer cleared his throat and shuffled papers. "You don't tell us what to do." He smoothed his tie down. "Why don't you tell us what you know about the attack."

"I don't know anything. I was eating breakfast then all hell broke loose. When it didn't stop, I got out of the way."

"What if I say I have a witness saying you're responsible for the attack and subsequent death of Boen Jones?"

"I'd say either you're lying or that person is. I had nothing to do with it."

Spencer tapped his pen on the table. "I'm going to get to the bottom of this. The person responsible will suffer the consequences."

"Good luck with that."

"Too many of you think you're so goddamn smart. Get the hell out of my office."

Starks didn't hesitate. His knees shook so he started walking—fast. At the end of the corridor were two Hermanos he recognized. He passed them; nods were exchanged. All the way back to his cell, inmates glanced his way. Some gave him subtle nods, others stared then looked away.

Jackson jumped up when Starks entered the cell. "What was that about?"

"Smoke and mirrors. Trying to scare me into confessing or snitching."

"What did the council say?"

"Tony Spencer did all the talking. Asked me what I'd say if he told me a witness said I killed Bo."

"Shit. What did you say?"

"That someone was lying. Told him to check the tapes."

"And?"

"I think my man came through for me."

A wide smile broke across Jackson's face. "You're the man!" He raised his hand for a high-five, which Starks ignored.

Starks put a foot on the edge of Jackson's bunk, hoisting himself onto his own bed. He'd gone head-to-head with surly opponents in business dealings, but his actual life had never depended on his staying in control before. Despite how his insides had quivered these last few days, on the outside he appeared collected. It was a façade but an important one, one that although exhausting was gradually becoming easier to maintain.

Bo had been dealt with. This wasn't to say there wouldn't be other challenges while he was in here—he was too logical to think otherwise—but his taking action against Bo seemed to be working in his favor. So far.

The foe he'd soon have to deal with was the one who'd borne three children with him.

CHAPTER 89

DEMORY OPENED THE file in front of him. On his notepad he jotted a reminder of what he wanted to discuss with Starks, if the inmate cooperated, that is. This reminder included asking who the distraught Cathy and Emma were; what Starks's state of mind was since he'd been stabbed; and the big one—how he felt about Bo's death. In parentheses he added, *and did he have anything to do with it.*

He tapped his pen against his lips. Retaliation was not a far-fetched idea. But from what he'd been told, something elaborate had gone down. Could Starks have coordinated that kind of attack, and when could he have planned it? He'd verified with the hospital that at no time had Starks had access to a phone, and certainly no visitors other than himself.

Demory looked up when he heard a knock on his door. "Come in."

Starks opened the door. Smiling broadly, he closed the door behind him and started toward the chair he hadn't sat in for months.

"Hi, Doc. It's good to see you again. How's your son doing?"

"He's completely healed and back to himself, like nothing ever happened. I'm wondering if the same can be said about you. You do look stronger than the last time I saw you."

"Progress happens every day, Doc."

"Take a seat. I know it's been a while but are you ready to get started with our sessions again."

"Looking forward to it."

Starks pulled his chair closer to the desk. He stared at the stack of newsletters in front of him for a few moments then began to straighten them, making sure all the edges were even.

Demory waited until Starks completed his compulsion then got comfortable in his chair. "I want to discuss how you're feeling emotionally since the attack on you, but there's something else directly related to that topic that needs to be included. Do you know what I'm referring to?"

"I'd rather be certain."

"Bo, and the fact that he died within forty-eight hours, with nothing more than a small puncture wound."

Starks said with controlled casualness, "That's what I heard, too."

Demory tilted his head to the side. "Any possibility you did more than just hear about it?"

Starks shrugged and folded his hands in his lap. "I was there but too much was going on for me to see what happened."

"How did news of his death affect you?"

"My troubles will never be over—in here or out there—but that's one part of my life that's no longer an issue."

Demory waited a few moments then said, "Let's focus on you and your close brush with death. That can change a person. Some people become more spiritual. Others become more determined about taking control over their lives and environment. I'm wondering which one of those groups you now fit into."

Starks rose and went to the row of framed certificates hung on Demory's wall. He studied the position of each, making micro-adjustments, staying silent until he returned to his chair.

"I nearly died. It sucks but that happens in here. I've adjusted to the fact that I have to watch my back . . . differently. I'm learning as I go."

He rubbed his chest and abdomen. "Some lessons are harder than others. But I'll say this about Bo's . . . absence: I like life to be tidy. I realize how difficult that is to maintain here, but any bit helps."

"And you feel his death has—"

"Gotten rid of some garbage."

"You realize someone else will take his place."

"I know."

"What will you do about that person?"

Starks smiled. "Hopefully find him an easier fellow to get along with."

Demory wrote on his tablet. "I suppose if he isn't, he'll find himself going the way of Bo."

Starks shrugged and stayed quiet.

With his head still down, Demory asked, "What you've been doing with yourself since you got back."

"I took on a work assignment in the library."

Demory looked up. "How's that going?"

"Sorry I didn't do it sooner."

"Anyone come to see you since you've returned?"

"Jeffrey. It was great to see him again." Starks faced Demory. "Speaking of Jeffrey, I understand there was a big screw-up about my being dead or not."

"I'm going to regret my part in that forever. I'd like to explain."

Starks waved him off. "Jeffrey did that. But, Doc—"

"Believe me, I know. I called everyone and apologized. It'll never make up for what happened but it was the best I could do."

"It's over. Let's move on. You'll like this. My mother and two other relatives are visiting next week. Arrangements are being made for me to see my children as well. Too bad the total number of people who can visit at one time is three. Visits with my kids will have to be staggered."

"How do you feel about seeing your children here?"

"Not great but that can't be helped. I have to get over that aversion or I'll never see them. So, yes, I'm frightened about their reactions but eager to see them."

"I think it'll be therapeutic for you. And even for them. They'll see you're all right. I know the visits with Jeffrey have been good for you. But keep in mind these family visits may be different. It's best if you don't attach too much expectation to them, especially regarding the children."

"I'm not following you."

"Don't have expectations about how the visits should go. Pay more attention to how your children act or respond than to your own feelings. That's very important with children. Any feelings you need to deal with, we'll deal with them in here."

"Sound advice. Thanks for that."

"What about Kayla? Has she asked to visit you?"

"She told Jeffrey she wants to. I told him to tell her I have the right to refuse the visit and will." Starks scratched the back of his head. "I especially don't want to see her now. I got a letter from her letting me know she's filed for divorce and that the papers will be sent here when they're ready to be signed." He shook his head. "I was beaten and stabbed but I'm managing to cope with that. What Kayla's done to me feels worse."

"As we said before, physical wounds can heal relatively quickly. That's not always the case with emotional wounds."

"That's the truth. I'm staying busy now, and that helps. But when I'm not doing something that occupies my mind or when I go to bed at night, it's as though it all happened yesterday. You'd think I'd be able to get over it by now. Maybe there's something wrong with me."

"We're each unique, Starks. Some handle emotional pain better than others. You're not weak because you're still feeling what you feel. Grief happens in stages, anger being one of the stages. Grief lasts as long as it lasts, and that's different for every individual."

"I think what gets to me most was learning she was a habitual cheater, and that she lied about it for so long."

"But you had your suspicions?"

"Yes. And there were times I checked up on her and found out she was engaged in sexual conversations with men. Lots of text messages and so forth. And telephone numbers I checked on. But I didn't want to believe it was more than that. That was bad enough. So I accepted her excuses. Including that it was girlfriends I didn't know who she was going out with at night. Her argument was that I went out, so she should be able to as well. She's lucky she didn't kill herself or someone else, considering how drunk she sometimes was when she came back in the middle of the night."

"She was right about your going out, though, and that you were with other women."

Starks began to pace. "Yes, but I'm a man. She's a wife and mother. Her behavior is supposed to be beyond reproach. She didn't respect that or me."

"Can you see why your behaviors may have triggered hers?"

Starks's pacing came to a stop. "Which do you think is worse, a man sleeping with a hundred women or a woman sleeping with a hundred men?"

"I'm pretty sure you mean your woman, not just any woman. Were you ever with a prostitute, even a professional one?"

"If you answer my question, Doc, I'll answer yours."

"We both know what your thoughts are about this, don't we?"

"We're going in circles." Starks faced Demory. "Listen, I heard about the problems you're having with your license. I don't want to intrude into your personal business, but if you need legal help, there's a guy you can call. Michael Parker. Brilliant attorney. Tell him I referred you; it'll make a difference. There was only so much he could do about this mess I got myself into, but he may be able to help you."

"I'll think about it." Demory checked his watch. "I'd like to talk about who Cathy and Emma are."

Starks got up from his chair and stretched his arms. "Another time. I'm tightening up from sitting. How about we end early today? I really need to rest. Same time next week?"

Demory recognized avoidance when he saw it but knew it was better, at least for now, to act sympathetic. "Sure. You need to take care of yourself."

He watched his patient leave the office. Starks was a hard one to reach. The man had his feet planted deep in his beliefs and it seemed he wasn't about to shake them loose any time soon.

What concerned him more was what had Starks been up to besides shelving books?

CHAPTER 90

STARKS FOUND JACKSON pacing up and down the cell, sweat dripping from his chin onto his scrub shirt.

"Thank God, Starks! You're back in one piece."

"It was just a session with Demory."

Jackson shook his head. "No, man. Bo's gang is after us, but especially *you*."

"What've you heard?"

"They're coming after us. That's the word around the yard." Jackson collapsed into his chair.

"Let them come."

"You're shitting me, right?"

Starks looked at Jackson. "Is this a matter of honor or something? Did they like Bo that much, feel that loyal to him?"

"That's not it at all. It's not because Bo's dead. It's because they don't have the same clout around here Bo did. They've lost alliances and allegiances—COs, inmates. They're seriously pissed off, man." Jackson stared at his hands, which he wrung as though trying to get something sticky off.

Starks pulled out his chair and straddled it. Facing Jackson, he smiled. "I'll prep the knitting needle and keep it with me at all times."

Jackson flung his hands up. "Great. That's you. What about me?"

"To use your words, you need to calm down so you can focus."

Jackson nodded. "Right. You're right. I gotta get my thoughts working." He pointed at Starks. "You've started a war."

"*We*. We've started a war. One you were planning before we met, remember?"

"Again, you're right." Both men stayed silent for a few moments. "If it's a war, we need an army."

Starks grinned. "So, we need to recruit some people. Let's start with the Hermanos. They protect you, and I've notice some of them watching my back as well. Set up a meeting for me."

Jackson slapped his hand against his thigh. "It doesn't work that way. It's a favor for a favor, man. They helped out in the chow hall because they owed me. You don't want to get involved with those guys."

"Too late. Set it up for tomorrow afternoon. My shift in the library ends at four. Make it after that. Don't worry about my involvement with them. Let me handle that."

"You're crazy if you think you can handle the Hermanos."

"I'll think of something."

"Man, it's like your head's up your ass, and it's too dark in there for you to see what you're doing."

Starks sighed. "Are you going to set it up or not?"

Jackson shook his head. "You're crazy. But, yeah, I'll set it up. Or try to. We can't do nothing."

The familiar sound of nightsticks striking metal bars grew louder in their corridor. Starks and Jackson watched the cell door, waiting to see what was going on. Three COs stopped at their open cell.

Ted stood in the middle of Roberts and Simmons.

In a voice just below a shout, Ted said, "Shake down. Jackson, step out of the cell so we can search you."

Jackson swallowed hard, glanced at Starks then got up.

Starks started to follow.

Roberts said, "Not you. You stay inside. Place your hands against the wall and stay there."

Outside the cell, placed where he couldn't see what was going on inside, Jackson was ordered to assume a similar position. Simmons began a pat-down while Ted stayed at the door, his focus on the corridor.

Starks watched Roberts move things around, but it was obvious the CO's effort was half-hearted, more for show than efficacy.

The guard cast a quick glance toward the door then positioned himself next to Starks, his back facing the entrance. In a low voice he said, "Name's Luke."

"And?"

"I took care of the cameras."

Starks lifted his hands away from the wall.

"Best if you don't do that, Mr. Starks."

"Got it. Thanks for handling that. You'll get paid in the next few days. Ted will arrange it, once I get it set up. Five thousand to each of you, as promised."

"Much appreciated." Roberts gave a quick glance over his shoulder then faced Starks. "So, you took Bo down. Impressive." He grinned.

"I don't know what you're talking about."

"Right. I get it. But, hey, anything you need, you let me know. And," the guard looked toward the door then back, "there are others who'd be willing to help you out. The pay's not that good here. Every extra bit helps."

Starks looked straight at the guard. "I always take care of those who take care of me."

"That's what I've been told."

A muscle in Starks's right temple twitched. "How far has that spread?"

"Just Ted, me, Simmons and a few others we know we can trust."

"I want assistance but I don't want this to get out of control. Okay. It's a deal. But I want to speak with the others."

"Not a problem. I know you're working tomorrow. I'll make sure they stop by the library in the morning."

Starks nodded.

Roberts called out, "All clear."

The COs strolled away from the cell.

Jackson entered the cell; he ran a trembling hand over his head. "What the hell was that about?"

Starks said with a knowing smile, "Turning my sixteen into a twenty-one."

"I'm not following you."

"You said we needed an army. You didn't say there were restrictions about who could be recruited."

Jackson glanced at the empty doorway then back. "Them? Son of a bitch. How'd you manage that?"

"I speak a language they understand."

CHAPTER 91

STARKS ROLLED ONTO his back. Red numerals on the clock-radio he'd recently purchased in the commissary shifted to 6:07. He hadn't slept well, despite what he considered his recent accomplishments.

He started his new morning routine early—push-ups, lunges, making sure everything on his desk and shelf was in order—and after the count had been taken, he had fifteen minutes to make it to the library for his shift, which was plenty of time. Being late, even by a few seconds, made him feel as anxious as an untidy space did.

Starks opened the wrapper of a packaged sweet roll, and ate as he started toward the library. He turned into the second corridor. One of Bo's soldiers blocked his way, the same inmate who'd mouthed "You die" what seemed a lifetime ago.

The man crossed his muscular arms in front of his chest and jutted out his chin. He flexed his arm muscles. The lion tattooed on his left arm seemed to leap forward. Glaring down at Starks he said, "We know you did Bo."

"You'd be wise to get out of my way."

The man's lips drew back over yellowed teeth. "I oughta fuck you up right here, right now."

Starks smiled. "You could try. You might even succeed." He leaned in, a hard expression in his eyes. "Either way, you'd end up like Bo. Life in here sucks, but are you really ready to kiss it goodbye?"

Surprise then fear registered on the inmate's face, followed by a scowl.

"You ain't gonna get away with killing Bo. You nothing in here, you cocky little prick."

Starks made his posture erect. "From now on, address me as Mr. Starks."

The inmate barked a laugh. "You ain't never gonna hear me call you *mister* any-fucking-thing."

"If you understood what you just said, you'd . . . Forget it. Wasting my breath."

Two guards making rounds crossed the corridor and moved toward them. One of them was Simmons, who kept eye contact with Bo's man and said, "Looking a little tense there, fellas. Move along or get sprayed."

Starks took another bite of the sweet roll and waited.

The inmate muttered, "We ain't done with you, fucker," then moved on.

Starks kept his arms at his side as he hurried to his job, desperate to keep the wet stains from his armpits out of sight.

He needed to act fast. In life, death, and trains, timing mattered.

CHAPTER 92

S TARKS STEPPED THREE feet into the library and stopped. It was as though all his organization efforts the day before had never happened. He moved through the first room, scanning the tall shelves. It would take hours to align all the book edges again. Desks were occupied and cluttered with crumpled papers that belonged in the trash receptacles being ignored.

His mother had kept their house spotless; had taught him that everything had a place where it was stored and returned to after it was used, especially books. In his own home, he'd made certain the only open shelving was in the library in his home office. Expensive closets and cupboards had been custom-built for each room, including in the children's rooms. A cluttered space meant a cluttered mind, he'd told them. They'd learned that every book, toy, or gadget had to be put away, if not once they were finished with it, before they went to bed.

The eight computers in the library had inmates seated at each; some of the desktops bore still-wet rings of coffee and soda, as well as what was intended as breakfast, next to opened books. He fought the urge to shout at the inmates, to order them to keep everything clean and organized.

Instead, he turned and went into the small room at the back, where only authorized staff was allowed. He stood behind the metal desk bolted to the floor and gazed through the partition of safety glass, noting fingerprints and palm prints that needed to be cleaned from its surface.

Starks pressed the button to turn on the computer on the desk and thought about the right words for notices he'd decided to tape up around the library, informing inmates how the library and its contents were to be treated from now on. Conversation in the next room grew softer then halted. He looked up. Two guards were heading his way. He sat back in his chair, watching and waiting.

Jakes and Simmons entered the office, closing the door behind them. Starks fought back a satisfied smile. Roberts had told him Simmons was in on it; the CO was okay enough. Jakes, on the other hand, had given him shit at every opportunity. The tide was turning.

Jakes rested his hands on his hips. "Luke Roberts said we should come by; that you'd know why. You're the guy took down Bo, right?"

Starks snickered. "I understand why people assume that but they're wrong. I had nothing to do with it."

Jakes winked and pointed a finger like a pistol at Starks. "I hear ya. Okay, the way this works is you need something, we take care of it and get something in return."

Starks rested his back against the chair. "That is how it works. What fee did you have in mind?" He glanced from one man to the other.

Simmons answered. "Depends on what you want."

"How about this? I'm going to arrange a regular pay schedule, like a retainer fee. Long-term, if it works out. I'll set things up with my guy on the outside. Any conversations or meetings with him happen away from here, of course." The COs nodded. "How many others are we talking about?"

Jakes pointed at himself then Simmons. "Three more makes five of us."

"You two, Ted, Roberts, and who else?"

Simmons said, "Ted's out."

Starks narrowed his eyes. "Why?"

"He's a fucking goody-two-shoes," Jakes replied. "He doesn't wanna be involved in anything."

Starks ran a finger slowly back and forth across his lips. Ted had more honor than these two put together; he could've kept his hand out for more but didn't.

"Tell you what I'm going to do. Once I get things set up, whoever meets with my guy, whether it's one or all of you, my guy gets a copy of your last paystub. He'll calculate your gross salary for the year. I'll match that through weekly payments for you two and Roberts. The other two guards will get ten thousand a year."

Jakes shook his head and said, "Everyone gets treated the same or we're not playing."

"Nice of you to want to play fair, but my offer stands."

Jakes and Simmons looked at each other. Jakes replied, "All right, but orders go through us. And we handle giving the other two their ten thou each."

Starks blew out a breath. "I'll agree about the orders going through you, or Roberts, but I don't want jealousy about who's getting paid what mucking things up. And, I need to know who the other two are; I need to be able to contact them directly."

Jakes placed his hands palms-down on the desk. "Look where you are, Starks. You're treating this like some business deal you're in charge of instead of a favor."

Starks replied, "That's exactly what this is, gentlemen. And this isn't small trade for small favors I'm offering; it's payment for services. Generous payment. Let me put it to you this way, if you don't like the terms, I'm certain I can find others who will."

Jakes looked at Simmons, who nodded. "We're good. When we gonna see the money?"

"I'll arrange it to start next week."

"Cash, right?" Simmons asked.

"No W2s or 1099s from me, fellas."

"Okay," Jakes said. "I'll get word to the other two to talk to you. At least one of the five of us is around day or night, depending on our shift schedule. When you need one of us, catch our eye. Scratch your right ear then your left arm. We'll get to you as soon as we can."

"Got it. Simmons, thanks for what you did in the corridor. Keep an eye on that guy for me, and on the other gang members. Word's out that they blame me for what happened to Bo and plan to take revenge. I want each of you in on the deal to watch my back . . . and Jackson's."

"What's Jackson got to do with it?" Jakes asked.

"Finding a cellmate you get along with isn't easy."

"Yeah, your last one was—"

Starks rubbed his abdomen. "You don't have to tell me." He stood. "I'll instruct my guy to continue payments for services as long as I'm alive and healthy. Any injuries and the payments get cut in half. Same deal about Jackson. If I die . . . so does your funding."

Jakes replied, "We'll watch those assholes. Any word we hear, or we see them up to anything, we'll take care of it."

"We're all settled, then. One more thing. Where's Mike Lawson?"

Simmons looked at Jakes, grinned then answered, "Weasel's still in PC."

"Where's it located?"

"Farthest wing. It's where all snitches and bitches like him are kept."

Starks walked up to the glass and scoped out the library. Not one inmate had hung around after the COs arrived. He turned to face the guards. "We have a deal. You'll be hearing from me."

Jakes's face was florid. "About how I treated you before . . ."

"You take care of me; I'll take care of you."

Lunchtime. Only the usual three inmates in the library at this time every day were using the computers.

Starks walked up to the inmate seated closest to the door. "Hey, Paco. How's the memoir going?"

"Going slow, amigo. But I got time." He laughed.

"Keep an eye on things for me for a few minutes, will you? I'm running over to the commissary to get something for lunch. You want me to bring you anything?"

"Ham sandwich and a soda."

"You got it. I'll even throw in some chips. Don't let anyone do what they shouldn't in here."

"If they even look like it, I'll threaten to take them out of my memoir."

Starks hurried to the telephones to make his collect call.

"Jeffrey, I need you again."

"Ask and you shall receive."

"Get a visit set up as soon as possible. But it has to be within the next six days. The sooner the better."

"I'm on it."

"Thanks. Gotta run. Ham sandwiches sell out first."

Starks smiled as he speed-walked to the commissary. Everything was falling into place nicely.

CHAPTER 93

B Y TEN AFTER four, Starks hadn't heard from Jackson about a meeting with the Hermanos, nor was he in their cell or block.

This was as good a time as any to face the showers. Days of sponge-baths had left him feeling like he needed to scrape grime off his skin. He needed hot water and lots of it.

His back stayed toward the wall and his eyes were kept open as hot water from the showerhead sprayed his face and body. Someone had cleaned the shower not too long ago and had gone overboard with the bleach; the odor of chlorine stung his nose and sinuses. Scars from shanks driven into the gray tiles beneath his feet during successful and unsuccessful fights reminded him of walking barefoot on gravel as a child.

He tried to get a lather going from the only soap available the last time he'd bought some in the commissary, but it wasn't happening. This was so far removed from his marble shower with temperature and pressure controls, steam jets, and his abundant supply of expensive gel and shampoo. He was tempted to ask Jeffrey to bring him some, but that would invite problems he didn't want.

Starks occasionally glanced at the other four inmates showering. He'd seen each of them in passing, and to his knowledge, none of them belonged to a gang. They looked his way as well, turning away just as quickly. He dipped his head down and smiled. Sure, his scars would draw attention but it was easy enough to see suspicion or maybe even fear in their expressions.

His smile faded. Even with his plans, even with working at the library, none of that matched the fast-paced activity he not only was used to in his former life but needed; it fueled him. He'd never done monotony or boredom well; one reason that monogamy had soon felt stifling no matter how wonderful the woman was he was with.

He got dressed and made his way back to his cell, his eyes always taking in who and what was in his field of vision. Hidden in the clean shirt he wore was the prepped knitting needle, kept on hand at all times now, just as the fake thumbs stayed tucked into any pants he had on.

Jackson was reading at his desk. He slammed the book shut as Starks strolled to his own desk. "Where the hell have you been?"

"What's the problem?"

"The leader of the Hermanos, Hector Sanchez, is going to meet with us. Just so you know, they call him the Razor."

Starks folded and put his dirty clothes and damp towel into a cardboard box under his desk. "Can't wait for an explanation about how he got that nickname."

"You really need one?" Jackson walked to the toilet. "And, he's skilled at keeping it hidden." Over his shoulder he added, "Until he needs it. Even goes after members of his own gang to keep them in line." He faced forward and went silent. Jackson flushed; washed his hands. "The guy's ruthless. You sure you want to do this?"

Starks sat in his chair and linked his hands atop his head. "I've noticed something about you. You don't do well under pressure. Sure, you're good at planning. You read people well enough. Even follow through on what you say you'll do. But anything takes a turn for the worst or even looks like it might . . ." He shrugged.

"That's not true." Jackson plopped into his chair; his brows were knitted together. "This is some serious shit we're in."

"Part of being a good leader is being able to handle pressure. You have to keep your composure when things go wrong. That's true for managing anything . . . business, relationships, even gangs."

"Didn't do so well in the relationship department, though, did you? Didn't keep your cool when you visited your wife's lover."

Starks let his arms slide to his lap. "Okay, I slipped up there. I'm just trying to help you, Jackson. Your brain can't be turned on only if things are going well. You ought to know that by now, especially in here."

"We all have weak areas, man. Even you."

"Point taken."

Starks walked to the cell door, looked out, then returned. He leaned against the wall, crossing his arms at his chest. "Where's the meeting?"

"Laundry room. It has to look natural so the COs won't suspect anything."

"When?"

"Ten minutes. That's another reason I was so anxious when you walked in. Sanchez doesn't like to be kept waiting."

"And I don't like to be late." He grinned. "Looks like he and I have something we agree on already."

Starks handed a small box of soap powder to Jackson. "Carry this." He bundled his dirty clothes and towels. "Let's go."

"The laundry I get but why are you bringing that?" He pointed at the hem of Starks's shirt. "What if he frisks you?"

"Jesus, Jackson. Will you relax? Be smart. It's not just Sanchez we have to worry about. It's the walk from here to there. I'm sure he'd understand why I carry it."

"Oh sure." Jackson dragged out the last word. "Razor's known as a real understanding kind of guy."

"I can be very persuasive."

"You gotta learn that it's different in here."

"Only in some ways. In others, it no different at all."

CHAPTER 94

A SHORT, MUSCULAR MAN with black hair that hung in a ponytail down his back turned when he heard Starks and Jackson enter the laundry room. On his cheeks and centered beneath each of his eyes was a teardrop tattooed in blue. Three other Hermanos, arms crossed at their chests, stood behind him.

Two inmates assigned to work in the laundry room were at a long table in the middle of the space. They left the clothes they were folding for other inmates and made hasty exits.

A CO surveying the area walked in. The three Hermanos went to the table and began folding clothes. Ponytail guy, who Starks was fairly certain had to be Hector Sanchez, positioned himself in front of a dryer that had seven minutes left to spin.

Starks walked to the one unused of the ten commercial-sized washing machines and tossed in his laundry. Jackson added soap powder while Starks inserted coins into the slots. Five machines made a racket as their individual wash cycles engaged. Starks leaned against the washer; Jackson followed suit. They spoke to each other as though having a chat while they waited.

The guard walked the room. After one pointed glance at each of the men, he left.

The three at the table positioned themselves behind Sanchez. Starks, Jackson, and Sanchez walked toward each other, stopping when there was a distance of three feet between them.

"Hector Sanchez, I'm Starks." The dark eyes he looked into were flat, emotionless. This wasn't a man to assume too much about. And acting arrogant with him in the wrong way could be fatal.

Sanchez puffed out his chest. "I know who you are. What I want to know is what you want from me?"

"It's what you want from me."

Sanchez glanced at his buddies and laughed; they joined him. "What you got that I want?"

"You know I killed Bo."

"So what?"

"Some of your soldiers helped me."

"They didn't help you. They helped him." Sanchez pointed at Jackson but kept his eyes focused on Starks.

"And he was helping me. The question you should ask yourself is this: how did a guy like me take out Bo."

Sanchez grimaced and replied, "Like I give a shit."

In one fluid motion, Starks had the knitting needle in his right hand. The three Hermanos bolted forward. They and Sanchez stared at the needle then at Starks and began to laugh.

Sanchez said, "Jackson, you didn't tell me your cellmate was a *bufo* . . . a clown."

"No, man. He's serious."

Sanchez cocked his head. "No stab wound with that could make Bo as *infermo* as he was. No matter how far you stuck it in."

"It's not the knitting needle." Starks pointed to the tip. "It's what's on it. My secret ingredient. Once it hits the bloodstream, you're dead in forty-eight hours. And those are the worst fucking hours of your life, unless you're lucky enough to lose consciousness." He thrust the needle forward a few inches. "You jab it in. The pain from what's on the needle—or anything sharp—renders the person unable to fight."

Sanchez eyed the needle; he rubbed the fingertips of each hand together. "Maybe I take that from you."

"You could. But you're not going to do that."

"You don't know what I'm gonna do or not do, *poco*."

Starks held the needle as though ready to strike. "Anyone tries to get it away from me and we'll all be dead. I have another two hidden on me." He nodded toward Jackson. "He has a couple on him, as well."

"How do I know you're not full of shit? Maybe there's nothing but your spit on there."

"You can try it out. If it doesn't work, you can kill me."

One of the others moved up. "We will. No one fucks with los Hermanos."

Sanchez silenced the man with a look. "Okay, homes, how I'm gonna do that?"

"Test it on Mike Lawson. He's in PC."

"Weasel didn't do nothing to us. You got a problem with Weasel, you deal with it."

Starks smiled and nodded his head a few times. "Right. Not your problem. Tell me, how many times have you and your soldiers had random cell and body checks done since Lawson's been in there? If they haven't started yet, they're about to."

The men looked at each other.

Starks continued. "I have it on good authority that Weasel's in there because he's a snitch. He's telling everything he knows about everyone," he wagged his finger at Sanchez, "and that includes you. Every time he gives them something useful, they reward him. They're feeding him rib-eye steaks in there, cooked just the way he likes them. You say it's not your problem? Fine with me."

One of the men kicked a washing machine. "*Cabron!*"

Sanchez turned to the man and said, "*Calmate.*"

He faced Starks, glancing at the needle then back at the man who held it. "It don't work, I cut you."

"That's only fair," Starks replied. "How are you going to reach Lawson?"

"Let me worry about that."

"When you're ready, let me know a day in advance. I'll provide what you need."

"I give you this: you got *pelotas grande.*"

Starks turned to Jackson who said, "Big balls."

The two inmates who'd left earlier hurried into the room. One of them said, "CO's coming." They returned to folding laundry.

Starks and Jackson assumed their prior positions at the washer and the four Hermanos left seconds before the guard who'd been there before returned.

The guard's gaze was hard when he passed by the washing machines. Starks smiled and said, "How 'bout those Red Sox."

"Up yours, asswipe." The guard made his exit deliberately slow.

"It's the charm of the place and the people," Starks said, "that keeps me coming back."

Jackson shook his head. "I think you like playing with fire, man."

"Wrong. In here you have to fight fire with fire, as the saying goes."

"Yeah, but looks to me like you're really starting to get into looking for timber to ignite."

Starks and Jackson entered the corridor of their cellblock. An inmate leaning against the wall next to his cell shook his head as they approached. "Y'all missed the count. Tier one ticket, man."

Starks asked, "What's a tier one ticket?"

Jackson faced him. "Different offenses get different punishments. Tier one means temporary loss of some privileges."

"Thanks for the heads-up," Starks said to the inmate. He pulled on Jackson's arm. "Let's go."

When they were almost to their cell he said, "Don't worry about it, Jackson. I'll take care of it."

Jackson stomped into the cell. "I think you're developing delusions of grandeur or something."

Starks put his folded laundry on top of his desk, pulled his chair out and took a seat, stretching his legs out in front of him. "No delusions. Reality."

Jackson sat at his desk, keeping his back to Starks. He opened a book; no pages moved during the next ten minutes.

Both men's head swiveled toward the door when someone cleared his throat. CO Roberts said, "Starks, Jackson, you missed the count."

"Officer Roberts," Starks said. "We apologize." He gestured at the folded clothes and towels. "We," he pointed at himself and Jackson, "lost track of time and didn't hear the call with all the machines running. It won't happen again."

"It's better for everyone if it doesn't." The CO nodded at both men then returned the way he'd come.

Jackson pointed at where the guard had stood and asked, "He's a recruit, right?"

"Yes. But we need to be more careful. Last thing we want to do is create problems for *our* soldiers because of what we do."

"How'd you know Sanchez and his guys were getting searched?"

Starks grinned. "It was a calculated guess. Keep in mind how the fight in the chow hall got started. Enough people saw one of Hector's gang was involved, and that others with him joined in."

Jackson nodded. "What about Lawson? Was the steaks and rewards stuff the truth or were you bullshitting?"

"What do you think?"

"Listen, man, you're keeping shit from me. I'm your fucking right-hand man. Or I thought I was."

Starks placed a hand on his cellmate's right shoulder. "Look at me, Jackson. You are. Anything you need to know, I'll tell you. Anything I don't tell you is for your own protection. You got that?"

Jackson's shoulders sagged. "Trust doesn't come easy in this place."

"No, it doesn't. Trust can't be bought but certain guarantees can be."

CHAPTER 95

STARKS FOUND AN opened box of new books for the library on the office desk. He took a seat and began the task of entering the titles into the computer. Movement in his peripheral vision caught his attention; three COs were heading his way.

He propped an elbow on the chair arm and waited for the men to walk in. He nodded at the first guard. "Officer Roberts. How can I help you?"

"These are the other two I told you about. Bill McKay," he pointed to a tall, slender man with blond hair and blue eyes, "and Mikey Camello." He pointed to the guard with wavy black hair and brown eyes, who was a foot shorter than McKay. "I briefed them," Roberts added.

Starks remembered Camello. He scanned the CO's faces. "We have an understanding?"

The two guards nodded.

Roberts said, "We're all on the same page."

Camello grinned at Starks. "Simmons had a talk with the inmate that confronted you yesterday. He shouldn't bother you anymore."

"Let's hope he listens."

"We got ways to make him listen." Camello's grin widened.

Starks kept his focus on the man. "How was the problem handled?"

The guard laughed. "Threw his ass in the SHU. Did it personally. Told him if he can't treat you right, he needs to keep his trap shut and walk his sorry ass in the other direction."

"He must've taken that well."

"All I care about was that he took it."

"He's probably going to tell others when he gets out."

"Nah. Told him any peep outta him gets him more time in there."

Starks's eyes narrowed. "Won't his being in the SHU be suspicious? If he didn't do anything, won't people question why he's there? Anyone getting that kind of punishment is supposed to go before the council first."

"The council doesn't have to know." Camello stopped smiling. "Let us worry about what we do. You just keep the green coming our way."

"I'm setting it up tomorrow."

"Tomorrow's a lucky day, then." Camello scratched his crotch.

Starks had always been able to handpick employees who were the best. In here, he had to settle for who he could buy. Services for payment was one thing, loyalty was another.

He made a mental note to keep that reality foremost in his mind.

CHAPTER 96

JEFFREY WAVED AT Starks, who joined him at the table in the visitation room. He extended his hand, which Starks shook, and said, "You're looking good, bro."

"It means a lot to me that you got here this soon."

"Before you tell me what's on your mind, Cathy's calling me every day. She wants to see you. She's annoying the hell out of me. I tried not answering her calls, but she calls back every five minutes until I do. She knows her name isn't on the list and she begged me to get you to add it."

"No way. Tell her that when she killed my son, she killed any feelings I had for her. I don't want to see her face. I don't want to hear her name. Tell her to keep taking the money as she has been and leave me, and you, alone. Tell her if she doesn't—if she talks about me to anyone at all, I'll cut her off."

"That's harsh."

"I promise you that her lifestyle, which she likes not having to work for, is way more important to her than I am. She's making a show, and I don't appreciate it. The last thing I want is for her to come here weeping and wailing. The woman has no sense. She was a mistake. I bury my mistakes." Starks covered his face with his hands. "Oh God. I don't mean that my son with her was a mistake. He was never a mistake."

Jeffrey stretched a hand out but didn't touch his friend. "I knew what you meant. I'll take care of it." He waited for Starks to compose himself then asked, "What do you need me to do?"

"I don't think I could take any of this if it wasn't for you." He cleared his throat. "I know I keep asking for favors, and this is probably the biggest one I'm going to ask."

"Bigger than fifty grand to the nurse? Which, by the way, I still don't get."

"You don't need to get it. As for this new deal, it has a long-term aspect to it. And it's imperative that it's handled right."

"Consider it done."

"You don't know what it is yet."

"Doesn't matter, and you know it."

"I don't have size going for me in here. I don't have real clout, either; though, I'm doing what I can to help that wind change direction. There's one thing I have, and it speaks everyone's language."

Jeffrey leaned back. "Good thing our money grows on trees."

"I know this is adding up but it's necessary. First, arrange a ten grand payment with Ted—cash, two stacks, five thousand each. He knows what to do with it."

"What's second?"

Starks scanned the area. He leaned toward Jeffrey. Lowering his voice he said, "I need protection. A lot of it."

Jeffrey's eyebrows rose. "What's going on in this fucking place?"

"Keep your voice down." Starks made sure no one's attention was on them. "More than you could imagine. But this time it's because Mason's solution—no pun intended—worked."

"I wasn't sure when you were going to . . . Want to share details?"

"Another time."

Jeffrey raked his eyes over his friend. "No obvious scratches or bruises on you. And, you obviously didn't get caught."

"You could say it was a well-executed plan as much as a well-planned execution."

Jeffrey was quiet a moment. "I'm glad it worked but I thought it was supposed to solve the problem."

"It solved that one. But he had followers. Word's out they want me."

"And your new plan is what?"

"I've put five guards on payroll, I guess you'd call it. Cash only."

Starks filled Jeffrey in on the details. "I don't want you to put yourself in jeopardy. I need someone reliable to meet with one of the guards, away from the prison, on a weekly basis. He'll take care of paying the others."

Jeffrey scratched his head. "I see." He watched a guard saunter in their direction then turn and exit the room. "Jim's our guy. He's the best person for this. He has connections. He'll know who can do it right *and* keep his mouth shut. Of course, both will have to be compensated."

"Keep everyone happy." Starks moved to the edge of his chair. "This has to be done fast. I promised the payments would start within a week. That was a few days ago. If they don't get paid pronto, it's my ass."

Jeffrey leaned back and smiled.

Starks studied his friend. "Why are you grinning like that?"

"We used to think what we got up to was risky. This is a whole other level, bro."

"I'm on an elevator that already went down as far as it could go—short of dying, that is. I didn't care for the view."

"You always said, 'If you don't like where you are, move up.'"

CHAPTER 97

THE NEXT MORNING, Starks strolled into the weight room. Other than the push-ups and lunges he did in his cell, he'd been neglecting his strengthening exercises for too long. It wasn't only about neglect, though, it was also fear of damaging something inside. His outer scars were obvious but he didn't know what the healed tissue was like under the skin. The crappy food he was forced to eat was giving him the start of a flabby roll around his middle. It was time to get back into the program and strengthen his body. Hard muscles were more difficult to insult with fists. He'd take it slow and easy to start.

For several moments, he stood with his towel around his neck, shaking his head at the disorder of the weights. No way could he have an effective workout until everything in his confined area was in its place. One by one he shifted the weights until their measured numbers were in ascending order.

He decided to start with the bench press and had just gotten into position when Luke Roberts walked up.

"Jackson told me where to find you, Mr. Starks. You have a visitor."

"I wasn't expecting anyone. Do you know who?"

"Just that whoever it is, is waiting in the visitors' room."

"Thanks."

Grateful that he hadn't worked up a sweat, Starks started toward the visitation area, thinking it had to be his mother waiting to see him. Lost in thought about how that conversation might go, Starks was surprised when the inmate who'd confronted him before blocked his way again. He'd wrongly assumed the guy was still in the SHU.

The man glared at him in silence.

Starks placed his hands on his hips. "If you have something to say, say it. I'm in a hurry."

"Yeah, I got something to say. Fuck you." He curled his hands into fists and altered his stance to one ready to strike.

Starks twisted his lips into a wry smile. "You need to back down. Now. Or maybe you'd like to become the old man who lived in the SHU. Look around, asshole. See who's watching you."

The inmate held his stance, letting only his eyes survey the area. Simmons and Camello had their eyes fixed on him and their hands resting on their tasers. "This ain't over. You gonna get what you deserve."

Starks walked around the man. After he turned the corner, he wiped his forehead on his shirtsleeve and took a few deep breaths to calm down. He had to look composed when he saw his mother.

He entered the visitation room and stopped, looking around slowly for his mother's face. It wasn't his mother at a table to the far right of the area, but Emma. He had put her name on the list of approved visitors, in case he eventually changed his mind, but he'd been adamant that she should stay away.

Emma leapt to her feet, waving, as he wound his way through the tables toward her. The short, low-cut dress she wore had every man in the room staring at her cleavage and shapely legs. He remembered the feel of those legs wrapped around his back. The memory of what he could see, smell, feel, and taste between those legs rushed over him.

Emma opened her arms wide when he reached her. "Baby, how are you?"

Starks held up his right hand to stop her. "They don't like hugs here."

"But I've missed you so much."

"Screw it." He wrapped his arms around her, holding her tight.

"I was afraid you'd be mad at me for coming here but I can *feel* how happy you are to see me."

A guard walking by said, "Limited contact."

"See what I mean," Starks said. "Besides, I need to sit down before I embarrass myself."

Emma's laugh was like sunlight.

"Baby, why haven't you called me?"

"You know I didn't want you to see me like this." He waved a hand. "In here."

"I know how you really look." She licked her lips. "From head to toe."

"You have to stop that. You don't know how difficult it is to be without you."

"I love you. I want to be here for you. Don't worry about how you look. I don't care about that." She stroked his hand. "I care about you. I care about us. If you think I'm the kind of woman who'll let you go through this alone, you're wrong."

"I appreciate that. But maybe you can understand how I feel."

"You need to understand how *I* feel, baby. First I got that scary letter from you. Then my heart stopped when I heard you'd been killed. I could breathe again when Jeffrey told me you were still alive, and was so worried when I found out your condition." Her lips stained red formed a pout. "And they wouldn't let me see you at the hospital, or even get information, because I'm not considered family. I was going crazy. I was so scared I was going to lose you."

"I discovered I'm tougher than even I thought." He patted her hand. "You don't need to worry. The guys who attacked me won't be doing it again."

"You sure?"

"I'm certain."

"How are you holding up here?" She glanced around the room and frowned. "I watched a program about prisons and got freaked out. Rapes, stabbings, killings, the horrible conditions. This is not the life you were made for."

"It's certainly different from what I'm used to but you know how reality shows are. They always make everything sound and look worse than it is."

One hand covered her cleavage. "I'm so relieved. I wanted to bring you a cake or some food, but they told me I couldn't."

"I appreciate the thought. You always did special things for me." He stared down at his hands. "It's best if I don't think too much about what's out there. What I'm missing. It's just . . . easier that way."

"Does that include me?" When Starks didn't answer, tears welled in her eyes and spilled over. "It's so hard being without you. Life's no fun anymore." She flipped her blonde hair from her shoulders. "You don't deserve this. You should be enjoying life. With me."

"Please stop crying. I can't stand it."

"If you want I can visit you next week. Every week . . . if you'd like." Her smile was hesitant.

"As nice as that would be, it's not a good idea, babe."

Emma sniffed a few times then smiled. "I brought you something." She reached into her handbag and waved her gift. "Calvin Klein underwear. They said underwear was okay."

Starks blushed and laughed. "It's prison, babe." He gazed into her eyes. "You're a good woman, Em. I knew from our first date that you were the one for me."

"The only one?"

"Believe it."

CHAPTER 98

THE HOUR-LONG VISIT with Emma had ended with some things said and others left unspoken. They couldn't leave the room together, so Starks asked Emma to leave first. He noticed inmates and guards appreciating the sway of her hips as much as he did. Word of her visit would likely get around, which he realized could benefit his reputation with some of the inmates.

It was recreation time, so Starks went straight to the yard. He squinted against the bright sunlight. Vulgarities, laughter, and shouts reverberated in the large enclosure. A few of the Hermanos sitting on benches several yards away nodded at him; he returned the gesture then ambled forward, trying to decide what to do, if anything, noticing nods coming from other inmates, some he'd seen before and others he hadn't. He stopped at the basketball court, where seven inmates were taking turns shooting hoops.

"Hey, Starks," one of the inmates on the paved court said, "You wanna play?"

"Sounds good."

He didn't know how to feel about this invitation. It was the first time any inmates had asked him to participate in whatever they were doing, especially a game. And, they knew his name, which wasn't too hard to understand. Still, it made him feel a number of things at once: less unknown or forgotten, and it carried the familiarity of status he'd once counted on as a given.

The game of four-on-four went on for a while amid laughs, lots of shouting, some cursing at missed shots, whether by the inmate who missed it or those who chided him. Each man's scrubs clung in wet patches to his skin; when two or more players collided, sweat sprayed from their bodies. Despite how the scar tissue pulled, Starks played well enough. His side lost, threatened to win the next time, asked Starks to promise to join them again.

He rested his hands on his thighs, and stayed bent over for a few seconds to catch his breath. When he straightened, he saw Luke Roberts walking the yard. The CO looked his way. Starks scratched his ear and arm as instructed. A subtle nod was returned by the CO.

Starks said his goodbyes then sauntered over to where Roberts waited at the gate.

Speaking low he said, "You're not doing your job."

Roberts glanced around. "I'm gonna take your arm and walk you inside so it looks like we have a reason to talk."

"Got it."

"What do you mean . . . about not doing the job?"

"Our mutual 'friend.' The one who recently paid a visit to the SHU approached me again. About two hours ago. Made his threats, basically saying my days are numbered. Maybe even my hours. He wasn't forthcoming with details."

"The man must've had too easy a time in the hole. He's going back in. Soon as I leave you. These next several days are gonna make him call out to Jesus."

"Good. Because I've already set my side of things in motion. Everything's getting arranged as we speak."

"Can't happen too soon."

The two men stood inside the prison. Roberts let go of Starks's arm. "I'm gonna handle that numbnuts right now."

"Give him a kiss from me."

Roberts rested his right hand on his taser. "He'll get *kissed* in a few places."

Starks looked down at his shoes. "You might want to monitor the other four. I'm sure you picked them for a reason, but you can't be too careful."

"Anything you're not telling me?"

"Just stay sharp."

The CO winked and walked off, swinging his nightstick in slow circles.

Starks watched the CO move away and muttered to himself, "As my grandfather always said, we teach people how to treat us."

CHAPTER 99

THE NEXT TWO days were as quiet and uneventful as Starks could hope to experience at Sands, that is, until the fact he had three visitors was announced. CO Ted Landers was the one who had found him. Guard and inmate walked the corridors together, enough time for Ted to quietly give an update about his wife's slow but gradual improvement and express more gratitude for the help they were receiving.

Starks stopped just outside the visitation room, watching Ted walk away, noting how the man didn't walk like the weight of his burdens were as heavy as before. To be able to do something that mattered so much for someone, especially while trapped in here, felt good. More than that, he thought, it felt redeeming.

For my sins.

Starks entered the visitation room, searching for familiar faces. He found them: His mother, his aunt Anita, and his cousin Hank watched him from the table where they sat. Their expressions were easy to read: anxious, fearful.

He fixed a smile on his face and waved; they rose to greet him. He walked in their direction and watched his mother's face contort; people turned and stared as her sobs grew louder.

Starks was three feet from the table. He paused and said, "There are restrictions about hugging. Only the briefest contact is allowed. Any more than that and I could get into trouble. Before I come closer, do each of you understand this?"

Anita and Hank nodded. His mother wrung her hands, her eyes conveying a clear message that this restriction didn't apply to her. When she saw he wasn't moving, she nodded as well. Appropriate hugs were exchanged. The four took their seats.

Lynn Starks studied her son's face. In a normal voice that grew louder with each sentence, she said, "I can't believe you're in this place. With these . . . criminals. I can't believe my brilliant son has to mingle with people such as these, like that hideous man over there sitting with that tattooed woman. What kind of woman does that?"

"Mom, keep your voice down." He grasped one of her hands then let it go, saying "It's okay. Really. It's not as bad as it looks. Most people in here are doing their best to get by until they can leave. I promise I'm doing all right in here."

Lynn sat rigid in her chair. "How can you say that, after what happened?"

"The people who hurt me can't hurt me anymore."

"If not them, someone else. I didn't raise you for this." She flicked a hand in the air. "If only you'd listened to me about that bitch. She was never good enough for you."

Anita placed one of her hands atop one of Lynn's. "This is not the time. You have to be strong for your son." She turned to Starks. "How are you truly doing, nephew?"

Starks stretched out his arms then slapped his chest. "Look at me. I'm fine. Really."

Hank leaned forward. "Did you actually get stabbed?"

"Yes." Starks cast a quick glance toward his mother. "But we don't need to talk about that."

"That's gangsta, cousin." Hank drew back when Anita slapped him. "Sorry," he said. "But look at him. He's okay. Starks, I didn't mean to dis you or anything."

"I know. When you live outside prison walls, it may seem like life inside has a romanticized veneer on it, like you're watching a movie or reading a novel. When you live it, the veneer comes off."

Anita pinched Hank's arm. "What the hell's wrong with you for asking a question like that? And in front of your cousin's mother?"

"Sorry, auntie."

Anita eyed Starks up and down. "You've gained a few pounds, I see."

"Thanks to the food I get in the commissary. The food in the chow hall is . . . it could be better."

"Shame's been brought to our family. All because of her. I can't say enough bad things about her. I'd like to say them to her face. That slut." She wagged a finger at him. "Your grandfather and I both warned you about her but you were too damn stubborn, too damn horny, to listen."

One of the guards was watching them, his posture indicating he considered walking over to their table.

Starks said, "You have to keep your voice down. You're drawing attention from the guards. You stir up trouble and he'll make you leave. They may even force me to remove your name from the visitors' list. Look, Mom, I understand why you're upset, and I appreciate it. But what happened is in the past. Nothing any of us can do about it now. I'm making the best of this situation. And one way I can do that is to put the past behind me."

Anita nodded. "That's the best way to deal with it. Before you know it, you'll be out of here." She blushed and added, "So to speak."

Lynn crossed her arms at her chest, her hands balling once again into fists. "All the money you paid those damn lawyers. They should have gotten you off. It's Kayla who should be in prison," she turned her face to the room, saying loudly, "not my son."

Starks placed a hand on her right arm to try to persuade her to calm down. She turned her face toward him. "She should suffer for what she's done to you and your children. Your children need you. They don't need their whore of a mother."

Starks sat back in his chair, realizing his mother was geared up for one of her loud rants about Kayla, no matter what he said or what any guard might say. The truth was that he'd appreciate her words and emotions if he were living free; he would even enjoy her anger on his behalf and join in, revel in the self-righteousness of it. But her carrying on was exactly the reason he didn't want his family, particularly his mother, to visit.

Starks glanced at the faces at his table, with a plea for compliance in his eyes. "Let's talk about something else. Give me news of the family. Share some good things with me. We only have twenty minutes for our visit; we've already used ten. Let's not use that time talking about anything or anyone unpleasant."

Lynn's expression was one of surprise. "I thought we had a few hours."

The lies came easily and from a true desire to get away from his family. "There's a long list today of people waiting for a visit. Plus, I have a job at the library. I had to get someone to cover for me, but his time's limited. I promised to get back as soon as possible so he can be on time for his job."

"You have a job?" Anita asked.

"I like it. It keeps me busy. The place needs a lot of reorganization."

"My son is working in a prison library. The shame never ends." Lynn shook her head slowly from side to side.

Ten more minutes was all Starks could take. The digital numerals on the wall clock had changed in what felt like slow motion. He hurried through the tearful goodbyes on the part of his mother and aunt, slapped Hank's back and told him to stay out of trouble, then made a hasty exit.

Being with his family had always been a comfort, especially once his structured life had begun to collapse. Now, he couldn't get away from them fast enough.

CHAPTER 100

STARKS KNOCKED ON Demory's door, waited to be told to enter then closed the door behind him. Demory was smiling at him. He smiled back as he took a seat in his usual chair.

"I called your attorney—Parker. Very knowledgeable man. Thanks for the referral."

"He's the best money can buy. Was he able to help?"

"He said I have nothing to worry about. I hope he's right."

"Usually is."

"So, Starks, how are things going with you?"

Starks pulled Demory's pen holder to him and began rearranging its contents. "A few family members visited. My mother, an aunt, a cousin."

"Were you happy to see them?"

"I was and I wasn't. Of course I miss them. But there was some drama." He glanced up. "My mother."

"What happened?"

"She was tearful, which I expected. And she wanted to carry on about Kayla. Loudly. I get that better than anyone; I'm the one who loved Kayla and married her." He slid the pen holder back to its original place on the desk. "I lied about how long the visit could last. They were disappointed, especially my mother. But I couldn't listen to her for an hour or more. No matter how many times I warned her, she kept raising her voice, getting the guards' attention."

"Maybe the next visit will go better."

Starks leaned back, linking his hands behind his head. He fixed his eyes on the ceiling. "Maybe. I may need to restrict how often they can visit. I'll have to see how I feel about that."

"You know best what you feel, and what you need."

"Yeah." He sat up, brought his hands to his lap and picked at his cuticles. "Emma—the woman I became involved with after Kayla and I separated—came to see me."

"How did that go?"

Starks chuckled. "Better than with family. Emma's great. She turned every head when she came here. She turns heads everywhere she goes. Smart, too. We met at an engineering conference after Kayla and I were separated. She teaches molecular biology at U.M."

"Was she the first woman you got involved with after the separation?"

"There was another woman before her; it lasted only four months. Emma was different, though. It got serious with her, enough that she and her son moved in with me."

Demory scribbled on his notepad. "What was it about the first woman that didn't work out?"

"She was messy. I mean like pigsty messy. I didn't care how good in bed she was, that habit of hers was damn annoying. And, she was also one of those people who always had ideas but never implemented them. That annoyed me, as well. It was the lack of discipline that turned me off. And the excuses. Every time I said anything to her about any of it, she'd start the tears. I had to watch everything I said. I won't live like that so ended the relationship."

"What about Emma?"

"Emma's reasonable, rational, cares about family. She has a close relationship with her mother, who acts the way a mother should. Emma's a far better person than Kayla ever was or ever will be, *and* she appreciates me. All characteristics of a good wife."

Starks flung back in the chair. "I can't believe the senseless decisions Kayla's made these last several years. As bad a choice as Ozy was, now Kayla's involved with that good-for-nothing Bret. He's not doing anything about contributing or providing for her financially. If something happens to her, you can bet he'll be gone in a flash. No way would he stay around and take care of her. And she's carrying his child, for God's sake. What the hell is she thinking? She barely knows him. Has him and his daughters living in *our* house, with *our* children.

"Sure, he caters to her; she's paying for his life. What Kayla doesn't get is that Bret's put his best face forward. That'll last awhile then the real person he is will surface. He's using her—financially, sexually, emotionally. Using isn't loving."

Demory tapped his pen against his chin and stared at Starks.

"I know why you're looking at me like that, Doc. But this is different. I loved Kayla. Bret's just using her and her money. Correction: my money."

"You seem to still care a lot about what's happening with Kayla."

"She's the mother of my children. I have to care a certain amount, for their sakes. Especially because I'm in here. If I don't do right by her, what will my children think about me? I have to let her get away with her shit. She's got my balls in a vice."

"How well do you know Emma?"

Starks's face reddened. "Well enough, Doc. After Kayla, I know how to recognize a good woman when I see one. But, I can't stop worrying about the effects of all of this on my children. How do they feel about another man sleeping with their mother in our bed? How do they feel about having a man other than their father living at their house? Does he correct them? Does he ever take care of them? Drives me crazy wondering what's going on there."

"Starks," Demory put his pen down, "you're justified, to a point, to care about what Kayla does, because your children are involved. But some of what she does is no longer your call or concern, difficult as that may be to live with. At some point, you need to let go; you're holding on too tight to what was rather than adapting to what is. Her relationship with Bret may succeed. If it fails, it's up to her to deal with it, even learn from it, if she chooses to do that. That's another thing you have no control over."

"I've always taken care of her, did all I could for her. I don't know how to stop doing that."

"You'll probably care about her in some measure for the rest of your life but you'll find life easier if you focus more on your own situation here. I'm not saying to let go of concern for your children's well-being, just that there's only so much control you have about that while they're in her care. If anything happens, I'm sure Jeffrey will let you know. You have a right to legal recourse if the safety and well-being of your children come into question. Until you hear anything like that, you're torturing yourself with what-if's and about matters you have no control over. You're in here suffering and she's out there dancing, so to speak."

Starks got up and began to pace.

"Look, I'm hearing what you're saying, Doc, and I know it makes sense, up to a point. But I want you to understand what some of my anger is about. She's using the money I provide for her and our children to give him a lifestyle he didn't have before. Tailored suits and shirts, handmade shoes, trips to exotic places while leaving our kids and his with the nanny to look after. And on and on. Hell, he has to get money from her if he needs to buy her a gift. He's not just living off of her he's living off me. And the fact that she's going along with this? It would be one thing if she was in a relationship with a man who could afford everything and was man enough to pay for everything. This is different. And what the hell are our children learning from her?"

"Legally, as long as your children's needs are met and they're being cared for, even if primarily by their nanny, you have no say in how she spends the funds you provide for her use. As for your children, you can write to them. You can guide them, especially as they get older and can understand more. You just have to do that in a way that doesn't criticize their mother. You have to come to terms with what you can do and let go of thoughts about what you want to do but can't. Is any of this landing?"

Starks's posture was rigid. He didn't look at Demory when he answered, "I hear you." He placed a fist to the wall and pushed against it.

"While we're on this topic, what about Emma? She and her son were living with you before things changed. Were you paying for everything for both of them?"

Starks held up a finger. "One. That's different. I'm the man." He held up another finger. "Two. Emma never needed me to pay for her life. She was supporting herself and her son before we met and continued to do so even after we were together; although, I took care of all the household

expenses and treated her and her son to things like gifts, new clothes, out-
ings . . . that kind of thing. She said she didn't want to be a burden."

"Is it possible you feel about Emma as you do because she's easier to
deal with?"

"Absolutely. No way was I going to go through what I'd been through
with Kayla."

"I wonder how long your relationship with Emma would have lasted?"

"What the hell do you mean by that?"

"Are you confident Emma's going to wait? Is it fair to ask her to? You'll
both be different people when you get out, no matter how many visits or
calls you have."

Starks didn't respond.

"Look at your life . . . before and since you've been here. You like a
challenge. I think it's possible you thrive on them. I'm just wondering how
well and for how long you would have coped with a relationship that went
along smoothly, perhaps too smoothly."

"You're way off the mark, Doc. Way off. I have—had—enough challenges in business to entertain me. I didn't need or want any in my intimate relationship ever again."

"People can become addicted to drama. I could give you the bio-chem-
ical explanation for this fact, but I promise you it's a very real experience."

"Not for me. You're wrong."

"Do you see any parallel between what you were doing with Emma
and what Kayla's doing with Bret?"

"What is this—annoy patient day?" Starks sighed. "The situations
are altogether different. Emma's not using me. And she has enough self-
respect to choose a man who's successful, not eager to live off a woman so
he doesn't have to work."

"So you believe that, even under the current circumstances, things will
continue to go well with Emma?"

"Oh yeah. She was as happy to see me as I was to see her. I was surprised, though. I'd listed her but told her not to come." Starks, smiling,
stared out the small window. "Said she misses me too much to stay away."

"How did you feel when you realized she'd ignored your request?"

"Surprised. Happy. Guarded."

"Why guarded?"

"You think after Kayla I can ever afford to trust a woman again?"

"You don't trust Emma?"

"I'm not a fool, Doc. Sure, Emma's a thoroughbred, but I learned a big lesson about trust." He snickered. "Learning it even better in here."

"Do you think it's possible to open your heart fully to someone if you can't or won't trust her?"

Starks, his face flushed, turned to Demory. "Fuck trust. People have to prove to me they've earned it. People can and will fool you—as much as you let them get away with, but there's a time limit on how long they can keep it up. So I watch and wait." He waved a hand in the air. "If I get what I want from them while I wait, so much the better."

"Part of what you just said is a guaranteed road to a life of selfishness."

"None of us ever knows how long we're going to live. You have to put yourself first in this life." Sneering, Starks said, "I learned that from my father."

Demory glanced at his watch and hurried to scribble a note.

"Look, Doc, I know what you're trying to do. You want me to look at my faults rather than at who's really to blame. That's your job; I get that. But that doesn't mean it's right."

Demory put his pen down and leaned back. "In a couple of weeks, I'm taking some necessary time off, for around two months. Another counselor will cover for me until I return. I'm sure you'll find he's okay to—"

Starks shot up. "I'm not talking to another counselor. I'll wait until you come back. Whatever you're doing, I hope it goes well. But don't expect me to talk to anyone but you. I think our time's up."

Starks's stride was deliberate as he left the session. Demory just didn't get it: *He* wasn't in the wrong; Kayla was.

Why was that fact so damn difficult for people outside of his family to get?

CHAPTER 101

STARKS NOTED HIS pile of dirty clothes was getting too high for the cardboard box he stored them in. Jackson had taunted him, back when they'd first been put together in the cell, about neatly folding what needed to go to the laundry—"Who does that?"—his cellmate had asked.

"This place may be a sty," he'd responded, "but that's no reason to live like pigs."

The word pigs reminded him of Lawson, who still needed to be dealt with. What was taking Sanchez so long to get back to him?

Starks removed the knitting needle from the hem then slid his scrub top off, followed by his undershirt. He sniffed at the garment, wrinkling his nose at its pungent odor. He blamed the stink on the cheap soap and deodorant the commissary carried. The shirts, followed by the pants, were folded and added to the stack.

The last thing he felt like doing was standing around in the laundry room for over an hour. In any prison, it was a favor for a favor, or payment—cigarettes, drugs, exchanges of items bought at the commissary, or cash, even with inmates whose paid work assignments involved doing laundry for inmates. He decided to arrange whatever was required. Dressed in clean clothes, and his slender, primed weapon tucked into place, he picked up the box and made his way through the two corridors that led to his destination.

Once inside the laundry room, he selected the smaller of the two inmates working that shift and approached him, introducing himself.

The inmate replied, "Name's Nick."

The details were handled quickly: Nick wanted nothing for doing the laundry; said it was his job, and that he'd be happy to do the favor.

Starks stared at the man for a moment then asked, "When will my stuff be ready?"

"For you, two hours. Clean and folded. If you need anything else, you let me know."

"I'd like the clothes put back in that box."

"Will do. And, I'll deliver them to your cell as part of the service."

"Appreciate it."

Whether Nick wanted anything for his services or not he was going to get something. It bothered Starks to accept favors or services for nothing, especially in here. His grandfather had taught him that money was the cheapest way to pay. Even after the time he'd been in here, he still didn't know the lay of the land well enough to determine whether accepting something for nothing would work against him. Some "big-house" rules stayed the same; some changed on a whim.

Starks was about to exit the laundry room when his heartbeat began to gallop in his chest. The inmate with the lion tattoo was at the entrance; he'd stopped and was staring, his expression unreadable.

The inmate pulled himself to his full height and put a smile on his face. "*Mister* Starks."

Starks hesitated, trying to figure out what the man was up to. Erring on the side of caution, he nodded but stayed silent.

The inmate returned the nod then went into the laundry room. Starks was hit with a sudden thought of concern about his laundry then shrugged it off. Everything in the box had been provided by the prison. If an inmate destroyed the clothes, the prison would replace them. He'd hidden the underwear Emma had given him. No way was he going to be caught wearing them but they might come in handy as an exchange with the right inmate.

This new behavior of the guy with the tattoo must be a result of the COs keeping their promise. He looked behind him. The tattooed inmate hadn't come out of the laundry room. Starks glanced at the round clock mounted high on the wall. It was lunchtime, and he wanted something from the commissary. He wasn't feeling up to what the chow hall might serve.

He made a right turn into a nearly empty corridor and stopped short. Three Caucasian inmates cornered an unusually large African-American man whose hair was in long dreadlocks. Guards and other inmates were conspicuously out of sight. None of the four men noticed he was there. He kept his distance, stayed silent, not yet certain what was going on or about to go down.

Two of the men pinned the huge man's arms behind his back. The other delivered blows to the man's face; kicked the man's legs out from under him. The man fell; the thud of his head striking the concrete floor made Starks's stomach constrict. The three began to kick the downed inmate. Red splatters took shape briefly on the gray walls, before trailing toward the floor.

Starks shouted, "Leave him alone."

Too involved in the moment, no one but the man being beaten took notice of him.

He edged closer, his right hand grasping the left side of his scrub shirt. The last thing he wanted to do was reveal his weapon, or worse, have it taken from him, used on him.

The victim pressed his hands against the wall, using the surface to drag himself up, despite the blows and kicks still being delivered to him. He turned, swinging at the nearest man; his fist made contact with the attacker's right temple. The man fell and stayed unmoving. Rage was evident in the large man's eyes and on his face. He lifted one of the two men standing and slammed him to the floor; the man moaned and stayed down. The other inmate took off, running in the direction opposite where Starks stood.

The bloodied man's fists stayed clenched; his breathing was hard and fast. He looked down at the men at his feet, wobbled then fell against the wall.

Starks rushed to him. "Are you okay? Do you want me to help you to the infirmary?"

The man held his hand out, not to accept assistance but to keep Starks from coming closer. He took a few shallow breaths then answered, "I'm okay, mon."

"What was that about?"

"Dem *batty* boys."

"I don't understand."

"Dey want me to be dey *girlfriend*. You understand dat, yeah?"

Starks's eyes took in the man's bulk. "They must be idiots to mess with you." The man's smile was slight but genuine. "Although, some might say the same about me."

"What you mean?"

"I'll tell you another time. I'm Starks."

"Skullars Bailey. Just call me Skullars."

"I'd like to help you, if you need help, that is. You want me to flag down one of the guards?"

"No, mon. No doctor, no guards for me." He winced when he straightened up then stuck out his chest. "I handle my own business. But I tank you for tryin' to make dem stop."

"I've never seen you before."

"First week out here. Just outta da SHU. Dem fools try somethin' wid me da first day. Don' wanna go back in da SHU."

"Believe me, I understand. All of it." Starks glanced left then right. "I like how you handled yourself. Listen, if you ever need anything or just want to talk, I'm in D block."

"Dey jus' move me inna same block. First cell on da right."

"I'm in the fifth cell on the left. Look me up."

"You not *batty* man, are you?"

"I assure you that I bat for the usual team."

CHAPTER 102

STARKS CHANGED HIS mind about getting something from the commissary. Jackson would be in the chow hall; he felt like having some company. He couldn't fathom why his roommate went there for meals as often as he did, nor had he asked. Maybe Jackson's funds had something to do with it. He wondered why he'd never thought of that before.

Jackson had never asked for payment, or anything, in fact, in exchange for his assistance with the attack on Bo. He needed to give this matter more consideration.

He spotted Jackson moving forward in the tray line and waved when his cellmate looked his way. Starks pointed toward their usual table; Jackson nodded.

Two minutes later, they sat across from each other.

Starks put a bite of potatoes and part of a meatball on his fork and grimaced when he tasted them. "Everything's cold and bland."

"Ah, the sweet consistencies of life," Jackson said. "Hey, I got a new gig in the kitchen, starting tomorrow."

"Maybe you can do something about the quality of this crap."

Jackson snorted. "Sure thing. You can expect gourmet meals from now on." He chewed thoughtfully. "I'll have more influence working in here. Inmates will want favors."

He pointed his fork at Starks. "People are talking about you."

"That's not news."

"Well, this is. The Beast is stirring things up."

"Who the hell's the Beast?"

"One of Bo's soldiers—former soldiers. Has a lion tattoo."

Starks frowned. "We've met."

"He's saying you have all the COs in your pocket. That he already spent time in the SHU twice in one week because of you."

Starks grinned. "He's wrong. I don't have all of them in my pocket."

"How many so far?"

"You know how many."

"If you add anymore, it would help if I knew who. Do you trust them?"

"I don't need to trust them; I just need to motivate them."

"Word's getting out that you have a secret weapon."

Starks's fork stopped halfway to his mouth. "That's not good."

Jackson shrugged. "Depends on how you look at it. The ones that helped that day think you just knew where to strike to cause the most damage. Others believe it's just part of the rumor mill. But you've probably noticed more people being nice to you. Maybe even treating you with respect."

Starks put his fork down, pushed his tray away, and folded his arms on the table.

Jackson grinned. "Man, it's like you're becoming mythical in their minds. It's like a fish story. Every time it's told, the fish gets bigger, more powerful."

Starks pulled his tray back, picking up his fork to poke at the food. "People will say what they say. If it helps me, great. If it gets me into trouble, that's not good."

"Won't be long before people start coming to you for favors and contraband."

"If I can help with favors, and if they're favors I'm on board with, no problem. As for contraband? I'll leave that up to someone else. I have no interest in becoming a broker."

Jackson leaned forward and lowered his voice. "You ought to reconsider, man. Things like cigarettes, drugs, booze, cell phones, and other such shit keep prisoners going. It's the infrastructure, if you get my drift. Might as well get a share of it, if not the biggest piece of it."

"I'm not interested."

"Then you wouldn't get pissed if I got involved, maybe even became point man?"

"Knock yourself out, as long as my name's not dragged into it."

"Like it or not, people are gonna assume you're lead man. They're wanting to lean that way now."

"Let them lean."

"Just give it some thought. You've got assets I don't have. I'd handle the administrative parts but it'd go a lot smoother if people thought it's you they're dealing with in the long run. I've got some guys in mind . . . for muscle. You know? They can be the runners, the go-between people. They can keep people in line."

Starks dropped his fork into the food on his tray. "Lost my appetite."

"Look, this would amp up my rep in here, but man, this would give you some serious clout. It's a big fucking pond. You really want to stay a little fish in it? It's one thing to take care of a few COs; it's another to get a large number of inmates in your corner. Easier to get recruits if they already depend on you. Get enough of them on your side and no one's gonna want to challenge you, and they'll go against anyone who does."

"Do you stay awake at night thinking up this bullshit?"

"I'm looking out for your interests." He glanced at Starks then quickly looked down. "I'd like to think we're kind of, you know, partners. At least think about it."

Starks's brow wrinkled. "I'm not trying to secure profits; I'm trying to stay alive and un-mangled. I'll catch up with you later."

He knocked on the table, got up and dumped his tray then headed for the yard. His scowl eased into a smile.

CHAPTER 103

THIRTY-FIVE MINUTES INTO his next session, after Starks had shared more about the past, he confessed something that caught Demory by surprise.

He avoided looking at the counselor as he spoke.

"My attempt on my life when I was in isolation wasn't the first time. When I learned the whole truth about Kayla, I had no soul left. If I'd had a gun, I would have killed myself. The range of emotions I felt are too hard to describe. I can say I was hurt to my core. That hurt battled with denial, until I had to face facts: I was married to a total stranger. Then I'd be angry one minute and despondent the next, feeling like I couldn't breathe. Other times it was like I was having a bad dream, and I waited for my wife to shake me awake.

"Something came over me and I convinced myself the best way to get rid of this pain was to meet my maker. I got into my car, looked for the nearest sturdy pole, punched the gas and hit it head-on. My head struck the steering wheel, and that was all I could remember about the incident. I woke up in the hospital with a broken arm, contusions, and facial lacerations."

"How long did these suicidal thoughts continue?"

"The thought entered my mind several times. I wasn't able to deal with the humiliation and betrayal."

"There're always three sides to a story: Yours, hers, and the truth. You made mistakes, just as she did."

Starks stayed motionless.

"Tell me what you're thinking," Demory said.

Starks rested his forearms on his thighs. "You're right that I've made some mistakes as well. There was a woman." He paused. "Cathy."

"I've wanted to ask about her."

"She got pregnant; we had a son. He drowned when he was five. I still have nightmares about him."

"You're dealing with more than I realized. Tell me more about—"

"I'm telling you this for a reason, Doc. You have a lot of opinions, and I'm sure it's easy to state them from where you're sitting. But all your advice and platitudes won't solve my problems or make my hurt and anger go away. I can't do this right now; I'm stopping this session." Starks rubbed his face and stood up. "Are you here next week?"

"Yes, and probably the week after that as well. There's a delay in getting a replacement."

"Next week, then."

Starks left Demory's office, wondering if there was anyone anywhere who could relate to what he felt, and could do so without judging him. Demory hadn't mentioned forgiveness for a while, and a good thing, too—he would've told him where to stick it. Some people didn't deserve forgiveness. Like Kayla, Ozy, Bo, and Lawson, and anyone else who trampled him in a similarly egregious way.

Whatever he'd done that hurt Kayla, it would never match what she'd done to him then—and now.

Betrayal was unforgivable.

He was reading at his desk when Jackson strolled into the cell after his kitchen shift.

Jackson clapped his hands together once. "We're in, man. The guys in the kitchen cut me in on the cell phone racket they've got going. It's my foot in the door." Still smiling, he plunked down into his chair. "They wanna meet with us."

Starks turned his head back to his book. "No reason to meet with me. That's your gig."

"Don't be such a selfish prick."

Starks faced his cellmate; his expression was threatening. "You sure you want to go down that path, Jackson?"

"Not everybody is loaded like you. Maybe this doesn't matter to you but it sure as hell does to me. You're gaining respect in here, man. I need that too."

"Any respect I have in here, I earned. The hard way."

"Yeah, you earned it. I've earned some but I need more." He pointed at Starks. "You'd probably still be planning what to do about Bo if it hadn't been for me."

"Point taken. But I told you—"

"You know what? Fuck it. I have to do this, with or without you. But I'd prefer it be with you. Don't you get it? I'd be safer if people thought you had my back."

"I have your back. As much as I can."

Jackson crossed the narrow space. "Then come with me. Meet with these three guys. Look, it's one thing to have the Hermanos sort of watching out for us. But that's not your safest bet. Same for the COs. You need more levels of protection. We need our own people. It's strategy, man. You see that, don't you?"

"When and where is the meeting?"

CHAPTER 104

THE NEXT DAY, Starks left the library under Paco's watch, giving him five dollars to buy lunch once Starks returned. He rushed to get a couple of ham sandwiches from the commissary then hurried to meet Jackson, who didn't start his shift in the kitchen until two that day. Jackson was waiting for him at the door that exited to the yard. They ate quickly as they made their way to the small set of bleachers by the track at the far end of the field. Three inmates waited there, all of them African-American. They talked among themselves in hushed tones and went silent when Starks and Jackson approached them.

Starks nodded at the tall, slender inmate sitting one row above the other two then at the one with average height and build, then at the short one built like a pit bull. His gaze returned to the *average* man; he looked familiar. A breeze blew from behind the men. Starks backed up, throwing his hand over his nose. "What the hell is that stench?"

Everyone but Starks laughed. The tall one pointed at the short, muscular guy. "That's why we call him Stinky. He doesn't like to shower more than once a week."

Starks looked directly at the odorous man. "Why the hell not?"

"No one can get it up and keep it up with a smell this bad hitting him in the face. They leave me the fuck alone."

"What do you do on the days you shower?" Starks asked.

"*Anyway,*" Jackson said, "this is Starks."

"We know who he is." This was from the tall guy. He looked directly at Starks. "Name's Pete. This guy," he pointed to the third inmate, "is Tommy."

Jackson continued. "I already discussed with you what we're looking for. What I—we—want to know is if you're in."

The three looked at each other. Tommy said, "I'm in."

Starks recognized the voice; a brief replay ran through his mind. "No one's in unless I say they're in. You're the guy who started the fight with one of the Hermanos in the chow hall."

"Yeah. I'm on your side. Proved it that day."

"You *were* on Bo's side. I don't know that I can trust a man whose loyalties shift so easily."

"I get that. Gotta prove myself to you. Earn my stripes." He pointed to himself and the other two men. "Give us a chance. Whatever you want us to do, we'll do."

"Why'd you betray Bo?"

"Man was a prick. He thought the more people he could make afraid of him the more powerful motherfucker he was. Making enemies . . . pissing people off right and left. Caused us a lot a shit. Had to clean up after the stupid bastard all the damn time. *You're* not stupid, though. You're not gonna put us in the shit like Bo did. Plus, Bo was a stingy mother. Word is you're generous."

Starks fixed his gaze on the man. "Loyalty isn't a buzzword with me. I take it seriously."

Tommy jumped up. "I showed my loyalty that day. What the fuck I get for it? Two days in the SHU and a bust-down on my parole—for you. Never got no thank-you, neither."

"You're right. Thank you." Starks looked at Jackson then back at the men. "I'll let you know."

He walked away from the sound of their mutterings and Jackson trying to persuade them to be patient. An image flashed in his mind: The Hall of Mirrors found at funhouses and carnivals. No matter how anyone moved in front of the mirrors, reality got and stayed distorted. It's the same here, he thought.

* * *

Starks nodded at Paco then went directly to the back office. He sat at his desk, fuming. Waiting. He didn't wait long.

Jackson stormed in.

"Close the door," Starks told him.

Jackson did, stopping just short of slamming it.

"Act right. The inmates are watching."

"Fuck them. What happened back there? You have any idea how much talking I had to do to convince those guys to be on my side—our side?"

"Not according to Bo's guy. He said he's 'loyal' to me. You want to be point man and you call in people like him? I can't trust him. And since the other two were with him, I can't trust them, either. And neither should you."

"If trust is the big fucking issue, you're gonna have a hell of a time finding anyone. They have to earn your trust? They have to prove their loyalty? You don't think you have to prove *your* loyalty to them? It's a two-way street, man. Who're you gonna find in this place to fit your," he used his fingers to make quotation marks in the air, "requirements?"

"You mean after you?"

Jackson's angry expression shifted. "Shit." He kicked at the desk. "Sorry, man."

"Skullars Bailey."

"You lost me."

"I'll start with him."

"I don't know him."

"You'll meet him soon enough." Starks trained his eyes on the ceiling. "I saw him in action. Strong. Fearless. Already did time in the SHU and didn't care for it."

"Why would he hook up with you?"

"I helped him, in a manner of speaking. Look, Jackson, you know the saying: You're as strong as your weakest link. You can't pick just anyone. I think *your* own delusions of grandeur are interfering with your common sense. You have people-reading skills, so use them the right way."

"Is Skullars smart?"

"I don't know him well enough to say he could be the brains behind anything but he isn't stupid. You said you need muscle. He's definitely that."

"Since you know him, you'll have to talk to him."

"I intend to."

Jackson, grinning, bounced up on his toes and back down a few times. "So . . . this mean you're in?"

Starks sighed. "I'm in, and getting deeper."

CHAPTER 105

S IMMONS FOUND STARKS working his shift in the library.
"Starks. Visitor waiting."
"Any idea who it is?"
"Real pretty . . . and ripe . . . least, that's what I heard."
"Thanks. I just need to finish this one entry and I'm on my way."
"Later."

Starks felt two things at once: Annoyed that Emma had returned, despite what he'd said, and excited that she still wanted to see him enough that she'd ignore his wishes.

He paused just inside the door of the crowded visitation room. It took a moment before he found the familiar face. The fucking bitch had her nerve.

Kayla was familiar enough with his expression of rage to first open her eyes wide then cast her eyes at the two visitors sitting next to her, whom he hadn't seen. His sons, Blake and Nathan, sat open-mouthed as they looked at people unlike any they'd ever been exposed to during their mostly sheltered life.

Kayla stood to greet him; every muscle in his body constricted when he saw her swollen belly. She instinctively placed both hands across her abdomen. This protective action was more than familiar to him. His heart wrenched at how beautiful she looked; the memories of how she'd glowed when she'd carried his children were driven to the surface as though fresh.

He was both anxious and delighted to see his sons but he wasn't fooled: she'd brought them with her to ensure he'd be on his best behavior.

"Hey, Starks." Kayla lowered her eyes when he didn't respond.

Blake and Nathan turned their heads in unison at the sound of their father's name. They leaped from their chairs, calling over and over, "Daddy!"

Their chairs were knocked over in their rush to get to their father. Starks bent down, wrapping his arms around the boys clinging to him. He glanced at the guard nearest them to see if there was about to be trouble for the noise and contact. The plea in his eyes, or the guard's empathy, made the CO nod and look away.

"Let me look at you both. You're getting so big."

Blake tugged on his arm. "Dad! Dad! I got straight A's. Mom said we can get a Playstation. And . . . and . . . Kaitlin couldn't come 'cause only three people can come. That's *sooo* unfair. She cried and cried. We left her with grandma so Nanny Anita could have some personal time." Starks didn't ask which grandmother but was fairly certain it was not his mother.

"I'm sorry to miss her. Tell her I send a big kiss and hug. And about your grades, that's great, Blake." He turned to his other son. "What about you, Nate? Did you get good grades?"

Nathan looked down at his shoes. "Yeah." He shuffled his feet. "I don't know why you're here. Only bad people go to jail. You're not bad." He looked at his father with such earnestness in his eyes, Starks choked up. The boy glanced at the nearest guard then back at his father. "I'll tell them, Dad. I'll tell them you're not bad and they'll let you come home with us now. They'll have to."

"I'm sorry, Nate. It doesn't work that way."

"When *are* you coming home, Dad?"

"Let's sit. We need to keep our voices down so we don't disturb the other visitors."

It took a few moments to noisily get the chairs up and in place and the boys seated. Starks continued to ignore Kayla. He knew she was studying his face; knew she could easily recognize the emotions he struggled to manage at one time: Anger, hurt, love, loathing, delight, disgust. And he knew she knew which emotions were for the boys and which were for her.

He looked back and forth between his sons, holding their attention. "How are things at the house? Bret and his girls treating you right?"

Nathan shifted in his chair. "He—" His brother elbowed him hard. "Ow! Blake hit me."

"I didn't hit you; I elbowed you. Mom said not to talk about what happens in her house, and you know it."

"Look at me, boys. I'm not asking about what happens there. I just want to know if Bret is looking out for you—taking care of you—in a way that's . . . comfortable and okay with you."

There was a flicker of something in each of their faces. Whether it was fear about Bret or fear their mother would be angry if they said anything at all was unclear. Nor did he want to put them in a bad position; he well knew what kind of ride home they'd have if they said more than their mother wanted them to. Still, he craved an answer that assured him they were safe.

Blake swung his legs for a few moments then answered. "We're all right. But we miss you."

"I miss you and Kaitlin too. Listen, boys. I want you to pay careful attention to what I'm about to say. Are you both listening?" He waited for nods from his sons, who kept their eyes fixed on his. "Anybody ever tries to hurt you or mistreat you, or does, you call your uncle Jeffrey and tell him. He'll take care of you. You both still know his number, right?" Both boys in turn said, "Yes, Dad."

"Now, tell me what's been going on with you guys and your sister."

It was a bittersweet visit that lasted an hour, with the boys interrupting each other repeatedly while trying to tell Starks all their news and pour out the usual chatter they engaged in. It was so much like their time together before everything changed that it ached in a way he thought he couldn't stand. He struggled to keep the gnawing emotion from them.

The boys handled the visit better than he did, and he was proud of them. At the same time, he'd noted how often Kayla shifted in her chair, uncomfortable because of its design and her pregnancy. He also knew, from experience, that she needed a restroom but didn't want to leave the boys alone with him or use one here. He kept his smile of satisfaction about this to himself.

Toward the end of the visit, Kayla finally spoke.

"There's something I need to discuss with you."

"You'll have to be disappointed."

"It's about the letter you sent. I was surprised to hear that you felt that way after all that's happened."

"I wrote that in another lifetime."

"Oh. Well, then, about the divorce. The papers were filed before you went to the hospital."

Starks turned away from her. "Boys, I'm sorry but visitation time for me is over. Give your dad a big hug."

The boys hopped off their chairs and wrapped their arms around him, holding on tight. He buried his nose in Blake's hair, closed his eyes and inhaled his son's scent. He did the same with Nathan. It wasn't that he'd forgotten their scents, but that he wanted to make sure he never did. He wanted to be able to call this to mind when he needed to remind himself who everything he did and had to do from this moment on was for.

"Remember what I said about telling Kaitlin I'm sending her a big hug and kiss. And tell her I miss her and love her." He hugged his boys again then held them a few inches away. He looked back and forth at them and said, "I love you. I always have. I always will."

Nathan's eyes filled; he aimed them downward. Blake put an arm around his brother. "I'll watch out for Nate and Kaitlin, Dad."

"You're growing up so fast and doing a good job of it." He stroked each son's cheek. "I'm proud of each one of you."

Starks cast one quick glance at Kayla, shook his head slowly from side to side then left the room.

Once he was certain he was out of their sight, Starks leaned against a wall, gulping air, stifling tears his body strained to release. The pain was palpable; he placed a hand over his heart.

He wanted to see his children again but he'd do what he could to make damn sure it wasn't their mother who brought them. God how it had hurt to see her carrying another man's child . . . while still married to him. He had to acknowledge the fact it would feel as crushing if they'd been divorced for years. His family's demise was now clearly a fact.

He needed air, light, and something to take his mind off what had just happened and what he was feeling. But he had a few hours left to work in the library. He walked into the book-filled space, noticing, but not caring, that books and magazines had been left out rather than returned to their proper places; that crumpled papers pitched at trash cans had missed their mark. He went into the back office and busied himself with task after task, waiting until his shift was over and recreation time allowed him to go outside.

When that time came, he sped to the yard, looking around for something to occupy his mind. He found it in one corner of the enclosure. Hector Sanchez occupied that space with the same three Hermanos who'd been with him in the laundry room.

Starks joined them.

Sanchez said, "What we talked about? It goes down next week."

"Get word to me the day before. One of you four find me. No one I don't know, or it won't happen; I'll deny knowing what they're talking about. Whichever one of you comes, bring me the shank you're going to use. I'll tell you then when and where to pick it up the next day. You have less than eight hours to use it or it won't work. You understand?"

"Si, amigo. You'll hear from one of us."

Starks nodded then kept walking, going around the perimeter of the yard several times, making it appear that he was exercising, rather than trying and barely succeeding to exorcise demons.

CHAPTER 106

STARKS SAT IN his chair in the cell, staring unseeing at the unopened book in front of him on his desk. He glanced at Jackson when he strolled in then back at the book.

"Man, you don't look so good," Jackson said. "What's up?"

"I saw her." Starks lifted and lowered the book cover with one finger, and continued to do so.

"I'm gonna take that to mean you saw the dragon lady."

The corners of Starks's lips went up slightly. "That's an apt description."

Jackson pulled his own chair out, turning it around so he could face his cellmate. "Wanna tell me about it?"

Starks turned sideways in his chair, keeping his left side to Jackson, rather than looking directly at him. "I'd made it clear I didn't want to see her. As usual, she did whatever the hell she wanted. My fault for leaving her name on the list. That was bad enough. Seeing her pregnant—knowing it's not mine—hit me hard."

"What'd you say to her?"

"I gave her the silent treatment, for the most part. I didn't dare say what I wanted to. Far as I'm concerned, she's put the nail in the coffin for our ever getting back together." Once again he stared out into the corridor. "She brought my sons."

"I don't have kids but I've heard how tough that can be. How'd they handle it?"

"They were . . . I guess you'd say fascinated by what they saw, like seeing the bearded lady for the first time at a carnival. They were excited to see me. I had to cope with a lot of stuff going on in my head all at once—for their sakes, you know?" He looked at Jackson, who nodded. "When I asked them how things were at home, I didn't like the looks on their faces. Kayla made sure to tell them not to say anything about what's going on at the house with the father of her child and his daughters."

"You think he's maybe messing with your kids?"

Starks clenched his hands into fists. "I don't know. And as I said, Kayla made sure they're not talking about what's what there. I just hope to God the nanny's doing her job and keeping them safe."

"Just because they're not his doesn't mean he doesn't care for them."

"Maybe he isn't mistreating them—he'd lose his ticket to ride, if he did; at least I hope Kayla would have enough sense to protect the children—but the guy's a phony. Even if he acts like he cares, that's all it is, an act. He's only in it for himself. That's something he and Kayla have in common."

Starks walked to the sink to splash cold water on his face and neck.

Jackson watched as his cellmate studied his reflection in the mirror. "You have a woman in your life. Emma, right?"

"Yeah. So?" Starks turned around.

"How was she around your kids?"

"She treated my kids with respect and kindness. I watched her anyway, of course, but it was obvious she was sincere; wasn't putting on a show for my benefit. My kids said they liked her. Not always easy for kids to do, especially when they want their parents back together."

"Do you get along with Kayla's . . . uh . . . guy?"

"No. But I didn't act like an asshole to him in front of my kids either. When I picked them up from the house, I'd wait in my car. Same for when I dropped them off, until they got inside. Bret came out of the house the first time I picked them up, waving them off like he really gave a fuck. He was dressed in a short robe. Eleven o'clock in the morning and he's still in a fucking robe, with his tanned legs showing—tanned out by *my* swimming pool. Who knows what he was wearing under the robe, if anything. With kids in the house, he should get dressed before he leaves the bedroom—*my* bedroom. Anyway, I got out of my car. Stood by the driver's side and gave him a look he couldn't misunderstand. After that he stayed inside when-ever I showed up."

"How does Kayla act about Emma?"

"Like she's not a threat."

"Is she right?"

Starks glared at Jackson then shrugged and looked away.

"This is some complicated shit, man."

Starks rubbed the nape of his neck then returned to his chair. He crossed his arms in front of his chest. "Yeah. I'd like to say—and mean it—that she's his problem now. But that's not the fact. They're all my fucking problems. Whatever. I need to find out what's happening there. Make sure my kids are okay."

"If they're not?"

Starks looked at Jackson with eyes so cold his cellmate shivered. "Someone better hope they are."

CHAPTER 107

H E WASTED NO time once he was seated across from Demory. "Look doc, I've been thinking about what we talked about last week."

"What's on your mind?"

"That woman knew what she was doing, and she's still not sorry for any of it. Time I face the fact that what she did is her nature."

"When you talk about Kayla, all I hear is animosity. When you talk about Emma, your face lights up. It seems Emma should be better for you, yet you're still stuck on Kayla."

Starks, radiating tension, raised himself from the chair and stood in front of the framed certificates hung on the wall to the left of Demory's desk.

"No response?" Demory said.

"I've always had a thing for Kayla. Doesn't mean I don't love Emma."

"You need to figure out where your loyalties are."

"My loyalties were clear before. It was always my marriage and my kids. I admit I contributed to the degradation of the marriage. We both caused a lot of hurt. But I wanted to save the marriage for the sake of my children and for the fact that I did love her. I told her I was sorry for what I did. She started calling me day and night, saying how she wanted me back, even though she was still seeing Ozy. I told her if she didn't call him and end it, we were over. By that point I was so disgusted with her I—"

"Would you have started over with her?"

"I don't really know, now. It wouldn't have been easy but I'd like to think I was willing to work on it." He rocked forward. "I realize now that I wouldn't be a man if I went back to her. And if I'd gone back then, she wouldn't have respected me and damn sure wouldn't take me seriously. All I can say is what goes around comes around. Her relationship with Bret isn't going to last. I'd bet money on it and win."

"Why do you say that?"

"Kayla was already cheating on Bret. As I said, it's her nature. It's just taken me this long to get that. One guess about who she cheated with. If that kid she's carrying comes out with blond hair, I don't know how she'll get out of it with lover boy. She and Bret both have dark hair and no blonds in their families."

"Is that the reason you attacked Ozy, because she went back to him?"

"Partly. It wasn't fair that Ozy destroyed my relationship, and went back to his normal family life as if nothing had happened. I didn't go there to hurt him. I just wanted his wife to know the truth. I wanted to destroy his life just like he destroyed mine. That's when I went to his house and that's what landed me in here."

"It's human nature to want revenge."

Starks returned to the chair. "Kayla came to see me last week."

"How'd that go?"

"She tried to talk to me but I didn't give her the satisfaction. She brought our sons so I'd behave. Hurt like hell to see her carrying someone else's child."

"But you stayed in control."

"Had to."

"I'm sorry I'm going to be away, especially now, with all you're dealing with. Still, I'm encouraged. You've made some right choices—keeping calm with Kayla, cutting short an unpleasant visit with your mother. Two conscious decisions you made in stressful moments."

"You really think I'm making progress, Doc?"

"You're doing better. Still have a ways to go. Now, to the matter of my absence . . . The temporary counselor's name is—"

"I don't care who he is; I'm not talking to him."

"If you change your mind, ask someone in the infirmary to set up an appointment for you."

"I won't."

"Since I won't see you for a while, there's something I want to say. I'm sure you've heard that line about the woman who protests too much. I'm referring to how much you talk about Kayla and dwell on what happened. It's obvious you still have strong feelings; I'm just not sure I'd call it love at this point. If you're right about her nature, she won't change. Plus, she's having another man's child. Sometimes we want something we can't have, and are probably better off if we don't get it. But we'll ride that merry-go-round until we make ourselves sick. The wisest choice is to get off. Starks, at some point—and I hope it's soon—you need to get the nail of bitterness out of your shoe so you stop spinning in circles about her and move on."

"Quite a parting speech. I'll think on it." Starks went to the door then looked back. "Two months away from here. I envy you, Doc. Do me a favor and don't miss us or this place."

"I will, if you'll promise to keep making the best choices."

"I'm getting smarter about that all the time."

CHAPTER 108

I T WASN'T THAT Starks wanted to eat lunch in the chow hall but that he needed to find Jackson, who was working his kitchen shift. Skullars Bailey was eating alone at a table near the entrance. He approached the inmate, calling out ahead of time, respecting the fact that deliberately surprising inmates was never a good practice.

"Hey, Skullars. Remember me?"

"Yeah, mon. What gwan on?"

"Mind if I get a tray and join you?"

"Okay wit me."

Starks found Jackson and raised one eyebrow in question when his cellmate saw him. Jackson nodded once. It was their agreed-on sign that the hastily formed plan was underway; that at that moment, Mike Lawson, aka The Weasel, was sitting in his isolation cell wondering why he was enjoying a large steak cooked medium-rare. It would take more than a day for the lingering aroma to diminish in the enclosed space.

Two minutes later, Starks sat across from Skullars.

The men ate in silence until Skullars said, "Dis food is shit."

Starks laughed. "It's better to get something from the commissary."

"Dat costs money, mon."

"Yes, it does." He waited a few moments then asked, "Mind telling me what put you in here?"

"I killed a mon."

"That would do it. If you don't mind my asking, any other time done for other . . . activities?"

Skullars flicked his head, sending dreadlocks behind his shoulders. "Neva stole. Neva sold drugs. Neva got into trouble. I worked hard to get to dis country wit my fam'ly. Work hard for my fam'ly . . . till it all turn to shit. I was a truck driver. Was on a run when fucking punks broke into my apartment. Dey kill my wife and . . ." He clenched the fork in his hand. "And my boy, fourteen years old. I found out who dey were. I beat dem. One got away. I kill de other. If I hadn't been arrested, de other one be burnin' in Hell also."

"I'm sorry for your loss, Skullars. And," he waited until the man was looking at him, "I'm sorry you got arrested before you could finish what you needed to."

"No mon ever say dat to me before. Make me tink you really understand."

"I do." Starks speared a piece of meatloaf on his fork and stared at it before putting it into his mouth, chewing twice then swallowing hard. "Things any better since I last saw you? People leaving you alone?"

Skullars shrugged.

"Like you, I worked hard for my family. My wife wasn't the good woman yours was; mine betrayed me in more ways than I can still believe. Broke my heart and the hearts of my three children. I have two sons and a daughter, all young."

"Dat's hard. To be here, away from dem."

"It isn't the kind of loss you're dealing with."

"It still hurt."

"Thanks for saying that. Anyway, I confronted the man who destroyed my family. And now I'm in here."

"You kill him?"

"No. But it wasn't for lack of trying."

"Mebbe you didn' try hard enough."

"Police stopped me." Starks pointed his fork at his companion. "But I messed him up good; put him in a coma for a long time." He speared a couple of green beans. "His wife's divorcing him, and my wife no longer wants him. That's something, at least."

"We kinda da same."

Starks nodded. "Listen," he moved his head closer, "one thing that helps in here is to have some protection. Someone looking out for you. They look out for you, you look out for them. I've been here longer than you have—not a lot longer—not even a year yet, but I've learned some things. Been through a lot." He rubbed his abdomen. "Have the scars to prove it. I'm setting up protection for myself and a few others. If you'd like to be included in that, I'm inviting you."

Skullars's eyes narrowed. "What I have to do for dat protection? You seem okay but I don't know you."

"I understand. And I like that you're smart enough to look at it that way. That's how you have to be in here." Starks paused then continued. "I have a meeting in a little while. Just some business I have to take care of. Why don't you come with me? See what's what."

"Why you wan me go wit you?"

"I like how you handled yourself the other day. And I know what it's like to get here and feel alone, to not know anyone, not know who to trust." He lifted his shirt just enough, satisfied when Skullars gasped. "I know what it's like to trust the wrong people in here." Starks smoothed his shirt into place. "No pressure. It's up to you."

Skullars sat for a moment, staring at Starks, then said, "You coulda let dem batty boys do dey worst wit me de other day but you didn't. What da fuck. I go wit you and see what's what, like you say."

"Great. Eat up. We have to be in the laundry room in twelve minutes. When we're in there, stand behind me. Pretend you're my muscle guy."

"Mebbe I don' pretend, mon."

"Skullars, I like your style."

The inmate scowled at the food and pushed his tray away. "I heard somethin' once: 'I felt bad 'cause I had me no shoes, till I saw a mon without no style.'"

Starks laughed. "You'll do just fine."

The two men exited the chow hall then walked down the corridors, drawing attention from other inmates.

Fortune, Starks thought, is smiling on me.

At least, for the moment.

CHAPTER 109

HECTOR SANCHEZ AND two of the Hermanos Starks recognized were waiting in the laundry room. The posture of all three men stiffened when they saw Starks wasn't alone and that his sidekick wasn't Jackson.

Starks stopped three feet away. He nodded at the men and said, "This is Skullars. He's okay, or I wouldn't have brought him. Skullars, this is Hector Sanchez."

One of the Hermanos leaned forward, making eye contact with Skullars. "Sanchez is called The Razor, amigo. For good reason. You be sure you remember that."

Skullars stared the man down and didn't reply.

Starks cocked his head at Sanchez. "You have it?"

Sanchez reached behind him, pulling out an ice pick from the back of his waistband. Skullars shifted in place. Starks looked at him in a way that let him know everything was all right. He also wondered where the razor Sanchez was infamous for was kept. "Give me a second," he told Sanchez.

Starks moved to stand behind Skullars. It took all of two seconds to carefully jab the ice pick through the thin cellophane and coat a few inches of the metal with the still-moist paste. He palmed the remaining wrapped paste in his left hand and stepped out.

Sanchez reached for the pick. Starks pulled it back. "Show me your hands."

"What the fuck?"

"To make sure there isn't any open skin on them. This stuff gets into your system and you go the way of Bo."

Sanchez stared at him as though he was crazy then extended his arms, slowly turning his hands over for examination.

"Remember what I told you," Starks said. "You have eight hours or less."

"My memory's good."

"Hold it from this end." Starks handed the pick over. "Give it about two minutes to dry completely."

"After that, can it touch my skin?"

"As long as it's unbroken skin. Make sure the pick can't puncture you. Just be smart, not scared, when you hold it."

"Hey, *vato*, I ain't scared a nothing."

Starks pointed at the pick. "That isn't nothing. Let me know when it's done."

Skullars impressed Starks yet again: he asked no questions about what he'd seen, but neither did he seem put-off by what he'd witnessed.

"About what just happened—" Starks said.

Skullars held up his hand to stop him. "Mon's gotta do what he's got to." Then he went on his way.

CHAPTER 110

THERE WAS AN hour left to go on his shift in the library, time that was cut short when a CO came for him.

Starks wasn't expecting a visitor, so was surprised to see Jeffrey seated at a table in the visitation room. It was immediately obvious that his friend was upset.

Concern for his children sent him rushing to the table. "What is it? What's the matter?"

"Kayla's in the hospital."

Starks dropped into a chair, his posture relaxing. "Thank God." At his friend's expression of surprise he said, "I thought maybe one of the kids . . . As long as they're okay . . ." He shrugged. "She looked well enough when I saw her a few days ago. She brought Blake and Nate along. What's wrong with her?"

"She might lose the baby."

Starks drove his hands into his pockets, fingered the fake thumbs tucked inside. "How am I supposed to feel about this? I mean, it's not my child, it's his. I suppose that's beside the point. How'd you find out?"

"She called me from her hospital room. You know how prideful she is; didn't want to come out and say she's scared or admit it's potentially serious."

"How's she doing?"

"Stable. They want to monitor her and the baby for a few days. If they think it's safe, they'll let her go home. But they may want her to stay in bed or move around as little as possible until delivery time."

"Maybe now she'll realize what she gave up. Should've stayed faithful to the one man who ever really loved her, who'd make sure she was taken care of. You think Bret or Ozy or any man she spread her legs for is going to look after her?" He slumped forward and let out a ragged sigh. "Make sure she has whatever she needs. I wonder if Bret's going to hang around if she needs care, especially if she loses the baby. He's used to her taking care of him, not the other way around. I know her. I know what she's like. Bret's there to party and be catered to, and the last thing it's going to be with her if she loses his kid is a party. By the way, how are my kids? Did you check on them?"

"I called the nanny. She said they're scared but as okay as can be expected."

"If Kayla needs anything—"

"I'll make sure she gets it. If she has to stay in the hospital a while, I'll see what's what about letting the kids visit her. At the very least, I'll set it up so they can see and talk to each other electronically." Jeffrey cracked his knuckles. "I knew you'd be upset. I hate bringing you this kind of news."

Some of the tension drained from Starks's body. "No. I appreciate it. I appreciate how you're looking out for me and for my family. And, yes, that includes Kayla. For the sake of *our* children, I hope she's okay."

"I'm sorry, bro . . . I have to run. I'll stay longer the next time but I planned just enough time on my way to an appointment. Thought it best to tell you in person."

"No problem."

Starks stayed seated and watched until Jeffrey swiveled around at the door to wave.

He'd always had to contend with a lot of things happening at once and had become adept at doing so before prison. But he had to say it again: Thank God for Jeffrey. Trusting anyone had never come easy. Jeffrey was the one person in his life he could trust absolutely. It had been a stroke of the best kind of luck that life had put them together in friendship and in business, had made them wealthy together so there was never any jealousy that sometimes happened between friends who had and those who didn't.

He may not be able to rest easy entirely, but some of the pressure was off knowing Jeffrey was looking out for his family and his interests.

Starks got to his feet and stretched. He still had time to go into the yard and walk off the feelings competing for his attention.

CHAPTER 111

STARKS SIGHTED HECTOR Sanchez in the yard with his usual cronies, so strolled in their direction. "What's the word?" he asked.

Sanchez replied, "Weasel's on his way to hell. You were right: The fucking smell of steak he had for lunch reached me before I even opened the door. Tray was still in his cell. Sucker lied and told me he didn't know why they'd brought it to him. Just before I stuck him in the heart with the pick, I told him they'd brought it because he was a dead man and that was his last fucking meal." He spit on the ground. "Weasel's not talking his shit now. Weasel's not talking, period."

"You got rid of the pick?"

"I know what I'm doing, gringo. Cleaned it good. Put it back in the kitchen. I need it again, I wanna get my hands on it pronto."

Starks made a subtle thumbs-up sign and kept walking.

There was no way the similarity of what had happened to Bo then Lawson would be missed. There was also no way that what had happened to Lawson could be attached to him, unless someone talked, and the chances of that, considering who'd done the deed, were so remote it didn't bear further thought. Any suspicions they had about his involvement with Bo's death would have to be dropped. It was logical; the evidence was in his favor.

He strolled around the perimeter of the yard, eyes aimed at the ground. Minutes later he noticed he was near the weight equipment kept out in the yard. Someone had left a fifteen-pound dumbbell on the ground. He bent over to pick it up, wincing as the scar tissue inside and out reminded him that he may never be the same again.

Who was he kidding? He'd never be the same ever again.

He placed the dumbbell on the rack where it belonged. It seemed an eon ago that he'd hit Bo with a weight five pounds heavier. The quote about how the journey of a thousand miles begins with a single step flashed through his mind. For him and others like him in this place, their journey had begun with a single *misstep*. This was never how he would have predicted his life to play out, here in this place, in the thick of it with misfits and missteps.

He kicked at a pebble, watching it sail through the chain-link fence to the grassy expanse between the fence and the wall. Head up, watchful, he made his way slowly to the door that led back inside.

Starks was almost to the door when CO Roberts opened it and held it open.

"Your attorney's here. I'll take you to where he's waiting."

CHAPTER 112

ROBERTS AND STARKS walked quickly and in silence to a small, windowless room fitted with a table and two chairs. The CO nodded then left.

Michael Parker was seated so that he faced the door. He stood when his client entered the room. Starks closed the door behind him, walked to where Parker waited and shook his hand.

"This is a surprise, Mike. Hadn't heard from you since the trial. What's going on?"

"A few things. Things I needed to see you in person about. Better that way, I think."

"Should I be as anxious as I'm starting to feel?"

Parker cleared his throat. "Take a seat."

"I have a feeling I'm not going to like this."

"The first matter. We're working on your appeal. Unfortunately, even though I advised you to keep your nose clean in here, that didn't happen." He held up a hand to stop Starks from speaking. "I'm truly sorry about what happened to you, and I'm glad you made it through that horrible ordeal. Still—"

"Before you continue, let me remind you that you know the kind of stuff that goes on in here. It's practically impossible to avoid trouble, unless you don't mind becoming one or more inmates' bitch, or dying early."

"I can only imagine what it's like for you."

"It's one thing to imagine it; it's another to live it every fucking day of your life."

Parker cleared his throat again. "The fact still is that what's now on your record affects your parole and, possibly, your appeal."

"They get you coming and going. I know you'll figure something out. What else?"

Parker linked his fingers and stared at them for a few moments before speaking.

"When you brought me and my firm on board for this situation, you asked me to look into Kayla's infidelities, specifically all the way back to high school."

"You said it was impossible."

"And you said enough money can accomplish anything."

Starks motioned at the room. "Obviously not everything."

"There are limits to what money can buy. Not often, but it happens. Anyway, without going into all the details, it took a lot of manpower to track down anyone who knew Kayla in high school and in college, and interview them."

"Did you have to pay them for information?"

"Sorry to say that the fact you're in here made some of them more than eager to talk. There are always those who delight in tearing down others who do well for themselves."

"Forget them. What did you find out?" Starks fixed his focus on Parker, who was obviously uncomfortable. "Go ahead, Mike. Or is it really that bad?" Uneasiness gripped him.

Parker exhaled, keeping his eyes on his joined hands. "Several men readily recalled one college classmate who told them about his secret relationship with Kayla. We were careful to interview them separately and simultaneously, so they had no opportunity to arrange their stories ahead of time. According to these men, with the exception of intercourse, the guy and Kayla did everything the law allowed, and didn't. I paraphrased their more explicit information."

Starks sat still for a moment then waved it off. "Sounds like bragging to me. The guy made it up. At that age, especially back then, even college-age guys always lied about conquests they never had a chance in hell to make happen. These days, it's all different, of course."

Parker's shoulders stayed tense. "Maybe you're right. However—"

"Where were these assignations supposed to have happened?"

Parker rubbed his eyes then looked directly at Starks. "The basement of your family home. According to the interviewees, there were two days a week you were in class that Kayla went to your house to study in the basement, and to wait for you."

"Grandpa and Mom were at work all day. I'd meet up with Kayla at the house after my morning classes and we'd go at it like rabbits until we both had to leave for afternoon classes. No." He shook his head. "I don't believe them. I'd need proof, and how can you get *that* after all these years?" Starks hesitated. "Unless . . . unless you're telling me it was Bernard Hazely. If Kayla brought that slug to my house—"

"It wasn't Hazely. As for proof, there's one thing each of them remembered, something distinctive they said the classmate told them about. It's something you'd know that would confirm whether the story is truth or a lie."

Starks sat at attention. "Such as?"

"The guy told them Kayla had a small, almost heart-shaped pinkish-red mole on the area just above her . . . you know."

Blood rushed from Starks's face, his breathing became shallow.

"There's something else. Your mother knew about the basement. Not who, just that it was a fact."

"No! She would have told me."

"I spoke with her myself. She didn't tell you, because she knew you wouldn't believe her. She knew it was a fact because she saw a guy running off when she came home unexpectedly one day, but not who it was. Your mother made it a point to see if she could catch them again, but it seemed her showing up that first time must have scared him off. She said after all the fuss you made about being with Kayla, it was better to let you find out on your own what she was really like."

"My God. She should have told me. All of this . . . all of it could have been . . ." Color drained from Starks's face.

"Are you okay?" Parker asked.

Starks sat with his face buried in his hands for several moments. When he looked up, he shouted, "That lying, conniving bitch. I never fucking told anyone about that mole. No one. It was mine, just as she was."

Starks lurched forward. "Who was it? God damn it, Mike, tell me." He slammed his fist on the table. "Tell me!" He pulled back and studied his attorney's face and posture. "What's wrong with you?"

He watched the attorney struggle to form a word—a name, and fail. Parker's anguished expression made it clear he wished he didn't have to.

"Starks . . . God . . . I'm so sorry."

"No." Starks's eyes were wild. His rush to get away knocked his chair over. He staggered around the room as a man seriously wounded might.

The air in the room had thinned for Starks, who stood gasping and gaping at Parker. A gagging sound came from within him and he stumbled to the plastic trash can in a corner of the room and vomited into it, before collapsing to the floor. He emptied his stomach of its bile twice more. The sour odor permeated the small, closed space. A few minutes went by, as he waited for dry heaves to stop. Then he got up, unsteady on his feet.

Parker stayed silent and waited.

Starks, after several minutes of pacing, faced Parker. "What about after college? What about all *those* years? What about lately? Tell me, Mike. Tell me. Did Jeffrey and Kayla . . . Have they all along been . . ."

Parker rubbed a vein that throbbed in the middle of his forehead.

"Jesus." A chord of restraint and hope snapped inside Starks. He walked to the door, placing his hand on the knob. His back to his attorney he said, "Mike, I can't continue today. I know we have more to discuss. If you would, please come back next week. I need time. There are some arrangements I need to discuss with you. Some matters I need you to take over for me."

"I understand."

Starks looked over his shoulder, met Parker's eyes. "I don't."

He opened the door wide and left the room, taking the burden of betrayal like a dead body with him.

And he wondered whose child Kayla was carrying.

CHAPTER 113

THE NEXT MORNING, immediately after the 8 a.m. count, Starks headed to the barbershop. One person was in the room.

The man lifted his gaze from the tabloid he was reading and sang out, "Business. Yay!"

"How's it going, Steve?"

"Honey, you saved me from boredom that was about to swallow me whole." He swished to the chair and patted it. "The usual trim, Starks? Or do you want to try something new?"

"Shave it."

Steve's hands went to his cheeks. He stared at Starks's reflection in the mirror with his eyes wide and his mouth open. "You want me to shave it . . . as in off . . . all your gorgeous hair?"

Starks nodded.

"I need a few moments to catch my breath." Steve studied Starks from all sides. "You do have the bone structure for it, but don't you want to reconsider?"

"I have other things to do today, so I'd appreciate it if you'd get going."

"I may cry, but here we go."

Steve wrapped a towel around Starks's neck, clicked the switch on the clippers, filling the space with its electric buzz, sniffling as dark locks fell to the floor. Over the racket he said, "You know, the last couple years of your life can be found in your hair, chemically, that is."

"Another reason to get rid of it."

When it was done and the room was silent, Starks asked, "Inmates don't bother you, Steve. Why is that?"

"You know how good I am with hair." He waited for Starks to agree then continued. "Honey, I was the best in Boston. Won every national and international hair show I competed in. With all that sucks in here, getting your hair done right is something no one wants to mess with. My skill is my golden ticket; I'm protected. Plus, I don't bother anyone who doesn't want to be bothered." He winked.

"What are you in for?"

"Murder. My lover of eleven years did the one thing he wasn't supposed to do: He fell in love with one of the sex partners in his stable. It was a no-no we both agreed on when we got together."

"I kind of get that."

"Of course you do, Starks. The similarities of our situations are obvious." Steve removed the towel. "So, what do you think of your new look?"

"Just what I wanted."

After several more comments were exchanged, Starks paused for a moment at the threshold to watch Steve sweep some of his history into a pile.

If only it were that simple.

CHAPTER 114

STARKS TOOK TWO left turns after leaving the barbershop, and then a right turn into the first cell in Block B, where he found Joe "Tat Man" Reynolds in his cell.

Reynolds sat up in his lower bunk. He frowned at the stranger disturbing him then recognition registered. "Damn, man. Took me a moment to know you. You've never even said hi to me before, and here you are. What can I do for you?"

"I hear you're the best tattoo man here."

"Going for a whole new look, then? C'mon in; take a seat. I was an ink artiste before I landed myself in here, and still am." He handed Starks a spiral notebook. "My sketches. Twelve to a page. Twenty bucks or four packs of cigs a tat"

Starks opened the notebook. "These sketches are good. You drew them?"

"Of course."

Starks continued to go through the drawings, spending a few minutes on each page until one drawing located at the top left corner held his attention. He pointed to a coiled serpent with vicious eyes and an open mouth with fangs ready to strike. "This one."

He was about to hand the notebook to Reynolds when his eyes were drawn to the last image on the page. He studied it a moment, his eyes narrowing into slits. "No." He held a finger on the sketch. "This one."

"Nice. No one's ever asked for that."

"And no one is to ever ask for it again. I'll pay you a hundred to do it and another hundred to never use it again. Is it a deal?"

"I can live with that. When do you want it?"

"You don't look busy now."

"I'm not. It'll take a while, though."

"If you do a good job, it should."

"Where you want it? Back of your hand? Upper arm? Middle of your chest? Scalp?"

"Start on my hand and let it go up my arm. I want it big enough for people to see it coming. Give it red eyes and lots of colors on the body."

"That'a a lotta ink. It's going to be painful."

"It's what I need."

Reynolds sterilized Starks's hand, arm, and the equipment with a smuggled-in bottle of Rivers Rum.

"You better take a couple hits of that yourself," he told Starks.

Starks took several deep swigs. "I'll replenish your stock."

With the precision of skill and experience, Reynolds began to make the fierce dragon spewing flames from its sharp-toothed mouth a permanent part of Frederick Starks.

"This tat's heavy-duty, man. Sends a message. A message of a man with a plan. You got a plan?"

"Not yet, but I'll think of something." Starks watched the needlework in silence for a moment then said, "My life went to shit because of me. All my fault. I trusted others—their love, loyalty. Never again. They can all go to hell."

"I hear you, man."

Starks allowed the pain from the needle repeatedly piercing his skin to fuel him. Once the beast was completed, he walked to the mirror. He didn't recognize himself. It was unsettling for several seconds then clarity overtook him: the old Starks no longer existed.

The dragon is born.

ABOUT THE AUTHOR

NESLY CLERGE RECEIVED his bachelor's degree in physiology and neurobiology at the University of Maryland, and later pursued a doctoral degree in the field of chiropractic medicine. Although his background is primarily science-based, he has finally embraced his lifelong passion for writing. Clerge's debut novel, *When the Serpent Bites*, is due out in 2015, with the sequel to follow. His debut novel explores choices, consequences, and the complexities of human emotions, especially when we are placed in a less-than-desirable setting. When he is not writing, Clerge manages several multidisciplinary clinics. He enjoys reading, chess, traveling, exploring the outdoors, and spending time with his significant other and his sons. For more information regarding the book please visit Clergebooks.com

59355566R00224

Made in the USA
Lexington, KY
02 January 2017